BLOODY MARGARET

Mark Lawson was born in London in 1962. After writing for *The Universe*, a weekly Catholic newspaper, and as freelance for *The Times* and *The Sunday Times*, he joined *The Independent* in 1986, as television critic and then parliamentary sketchwriter. Since 1988 he has been Chief Feature Writer for *The Independent Magazine*. From 1990-91, he was television critic for *The Independent on Sunday*. He has written and presented two television documentaries: 'Vote for Ron' in the BBC *Byline* series and *J'Accuse: Coronation Street* for Channel 4. He has appeared regularly on TV and radio, including *Start the Week, Behind the Headlines* and *The Late Show*. He has written a travel book entitled *The Battle for Room Service: Or All the Safe Places,* also published by Picador. He lives in London.

This début work of fiction by an award-winning journalist takes images from real politics, elections, television and many other things and combines them with imagined ones in three fantasies set in contemporary Britain and America.

In 'The Nice Man Cometh', set in Britain during the last decade, Graham Sterline, a young man obsessed with doing good deeds in a naughty world, is drawn to a new political group which promises to be The Nice People's Party. But can it do any good? And can Graham stay nice?

In 'Bloody Margaret' various members of the entourage of a British Prime Minister – including her admirers, her rivals, her image consultant, her chaplain, her porcelain cleaner and her electric-shock consultant – reflect on their parts in her rise and downfall.

In 'Teach Yourself American In Seven Days', set in the present day in London and New York, a City banker, whose firm is taken over by a Wall Street giant, finds himself taken over by strange new appetites and impulses. The Kafka character who turned into an insect had it easy by comparison.

BLOODY MARGARET

MARGARET

Three political fantasies

Mark Lawson

First published in hardback by Pan Books

This edition published 1992 by Picador
an imprint of Macmillan Publishers Ltd
25 Eccleston Place, London SW1W 9NF
and Basingstoke

Associated companies throughout the world

ISBN 0 330 32387 3

7 9 8 6

A CIP catalogue record for this book is available from
the British Library.

Phototypeset by Intype, London
Printed and bound in Great Britain by
Mackays of Chatham PLC, Chatham, Kent

Permission is gratefully acknowledged to quote from the poem 'Dockery & Son'
in 'The Whitsun Weddings' by Philip Larkin, published by Faber & Faber,
and to quote from Graham Greene's play *The Complaisant Lover*, published
by William Heinemann Limited.

FOR SARAH BULL

Contents

BLOODY MARGARET:
Three Political Fantasies

This book consists of three pieces of fiction: *The Nice Man Cometh*, *Bloody Margaret*, and *Teach Yourself American In Seven Days*. They are all quite different in form, but have certain links between them and are all concerned with the politics of the 1980s and 1990s in Britain, America, and elsewhere. They appear in descending order of length and are intended to be read in that sequence. The first two stories draw on actual events and a note at the end of the book clarifies further what is real and what is not.

ML

The Nice Man Cometh

'I'm a man of no convictions. (Pause) At least I think I am.'

The Philanthropist   CHRISTOPHER HAMPTON

'All streets in time are visited'

PHILLIP LARKIN   "Ambulances"

'Many of his disciples, when they heard this, said: Master, this is a hard teaching. Who can follow it?'

JOHN v, 60

'Every public philosophy that gains credence . . . . contains some truth. If it did not, the parable would not resonate so powerfully in our collective consciousness. But a public philosophy is a simplification of reality. Without some simplifying fables, citizens would be awash in disconnected data. The world is too complex for wholly empirical politics.'

ROBERT B. REICH   *The Resurgent Liberal*

The Nice Man Cometh

1

Left, Right, Left, Right

GRAHAM STERLING was disturbed, in his twenty-fourth year, by the thought that he was almost certainly the only man of his generation who had the words 'Left' and 'Right' scrawled as reminders inside the lips of his Wellington boots. This detail had been added by his wife Eliza, as a precaution after he had been spotted walking with pinched feet on a weekend ramble. Graham owned a small cottage on – well, in truth, some way off – Exmoor, bought with Eliza's earnings. A Londoner who had really seen animals only in a zoo or a stew, her husband had never thought to possess Wellingtons until they became weekenders. Scarcely had they won their first splash of mud when, on inspection, the toe-caps had been shown to be pointing in suspicious directions.

'Are they comfortable?' Eliza had asked.

Of course, she knew that they were not, but this was how she operated. It was as if the chairman of a government inquiry, which had already gathered enough evidence to damn the investigatee, addressed the central question to them once again. It looks like an opportunity to reduce the hypocrisy, by admission, but it is a safe bet that the culprit will elect to increase it, by denial, thus adding to the impact of the inquiry's findings.

'They're fine,' said Graham.

He chose a tone as either-side as he could find; he had already guessed the conclusions of the report.

'Really?' queried Eliza. She smiled. It was a mother's smile,

7

not a lover's, which at first alarmed him, but then he was forced to accept that this could not be a scene often played between adults. It was hard for the diagnosis of mis-shod galoshes to have much undertow of sex.

'They're on the wrong feet,' she had said.

This was in the first year of their marriage – 1979 – and although, in retrospect, it could be seen as the period in which they heard the political speech which would ultimately lead to their divorce, she would have said 'they're on the wrong feet' with essentially a taut affection. In the same way, when she subsequently inked his shame inside the boots with a prep-school marker, she did so with a certain what-will-we-do-with-you good humour. Later, she would have the same lines – it was the script you got, living with him – but deliver them with a different intonation.

Graham's political friends – or, rather, friends of political positions more fixed than his – liked to joke that both the boots should have written on them 'Middle'. For Graham Sterling was a man of the ideological centre. At university – London, because, he would quietly explain, his school had not gone in for Oxbridge – he had chosen from an article in his impeccably solemn and fretful morning newspaper the phrase 'liberal humanist' to corset his confusions. It gave intellectual credibility to his uncertainty, although he reflected after a nervous visit to the basement of the local hospital in his second year at college (his first as a non-virgin), that it might be the political equivalent of saying non-specific urethritis, not venereal disease.

Now, in his thirty-fifth year – which was 1990 – he would say that he was 'disenfranchised'. It was another borrowing from a columnist and summed up his new ideological imprecision. Which was: not only did he have no idea what he actually thought about anything (which was usual), he had no idea what to do about it (which was new). He was a voter without a home, an orphan of the death of the old consensus.

While the oppressed peoples of Eastern Europe were moving towards democracy, Graham Sterling, a Western citizen conscious of his responsibilities, a man who aimed to read every page of his serious newspaper every day, had decided that he would probably not vote at all in the next election. The explanation of this paradox lay in events between the years of 1979 and 1990 and were also recorded in the pages of two secret documents which guided his life. He called them, respectively, the Biography and the Questionnaire and hoped that they would not be found among his papers when he died.

Although, even in his early twenties, he no longer hoped to be celebrated, Graham still filed in his mind stories for a biography of himself. Even as he admitted that his condition of solid anonymity made such a volume improbable, he held in his head two fat folders, one containing anecdotes for inclusion and another holding those he planned to have suppressed.

The censorship involved aspects of his character or existence which were simply too revealing. He intended, for example, to prevent publication of the Wellington boots story. A keen reader of the heavyweight book pages, he was well aware of the sensationalist direction which the genre of biography seemed to have taken, and was intent on keeping out of his memoir – for which his private working title was *A Good Man in a Bad Time: The Life and Ideas of Graham Sterling* – details of his ejaculation problem, of which the reader will learn more later.

He was also keen to keep secret a part of his extensive book collection, the revelation of which would surely reduce his standing in the eyes of normal people. Graham was convinced that he must be one of the very few men – of his or any other generation – who possessed a dozen copies of the London A-Z. It would be wrong to suggest that he had purchased twelve editions of the same book. There were subtle variations. The title of one was *Streetfinder*, of another *London Street Plan* and of yet another – a breezy publication, slight on detail, aimed at monolinguist visitors – *Get Lost?* There was also a range of scales. By some of them, the West London road in which he

9

lived was as long as your index-finger; by others, it was as squat as your thumb.

And one of them, he had grim reason to recall, simply did not include the West End address of the restaurant in which his wife had elected to meet him one evening. She had provided directions, up to and including where the taxi should drop him off, but he had failed to find the place from there. So, all things considered, and Graham's temperament led him always to consider all things, it was a calumny to say that he had a dozen identical publications. You might as well say – although he never had said it in case it sounded pretentious – that a man who possessed a folio *What You Will* and a quarto *Twelfth Night* had bought the same book twice. Graham had read English literature at university.

And it happened to be the case, whatever Eliza said, and she made it clear that she did not believe him, that the particular text he was working from, on that sweaty night of searching for the restaurant, did not include the necessary reference. He had asked for directions but suffered from an allied inability to retain in his memory any suggested turns but the first. He had tried an intuitive foray along one street and down another – when lost, he had an almost Aboriginal belief in a long-existent path which might be divined – but had been forced to resort again to a tobacconists'. Assuming that his failing was as obvious to others as to himself, he bought street atlases furtively now, like a bulimic might purchase chocolate or a fifties Catholic condoms.

He always hoped that the assistant would be an Asian because – understand he wasn't being racist; Graham was a man of the centre – they would accept his money without question. What he dreaded were big-hearted and very probably big-chested – an irrelevant personal detail; he was sorry – East End women who would say: 'Where is it you're going, love? Save your cash.' This was Graham's nightmare, for he could never remember the directions. His only option then was to dart for the next newsagent's, where he might be sold an A-Z. Once, inadvertently circling the block, he had returned to the shop from which he had just been dispatched and known, in the slack-jawed recognition of the bosomy cockney behind the counter, the horror of the drug addict when the assistant shouts for the pharmacist.

On the night of the disappearing restaurant, the (Asian) tobacconist had sold him a map without demur. This one was called *Capital Pathfinder*, a title new to the collection. Thankfully, the emphasis of Margaret Thatcher's government on personal financial gain had reduced the likelihood of a shop-owner throwing up a sale. Graham's gratitude for this development was, it must be understood, a result of selfish expedience, not political belief, in which he was wholly opposed to the government. He had thumbed through the book on the pavement outside. It is a peculiar shame to hope, in your own country, to be taken for a tourist but that is what Graham always prayed when reduced to this manoeuvre. He had walked to the end of one street, stopped and stared at the grid made by D and 5 on page 76 of *Capital Pathfinder*.

'Are you lost?' said a slow, kind voice.

It was at moments like this that Graham, as neurotically and undiscussedly agnostic as the rest of his post-faith generation, believed in God. For, behold, He had sent forth His messenger to clear a path in the wilderness.

'Yeh,' Graham said.

The trick, in his experience, was to produce a reply vaguely between the lazy English 'Yeah', the upper-class English 'Yah' and the German 'Jah!' With muddy-straw hair, a gash of pink scalp showing above the beginning of his fringe and early foundations of the convex belly of a comfort-eater, Graham did not look giveaway-British.

'Where er do er you er want?' said the Samaritan, interspacing the words with the short pause for clarity which he believed to be the least patronizing way of dealing with the foreigner for which he had blessedly taken Graham. The pseudo-tourist was impressed. As a liberal humanist, and, even now, as a member of the disenfranchised centre, he had always been careful to avoid the typical British response – 'ignorant, vestigial colonialism', he considered it, in another borrowing from his favourite columnist – of yelling directions at those who had selfishly omitted to learn your language.

Admittedly, Graham only had the opportunity to display his sensitivity on the, thankfully rare, occasions when a foreign tourist was so unfortunate as to mistake his chosen facial expression of benevolent non-aggression for that of someone who might willingly give directions. He gave them smilingly but inaccurately, helpfully but unhelpfully. Eliza, for whom, in her husband's opinion, humour was a low priority and an infrequent event, had once been forced to turn away to mask her mirth when such an encounter had occurred.

On the evening of the uncharted eaterie, when the roles were more traditional, with Eliza glaring at an empty chair and Graham taking directions from a kindly passer-by, Graham had told the stranger the name of the restaurant he sought – 'Tardelli's' which he pronounced with a guttural undertow which could pass either for catarrh or foreign nationality – and the man, glad to be so easily of assistance, had smitten the air and said 'behind you!'

Which indeed it was, though you had to admit that the writing above the door was tiny and curled for effect. When Graham entered, cursing the nervous sweatiness which made him appear balder than he was, Eliza was sitting at a corner table, reaching for the phone which a waiter had just wheeled to her. She saw her muddled husband.

'It's all right,' she told the waiter. 'He's here.' There was a stress on the 'he' which told him that his absence had been discussed with this Italian, in trousers tight for emphasis. As he often did when he arrived late or returned from one of his fretfully-frequent visits to the gents, he had a feeling that Eliza had entered into a conspiracy about his stupidity, sometimes as little as a matter of ironic eye-contact, with a stranger. The cock-walking waiter swung away. Graham, trying not to suspect that the Italian – not, of course, that his nationality was relevant – was thinking 'her and him!', sat down opposite his wife.

'The late Graham Sterling,' she said quietly.

This was an habitual greeting but even though this was a time, just before the 1983 general election, when their marriage had been at its happiest, she said it with more of an edge than was normal. He leaned across the table to kiss her on the cheek. She did not resist but took it with no more reciprocity than a plaster Mary takes the halitosic Easter devotions of believers.

'You are hopeless,' Eliza said, as slowly as, but far less benevolently than, the Samaritan had spoken to Graham outside the restaurant. 'What happened?'

He fashioned a justification around the fact that the restaurant, while listed in the telephone directory under one address, had its entrance in another but he knew that, when they got home, it would take her only two minutes to prove him wrong, which it did.

His locational aphasia was one of the many qualities about Graham – not that he would want to suggest that he had many qualities, but, well, you know what he meant – which his wife had found first erotic then emetic. With a dull wonder which merely increased his habitual state of confusion, Graham would recall how she had been – well, he didn't want to brag, but what other phrase was there? – turned on the first few times when – she at the wheel, he navigating; Graham had failed his driving test six times – he had sent her the wrong way.

In retrospect, it was completely her temperament to have been quickly irritated by this, but she had not been. Perhaps she had been relieved to meet a man so completely without car cockiness; who could not be accused of treating his vehicle as his penis, because he did not have one; who was wholly unlikely to grab the wheel, while his wife was driving, and say things like: 'Notting Hill'll be solid. If we do a sly u-ee here, we can come back on at the Castle.'

The roots of Graham's geographical incompetence were twofold. There was the vanity – well, the way he looked, he couldn't

13

risk getting worse, he would explain – which prevented him from wearing spectacles, although he now needed to squint at bus numbers even when the vehicle reached the stop. This left him, when walking, unable to ascertain exactly where he didn't know he was. That was a practical explanation. The second factor in his tendency to become lost is more a matter of speculation, but worth mentioning. Perhaps Graham's inability to read a map, like his difficulty in inserting the correct foot into the approved Wellington boot, was characteristic of a particular personality: apologetic, non-assertive, dominated.

In moments of depression, he would reflect that liberal humanism, or now disenfranchisement, was the political projection of those character failings. Perhaps in politics, as in all areas of human activity, there were the fuckers and the fucked, their fates pre-ordained by something other than elections. He had once read that the unsuccessful American presidential campaign of George McGovern in 1972 had been remarkable for the number of glandular fatties – real solo lift-users in special-shop suits – on the senator's staff.

As a liberal, and one who already wore his trousers two belt-notches on from in his teens, Graham was certainly not going to be caught equating girth with worth but he wondered whether McGovern's attraction to people who might have been led to believe that they were, by conventional measurements, failures – he would go so far in judgement – had any connection with the result of the campaign. He considered the possibility that the politics of moderation attracted the personalities of failure. He had a hunch that, if you stopped a man arriving breathlessly late at a restaurant with his Wellingtons on the wrong feet and asked his politics, he would probably not prove to be a Conservative or a Republican.

What worried Graham most was that, however often he told himself that people got lost all the time and that a left foot looked very like a right one in a country light, he knew that his condition was almost certainly not normal. In moments of especially profound self-doubt, he would sit and stare at the dozen A-Zs on the shelves which he had constructed and therefore for whose fall he daily braced himself. Sometimes, he hoped he would be sitting there when it happened: the foolproof undetectable suicide.

Filling nearly a foot of wood, competing in length with his Kingsley Amises and his Evelyn Waughs, and only behind Graham Greene if you counted in his travel books as well, they were like the life's work of a diligent but rather repetitive author. His habit since college had been to store all his books alphabetically. On the day that he and Eliza occupied their first home, Graham, cataloguing his library, had come to the street plans, then only six or seven of them. He had wondered, half jokingly, whether to shelve them under A or Z: beside all the Amises, of both ages, or the single inked and chocolated Zola, left from school. Eliza had advised, half sternly, that it didn't really matter: 'If you can't find it under one letter, look under the other.'

In the end, Graham had put three next to *Lucky Jim* and three next to *Germinal*. It worried him that not being able to find the A-Z was probably the definition of ultimate uselessness. Even now, he was troubled by the thought of dying in a road accident or disappearing – all those people who went missing every year, perhaps they had not deliberately absconded but were simply lost – and the police popping the lock on his flat and searching through it for a clue to his personality. He visualized their eyes falling on the line of books whose titles were letters not words. What could they think but that he was a man who, in a particularly serious way, lacked a sense of direction.

In the folder of anecdotes cleared for inclusion in the authorized biography were three from childhood. If Graham had been called before a tribunal and asked to account for the way he was, he would have brought these memories in evidence. He catalogued them as: 1) The Cake Day 2) The Boxing Lesson 3) The Perfect Patrick Affair.

The Cake Day took place at Graham's primary school in

1961. He was aged six, a solemn, podgy boy, saved from the fists or criticism of his more assured peers by a generous nature – he had been taught always to offer around his sweets to others first – and an encyclopaedic knowledge of soccer, which gave him playground credibility.

One day, their class teacher – either she had been called Mrs White or her hair had been white – announced that they or their mothers must bake bread, cakes, or scones – she had pronounced the word, in the pretentious English manner, to rhyme with tones – for a charity sale in the school hall. In the version of the event he now knew, the cause was famine, but this detail may have been a sardonic addition of his adult brain.

Graham remembered the school stage, on which house points and Birthday Badges were handed out, heavy with cellophaned gâteaux, fancies and loaves on paper plates. He remembered a crush of children, given money by their mothers, scrumming for the tastiest baking. Graham had a different mission. His mother, when she had pressed some coppers into his hand, with the reassuring smile which was still his favourite of her faces, had held up a separate coin and whispered: 'Buy a cake for Mrs White.'

Her son, true to his upbringing, had waited calmly at the back of the ruck until a gap cleared. Pushing through, he had grabbed and paid for an individual sponge cake – he saw it as pink-iced, scattered with the candy shrapnel called hundreds-and-thousands – sought out his teacher in the hall and handed it to her. 'But you haven't got one for yourself,' she said, gently. 'I got yours first, Miss,' he had replied. When he returned to the stage, there were only a few dull buns left unpurchased.

In class next morning, the teacher had announced the amount of money raised for the starving (if, indeed, it had been them) by the cakes, and then said: 'I just want to say something about yesterday. I saw some of the bigger boys pushing and shoving their way to the front of the queue, which I didn't think was a very good way of Showing That We Care For Others, which we talked about in assembly yesterday. But Graham – where are you, Graham . . . ?' He had been asked to stand up at his desk, while she told the story of the cake, ending with the words: 'Now, that's what I call a well brought-up boy.'

Graham sensed the hostility of his classmates even as the tribute was given and, after school that day, he was pushed and punched, bloodying his knee on the rough red-brick wall. On the way home, he had experienced a new emotion which he now identified as confusion. He had understood for the first time that, in the rules of Good and Bad, Nice and Nasty, there was a new, and dangerous category, called Goody-Goody. He had also learned that you could suffer for doing what your mother said.

The Cake Day led directly to the Boxing Lesson. When Graham's parents saw his bleeding knee and dusty blazer, they asked who had picked on him and why. He had stuttered out the cake tale. The look that passed between them told him that they took this for a cover story. 'Show me how you fight back?' said Graham's father thoughtfully. 'Put up your fists.' Graham, his eyes moistening, had shrugged that he didn't. 'You mean that you just let them thump you!' exclaimed his father. He tut-tutted to Graham's mother, who muttered something – he thought he remembered – about maybe having taught him to be too good.

That afternoon, Graham's father had knelt on the living-room carpet, bobbing around and throwing non-connecting punches, occasionally breaking off to arrange his son's hands in a convincing pugilistic stance, with as much success as the first attempts to dress a wriggling baby. 'Left, right, left, right,' he instructed his uncoordinated son. The mock-snarling father had also tried to teach the growling of the phrase 'Geroffff!' in preference to the weak and fully enunciated 'Stop it!', which had been Graham's first suggestion. After about half an hour, during which the boy had become tearful, dabbing at his eyes with the back of his inefficient fists and needing to urinate every few minutes, the lesson was abandoned. Graham resolved, while a teenager, to tell this story in the magistrates court, if ever called up to fight a war.

So that was the kind of boy he had been and the man he was carried the same shadows. The only interruption to the pattern, which was why the story fascinated him, was the family anecdote of the Perfect Patrick Affair. Graham's parents had been friendly with a couple they called the Perfect Pattersons. This had been, he guessed in restrospect, because the other family was obsessively concerned with social status and the creation of a lifestyle which others might envy. The Sterlings had always called the Pattersons' son, a boy of Graham's age, Perfect Patrick, presumably because he had been even more sickeningly spick and well-behaved than Graham. He thought he recalled that Patrick had written personal thank-you notes after every visit; a protocol which Graham was allowed to drop in cases where the visits were as regular as the Pattersons'.

However, one Saturday afternoon, after the boys had been playing in Graham's room, Perfect Patrick had whispered something in his mother's ear as goodbyes were said. Her face had paled and the friendship between the couples was subsequently ended, with no more telephone calls or Christmas cards. Graham's parents claimed that they could not make contact, because it had been the Pattersons' turn to invite them, so the mystery had never been solved. Graham could not even remember what game they had been playing, or any scrap of conversation. The event perplexed him, because it was the single illustration he had ever had of his ability to upset another with an opinion or statement.

As well as stories from the past which might help to explain his temperament, he accumulated anecdotes from the present which illustrated it. For example, he had been riding on the London Underground one morning to an assignment. It was the period between breakfast and lunch-time rush hours when only those workers in essentially deskless professions like Graham's were to be found travelling; his end of a satisfyingly empty carriage was shared with a pack of about a dozen mewling school children under the charge of a pasty, twitchy female teacher. Graham, who was himself generally taken for a decade older than he was, had no real feel for ages but would have put the children at about seven and the teacher at about twenty-five.

It was not an equal contest. Ten of the children were black. Graham hated himself for thinking that the other two, who, like the teacher, were white, must be the offspring of shout-about-it liberal parents. Graham, who was viewing his fellow travellers from behind a copy of Britain's only even nominally leftish serious newspaper, regarded himself as impeccably liberal but was not sure that his membership application would extend to permitting his (as yet theoretical) children to attend a school in which they constituted the ethnic minority. If a stand ever needed to be taken against such an establishment, Graham planned to blame the dogmatism of his wife, quietly suggesting that he had inadvertently wed a closet white supremacist, but he knew that he might come to regard Eliza's domination of the decision-making process as a convenient excuse.

It pleased Graham to note, however, that the two most irritatingly mischievous among the dozen children on the Tube were the pale-skinned ones. His pleasure at this observation made him feel fair-minded again. One of the two ill-behaved Caucasians – who seemed, from the teacher's frequent use of the stroppy vocative, to be called 'Danielle!' – leaned across the aisle between the seats and flicked her fingers hard, like a table-football player, against the front of Graham's newspaper.

'Oooh!' said the teacher; the sound of someone winded. 'Danielle!' she added, the admonitory vocative replacing the stroppy one. The other children were whooping and giggling, thrilled by Danielle's terrorism against adult targets. The teacher looked across at Graham, presumably to apologize, but saw that he had lowered his newspaper and was smiling with friendly indulgence at the triumphantly grinning girl, to whom the teacher now returned her attention.

'You're just lucky it was such a nice man!' the teacher said.

A nice man! Graham raised the newspaper again to hide what he feared might be an expression quite as smug as Danielle's. Few people outside politics and journalism actively desire to be regarded as nasty but it is certainly not true that niceness (the adjective of which was among the 'lazy words' which one of Graham's English teachers had counselled against ever using) is the quality which most people would like to overhear being praised.

The average man, offered the opportunity to stand behind the arras while two women discussed him, would probably choose to eavesdrop on the comment. 'Well, I've certainly never seen a bigger one!' The above-average man might select 'No one else has ever made me come like that!' or the businessman, behind the screen at a board meeting, 'He's just a fucking good operator – one of the A-Team'; but Graham would have wanted none of these. His whole life had been an attempt to be widely regarded as (and here he defied his English teacher) nice. Now there was independent confirmation from a stranger on the train.

It was true that, as the journey rattled on, Graham thought he detected, in Danielle's shrill impromptu press conference for her classmates, a reference to 'the bald man' (he still regarded the daily crushing evidence of the mirror as circumstantial), and was briefly not smug but blushing behind his barrier; but the teacher's public acknowledgement of an opinion which he had long held privately lifted his spirits for the rest of the day.

The tragedy (too strong a word but you knew what he meant) was that, even if he should improbably attain fame, there had been no witnesses to an event which he regarded as emblematic. He knew from a Catholic girlfriend at college that, in the process of making a saint, the Vatican called in stories of divine forbearance by the promising young soul trying to catch the selectors' eye. Graham thought of naughty Caucasian Danielle in middle age, gravely veiled before a bunch of clerics ('He just put down his paper and smiled, Monsignor'); but the truth was that it was secular rather than heavenly glory he sought. The story would be recorded only in his privately-non-published, very-limited-edition memoir.

Perhaps it was because both his parents and his teachers placed so much emphasis on reading that Graham was pursued through life not only by the Biography, but by another mythical written document: the Questionnaire.

This examination paper had afflicted him since adolescence, when he had first become conscious of the phenomenon of moral choice. Not all decisions were attended by it – and questions already answered could be presented again later – but he was always braced for its possible intervention. For example, one evening in the late 1980s, Graham, on his way to the theatre in London, passed a shivering young man, slumped on the steps of a railway station entrance: beggars were an increasingly common sight in the capital. This one held a cardboard notice which said: 'Homeless and Broke. Please help.' As Graham hesitated, he felt the onset of the questionnaire.

23: Do you believe that the man in front of you is:

☐ **A:** An innocent victim of the present government's economic policies.

☐ **B:** A beneficiary of the present government's economic policies; an entrepreneur brilliantly exploiting the middle-class guilt market.

☐ **C:** A tabloid newspaper reporter researching a story on the Fake Beggar syndrome.

☐ **D:** Someone who has wilfully refused to accept any of the huge number of unfilled jobs on the market.

☐ **E:** God's [*respondents may substitute Fate's or Nature's*] way of showing what will happen to you if you don't shell out.

☐ **F:** A genuinely deserving case, but if I handed out cash to everyone like him I met, I'd be sleeping next to him by next week. Let the authorities do something.

Graham had at least one friend who would have chosen each option: this was one of the factors which made debate, dinner parties, and even everyday conversation so problematical. He had a sneaking fear that he believed in E (premonition) – although an agnostic humanist, he had never quite lost the conviction that, for example, if you didn't put money in a cancer research tin, you got the disease – but his instinct was for A, although he would want to enter the caveat that the current government could not be entirely to blame.

He had stopped now in front of the beggar, who looked up with an expression between fear and anticipation. Graham was also conscious of the glances of the passers-by. He sensed that, in trying not to catch the eye or the sign of the youth, they were sneaking a look at Graham, wondering, presumably, whether he was a policeman, an evangelist, or a campaigning television reporter. He bunched some change in his pocket. But he had forgotten, as he often did, that, in his juggling of options, there might be supplementaries.

23a: Whose reaction would you find most embarrassing:

☐ **A:** The contempt of the beggar as you walk away full-pocketed.

☐ **B:** The aren't-you-a-goody-goody glares of other passers-by as you throw some money in the hat.

☐ **C:** Your own guilt later on about not having given.

This dilemma was the worst kind on the questionnaire – a three-way tie between morality, embarrassment, and guilt. Already late for the theatre – and uncertain of finding it easily – Graham, in a rare burst of certainty, let the coins jangle back against the stack in his pocket and strode away.

'And happy fuckin' Christmas to you,' yelled the beggar. Graham stopped, walked back, dropped a mid-denomination bank-note in the hat, where the youth – giving a rot-toothed grin

at having played the conscience joker with such easy success –
trapped it hastily, nervous of thieves or the breeze.

'God bless you,' he croaked.

Respondents may substitute Fate or Nature, thought Graham
as he began to work on an excuse for being late for his date.

The stories told by the Biography and the Questionnaire were
parallel narratives. They were private parables of Graham's
attempt to live up to the doctrine he had borrowed from the
newspaper: liberal humanism.

As far as Graham understood it, which was not completely,
a liberal humanist was someone who eschewed prejudice against
others, was kind as much to strangers as to friends, faithful to
their sexual partner, favoured peace over war and the improvement of society over personal advancement. These beliefs, or
working sketches for beliefs, intersected at many points Christianity, although the crucial new element was the humanism. If
liberal humanists remained monogamous or were charitable
towards another, they did so not because a charismatic community leader with a beard had told them to two thousand years
previously, or because they would burn for eternity if they failed
to comply, but because this was simply how any human being
ought to behave in their fleeting tenure of a rented planet. It
was, effectively, an attempt to establish goodness as the product
of personal will rather than of a big stick or a supernatural
carrot.

Although, the liberal humanist would stress at this point, if
a deist construct of reward and punishment worked for others,
then that was what worked for them. There were a lot of
'althoughs' for liberal humanists. He – or, the believer would
swiftly insist at this point, she – attempted to examine every
issue on its merits, not handcuffed by party instructions or
personal circumstance. There were, in theory, no Ten Com-
mandments. In truth, this was not practically possible. There
was an unwritten set of Moses' stones, particularly relating to
attitudes towards war, women, and those of different ethnic

backgrounds. In its own way, liberal humanism could be as prescriptive as Christianity.

It was often objected by traditional believers that, once God was removed from the equation, these were laws without a police force. There was no incentive to behave well. The liberal humanists replied that the motivation was that those who failed to comply earned the censure of civilized society. Regrettably, as Graham Sterling would learn, this theory proved to have particular weaknesses in the 1980s, when, it seemed to him, the nastier and more grasping and more insensitive you became, the more you earned the applause of civilized society.

He would also discover that, although liberal humanism was not a religion, it was still possible to lapse from it.

2

The Duke of Burgundy's Return

Mortgage rates were up again, Graham's edition of his London evening newspaper told him. He wondered whether to mention this to Eliza, who was reading at the other end of the sofa. It was just short of eight in the evening and they were on the last third of a 1976 French red wine which, if this had been the present day, would have been suggestive of striking wealth but, it being 1979, indicated only comfortable young-married money. Secure in his six-month-old marriage, Graham drank a splash of the three-year-old wine and looked at Eliza as she read. Most people in this pursuit and in these circumstances would have had their legs curled underneath them and a shoulder, at least, hunched over but Eliza sat with a rapt back and both feet (still in shoes; stocking-shod at home, she thought, was sloppy) flat on the whipped-cream carpet. It was an attitude more of examination than relaxation.

He tilted his head for the title. She was reading the book which had just won the big award for fiction. Graham – who scanned the arts pages second, after sport and before news – was dimly aware that it was by a woman and about some others living in a houseboat. He had at first resolved not to bother with it on the grounds that it sounded like a work for girls. That thought, however, had got him in to trouble with the in-head security service which anyone who aspires to the politics of the centre or left must employ.

Over in the ideological right-hand lane, you wrote your own Highway Code (why should everyone be forced to go at the same speed? It was unnatural). Almost any infringement could be justified by blaming other drivers. In the centre and left lanes, there were rules, ruthlessly enforced, for both your own comfort and that of other users. These stretches were closely patrolled. Sometimes, your thought was so awful that you saw the forensic detective, the judge, or even the shrink. This particular aberration ('A work for girls') brought only a WPC, flagging him to the side of the road.

'I expect you know why I've stopped you, sir?'

'Er, yes. I was signalling to the right.'

'And which way are you meant to be heading?'

'Er, centre or left.'

'Well, which? You've got to choose a lane and stick to it.'

'I, er, want to be sort of middle of the road.'

'Well, you'll have to be particularly careful, then. And that thought about "a work for girls," sir. That could easily be disturbing to women . . .'

'I didn't realize it was a built-up area.'

'Oh, almost everywhere's a built-up area nowadays, sir.'

He had got off with a caution and a warning not to veer to the right. He had pledged to read the houseboat book as soon as Eliza had finished with it. Finished with it rather than finished it was the correct usage. He suspected that she kept most novels for as long as they impressed when taken out on trains and that she probably read just enough to discuss them at dinner parties. He had detected a routine in her critiques, which veered away from detailed textual evidence. She would say a short book was 'a bit sketchy' and, of a brick thick fiction of the American kind, that it sagged in the middle or trailed off towards the end.

Graham's detection was correct. Eliza could have written a thesis on modern British novelists and the skill of the artful beginning but barely a third-form essay on their ability as finishers. Wise to this, John Durry, a college friend of Graham's with whom they still swapped dinner invitations, had caught her out when, over a dessert, he had suggested that the previous year's winner of the big prize – an Iris Murdoch work about the sea – had featured a particularly vivid hurricane scene at the end. 'Absolutely,' Eliza had said. 'Those phrases about the wind.' She had paused. 'And the waves.' John Durry had smirked and had explained the sting to Graham at their local team's next home match.

Now, inclining his left ear towards his shoulder again, he saw that there was a substantially thicker shank of pages beneath her right thumb than her left. It was the second chapter, at most, which she now followed across the pages with a learner driver's attention. Graham thought of offering a casual warning ('I've, er, heard the ending's well worth reading') to prevent Durry winning her innocent agreement that the bit at the end, when the pirates seized the houseboat, was really something, but he lacked the courage. His fear was always that Eliza would somehow guess what he was getting at. So he said nothing about the climaxes of contemporary novels and nothing about that day's rise in mortgage rates to 15 per cent – potentially a subject of controversy, as there was more of her cash and salary in their property than of his – but concentrated on a superficially less contentious topic: the evening's television programmes. Yet, even here, Graham had what politicians call a hidden agenda.

'Good book, darling?'

'Sorry? Mmm, really good beginning. What are you doing?'

'Looking at the paper. Nothing much on telly.'

'You surprise me. Sometimes I don't know why we have it. The news, your football. I only ever watch those wildlife documentaries . . .'

'It's the Dimbleby lecture tonight . . .'

'I can hardly wait.'

'No, seriously, darling, I er, think it's worth watching.'

'Who's doing it?'

'Er, R-R-R-Roy Jenkins.'

'Oh, really? The Duke of Burgundy's return!'

'Seriously, darling, I think it's our kind of thing – an appeal for moderation.'

'Oh, yes, right up your street – or right down the middle of it . . .'

'But I thought you . . .'

'Joking, darling, joking.'

The young, the foreign, and students of merely serious politics may need a little history here. This fiction is based around the life cycle of the Social Democratic Party or SDP (1981–1990), a new British outfit launched with the intention of altering irrevocably the democratic processes of the nation. In the British political theatre of the years between 1979 and 1989, the run of the SDP ranks, between the brash, big budget musical of Thatcherism and the corpse-strewn horror movie of Socialism, was a boulevard comedy always unlikely to last, but it attracted, for a while, a large and appreciative audience, whose doomed enthusiasm deserves remembrance and its roots investigation.

There is a currently popular branch of literary invention called faction; the word, like the stories it describes, a conflation of fact and fiction. There is the purest kind, in which all of the characters wear the names of real people; this is most common on television (in programmes with titles like *Suez 1956*, *Bomber Harris*, *Countdown to War*) where the physical similarity between actor and historical figure may attract much favourable comment from critics cooing like aunties seeing daddy's nose in baby.

A variant, commonest to the genre of the thriller, mixes invented characters with factual ones. The standard procedure is that a hero (usually a policeman or agent) with a perfunctory made-up name shares plot or conversation with some genuine headline meritocrat. In Jeffrey Archer's *Shall We tell the President?* (1977), special agent Marc Andrews co-habits paragraphs with Edward M. Kennedy, who, in make-believe at least, gets to be President; in Frederick Forsyth's *The Negotiator* (1989), secret agent Quinn is the subject of sentences in which Margaret Thatcher and Mikhail Gorbachov are objects, although, curiously, in this case, the President of the United States is the fictional John Cormack, Mr Forsyth presumably fearing that a thriller with George Bush in it might fail to justify its name.

Something of the same problem applies here. This is not a thriller – there is only one death, which is not violent, though it is premature – but it is a particular variant of faction in which the made-up names (Graham and Eliza Sterling and later, for example, Ben and Paula Waddle) ring no more real or false than those of headline meritocrats (David Owen, David Steel, Rosie Barnes). Which were invented by fiction and which by politics? It is hard now to remember. For what, in truth, do we remember of more conventionally significant events?

Take 1979. The first year of the Sterlings' marriage and the first of this story will be remembered with bitterness by many political figures who may console themselves by reflecting on the number who do not have the option of recalling it at all:

Nelson Rockefeller, an American millionaire denied the vice-presidency by what he regarded as scandal-mongering, died stiff inside his mistress, who, rumour had it, was forced to crawl out from underneath his corpse – always a potential drawback in intercourse between age-gap partners – to dial 911.

President Park Chung Hee of Korea was assassinated by a Head of Intelligence who had omitted to advise him of the threat.

Z. A. Bhutto, the former Prime Minister of Pakistan, was hanged for a murder for which he insisted, until the rope tensed around his neck, he had been framed by the military ruler, General Zia.

Others lived but left:

Pol Pot fled into the jungle in Cambodia after the Vietnamese ended his Khmer Rouge regime. The dredging out of a lake in Stung Treng revealed two thousand skeletons, believed to be those of middle-class intellectuals he had wished to purge

('If we'd been Cambodians, that would have been us,' said Eliza Sterling, seeing the story on the evening news).

President Idi Amin, the tyrant's tyrant (the one Pol Pot and the others looked up to, like small boys copying the shots of famous batsmen), was chased out of Uganda.

The Shah of Iran, formerly the Shah of Persia, the Western democrat's tyrant, was chased out of his country, fifty-four years after his father seized the throne. He took his cash and the cancer that was killing him to America, a friend in need.

General Anastasia Somoza Debayle, ruler of Nicaragua, was toppled by the Sandinista rebels. 'Takeaway Somoza', said one headline, succeeding in offending two ethnic groups simultaneously. (The headline's insensitivity, though not its long-awaited information, was condemned by Graham and Eliza's securely left-wing friends for whom Nicaragua knocked Northern Ireland off the top of the chart of subjects to be smug about at dinner.)

James Earl Carter, President of America, claimed to have been attacked by a swimming rabbit while on a fishing holiday. Responding to press scepticism, a White House spokesman was reported to have said: 'This is not being taken seriously enough. It was a goddam killer rabbit.' (Reading this, Graham asked Eliza if rabbits swam but she just looked at him.)

James Callaghan, British Prime Minister, lost a vote of confidence in the House of Commons, having continued to be at an international summit in Guadeloupe when, despite the promise of the song, rats ran in London's Berkeley Square as a result of a dustmen's strike, one of many large pay claims.

Dozens of Labour MPs in Britain feared for their careers, even after surviving the 1979 general election. The left wing of the party – at the annual conference – forced through 'mandatory reselection'. This permitted a constituency party to remove its MPs. As, generally, it was the hard left which had the energy and endurance to sit through branch meetings, there were fears of a holocaust of moderates.

But, for other politicians, the year was more promising:

Jeremy Thorpe, leader of the British Liberal Party, was tried at the Old Bailey on a charge of conspiring with others to kill Norman Scott, a male model. Scott, whose dog Rinka had been shot in one of the murkier aspects of the affair, claimed that Thorpe had seduced him, called him 'Poor Bunny' and come to his bedside with a tube of KY jelly and a copy of James Baldwin's *Giovanni's Room*. Thorpe was cleared. ('I'm a liberal but not a member of the Liberal party,' Graham told friends. 'Yeah, Liberalism's a dead dog,' one of them quipped.)

The Ayatollah Khomeini returned from exile in Paris to preside over Iran, now a Muslim Republic. 'Mad Mullah,' said the British popular press. The Foreign Office consoled themselves that he was too aged and frail to last too long or do much damage.

Mrs Margaret Hilda Thatcher, mother of twins and wife of an oil millionaire, became Britain's first female Prime Minister. The Opposition consoled themselves that, given her lack of senior ministerial experience and her disturbing personal manner, she was unlikely to last.

James Callaghan resigned as leader of what was now the Opposition and was replaced by Michael Foot, an elderly Byron enthusiast whose barber and tailor apparently cared little for the new religion of media beauty.

And Mr Roy Jenkins was said to be planning a major political statement. A former Home Secretary, he was blamed by the Right for the Permissive Society of the 1960s and was therefore directly responsible for Graham Sterling getting to sleep with Eliza Nicholas, as she then was, on only their third date in 1975. Alleged to have a passion for fine wine, Jenkins was known in the Labour Party as the Duke of Burgundy or Roy the Red or White or Rosé. He left British politics in 1976 and from 1977 served as President of the European Commission. In Europe, because of the grandeur of his bearing, he was known, in a bi-lingual pun, as Roi Jean Quinze. In 1979, he agreed to give the BBC's Dimbleby lecture, an annual televised address by a worthy on a matter of topical concern. This was scheduled for November 22nd, 1979.

'They were saying in the paper this morning,' said Graham, 'that he hopes to shift the political agenda.'

'Politics!' snorted Eliza, 'I think we had enough of politics on Saturday night!'

This was a reference to a dinner party given by the Sterlings five days previously – November 17th, 1979 – against the backdrop (as they say in stories with more acceptably dramatic historical settings) of the political situation outlined above. The six guests included, as was normal, more friends of Eliza than of her husband and, equally typically, the cooking was Graham's responsibility. It was not that he had a particular wish to do so but more that Eliza had a particular desire not to, which, in their relationship, constituted a casting vote. From the cookery column of his morning newspaper, two weeks previously, Graham had selected a recipe for 'Lamb in a Herby Crust'.

As that was a concentration job – real neurosis cuisine, given Graham's kitchen limitations – it would be paté starter, bought from the local delicatessen, and fruit salad afters. Giving himself four days to fret about the correct wine, he decided the menu on the Monday before the designated Saturday. On the Tuesday, John Durry, who had already accepted on behalf of himself and his newish girlfriend Jenny Cann, rang to say: 'I forgot to mention. You do know Jen's a veggie.' Graham hadn't known. 'A vegan, actually,' Durry went on, apologetically. The way he let out the information in stages suggested that he knew it was a problem. 'I mean, she doesn't mind what everyone else has, she's not, like, Stalinist.' Durry paused. 'Well, very pink meat makes her queasy. But it always did. I mean, that's nothing to do with being a vegan.'

Back on the sofa after taking the call, and relaying its train, Graham said to Eliza: 'Which one's vegan? I muddle them up.'

The bulge of Eliza's lips became a line, like waterwings hit by a pin.

'I think what it means,' she said, 'is that she won't eat anything that said ouch on the way to the supermarket. The jury's still out on Farmhouse Cheddar.'

'She doesn't mind what everyone else has,' explained Graham.

'I should bloody well hope she doesn't,' flared Eliza.

'I'm just wondering,' Graham mused, 'if it puts the mockers on Lamb in a Herby Crust.'

'Don't you dare,' said Eliza. 'She can eat the bloody crust.' But, even to her own ear, she must have sounded like a Grimm witch and she relented: 'We'll get her something nutty from the frozen counter at Sainsbury's. After all, it's her that's in the minority.'

Graham accepted this but, without consultation, decided that the pâté would be mackerel, which he thought Jenny Cann could allow. It seemed to him a decent Liberal compromise. And so, on the Saturday evening, with aperitifs emptied and a claret and a Chablis on the table (he didn't want to be dogmatic about what you drank with lamb), he was within acceptable reach of being calm as the guests took their places at the table and he carried in from the kitchen, scarcely ever in danger of dropping them, baskets of toast and warm rolls.

'Didn't John say anything?' asked Jenny Cann softly.

Graham showed her a smile which he intended to telegraph effortless tolerance.

'Oh, yes. Don't worry. There's an optional main-course for anyone who, well, opts for it.'

The sentence, which he realized might have been better constructed, was intended airily to suggest that, for all he knew, the entire gathering might be non-carnivorous. It was no problem; the chef was a liberal humanist.

'This smells like fish,' Jenny Cann said. Graham saw Eliza giving her the kind of look sarcastic schoolmasters give students who need four shots at the easy question which begins the text-book. Hoping Jenny hadn't noticed, Graham beamed at her as if she had split the atom in her first physics exam.

'What kind of fish?' she asked.

'Whale,' Eliza said suddenly. 'We're not sure which species but it's definitely one of the protected ones. I always think it's worth paying that little bit extra, because they taste better.'

'Mackerel,' Graham told her, lifting his voice above the laughter of everyone except himself, Jenny, and John Durry. Although, as the evening would prove, the other five wore quite different political badges, they had already ganged up against the faddist. The derision took some of the fire out of her individuality.

'I, er, it was still killed . . .'

'Suicide,' Eliza insisted. 'It craved the net. Pâté to fish is like heaven to Christians. I really wouldn't worry about it. Surely even vegetarians make an exception for *felo de se*.'

This was at least said in the tone which Eliza regarded as ironical. The sensitive would have argued about that definition but John Durry laughed and even Jenny discovered a pale smile. 'I'm sure it will be fine,' she said but Graham, when he was not worrying about whether everyone thought him a cheat for having bought the first course instead of making it, noticed that, although she mashed and divided the pâté on her plate, Jenny ate only unbuttered wholemeal roll. It was the evening's first defeat for tolerance.

For bigotry's subsequent victories, Eliza would afterwards blame Graham's seating plan. He, however, thought that harsh even by her standards. Their dining-room table was relatively plausible imitation pine. It would have fooled all of their friends except those who really worried about that kind of thing which, unfortunately, was most of them. It hinged in the middle and there was a hidden slab which swung out to make places for eight.

Graham had put himself at the head of the oblong with Ben Waddle, easily the least socially volcanic of those invited, at the foot. Eliza was on Ben's right and Hamster Macleod, who was potentially tiresome but not actively dangerous, on his left. Graham had Paula Waddle, as equable as Ben, on his right, and Jenny Cann, whom he hoped to protect from too much carnivore scorn, on his left. That left John Durry facing Alastair Macleod in mid-field, which, in view of their exactly contrary political convictions, was suicidal but there was no other way of getting boy-girl-boy-girl, which was one convention Graham absolutely refused to flout, given that Eliza refused to sit next to John Durry, whom she regarded as a communist.

Retrospectively, there were certain signs you might have noticed at the time – like the way John Durry had scowled when Graham, placing people, had quipped: 'Paula, you're on John's left – on the seating plan, that is!' – which suggested that he had come with his dogma bovverboots on. But, apart from the mackerel pâté incident, the early stages of the meal were exemplarily banal.

'Smashing big table,' Hamster Macleod enthused, her poetry-recital accent slightly scrambled by paté and toast. Graham had explained, perhaps in too much technical detail, its hinged extension system.

'What a super idea!' replied Hamster. 'Wouldn't it just be the perfect solution for those slum families with millions of kiddies and hardly any space? They could tuck it in the corner and get it out for meals!'

Everyone was staring at the tablecloth as if it were an exhibit by a new painter who the papers said was good. Graham glanced at Durry, who could be relied upon to know the exact cost of a pine *trompe-l'œil* table of this kind and precisely how long it would take the average inner-city family to save up for one, but he seemed to have decided not to pounce. Graham wondered what he could say about the table to multiply the conversation. He found: 'The great thing is it's only big when it needs to be.'

'Designed on the same principle as men,' said Paula Waddle wickedly, winning a laugh or smile from all except Eliza, who disliked talk about sex. Paula Waddle was a tall, confident girl of twenty-five with blonde hair lapping her shoulders and eyes and a voice Graham would have chosen to tell him any bad news he had to hear. Like her husband, Ben – a chubby, apparently anger-less man with amused blue eyes – she was a secondary school teacher in North London. Of the many qualities for which Graham liked them since they met at squash club, one was that they could be relied upon to kick-start dinner-party conversation for you.

'You must get sick of being asked,' said Paula, politely across John Durry, to Hamster Macleod, 'but surely you weren't christened Hamster?'

That's fine, thought Graham, although he would slightly have preferred 'surely isn't your real name' to 'christened', in case Hamster was part-Jewish and could be upset by the culturally assumptive participle. The first time she had been asked, at an earlier supper given by the Sterlings, the origin of her nickname, Graham had panicked in case she was so called because of her prominent upper and lower teeth, which forced her to speak and eat through a sort of funnel of enamel. This time, knowing the answer, he relaxed as she wooed the congregation with the cuteness of the story.

'When I was a little babbie,' she said, adopting a style of child's voice for the anecdote, 'I used to puff out my cheeks in my pram – like this.'

She made such pouches as a visual aid. It was not hard to imagine her plump, ruddied cheeks and buttery curls some quarter of a century earlier being cooed at in a sun-hat. 'Max, my big bro – he's a teacher too, Ben, actually, at Uppingham – said I looked like his hamster. It stuck. Family story, sorry. V. boring for anyone else.'

'And what's your real name?' asked John Durry. He was slight and intense, always hunting and expelling imaginary lice from tightly cropped brown hair, with a manner so permanently urgent and suspicious that anyone listening to the exchange on tape would have thought Hamster a criminal notorious for alibis.

'Ah, my dear chap, her real name's a state secret,' declared Alastair Macleod, four years older than his wife's twenty-seven;

long-browed and short-chinned, he was a totemic representative of all those routed from an old English (strictly Scottish) family, via a venerable public school and ancient university, to a long-established bank. None of his features took risks. It was a *status quo* face. Except that he could never have amassed the passion, he might have murdered half the residents of the south-west London street in which he lived and the Identikit would still have given him substantial crowd-cover. He could get away with most things; but not calling John Durry his *dear chap*.

'I mean,' Durry continued, 'to want to be called Hamster – not that I'm not admitting it isn't sweet – there must be something else you don't want to be called.'

'Wow! I'll set you as an exercise in negatives for my English GCEs,' smiled Paula Waddle. Hamster Macleod waited for the gurgle of laughter to drain away before revealing. 'I'll make an exception for you, John. My parents called me Emma-Jane.' Durry adopted his QED expression, having apparently proved something to his satisfaction.

'It causes one or two problems at the office,' admitted Eliza. 'Particularly the Japanese – pliz spik Miz Amzter.' Eliza and Hamster were joint partners in a public relations company called Dazzlem.

'There's no need for racism,' scowled Durry.

Even so, Graham was worrying more about the food than the guests as he served the main course: first, Jenny Cann's supermarket Vegetable Bake ('I'm really sorry to be such a pest!') and then the Lamb in a Herby Crust.

'Herby Crust!' said Ben Waddle. 'Sounds as if he ought to be a New Orleans saxophone legend. Blind, drunk, but when he blew that horn . . .'

Ben managed to be a jazz enthusiast without having yet hardened in to a jazz bore; something for which his many friends liked him all the more.

'I just hope it's not too red,' fretted Graham, carving. 'I never really know.'

He thought to himself that he sounded like a housewife but

then he saw the WPC, her patrol car half-hidden in the glade beside the centre lane, raising her arm as if about to flag him down, so he buried the reflection. Ben Waddle prodded at one of the thick slices on his plate and said: 'Looks OK to me. The trick is that it should look as if it needs bandaging but not stitching.' Jenny Cann looked as if she might be sick. Ben and Paula's uncomplicated attitude to the human body sometimes came out Rabelaisian.

There was a lot of yumming and mmming and 'Jolly good, Graham' as the meat, broccoli, potatoes, Chablis, claret and (in one case) Vegetable Bake went down. None of the conversation was particularly inflammatory. Alastair Macleod asked Graham how was work and Graham replied 'Oh, you know . . .' but no one went truffling on that subject, to his relief. Ben and Paula said that morale in the education profession was low because everyone thought the Tories had it in for teachers.

'Well, I'm not an expert,' said Hamster Macleod. 'But didn't I read somewhere that one of those hard left Labour councils has said that the blackboard has to be called the whiteboard. Or is it that they have to use black chalk. . . .'

'I think you've been reading the wrong newspapers, Gerbil,' said John Durry. Graham jumped but Paula could usually be relied on to play United Nations.

'Chalkboard, actually,' she said. 'Yeah, yeah. And all the little tots singing baa-baa-green-sheep while the staff room reels with the fumes of ganja and Nicaraguan coffee. Very little of it is true, actually, Hamster.'

Graham once again reflected on how difficult it was to have a serious conversation with someone who called themself Hamster. You had the constant subliminal impression that you were addressing a particularly cogent rodent.

'Sure you get educationalists, white and, er, coloured – ' Paula Waddle was now telling it – 'who want to ban the word black. But there are white parents at both our schools – and thousands more in the shires – who'd have every one of my coloured students in pens at Heathrow tomorrow. And that would include the ones who were born here. No political party has exclusive rights on head-cases.'

This was a draught of authentic liberalism and Graham, nodding support, breathed it in. He was pleased to notice that John Durry was nodding too.

'Absolutely,' said Durry. 'Paula mentions Nicaragua....' This was not so promising. In fact, Paula had made a fleeting ironic reference to that country's coffee. One of the things to which Graham objected about Durry was that he affected to pronounce the nation's name in what he claimed as the authentic manner: knee-har-rah-wah. Paula had said it the way Graham did, with a hint of rented undergarment: knicker-rag-wa. Durry was commencing a complaint about the way in which the Sandinista Revolution had been reported in the right-wing ('Almost a tautology') Western press.

After about ninety seconds, Eliza said: 'Couldn't we talk about something a bit jollier?'

'Hear! Hear!' Hamster Macleod added. 'After all, I don't expect the Nicaraguans are talking about us at their dinner parties!' Knicker-rag-wans.

'That comment,' frothed John Durry, 'encapsulates the tragedy of the Nicaraguans.' Knee-har-rah-wans.

Graham was about to change the subject to whether anyone had read anything decent lately, when he realized the danger of that opening. Not only did Durry probably have by his bedside at the moment *So Cry the Stones: The Tragedy of Nicaragua Now* but he might easily strike back at Eliza by discussing the big flood scene at the end of *Gone With The Wind*. He was seeking an innocuous alternative when Paula Waddle, helping out, asked: 'What exactly is it you do, Alastair?'

'I'm a banker,' Alastair explained and Graham guessed that the smile which swam across Durry's eyes betrayed a rhyme he had made privately. 'For Hanratty Forest Podge. We're in Cheapside.'

Paula was a big-league small-talker and came back with:

'And how is . . . do you ask a banker how trade is or does it, I don't know, just chunter along regardless?'

'Oh, yes, that's a perfectly reasonable question, my dear. Trade fluctuates. Actually, we're on an up curve again at the moment. A significant number of our clients had been making large withdrawals before the election . . .'

'To pay into the Tory slush fund?' Durry sneered.

'Not at all,' Alastair said. 'It was simple terror at the political situation. I would not expect you to believe me, my dear chap, but there was reason to believe that this country was on the brink of civil war. . . .'

There was keen amusement on the face of Ben Waddle. 'Good God!' he laughed. 'And your customers were funnelling the stuff out of the country, getting down the ten-cup tea-pot from the mantelpiece. . . . I had no idea. . . .'

Graham thought of the English upper-classes in their country homes; of the bolts jammed hard across at night like well-struck fours at Lord's; of the living members of families who could raise whole rugby teams in country graveyards lying awake at night, on mattresses mysteriously inches higher, listening for the tramp of workers' boots beside the fountains; of the metal detectors at Heathrow pinging the ingots. He could see it but he could not believe it. It struck him once again that to be a Liberal is often to feel like a foreigner in your own country. In America, of course, the arrangement was formalized and Liberals were regularly accused of being foreigners or at least of being in their pay.

'It, in fact, displays a quite touching stupidity,' John Durry was saying to Alastair. 'If there were a revolution, green and brown pictures of the dead queen's head would be as useful in a bank as up your chimney.'

'Well, yes,' conceded Alastair. 'We advance an argument along those lines.'

'I expect I would be one of the first to be shot,' Hamster claimed with an expression that should have been seen over footlights. 'Anyway, commonsense prevailed. . . .'

Paula asked Alastair, whom she rightly assumed to be a Conservative, whether he was a fan of Mrs Thatcher's. He puckered his lips like a duck's.

'I suppose the absolutely honest answer, Paula, is it?, is that she is perfect in almost every respect, except that one has qualms about her gender. I wouldn't want to take Communion from one. I wouldn't want one to open the England batting. And I'm not absolutely convinced I want one as First Lord of the Treasury. ....'

Graham had often observed how people of Alastair's class made a kind of full-stop with a drop of their chin at the end of some particularly illiberal statement. Politicians did the same. He had read that it was called an Applause Gap, cueing the howls of the crowd, but, in Alastair's case, it presumably invited a hum of approval or, possibly, the throwing of bread rolls. As was more often the case than Graham would ever have admitted, Durry spoke for him. The radical and the banker were eye to eye. Graham sensed that Eliza was blaming his seating plan.

Durry said: 'I suppose, where you come from, when people say that kind of thing, you all bang the table like fucking gorillas in fucking penguin suits, then get out your willies and wave them at the Cambridge sunrise. You wouldn't want *one* doing this. You wouldn't want *one* doing that. Just because she's a woman. Not that I think Thatcher is a woman, in the proper sense, in fact, but, even if she were, that would be even more reason for you not to like her. ....'

'I think I've lost track of your argument ...' laughed Paula Waddle. Graham was relieved because he had assumed that his own inability to follow the comment was the result of intellectual shallowness.

'What I think I'm saying,' spluttered Durry, 'is that the English nanny has a lot to answer for.'

A cheap shot, Graham thought. The good thing about the Left (and, for that matter, the Right) was that they always became immoderate just when you were in danger of agreeing with them. He sometimes worried that he had managed thus to excuse himself from every known political view, except a general one that deeply held convictions should be loosely rooted, but the truth was that he really wouldn't want to be either Alastair Macleod or John Durry for a day.

The table had become silent. Graham had long enjoyed a private joke with Paula Waddle that she ought to have been called Olive Branch and here she staggered again, waving a twig in a gale.

'Has anyone read anything good recently? I've just been ...' she began.

'So you think Mrs Thatcher is basically welcomed in the City?' cut in Graham, preferring this political devil to Paula's literary deep blue sea. Alastair, perhaps relieved to have been spared the strain of thinking of a book he might plausibly have read, plunged on.

'Well, of course, she's inherited a damn bloody mess from the Left – inflation, unemployment, and so on. We've got to mend the tools before we can do the job. . . .'

'I say it's about time a woman got the chance,' said Hamster Macleod. 'And jolly good luck to her!'

'She worries me,' said Ben Waddle, carefully, Liberally. 'Not just politically but something in her manner. And not even just the crowbar flirtatiousness with men. There was a girl at primary school, Little School, Fiona Fuller – Frosty Fuller we called her. She was in charge of dishing out the milk in the second years, although the actual term Milk Monitor had been abandoned ...' There was a precision of detail in Ben's reminiscences which may have reflected his dedication to balance. 'One day, as soon as we punched the foil in – those little bottles, always lukewarm, do you remember? – it was obvious the stuff was off. It never tasted like home milk but that day it was even sourer. So we're all saying "Ugh, Miss!" and holding our noses and people are saying "Pooh!", which would have been the word then. And Frosty – giving us looks like this is her milk, from her own tit, we're rejecting – says "There's absolutely nothing the matter with it, Miss. They're just being stupid."

And Miss – either she was called Miss Grey or she had grey hair, I forget which – said "If it's all right for Fiona Fuller, I think it's probably all right for the rest of you, even though you obviously aren't as grown-up." So we all drank it, holding our noses and churning up our faces. With the result that half the class at least was off next day with the squits – or a "tummy bug" as your mother would have called it on the note. Except, of course, Frosty, whose inevitably double-strength oesophagal bacteria saw her through unscathed. I often think of her when I look at our Margaret Hilda. . . .'

Ben took a sudden, savoured gulp of Chablis, as if to wash a taste away. Durry was nodding appreciatively but Graham thought he sensed that Waddle didn't want that man as an ally.

'She's probably a Tory candidate now,' said Durry.

'Ah, no. She died of leukaemia at college,' replied Ben.

'Oh, right.'

Graham found himself enjoying Durry's discomfiture, this rare ideological gaffe. But then he realized that, in effect, he was pleased that the premature death of another human being had permitted the scoring of a point at a dinner party. He trembled, expecting the arrival of either the internal police force or the questionnaire.

Durry, recovering more quickly from his own unease, said: 'And, of course, it was Thatcher who stopped free milk in schools, so that's a very resonant connection. . . .'

'Perhaps you all picked up a germ somewhere else,' suggested Hamster Macleod. 'Perhaps it actually wasn't the milk.'

'Ah. I can see you'll be voting for her again,' sneered Durry. There was a lull (contemplated-holidays and college-remin iscence stuff) through the fruit salad. Hamster wondered if she could taste papaya in there and Graham muttered that he wasn't very good on fruits but that there had been a yellow one and a green one he had brought from the Exotic Varieties section, which won an indulgent smile from everyone, including Eliza. Then, over the Muscat, which was served with the cheese for those who wanted it, Ben Waddle said to Durry, not at all in a threatening way: 'How are things in the People's Party?' Durry was an active member of his local constituency Labour Party branch.

'Inevitably, this is a period of reassessment on the Left,' began Durry, who, even on subjects which interested him, had a habit of sounding like the opening paragraph of a book you thought you ought to read but wouldn't.

'Losing the election must have been a bit of a blow,' said Hamster, who was usually uncomfortable in political discussion but regarded this as a safe observation. Durry, however, removed a particularly sizeable phantom infestation from his thatch.

'Well, yes and no. I mean, there is a view – with which my own, in fact, coincides – that it is better to be out and Socialist than in and closet Tory. . . .'

'You're right behind the scarecrow then?' asked Alastair Macleod.

'Michael Foot,' replied Durry, 'is an intelligent and cultivated man for whom the word Socialist would not – for once in the recent history of the British Labour Party – be a euphemism.'

Ben Waddle leaned forward with a regretful but compassionate smile, which Graham associated with Liberalism and had always wished he could do so well himself.

'Mmmm, John, that may very well be true but isn't it increasingly the case that a Socialist can only win an election in Britain by pretending that he isn't one? Then, after three state banquets, a Budget and a couple of briefings from the Joint Chiefs of Defence Staff, he isn't one anyway, so it hardly matters. What's more, your Mr Foot is shit on television, which shouldn't matter but it does. And ever more so.'

'I agree with what Ben says,' added Graham quietly and then, sensing that people were expecting him to carry on, said: 'All of it.'

'And do you have political ambitions yourself, John?' Paula asked him.

'You probably ought to specify,' said Eliza softly. 'I mean, with

John, it's as well to ascertain whether he means membership of an elected chamber or sorting things out solo in epaulettes.'

Graham frowned inwardly, although he did not risk doing so outwardly. Eliza, he reflected, did rather tend to over-state the case against; it was this, in the end, which distinguished her from a liberal like himself. Apart from anything else, she had given Durry another reason to dislike her.

He now hissed in her general direction: 'I have no personal ambitions to join the parliamentary Labour Party as it is presently constituted. I am, however, working, with others, to change its constitution. Or its constituencies. Or, specifically, the one constituency in which I have any substantive influence. The committee is fairly confident that it can have Reginald Fisher, MP – who is, for those of you who follow politics only from a distance, about as revolutionary as Dame Vera Lynn – deselected in good time for the next election.'

Graham wondered if there was ever a time – perhaps at breakfast with the startlingly silent Jenny Cann – when Durry spoke as if he was not reading a will in a wing collar in a period B-film. He also wondered who would take Durry on over this (as Graham viewed it) self-destructive witch hunt. He saw it was to be Paula Waddle, the evening's peace-maker, suddenly sick of pacifism.

'It's an interesting logic, isn't it,' began Paula, 'that a party, many of whose members lost their seats in a recent election, starts hounding out the ones who won?'

Alastair Macleod nodded at once, as did Hamster moments later and Graham after that, but Paula's husband was shaking his head.

'Ah, no,' said Ben. 'I can see the argument for a new start. I mean, stop me if I bang on about cricket for more than ten consecutive minutes but, sometimes, when you lose the Ashes, the players who've got decent averages or reputations have to be dropped as well. . . .'

'New broom!' was Hamster's contribution to the debate.

'I think Ben's right,' said Durry slowly. 'Reginald Fisher MP found an air pocket on a sinking ship. I think his biggest disappointment over the party's defeat was that it complicated his prospects of a knighthood . . .'

'As a matter of interest, how did Fisher get on in the last election?'

This was from Paula Waddle. Durry commenced a cranial inspection which would have given one of the old school nit nurses a tremor of professional anticipation. Graham wondered (internally, inevitably) whether, if you produced a transcript of this dinner party, with every comment presented anonymously, an absent friend could deduce the attributions. Was a conversation of this kind a debate or a laying down, like a wreath on cenotaph steps, of wholly predictable statements?

Invented insects expelled, Durry at last said: 'Eight thousand and seventy-four majority. But . . .'

But his but was butted in on. This was the touch-paper.

'Up or down from '74?' (Paula Waddle)

'Marginally up. But . . .' (John Durry)

'But up – against the national swing?' (Paula Waddle)

'Yes but . . .' (Durry)

'There's always a but!' (Hamster Macleod)

'I think his increase is very largely attributable just to residual local loyalty . . .' (John Durry)

'Just! Just!' (Ben Waddle)

'My dear chap . . .' (Alastair Macleod)

'The British electoral system as it stands will always give a false impression of the performance of those members who, though a liability to their party nationally, survive through strategic massage of the more old-fashioned factions of their constituencies . . .' (Durry)

'So you'd vote for proportional representation?' (Paula Waddle)

'I think there are more pressing anomalies on the agenda . . .' (Durry)

'If I've translated that correctly, to my considerable distress,

I find myself in agreement with you on something, old man.'
(Alastair Macleod)

'Whatever one's doubts about democracy, I do wonder how
many people, in what John would doubtless refer to as the final
analysis, would prefer the selection of MPs by a cabal of head-
scratching zealots clacking badges in disused Scout huts.' (Eliza
Sterling)

'She always goes too far – and that personal reference to his
itching . . .' (Graham Sterling, unvoiced thought)

'And what entry requirements must the successor to this, er,
Fisher chap fulfil?' (Alastair Macleod)

'Commitment – chiefly – to the established principles of
International Socialism. Not some wet Tory in a red
sweater . . .' (John Durry)

'So your belief – correct me if I've got this skewed because
I really want to understand – is that Labour lost the last election
because it wasn't left-wing enough?' (Ben Waddle)

'Yeah. Yeah, OK. That's a simplification of my analysis but
not a complete misrepresentation.' (John Durry)

'Jenny, you've been very quiet through all this. I expect you'd
probably agree with John, wouldn't you?' (Eliza Sterling)

'Er, no. Not really. We sort of agree not to talk about it. I
don't know what I am really. I suppose I'm sort of a lapsed
Liberal . . .' (Jenny Cann)

'Does anyone want more fruit salad? There's masses.'
(Graham Sterling)

A higher-than-expected 50 per cent of those asked were in
favour of having more fruit salad, including Jenny Cann. ('That
bowl is a holocaust for oranges,' smiled Eliza. 'A Cambodia for
citrus fruits in general.') For coffee, there was an even larger
turn-out of 80 per cent. As it was being served, Alastair
Macleod said: 'As a matter of interest, free country and secret
ballot notwithstanding – you don't have to answer if you don't
want to – if there was a general election tomorrow, which way
would everybody vote?'

There was a certain amount of fidgeting and discussion

before the count. Paula Waddle said: 'I would find it a lot easier if being a liberal and voting Liberal were the same thing, and more and more I think they're not. There really isn't a party for people like us.'

Graham thought: People like us! You'd need eight different political parties just to accommodate the eight views round this table. Finally, however, with Alastair Macleod acting as returning officer, the result of the dinner-table ballot was declared as follows:

Conservative 2 (Alastair and Hamster Macleod)
Labour 1 (John Durry)
Don't Knows 5 (Graham and Eliza Sterling, Ben and Paula Waddle, Jenny Cann)

After which, the dinner party passed to an unexplosive close, except for a troubling moment when John Durry claimed to have heard of a game based on famous last lines of novels. A majority of those present, however, voted against playing on the grounds of tiredness. Later still, 50 per cent of those present in the Sterling bedroom were in favour of sexual intercourse, but Madam Chairman's nay vote was regarded, under the rules of assembly, as decisive.

——Bob, looking at the results of this November 1979 dinner party ballot, is there anything, which strikes you immediately as interesting?
——Well, David, I think the one serious shock of the evening is the way Eliza Sterling voted.
——Regarded as a Tory stronghold?
——It had certainly looked that way but, Bob, note the rock solid traditional Tory support from the Macleods. I should say, however, that this isn't a complete picture – it is only a coffee poll, remember – as it includes no hint of the new band of Tory backing. For that, we'd need to include the Sterlings' cleaning lady . . .

——And, Bob, bad news for Labour?

——Well, yes, I think so. We're wondering, of course, how the party will fare in the battle between ideological purity and electoral pragmatism. And Durry's, obviously, a snapshot of that. But, you know, David, the most striking aspect of this poll must be the high number of unaligned voters. Around 60 per cent of those at the table opted for no party at all. This chart here – do we have that? – shows the Coffee and Mint poll projected across the whole country. One is tempted to joke that, on this sample, the don't knows would be forming a government . . .

——If they could decide what to do, Bob.

——Quite, David. But seriously, I think we're perhaps seeing the confirmation of a significant sector of the electorate which might be described as disenfranchised. I think a key finding of this poll is the number of people who would regard themselves as liberal, centrist or even soft right who have no one to vote for. That's very, very interesting, David.

——Thanks Bob. We've got to leave it there because we're going back to the Sterlings on their sofa on the evening of the 1979 Dimbleby Lecture. As we rejoin it, Eliza is remembering the dinner party we've just been discussing . . .

'Politics!' snorted Eliza. 'I think we had enough of politics on Saturday night.'

'Saturday night,' echoed Graham, aiming for a vocal effect – he characterized it as ironic sympathy – which he had often envied in Ben Waddle. 'I know. But I think his lecture is intended, in a way, for, well, people who are fed up of politics.'

He knew it was good as soon as he heard it in the room. It had sounded fine at the dress rehearsal in his head but, frequently in Graham's experience, a sentence with potential bombed when it went before the public. This time, it was clear he had a hit. Eliza gave it her standing ovation of acquiesence to her husband's view. It was agreed that they would watch the Dimbleby Lecture. Eliza returned to the early chapters of her novel.

Buoyed up by his recent conversational success, Graham even dared to say: 'You're whipping through that one. When do you think you'll have finished it?'

Eliza, smilingly, replied, 'Soonish. Do you want it next?'

'Mmmnoo,' said Graham. 'Well, yes, if you think . . .'

Rotund, orotund, but not (he insisted) moribund, Mr Roy Jenkins told his audience of a few hundred in Guildhall – and more, but probably not many more, watching at home – that he vividly recalled Richard Dimbleby, the lecture's memorial dedicatee, from long-ago appearances on television programmes presented by the late, generally acknowledged First Broadcaster of British Television. He was privileged to follow seven distinguished previous speakers: 'Four peers, two knights . . . only Mr Jack Jones and I unadorned!'

'Hint, hint, hint,' mocked Eliza. Graham risked a thought of irritation but not a facial signal of it.

'The Attlee Government,' plain Mister Jenkins was saying, 'is now widely regarded as a great administration.' In fact, to be cruelly accurate, he was describing it as being widely wegarded as a gweat administwation. His palate, fine for wine, was famously cleft with regard to speech. It had been responsible for a glut, during his political career, of indifferent impressionists in clubs and on television. There had been a time when anyone in Britain could do a passable Home Secretary or (later) Chancellor of the Exchequer; anyone, that is, except those few who talked like that already and would find people laughing and saying 'Nice one!' while merely asking, in their normal voices, for a roll and a packet of crisps.

'In 1951,' the lecturer was saying, '83 per cent of the electorate voted, and no fewer than 97 per cent of those who went to the polls voted for one or other of the two big parties.'

But this period of an enthusiastic electorate deciding between the two giants had, he explained, now ended. 'The Labour Party in 1951 polled 40 per cent of the total electorate, including those who stayed at home, and it just lost. In October 1974, it polled 28 per cent of the electorate and it just won. Even in 1979, with some recovery in the total vote and a substantial victory, the Conservatives polled only 33 per cent of the electorate.'

Graham knew this last statistic well: John Durry liked to refer to the Thatcher administration as the Third Reich ('An answer two-thirds of us never asked for') because of it. That was just Durry going too far, as usual, but Graham always found the figure powerful. It made any talk of government by mandate laughable. He had tested this conviction for holes, with the diligence of a quality controller in a sheath factory, and now felt safe to use it with Eliza.

'And they talk about a, er, mandate,' he ventured.

'Mmm,' said Eliza and then, directly at the television screen: 'Come on, Woy, Pworportional Wepwesentation! To end the thwee-horse-wace-with-one-wunner-handicapped we've got now!'

Graham feared that she was not taking it seriously but then reflected that, usually, when her contempt was as friendly as that, it was a sign of engagement. Her back and feet were fixed in the positions she employed for reading.

And so the Dimbleby Lecture continued, with Mr Roy Jenkins at Guildhall and interpolations, some silent, from Graham and Eliza Sterling; both, according to a recent poll, don't knows.

This, some people well say with howwor, is an unashamed plea for the strengthening of the political centre. Why not? (Roy Jenkins)

'Absolutely.' (Graham Sterling, unvoiced thought)

'The general mood is not that of reaction or of putting the clock back. But nor is it one of support for class selfishness or for revolution, whether it be utopian or malevolent.' (Roy Jenkins)

'I see nothing wrong with class selfishness *per se*. It depends which class is doing it . . .' (Eliza Sterling)

'Darling, you . . .' (Graham Sterling)

51

'Joking, darling, joking . . .' (Eliza Sterling)

'I believe that the case for proportional representation is overwhelming. The main argument for it lies . . .' (Roy Jenkins)

'Told you!' (Eliza Sterling)

'I wonder if she'll want, you know, rumpy-pumpy later. She's in quite a good mood . . .' (Graham Sterling, unvoiced thought)

'The onus of proof must be upon those who wish to defend the existing system under which you give only a handful of parliamentary seats to 20 per cent, or even 25 per cent, of the electorate . . .' (Roy Jenkins)

'The disenfranchised . . .' (Graham Sterling, unvoiced thought)

'This is not to argue against some dispute and tension within parties being inevitable and even desirable. Such reasonable and creative tension is, however, a far cry from a position in which internecine warfare is the constant and major purpose of a party's life . . .' (Roy Jenkins)

'Damn, I want to go to the loo. I wonder whether to go or . . . actually, it must be nearly over . . .' (Graham Sterling, glancing at watch, deciding to stay)

'Sssh! This isn't entirely uninteresting . . .' (Eliza Sterling)

'I believe that such a development could bring into political commitment the energies of many people of talent and goodwill who . . . are at present alienated from the business of government . . .' (Roy Jenkins)

'Darling, he's talking about you . . .' (Eliza Sterling)

'Is she being sarcastic?' (Graham Sterling, unvoiced thought)

'At least we can escape from the pessimism of Yeats's "Second Coming", where "the best lack all conviction, while the worst are full of passionate intensity" and "things fall apart; the centre cannot hold".' (Roy Jenkins)

With the distance of history, it can be seen that, for all its potential relevance, one of the most striking qualities of this passage of poetry is that it contains none of the consonants which the speaker was unable to say. Was Roi Jean Quinze deliberately allowing himself a peroration of unhandicapped clarity?

How does a public speech – that persistent prop of politicians and other demagogues through the ages – work? A thought is transported from the mind of the speaker to the brain of the spectator. But is the listener disposed to be receptive before the start? Can a reluctant ear really be seeded through the simple power of a voiced conceit?

Who can know? It can only be recorded that, on November 22nd, 1979, this robust appeal for powerful moderation was celebrated, in Guildhall, by applause and, in the residence of at least two potential recruits to the cause, by sexual intercourse.

Early in his erotic career, Graham had discovered that the surest method of delaying ejaculation was to think of Mrs Margaret Thatcher. The forestalling of orgasm was a social requirement of all middle-class liberal men by the mid-seventies; the aristocracy and the working classes, in both of which the link between alcohol and copulation was almost causal, were still permitted the grab, the lunge, the plunge, the thrust, the grunt, the cigarette.

The New (or even New-ish) Man, however, was required to follow a diligent rhythm of talk, finger, tongue, rhythmic friction, and position changing before throwing his load. Men achieved no tangible pleasure from any of this; it was just that, research showed, female sexual response required a longer run-up, so courtesy demanded that you put in the long-distance work before your individual sprint. Sexual athletics was now the exact opposite of the other kind: the more time on the clock the better.

The male brain, which (Graham had once read and now thought) was programmed for a quick spurt to further procreation, therefore needed to be sidetracked. Friends at university had suggested the solution, once intercourse was engaged, of algebraic equations. Graham had tried this once but lost his erection by the first minus sign, perhaps because, at school,

Maths had been for him a daily ordeal. At about this time, Graham and his friends were reading Martin Amis's brilliantly cocky novel *The Rachel Papers* and realizing – with a combination of gratitude and nostalgic regret – that this was the way things were now for men. Male pleasure was not the only end but, as it were, only at the end.

Cricket had sometimes worked for him. Running Test Match highlights through his head, he had once seen a pre-Eliza partner through three of what he thought were probably orgasms but felt it would be immodest to ask. Regrettably, by the mid–1970s, English batsmen were getting through partners more quickly than the most fecund student lover. Almost any anti-ejaculatory sequence you selected from an international match involved an Australian or West Indian fast bowler (their entire bodies built like the penis of your wettest dreams) uprooting a long thick stick with a sphere. This imagery could be detumescent or orgasmic, depending on your mood, but it was never merely anaesthetic, which was what these circumstances demanded.

Luckily, the beginning of Graham's sexual elevation almost coincided with Mrs Margaret Thatcher's election as leader of the Conservative Party. As soon as he first saw on television her (then) yellow hair, shrill voice (tutored to neuter her birthright vowels) and nervelessly certain eyes, he realized that, for almost the first time in his life as a man, he had encountered a woman for whom he felt not even a suppressed tremor of erotic curiosity. She was anti-sexual. And, therefore, the perfect desensitizing picture to divert the attention of the nerve-ends in the penis. (In political despair in the mid–1980s, Graham sometimes speculated about revealing his technique in a letter to a newspaper, thus assuring the government another conference ovation: 'And, thanks to Margaret Thatcher, the quantity of female sexual pleasure has increased substantially . . .' By then, however, to have written such a letter would have been the nearest the secular world could come to blasphemy.)

In bed, and inside Eliza, on the night of the Dimbleby Lecture in 1979, Graham was not thinking about Margaret Thatcher. For three basic reasons, he no longer used this mind dodge. The first was that even an implement as essentially stupid and immutable as the male penis can be trained to behave in a certain way. At some cell level, Graham's now knew that there would be no supper unless it spun out the fun for at least twenty minutes. The second explanation was a peculiarity in Eliza's sexual technique. A wholly passive participant in foreplay, she never touched her husband below his underpant-elastic indentations. Thus desensitized both by habit and present, local neglect, he could control his organ without recourse to thoughts of Britain's first female Prime Minister. After he entered Eliza, she would reach three or four of her orgasms-were-they? before terminating the encounter.

Now, for example, her lungs took up the rhythms of a runner for the third time in this particular bout.

'Coming!' she half-shouted, again, and, as usual, Graham distractedly reflected on how she sounded like someone hearing a door-bell downstairs.

In the unwritten Debrett's of sexual etiquette in the 1970s, the third lurch and gasp could be taken by the male as the equivalent of the last-lap bell in the ten thousand metres. Graham, accordingly, began to thrust without the safety-catch consciously on.

'Darling?' said Eliza, down quickly from her heights.

'Yeah-ah-Yuh?' gasped Graham, attempting to sound too viscerally involved for conversation, although, in fact, feelings were the one area in which he could avoid getting lost.

'Can we stop now?' she said, her tone as nondescript as that of a passenger on a weekend drive seeing a pub and wanting lunch.

'Really?' Graham dared to say on this occasion.

'I'm a bit sore.'

At first, when this had occurred, he had begun desultory discussions about creams and other treatments but he had soon realized that the phrase was a convention; like over-stretched hosts putting out the milk bottles. Graham halted, pulled back and slackened as he did so.

Husband and wife turned away from each other. Eliza was soon asleep, the post-orgasmic vortex of images which took her away including the face of a distant former lover, an exclusively dramatized scene from the houseboat book she was reading and the plump, bespectacled face of the President of the European Commission, intense at a lectern.

Graham, awake, was reflecting on a third, and recently emergent, aspect of his non-ejaculation. In furtive, urgent self-abuse, his first since marriage – one night when Eliza was away on business – he had been unable to come, abandoning hope of output after a sore, and pretty boring, twenty-five minutes. His new terror was that his diligent liberal humanism had produced a stage of evolution in which he had become non-orgasmic man.

For, as much as by the Biography and the Questionnaire, Graham's thoughts were charged and marshalled by the two conditions from which he suffered: one physiological, one psychological. The former was his inability to ejaculate. The latter was a complaint he called Donne's Syndrome. In his teens, Graham had discovered that he suffered the news of another's death – even someone he had never met: those standard paragraphs of carnage in each day's newspaper – intensely and personally. He seemed cursed, unlike those who could joke or snore or knit through a news bulletin dense with deaths, to fulfil the stiff injunction of the John Donne sermon: 'No man is an island, entire of itself . . . any man's death diminishes me, because I am involved in mankind; and therefore never send to know for whom the bell tolls; it tolls for thee.'

That bell disturbed Graham's work and disrupted his sleep. He had the ability to be, or the handicap of being, an all-purpose mourner. As his favourite living poet was Philip Larkin, that literary undertaker to mankind, his potential for gloom was further boosted. Already, through Donne's Syndrome, tormented by the mortality of others, he was also, from Larkin, obsessed with the fact of his own.

As he tried to sleep after the speech, both of his conditions affected his reflections. But as he lay there glumly, his seminal vesicles vainly plump with the potential of another generation of wrecked liberals, his thoughts also turned to the cleft, bespectacled lecturer and he had hope.

Politics was beginning again. And this was Year Zero.

3

What Graham Did

'ISN'T IT AMAZING,' said Appleton on the second day of Year Zero, 'how people with speech defects are so invariably given a name which includes the letters they can't say?'

Appleton, far from having a speech defect, had the perfect vocal asset for the times: a classless baritone which Graham, whose accent contained the wreckage of desultory school elocution lessons and frequent unbidden soprano notes of stress, had always coveted. It was November 23rd, 1979, the morning after the Dimbleby Lecture, and Graham and Appleton were reading the coverage of it – in their liberal and conservative newspapers respectively – as their Circle Line tube train rattled from the West to the East of London, where both worked; Appleton in a merchant bank, Graham in journalism.

Theirs was a commuter acquaintance, in which the primary source of talk was the inefficiency of the railway system, the secondary subject the events of the day as reported in the newspapers crumpled on their knees (or, on a bad morning, crushed against their chests) and a tertiary inspiration was tiny references to wife, car insurance, and summer travel plans. Graham was thankful that, because tubes ran, at least in theory, more frequently than mainline railways, a London Transport commuter friendship was less intense than a British Railways one, in which the travellers might catch the same train daily for thirty years. Graham and Appleton might travel on the same tube twice a fortnight. This meant that there were many things that Appleton didn't know, like the exact variety of journalism in which Graham was engaged. He had so far got away with technical, which, as a broad generical description, was accurate.

'I mean,' said Appleton, expanding on his theme of speech defects, 'when I was at school, there was a single chap in our year who couldn't say his r's properly.' The first 'r' in 'properly', as Appleton, said it, had a good strong hum and there was even a hint of the silent second. Again, Graham wished he had a voice like that.

'And guess what he was called? Brian Lawrence! I mean, Christ, Graham, imagine having to start every conversation with "Hello! I'm Bwyan Lawensh!" Even the sweetest of the teachers once accidentally called him Bwyan. Grew up with more complexes than a new town. I mean, what hope did he have of not turning out a premature ejaculator?

Appleton smiled. 'Pwwwematewa,' he mocked.

Graham felt uncomfortable, as he always did when he was with a man apparently secure enough in his virility to joke about sexual short-comings. Fleetingly, he visualized Appleton crumpling between the thighs of Mrs Appleton after a spell of mutually satisfactory intercourse. He imagined Appleton's wife, whom he had never met and about whom he had heard the merest details, as an air-brushed version of his own: a plumper, country-cheeked Eliza with a shy, becoming smile. It worried him that, married only a year, he always visualized the wives of other people, off-stage characters in a hundred business pleasantries, as being nicer than Eliza. Then he relaxed. All things considered, Appleton must assume Graham to be pretty competent in the bedroom or he wouldn't be cruel enough – Appleton struck him as one of those professional good blokes, whom your mother would call well brought-up – to taunt even a friend as tenuous as this with the phrases of sexual failure. Appleton would hardly make jokes about premature ejaculation if he began to suspect that, at this very moment, he was sitting next to a victimized non-ejaculator.

'I mean, take Roy Jenkins,' said Appleton, returning the

discussion from premature seed-shedding to the ejaculations, which many regarded as overdue, of the Dimbleby Lecture. 'Who can calculate the effect on him of all those years of being called Woy. Of – and this is the point – calling himself Woy. It's like Bwwyan Lawensh. Of all the bloody names to get . . .'

Graham contemplated saying something to the effect that, as children are named before they can talk, parents cannot be expected to know. Woy and Bwwyan were a result of bad luck, not malice. But, bruised at school and subsequently by the occasions on which he had been made to look stupid by hasty remarks, Graham now tended to weigh the sense and necessity of any comment before he made it. Graham also reflected that, in his own case, being allotted a name which his palate permitted him to say without difficulty had not entirely prevented him turning out a wreck. He had neither a stammer nor a stutter but still tended to falter when introducing himself. 'And the name on the card?' a telephone theatre-ticket clerk would say. 'G-G-G-Graham St-St-St-Sterling,' he invariably replied. His conversation was less like talking than the composition of a sentence by a slow, methodical writer who prized their style. The usual result was that the other person read the silence as a green light and carried on.

'Of course, christening precedes speech,' admitted Appleton. What generally happened, also, was that the other person said exactly what Graham had been contemplating. Equally, as here, they tended to express it rather more neatly.

'I mean,' Appleton went on. 'They could have called him Stan and found he had a stammer. But, even so, one can't help wondering if dear old Woy might not have been Prime Minister if his folks had called him Tony . . .'

'I think he might still be Prime Minister, anyway,' said Graham, quietly, as close to interrupting as he ever came in conversation. There, he had said it now. Mr Jenkins had been right: if the best did not show conviction – not that he, you understand, necessarily numbered himself among the best –

then the whole caboodle went down the tubes. Yeats had put it better but with that gist.

'Ah, you take all this new party farrago seriously, then?' asked Appleton. 'Ex-comwad Woy leads the acceptable face of Labour over the horizon and Labour goes down in the polls like ten red bottles?'

The newspapers were already speculating about the possibility of a fourth major political party founded on the kind of consensus socialism dispensed with by the present Labour Party Left. This time, Graham paused only momentarily before answering. It was not so much that he knew what he believed – he would hesitate ever to be so bold – as that he possessed the answer to this particular question.

'Yes,' he said. 'A new party. Labour's had the chance and they've blown it. It's like Eliza – my wife – was saying last night before we went to bed . . .' (Graham fleetingly wondered why he had included that irrelevant detail: was it to suggest to Appleton a healthy sex life?) '. . . she said, it's time we stood up and were counted . . .'

He wanted his voice to do a full-stop, perhaps even an exclamation mark, but it achieved something more like three dots instead.

'Time "we" stood up?' queried Appleton. 'Who are "we"?'

'The nice people,' said Graham, almost emphatically. Impress was probably too strong a word for what he had done to Appleton but he seemed to have had some effect. He felt temporarily uneasy at having attributed the definition to his wife but then he realized that a total stranger could not know the shocking blasphemy of Eliza's claim to represent that particular constituency. Then it occurred to him that this self-reassurance was disloyal and, for a moment, guilt replaced nerves as his primary insecurity.

'Ah,' said Appleton. 'It would be good. But don't the nice people always get fucked?'

It was Farringdon, where Graham got off, Appleton going on to Moorgate. As they began the customary, irritating wait for the doors to shudder open, Graham stood up. As was traditional, the train, without warning, break-danced a few more yards along the platform, causing Graham to lose his balance and slam the heel of his hand down hard into the knee, and blushingly close to the thigh, of the blonde girl on his right.

'Sorry,' gasped Graham, for whom that word was like warm and comfortable old clothes. In the opposite of the problem of the majority of people, about the only time he didn't feel shame was when he was apologizing. The girl smiled, so that was all right. At least he was so openly uncoordinated that his clumsiness was generally not assumed to be a cover for sexual interference.

'See you again,' he added, to Appleton; a ritual.

'I hope so,' came the reply; no less of one. His fellow traveller tapped the front of the newspaper. 'Interesting time for you, being a journalist.'

As the doors of the train finally opened, and Graham exited, he wondered, not for the first time, whether Appleton knew.

Five minutes later, Graham walked through the reception area of the address where he worked, flinching from the giant-sized skull, with its mouth in an inane gape, mounted on a plinth beside the door. In the newsroom, the large television screen in the corner was filled with the custard colour of firemen's waterproofs and the creamy spray – which, to Graham's shame, made him think of ejaculation – from their hosepipes, which were directed at the overturned Glasgow-London express.

They were pictures from the night before. When they faded, the newsreader, who still favoured striped shirts with white collars, although the fashion for them had passed, announced that the death toll had reached forty-seven, with the demise in hospital overnight of a father of three. Graham had a fleeting image of a middle-aged woman frozen by the telephone and young children shifting in their beds upstairs. He banished it. To a journalist, such casual human tragedy was work. It was no coincidence, he reflected, that newspaper reporters – though not, perhaps, those at this particular publication – were known as firemen. In those jobs, he thought portentously, you didn't get to cry. He knew what he would have to do.

Napier, the news editor, was standing amid the nest of desks which the reporters occupied; the television was in the corner. This arrangement was an architectural acknowledgement of the rules of the New Journalism, in which most of what appeared in newspapers was copied down from the television or the radio. Napier used to joke that his worst day in journalism was when the secretary forgot to get new batteries for the tranny. Hitching his trousers up somewhere nearer a D-shaped waist and searching out the bed of a missing tooth with the cap-end of a cheap blue biro, Napier had the channel-changer in his hand and was button-punching feverishly, seeking the best pictures. The look on his face was always about to break out into excitement but some vestige of conscience kept tugging it back. Graham had seen the look before, in Napier and others. Sudden death brought them to life. Disasters gave them a hard-on. This reflection alerted him to his own erection.

Fuck, thought Graham, still queasy from his retina throwing him the image of the ejaculating fire-hoses. You tried to be a liberal humanist and a feminist and a philogynist (the opposite of a misogynist, a female columnist had taught him), and yet every time you groped (look, shit, there he went) for a comparison, something – it surely could not be God – sent this parade of prick-imagery through your head. He had always known that being decent was dull but, if so, surely it ought to be easy. Fuck. Fuck. Fuck. Graham's swearing took place generally inside his head. He had never escaped enough from his upbringing to have the courage to do so in public without an involuntary lowering of the voice.

As Graham settled behind his desk, his body-language long adapted for obscurity, Napier spotted him. 'Morning, Bob,' he bawled, while, in a particularly frenzied burst of channel-hopping, settling for commercial television's angle on the Glasgow carnage over the BBC's. The name 'Bob' was a fiscal pun on

Graham's surname: Sterling. Readers of the periodical would probably have been alarmed to know that so much energy was expended on this redundant cleverness but it was widely believed that many of the older publications had people on the pay-roll charged with nothing other than the construction of arcane designations for members of staff.

'Bob,' said Napier, as the television pictures of the train smash were replaced by some of a camp young man with a cat-puppet on his hand, 'I expect you've guessed what you're going to have to do.'

Napier walked over to the single teleprinter the company could afford and tore off a hank of paper, which he dropped on Graham's desk. It was a Press Association report of the first names of the dead in the rail crash, issued by the police.

'Find out if any dentists died,' Napier said. 'Dental hygienists will do if you are pushed but, if you find a dentist, let me know. The front's still open.'

The periodical for which Graham worked was a weekly publication of a technical nature. Its name, which he had never quite told Appleton and which Eliza continued for as long as possible not to tell each new colleague or acquaintance, was *Dentists and Dentistry*. Hence the stark and staring skull in the reception area, a gift to the Display Advertising department from a prosthetics company. A casual visitor would have drawn the inference that the magazine was connected with illegal shipping or the occult but, on closer inspection, you saw the connection.

In one of the skull's back teeth was the kind of polyester prosthesis which the donating company had pioneered. Graham accepted that the group was at the forefront of oral engineering – he had written a piece on the subject the previous year – and that its advertising paid his salary but it was still a hideous intimation of mortality to have to face at 9 a.m. each morning. Graham had first come to this office, down among the ethnic restaurants and old-clothes and hooch-cassette markets of East

London, in 1977. He had graduated with a 2:2 in English, which meant either teaching or journalism.

This was the back-end of consensus socialism, with James Callaghan, the beneficiary of Harold Wilson's resignation, a Prime Minister never elected by the people. Schools, according to those newspapers (the majority) which supported Margaret Thatcher's opposition, were in ruin. There were stories of knives being drawn on teachers in the classroom. It was at about this time that Graham decided against a career in education. He was broadly with the Socialists on the policy of comprehensive schools but felt that someone of his delicate nerves might not be suited to the special responsibility of instructing the young.

Journalism, he guessed, might be safer, particularly if he could devote himself to the peace-zones of the world, the trouble-free spots. Fearless reporting from the front lines might be thrilling to read but he knew, in all humility, that it was not for him to write. Fearful reporting from the back lines was more his style. Admittedly, when he had made this accommodation with himself, he had not entirely appreciated the extent to which his career would be fearful reporting from the back teeth of the world, but there it was. Most of the people he had graduated with in 1977 had been unemployed for two or three years. It was true that when, in this period, Graham met jobless college friends, he would pretend to be unemployed as well but that was because people did not really understand dental journalism.

Occasionally, when a tooth story went national (invariably something banal like an original set of NHS dentures still functioning after thirty years), Fleet Street would send some of its frivolity operatives on to the circuit, where they would be patronizing to the representatives of the trade press while not declining to reproduce, nearly verbatim, articles the specialists had written. 'Where are you from?' they would sometimes ask. Once, when Graham had said, as usual with laryngitis of embarrassment, 'Er, you won't have heard of it – *Dentists and Dentistry*,' a man from a national broadsheet, with granny glasses and a green, waxed jacket, had said: 'Christ, I've got some mates who work for magazines that get left lying around in dentists' waiting rooms, but I've never heard of one that gets left lying around in dentists' surgeries!'

Graham had given the man a generous smile and shrug, as if to say 'I know, I know!' but this kind of response was robbing him of what confidence he had: a theft which, given his stock of it, was equivalent to embezzlement from a Third World country. At dinner parties, when he was lobbed that inevitable grenade of new acquaintance, 'And what do you do, Graham?', Eliza would parry with 'Graham's in medical journalism,' adding, in anticipation of the reaction she assumed politeness hid: 'Well, it's a smart move to have a specialism under your belt, if you're looking to get in to Fleet Street.'

Often a guest, usually a man thinner than Graham and with more hair, would ask: 'Which bit do you write about?' The stress of innuendo always irritated Graham because there were, in fact, no accredited cock correspondents, which made the question redundant of serious purpose and therefore no more than an attempt to introduce sex in to a conversation between his wife and Mr Wasp-Waist Bouffant. Eliza would retract her lips and tap the upper-front row with a varnished nail, like some coquettish contestant on *What's My Line?*

'Teeth!' someone would hazard. Laughter would almost always follow.

'What's it called?' someone would chortle. 'Don't think I know it!'

'Er, *D-D-D-D-Dentists and Dentistry*,' Graham would explain. Eliza, who willingly understudied most of his social replies, tended not to answer that one for him. The next test, invariably, was 'What kind of thing do you write about?'

It was a reasonable enquiry and Graham's defensive responses did not do full credit to the publication which employed him. *Dentists and Dentistry* was a tabloid newspaper, printed on glossy stock, with full-colour availability, which was intended to provide news and comment from and for those involved in what the paper's advertising department called 'the mouth industry'.

The publication had a regular staff of six. The editor, a man upwardly mobile in nothing but blood pressure, was George Elliott, but if his parents had christened him with a nod at literary precedent, they had been bitterly disappointed. A stooped and baffled man in his middle fifties – known to his staff as Emily Brontë – he had been absent for more than half of Graham's presence because of a volatile neurological history. Occasionally, Mrs Elliott, her own voice trembling with a more socially absorbable timidity, would telephone to review the likely date of his return. According to office legend, Elliott was a defrocked dentist. This had never been confirmed but there was much speculation among the staff he almost never saw about the nature of his valedictory offence. Napier claimed that Elliott had, one afternoon, borrowed the mouth of an anaesthetized female patient for fellatio but this tale was generally believed to be more revealing of Napier's fantasy life than of Elliott's enigmatic career.

More than one employee of what an ancient office joke designated the 'mouth organ' had remarked that Napier should be glad that journalism had no equivalent of defrocking. In the cursory staff file which the editorial secretary, the cheerfully uncomplicated Diane, would occasionally swap for a hunk of gossip, it was revealed that Napier had been commended in the news reporter category of the South-West England Regional Press Awards in 1949. From the late 1950s, he had been a fireman on various national news desks before leaving a tit-and-vicar tabloid in 1971 because, it was said (though not in the file), of a dispute over expenses. If so, it must have involved restaurant bills as now, in the middle of his sixth decade, he was a man so fat that the catch on his trousers was permanently undone; he clearly bought the widest waistband available off the peg. There was broken-glass Glasgow somewhere near the top of his speech but it was unclear whether he was actually

Scottish; news editors often pretended to be, in much the way that disc jockeys affect to be American.

Even his whisper was most other men's holler. It was generally directed at the only two reporters on the staff, who were Graham (also Chief Feature Writer and *de facto* Features Editor) and Timothy ('Timmy') Duvet-Hogg, who had joined from Oxford six months previously. A decade earlier, he would have gone straight to a job on a national newspaper – his uncle edited a tabloid gossip column – but Britain's new shop-front egalitarianism and an economic recession had blocked some opportunities. Timmy's father owned most of a London bank which bore two haughty Norman names joined by an ampersand; Timmy's pa's dentist (who deposited gold both in his vaults and in his mouth) was on the board of *Dentists and Dentistry*, so Timmy had been, in the phrases of those days, 'taken on board' to secure 'a foot on the ladder'. The response of his class to greater egalitarianism was greater nepotism, even if it was sometimes, of necessity, a little second-division. But Timmy, whose conversations with Napier were like the ones Anastasia Romanov might have had with Lenin, made it clear that his position in the dental press was transitional. He wasn't taking his coat off.

By contrast, Eric Foster-Thomas, one of the two sub-editors, never really put his coat on. Years ago, he had learned the office trick that, if you planned to be absent from your desk for lengthy periods, it was wise to drape a jacket across the back of your chair. 'I think he's around,' people would reassure callers in the second hour of his disappearance. 'His jacket's here.' Where Eric would be was in the office of a national newspaper; he worked for one each evening and others when requested. The imperative was financial. He was on his third marriage for an aggregate of seven children and there was said to be a stray eighth non-wedlock toddler for whom he also took the tab. The odd thing was, as Anne Colledge, the other sub-editor, put it, that you really couldn't imagine him doing it at all. His was not the conventional exterior of the *homme sensuel*.

He was trim enough for a man nudging sixty but the thinness was more the product of nicotine and worry than of vanity. Nor did his work-place conversation account for the speed with which he seemed to move from bar to bed to altar; but, perhaps, by this stage, his seductive repartee had been dulled by over-work and under-luck. The only explanation was that some people are just a magnet for sadness. Timmy Duvet-Hogg said: 'Let's face it. He's just fucked it up pretty cosmically!' Graham thought: People's lives!

Anne Colledge, on the other hand, you really could imagine doing it; moreover, you could imagine doing it with her. She was small and dark with good white teeth you saw a lot of (Graham often thought her picture in reception would set the tone better than the occult skull) and a sod-you look for bosses which had no direct effect when used on Napier but made everybody else feel good. Duvet-Hogg was attentive with coffee and compliments and she had become one of those women Graham saw as the road-model for which Eliza was the proto-type. She sometimes took phone calls with a blush but no one knew if there was a boyfriend.

This was the editorial staff of *Dentists and Dentistry*. George Elliott, when not called Emily Brontë, was also known as 'God'; Ernest Napier as 'Ape'; Eric Foster-Thomas (behind his back) as 'Stud'; and Timmy Duvet-Hogg as 'Bedspread' (or 'BS'), 'Lord Tim' or 'Cold Toes', which was arcane, even for a newspaper nickname, but what do you get if a duvet is hogged?

The prevailing editorial tone of the magazine was sombre and respectful of the profession's ruling bodies. 'Teeth not cheek,' Graham had been told as a trainee reporter and the main opportunity for circumventing this cautious orthodoxy was offered by writing headlines for lighter items, a duty which Graham, this being a small-staff operation, was expected to share with the enticing Anne and the mysteriously libidinous Foster-Thomas. He had, for example, been permitted 'Eee, by gum!' above a front-page picture of a Leeds-based root canal specialist who had received the CBE. Graham harboured mild hopes of a company which specialized in inter-dental waxing setting up in Bradford or the vicinity; he was sure there was a headline possibility of something like 'Floss on the Mills'. This would have had a second level of humour, given the editor of *Dentists and Dentistry*.

Apart from the news pages, filled with prizes, retirements, official reports, and raging debate about techniques of capping and extraction, there was a weekly, unsigned editorial called 'Mouthing Off'. Graham was now senior enough occasionally to be forced, by holiday rosters and influenza epidemics, to fill the hole. For someone like him, who went through events like a drugs courier through customs, terrified of being caught in possession of a view, this was an unpleasant experience. As a liberal, and furthermore an amateur affecting to advise professionals, he was keen to be generous to all ideological entrenchments.

The subject for his debut as a pundit had been the disagreement which existed in dentistry about extraction. One group of practitioners (which Graham's editorial called 'the pullers') held that a tooth ultimately, after decades of neglect or careless brushing, reached a stage at which there was no useful treatment but removal. The opposing view, proposed by dentists whom the 'Mouthing Off' column of June 15th, 1978, isolated as 'the fixers', was that modern dental methods allowed the sustenance of any tooth, even if part of it had rotted off. Cynics suggested that the fixers were merely financial pragmatists, who knew that a tooth still rooted remained a potential source of income. 'It's a milk tooth to you. It's a milk cow to them,' Napier had said at the weekly editorial conference. In his editorial, however, Graham had been careful to point out that the 'pullers' might equally be accused of ignoring the proven psychological disadvantages of tooth-removal. ('Aye,' Napier had remarked while subbing Graham's piece, 'never fuck a woman whose teeth are not her own.') Allotting two paragraphs to each side (one summarizing the pros, one the cons), Graham used the climactic fifth for the conclusion that each approach, while open to valid criticisms, had much to commend it; perhaps the best answer was a combination of the two methods.

'What exactly does your leader-writer have in mind?' a dentist from Loughborough had asked in a letter which Napier had gloatingly insisted on printing. 'Leaving the poor patient's tooth half in and half out? Perhaps your leader-writer might next turn his attention to the vexed question of anaesthesia. Would he, I wonder, advocate waking up the patient half-way through the operation?'

When he had been shown the letter by a beaming Napier, Graham had immediately felt the heat at his cheeks, a sensation which he recognized from school. 'Next week, laddie,' beamed Napier, 'we'll get you to consider the dilemma posed to Roman Catholics by coitus interruptus. Dr Graham writes: you can come inside her as long as you've pulled it half-way out.'

Blushing even more deeply – Napier's ejaculatory gags were surely coincidental, weren't they? – Graham had resolved never again to contribute to 'Mouthing Off'. But, by then, any embarrassment was just an echo. At supper, three days after he had written the piece, Eliza had flicked, as usual without involvement, through Graham's early copy of the magazine, sticky from the printers. Her progress through the pages followed an unbreakable pattern: flinching from the more graphic depictions of gum disease; involuntarily flashing her own near-perfect teeth at the glossy colour come-ons for new whiteners; promising to read Graham's longer features later and, finally, turning to the 'Mouthing Off' column. Eliza liked editorials, in any publication, because there was the possibility of disagreeing with them. As she read, Graham entertained the option of retreating to the bathroom but decided to take his chances.

'My God!' snorted Eliza. 'Who wrote this one?'

'I, er, haven't read it yet,' faltered Graham. 'What's wrong with it?'

'It's like some deliberately wicked parody of liberal thought. There are so many arguments against pulling them out and so many arguments against leaving them in. So – conclusion! – do a bit of both. Was Gormless George well enough to come in again this week or something?'

'No. He's, er, back on electro-convulsives. His wife rang. I, er, think Napier was doing "Mouthing Off" this week.'

'Napier! God, he might be an ape in many ways but you'd think he would have forceful opinions.'

'I know! You'd think he'd advocate tying a bit of string to a door!'

Eliza had smiled at Graham's brave rejoinder; doubly courageous, for he now had cause to wonder whether Eliza fancied Napier. He toyed with saying, quietly, 'Er, actually, I wrote it,' because doing so might rob her of her poise, but then he realized that confession would make him the object of her pity, which he thought he probably did not want. As a compromise, he continued throughout the evening to offer the opportunity to ask him what was wrong; but, though he acted sadness with an emphasis which would have been regarded as excessive in Greek tragedy, his wife continued to wear the careless face of a spectator at a comedy.

Not all assignments on *Dentists and Dentistry*, however, were so painful. There was a gossip column, 'Deep Throat', which accommodated what passed for tittle-tattle in the dental world: 'I hear that Tom Bollocks of Axminster is hotly tipped to be the new chairman of the British Society of Restorative Dentistry!' So stunned were they by the dullness of the copy submitted, the sub-editors would liberally (in the other sense, Graham would want us to note) insert exclamation marks; therefore according the page a rather distinctive tone of irrelevant pleasantries urgently revealed. Although the page was usually written by Graham and Timmy Duvet-Hogg, it was signed with the pseudonym Hal. E. Tosis. This excruciating pun was still too subtle for some of the publication's readers who, usually seeking a retraction for an alleged inaccuracy (perhaps Tom Bollocks was seeking the chairmanship of the European Society), would tetchily demand to speak to 'Mr Tosis'. The staff had concluded that dentists perhaps lacked a sense of humour.

The most popular regular feature in the magazine – according to recent market research in advance of a radical redesign, the third in five years – was an innovation of Graham's: a weekly first-person account of some eight hundred words called 'My Teeth'. Interviewed by Graham, who would then rework the conversation into continuous quotation, a celebrity discussed his or her dental history. The popularity of the column was a result both of its simplicity – 'Good idea, Graham. Everyone has – or has had – teeth,' George Elliott had sagely observed while briefly at the helm again between new treatments – and of its provision of anaesthetic banter for the profession: 'Olivia Newton-John had a brace when she was little!' a buck-toothed teenager would be reassured in the chair. Twice, revelations from Graham's pieces were followed up by the national tabloid press: a Hollywood actress, volatilely married, mentioned that her husband, a Sunset Boulevard bruiser, had broken one of her teeth in a fight, and a rugged actor, the latest Saturday night avenger on television, admitted that he was terrified of the dentist's chair. Predictably, there had been no acknowledgement of the source of the stories. Intrigued as to how the national press, whose monitoring of the tooth news was surely cursory, had discovered the columns, Graham did not for several years suspect the truth, which was that the entrepreneurial Timmy Duvet-Hogg had been the middle man.

No politician had been featured in the first eighteen months of 'My Teeth'. No one on the staff had ever met a dentist who was not right-wing ('I mean,' said Napier, 'who would want to poke around in people's gobs unless they could charge for it in the afternoons?'), but the publisher, whose more lucrative other products served drivers, bikers, golfers, and skiers, insisted on no party-political partisanship from his editors. The proprietor's view was that it was pointless to lose someone's thirty or forty pennies for the sake of irrelevant tirades for any flag. Accordingly, the closest *Dentists and Dentistry* had ever come to politics was a breezy Christmas double-issue feature in which a consultant orthodontist was given close-up pictures of leading ministers and shadow spokesmen and asked to assess them dentally. He had noted that Mrs Margaret Thatcher, the (then) Leader of the Opposition, had an aggravated over-bite. The orthodontist had pointed out that, in America, no man dare declare for the Presidency without corrective dentistry. He speculated how long it would be before election cosmetics were also the norm in Britain. The headline asked: Is it all in the Smile?

Risk was probably too strong a word for what Graham planned to do that morning but he certainly intended to take the 'My Teeth' column in new directions. As soon as he had ascertained whether any senior mouth-men were involved in the Glasgow disaster, he would put in a call to the office of Roy Jenkins, inviting him to be interviewed for the feature. No one could claim it was party political; Jenkins didn't belong to a party. Yet. Graham felt again a tingle of the excitement which he had known the night before.

It was ended by Napier, whose belly shuffled the mess of books and press releases at the front of Graham's desk. 'Bob,' he boomed. 'I'm holding the front for you. Bring me Top Dentist Dead in Glasgow Crash and I'll give you first fuck of my mother.' Napier, who made a moralistic fuss of his possession of short-hand and law certificates which journalists of Graham's and Duvet-Hogg's generation tended not to have obtained, also seemed to have done a course in Fleet Street Obscene. Graham found his sexually-metaphorical banter distressing. As Napier left to leer at someone else, Graham set the Press Association list of dead beside the National Register of Dentists and Orthodontists and began to compare names, initials, and addresses, while trying not to think about how much he disliked what he was doing.

'Don't worry, love,' Napier was saying to Anne. 'Graham's working on a story that will make you cream your knickers.' Anne did a conspiratorial roll-eyes in the direction of Graham, who idly wondered whether Adam, the first man, fashioned in God's image, had been, on balance, more like Graham Sterling or more like Ernest Napier.

Forty-five minutes later, Graham had found a coincidence between the two lists of names: Sayer, J. M., Glasgow. The police record of the first haul of corpses did not specify whether the deceased had a professional title, which would have helped as the J. M. Sayer in the office bible was a dental surgeon who took the prefix Dr. There was a comic side to specialist journalism – like the legend that the London correspondent of the *Irish Times* had reported, during a rail strike: 'Thousands of commuters, many of them Irish, struggled to work today . . .' – but it had its seedier aspects in the measuring of the significance of the dead by their profession.

Trembling with ethics, Graham reached for his telephone and dialled the work number listed in the register of dentists. The rings of the unanswered telephone were like the hissing of a scrapping cat. After a minute and a half, he replaced the receiver. He concluded that the surgery was closed. Because the dentist – what was left of him – lay mangled on a slab? Because it was a public holiday in Scotland? (His diary confirmed that it was not.) Or because Dr Sayer was fulfilling some prosaic morning engagement; like attendance at a funeral other than his own? The papers at the front of his desk were rearranged again. Graham looked up.

'Got anywhere?' asked Napier in the yell he regarded as friendly.

'Er, there's a J. M. Sayer of Glasgow in both lists,' replied Graham.

'Phone number?'

'Yes. The surgery's not answering. I'll try the house.'

'Good lad. Let's just pray he's dead.'

Remarks like the last could be taken the wrong way, out of context; what worried Graham was that, in men like Napier, they were meant the wrong way, in context. Their profession merely licensed their insensitivity. As Napier returned to the sexual harassment of any female employee under sixty, Graham dialled the home telephone number of the blameless Scot whom the mechanics of newspaper production wanted dead. On this occasion the angry feline was swiftly silenced.

'Hello?' answered a Scots voice, stretching the word into a tunnel of o's, but unusually soft, as if in church.

'Er, hello. Mrs Sayer?'

'Yes?' Nothing else. She was forcing him to be a reporter.

'I'm calling from . . . Mrs Sayer, I, er wondered if your husband wa . . . is a dentist?'

The conversation stopped for long enough for him to become conscious of Napier watching from the other side of the room with the swollen hopefulness of a parent at ballet exams.

'The surgery, er, won't be opening today,' said Mrs Sayer. At these words Graham's face clouded with an expression of profound distress. Napier, who had read it wrongly, gave a shrug, which his shape made an audition to be a belly-dancer, and started to riffle through agency copy for an alternative lead story.

'If you wait,' said Mrs Sayer, 'I can get you the number of another dentist.'

Christ, thought Graham, she's trying to make it easier for me. Anyone looking at him then – and no one in the office was, now that Dr J. P. Sayer was assumed to be irritatingly alive – would have seen a man who found a small rock in a sandwich and opted to swallow it to save his hosts embarrassment.

'Er,' said Graham. 'I didn't want a dentist . . .'

'Then, wha—?'

'I'm, er, a journalist . . .'

'For whom?'

'D-D-D-Dentists and Dentistry.'

'Och, yes, he gets that.'

The present tense briefly unsettled him but, on reflection, this phenomenon was mentioned in everything he had read about the relatives of the dead. After that, she spoon-fed him; he was the beneficiary of her decision that this was what the mangled dentist would have wanted. Dr J. P. Sayer, dental surgeon with a practice in Hillhead, her husband for thirty-two years and father of three children at those ages you called grown-up, had indeed died the night before. He had been taking the train to London for a meeting of the British Society of Restorative Dentistry. Would the paper like a nice photograph of him? She was sure she could hunt one out. Now, if he thought he had everything he needed, she had matters to attend to.

'Thank you,' said Graham. Even one of those brilliant young directors of Shakespeare he was told about on the Arts pages would have admired the amount he tried to force those two words to communicate. The subtext was: Look, it's a job and I hate it, this side of it anyway, but it's nice that other dentists get to read about him, maybe stop to reflect, look I don't believe in God but, well, I'll think of him, good luck.

Replacing the receiver, Graham thought: People's lives! He imagined that house in Glasgow with the curtains drawn and conversation in unnaturally soft voices and the neighbours greeting their spouses and offspring with particular force that morning; clutching their luck. For a moment, he made a sort of plate with his hands on the desk and laid his head on it. Observers with certain prejudices would have called it prayer but it was more a silent yell into an empty cave. The cave was soon invaded.

'Pecker up, Bob!' bellowed Napier. 'You look like it's your time of the month!'

If Graham had not been, in no particular order of weakness, a pacifist, devoid of muscle in his upper arm, and (though hefty) three stone lighter than his adversary, he would have hit Napier at this moment. He compromised by arranging his features in a pattern which even the ape would surely reconstruct as loathing and by looking up sharply.

'Bob! Bob!' roared Napier with what the man would have sworn in court was compassion. 'It's not your fault he isn't dead. In the end, that is the responsibility of God, not journalism.'

'He is dead,' said Graham flatly. The ape gave a poolswinner whoop and turned, like a juggernaut overtaking, towards the sub-editors. If he had been a lorry, you would have feared for the load.

'Anne, darlin'! Drop the Plastic Plate Breakthrough stuff. There's a hole on page four. Bob's got us a better story. Top Dentist Dead in Glasgow Crash. Two decks, forty-two point across four.' Momentarily troubled, he turned his head back towards Graham. 'He was quite a large banana, wasn't he?'

'Oh, yes,' said Graham. The words were surrogate punches.

'Six hundred words, Bob,' instructed Napier, easily ducking the laser of Graham's contempt, because he would never have thought to look for it. Top ought to be "Tributes have been flowing in . . ." I'll get Tim on to rustling some up. And Bob . . . ?'

'Yes?'

'I'll give my mother a ring.'

The six hundred words, none of them very long, which summarized the life of Dr J. M. Sayer, dentist, had been clawed from the rusty typewriter by Napier, who read through in about ten seconds with apparent satisfaction: 'Shit-hot, Bob, we'll make a hack of you yet.' Now came the part of the working week which Graham most enjoyed. The rice-paper constitution to which Napier broadly adhered guaranteed that he did not really victimize anyone for forty-eight hours after press day. The staff could do things they liked, which usually meant freelance work for other publications or, in Graham's case, arranging interviews for 'My Teeth'. On that day, with a particular spring in his finger, he dialled the office in Brussels of the President of the European Economic Commission.

'Bonjour. Bureau de President de . . .'

'Er, hello, does anyone speak English . . . ?'

'Certainly, hello. How can I help you?'

'Er, I work for the English publication *D-D-D-D* . . .'

'You require the Press Office, I think. I give you the number.'

She did. He dialled. The preliminaries were much the same. And then:

'*D-D-D-Dentists and Dentistry*. You probably won't have heard of it.'

'This is a newspaper of the teeth, Mr Sterling?'

'About the teeth. For all those in the mouth ind ... for dentists. We run a weekly column called ...'

Details were taken. This was certainly a most unusual – even amusing – request. Monsieur le Président would be advised of it on his return from London where, as Mr Sterling might know, he had fulfilled a speaking engagement.

'The only difficulty I foresee, Mr Sterling, is that perhaps the President's teeth are not his own.'

'That needn't matter. The area of denture-care is one ...'

'That remark was off-the-record. I should not have made it.'

Four days later, the Press Office of the Commission telephoned to say that they would, regretfully, be unable to accommodate Mr Sterling's most original request. But when, in 1989, the President, by then Lord Jenkins of Hillhead – in Britain, a politician's name becomes longer before they are forgotten – published *Brussels Diary*, an exhaustive memoir of his incumbency, the entries for the last week of November 1979 made no mention of the dental dilemma and Graham would always suspect that he had never been asked.

The following day – November 24th, 1979 – most broadsheet newspapers reported a speech made by Dr David Owen, former Labour Foreign Secretary, at Wolverhampton Polytechnic. Dr Owen, probably the most physically beautiful of post-war British male politicians, had been tipped as possible leader of a putative new centre party, but he told the students unequivocally: 'The most foolish course now for those who are determined to swing the Labour Party back to sensible Socialism would be to abandon the struggle within the Labour Party, to talk of founding new parties. ...'

'A pity,' said Eliza Sterling. 'He wasn't unattractive. ...'

4

However, Others Believe . . .

'SEVENTEEN.'

'Sorry?'

'Boy of seventeen. Jesus.'

It was Graham's habit, on every day when he failed to forget about it, to check the ages in the obituary column of the broadly right-wing paper which Eliza took in addition to and in preference to her husband's broadly left-wing one. The latter publication did not list deaths, for reasons which escaped Graham. Surely it could not be political ideology; the belief that, afterwards, we are all just dust, an equality of nothingness? The newspaper's position on this was further compromised by its willingness to record the celebrated corpses of the day. Whatever the reason, he was forced to wait until his wife had finished with her paper, before checking the deaths. You looked first at ages, then for verbs, adverbs, adjectives, any hint of the manner. Different numbers and constructions nudged forth different pictures, which were variously scaring or consoling.

What you were seeking, ideally, was 'aged 89, surrounded by his much loved/loving family' but the divisions of fear could be filigree. 'Aged 89, thanks to all at St Martha's/Kevin's', smelled of death alone, perhaps in rancid underpants. Similarly, '63, suddenly at home', with its comfortable suggestion of not knowing, out-ranked '63' with invitations to send money to a Fund or Unit, which spoke all too loudly of knowing only too well. Graham, who had begun this death-watch in his early teens, could remember a time when '55, on holiday in Spain' seemed unappalling but now – this was 1981 and he was twenty-six – anything around the fifties meant, subjectively extended, your children getting a phone call at university to tell them you were dead. Reading obituary columns now was like shells exploding closer to your trench.

Still, he had already outstripped this morning's first entrant (and first exit) by nine years.

' "Aged 17, after a heroic fight",' he read out to Eliza. 'Jesus.'

'An heroic, shouldn't it be?' she replied, mildly.

'What?'

'After an heroic fight, surely.'

There was still nothing much in the tone; friendly-antiseptic, a skilled teacher with a dim child. Graham's voice, however, was on the rise.

'Well, even so, seventeen. "Thanks to the Royal Marsden." Cancer place that, isn't it? Have to be. Bike accidents, stabbings, they always put "tragically" . . .'

'I mean, you'd think they'd have someone to correct that kind of thing,' Eliza added, on her parallel but distant track, flapping at toast crumbs with a napkin.

Correct what? thought Graham. Disease? Death? Grief? Anger had never been an emotion which he could achieve from a standing start but he was already half-way through the run-up. He was married to a woman more shocked by grammar than by cancer. Among the more depressing tendencies of English life was that of the educated to be more interested in syntax than sin. Graham had once read in a newspaper a letter protesting about a report that eight people had been 'Hung' in Uganda. 'The correct participle, sir,' the correspondent had roared, 'is "hanged". I fear for the standards of this country.' This apparent lack of fear for the standards of another country which was roping its people to a gallows had clearly been accepted by the editor with equanimity.

For the rest of that day, the number 17 jumped out at him, like the figure on the door of a house seen in a dream; a place of definite but unexplained significance.

This breakfast, which he would have wished a biographer to note, took place in January 1981. The year 1980, which has occurred between this chapter and the last, had been one in which Graham – and those of his friends and colleagues who were not members of what he regarded as the Rhino Right – feared the outbreak of World War III.

On the first day of the new decade, while the Capitalists fumbled with the headache pills and stomach settlers, Soviet Communist tanks entered Afganistan. John Durry, whom Graham and Eliza had met that evening at the Waddles' New Year party, insisted 'the Russians were invited' but Eliza replied: 'Ah, yes, John, but I invite you to my dinner parties.' Shortly afterwards, Andrev Sakharov, a Russian scientist who had criticized the action in Afganistan, was arrested and deported to Gorky.

From then on, if you were young, contemplating what you had previously thought of as your future, you really didn't have to listen very hard to hear four horsemen kicking at the stable door. On April 25th, 1980, President Jimmy Carter launched Operation Delta to rescue his nation's hostages in Iran. The mission ended amid eight deaths, the charred shells of Army helicopters and the mocking cackle of Ayatollah Khomenei. Hearing the first reports on the morning news, Graham was unable, on reaching the office, to proceed with a feature on advances in root canal surgery, of which he had written three paragraphs the night before. Having once heard a best-selling thriller writer advise in a radio interview that aspiring authors should always finish work in mid-sentence, the better to continue next day, he had stopped the previous evening on 'However, others believe, . . .'

Now, however, he could not get beyond the comma. The sentence was supposed to introduce direct quotation from orthodontists who feared the procedures were unproven but, each time he attempted to complete it, his fingers would freeze on the keys, distracted by the certainty of Soviet retaliation for Carter's folly. Two thoughts particularly appalled Graham. The first was that the fucking Third World War was to be started by the one truly fucking liberal President in recent American history. The second was that his own career, indeed what you might justifiably call his writing life, was to conclude with words which were a parody of centrist indecision: 'However, others believe, . . .' So this was the way the world ended; not with a noun but with a comma.

Moscow, however, stayed calm. John Durry commented, at a soccer match during this period, 'Whose foreign policy in the twentieth century is the more reprehensible? America's or Russia's?' and Graham almost agreed with the answer clearly implied. President Carter, in a nationwide television address, became the first politician in world history to say the words: 'The responsibility is mine alone.' Perhaps because of this, defeated in November, he was replaced by Ronald Reagan, who had shared the billing with a chimpanzee in Hollywood, had informed on fellow actors for the FBI and was now said, in newspaper profiles, to see the Book of Revelation as a screen-play for a movie due to start shooting any day then. Margaret Thatcher's government agreed to the siting of American nuclear missiles in rural Britain and Graham, although he thought more and more about death, ceased, during this period, to read the obituary columns with such zeal. Who could now care about the relative merits of expiring at fifty in a living room as opposed to ninety in a home or forty in a ward? They would all go together, one beside eighty-nine, suddenly at home, thanks to all at the Pentagon and the Kremlin, no flowers grow, with no families to mourn and no newspapers to record the departures alphabetically.

The possibility overshadowed everything else. Unemployment in Britain reached two million, the highest since 1936, John Lennon was shot by a liberal-minded reader of J. D.

Salinger, and Britain surrendered Rhodesia. But to a cynic, which Graham feared he was becoming, all events seemed headed to one end. On January 20th, 1981, Ronald Reagan was sworn in as fortieth President of the United States.

'And last,' said John Durry, over tagliatelle carbonara at the Sterlings. 'And last.'

It was the flags and the chanting which first disturbed him. Then, the language.

'Oi, watchit, mate, OK?'

This was said by John Durry on the fourth day of the Ronald Reagan presidency – Saturday 24th January, 1981 – to an anonymous yob who had just trodden on the feet of him and Graham. They were in the approach road leading to the stadium of their nearest first division football team. It was slow progress, behind the beating tail, steaming backsides, and sliding feet of lines of police horses. Periodically, as the crowd was funnelled by the rearing beasts and the raised truncheons of their riders, the two men would be elbowed or otherwise dented by some large, scarved slab of beer-belly and denim. It happened again.

'Ooooff!' splurted Graham. Then, ridiculously, pre-emptively, 'Sorry!'

'Oi, fucking watchit, fat cunt,' said Durry, his even, Varsity vowels roughening effortlessly to the required street grunt.

Graham always admired people who had more than one voice, who could adjust their timbre or vocabulary to the situation, but he still marvelled that the man whom Durry had just compared to an unappetizingly fleshy and slack vagina replied with nothing more heightened than a grin and a fraternal bang on the shoulder, which Graham first took as an assault and flinched. Then he realized that the exchange was agreed social currency, equivalent in its way to the requirement in gentrified England to reply to an invitation by copying it out on to another piece of paper before adding 'and has pleasure in accepting'.

It was by now standard in British football for the scheduled fixture to be preceded, punctuated and/or followed by a parallel match between teams of rival supporters. Refereed by mounted police, this encounter had no rules beyond those laws of the land which the participants were ignoring and no goals beyond the inflicting of injury (quite often fatal, now). The teams gave themselves names and kits and one of the popular English newspapers, with characteristic wit, began to publish league tables of results in the punch-ups.

'If I had a son,' said Graham (an expression as vague and fairy-tale for him as 'If I were King' would be for children), 'I wouldn't take him to football, I don't think, not now.'

They had reached their seats in the main stand. Suddenly, above the routine screech of the names of the two teams and their most celebrated players, they heard screams of real fear and saw the crush on the terraces to their left crumple and shudder at the front. It was the now traditional five to three fight.

'Farkin' arseholes,' said the man on Graham's right. He wore a camel-hair coat, which enclosed a camel-hump tummy. He smoked a thick Havana cigar but his conversation suggested that this was more probably homage to Churchill than Castro.

'They want putting up against a bleedin' wall, they do,' he continued, as the police ringing the pitch gathered in the corner where the fighting was.

'What makes people behave like that?' asked Graham in an art gallery whisper; he had a terror in football crowds, as indeed in any gatherings, of his conversation being overheard and mocked or challenged.

'Oh, Thatcherite tax breaks and incentives. Probably a builder. Get the coat and the smoke. Giveaway. Class traitor, naturally. Thinks he's different from the kids down there when the only thing different is that he sold out. Why are you smiling?'

'Not him, them. The . . .' Graham lowered his voice to chapel level. 'Hooligans.'

'Ah, well now,' said Durry. 'Hooligans is an emotive word. I mean, with two million unemployed, it's arguable that the really incredible thing is the limit of the social unrest is a few split heads at football matches . . .'

'People have died,' said Graham but his interjection had no more effect on the conversation than interference from another station on the radio.

'. . . I mean,' Durry continued, 'these people have been treated like shit. Benidorm and refrigerators in the '70s and now it's sorry, time up, can we have that back please? I think it's not in the end, entirely surprising that people are asking why? That people are saying: sorry, could I just check something?'

A particular trick of Durry's in debate was to apply the language of cerebral disagreement to the actions of physical conflict so that a fist became an interjection, a boot a donnish footnote. Graham didn't blame Durry for doing this; he merely feared its tendency to introduce a further confusion into another issue on which he was unsure of his opinion. Although he blinked his eyes, and tried to concentrate on the now quiescent violence on the terrace, he felt the questionnaire approaching.

15: Do you believe that violence involving football supporters is essentially the result of:

☐ A: Mass unemployment (Jan. 1981 figure: two million) and the forcible conclusion of the consumer dream in which the proletariat was encouraged to believe in the '70s?

☐ B: The end of National Service (or military conscription) in 1961?

☐ C: The innate evil in the heart of man?

☐ D: Antagonistic policing and the poor design of football grounds, most recently exacerbated by terrace fencing ('If you put people in cages, they will behave like animals' — newspaper columnist, 1981)?

(Remember: you may tick one box only)

Well, B was for buffers and the Rhino Right. Graham was

fiercely opposed to the re-introduction of National Service. This was partly, it was true, because of a personal conviction that NCO Sterling would have spent two-thirds of his army engagement – left, right, left, right, left, right – with Cherry Blossom bollocks or his head in a puddle, three miles behind the pack on a training run. But equally, as he didn't believe in wars, he could hardly justify the priming of a peace-time army.

More tempting than it should have been to an agnostic was C. A liberal humanist was meant not to believe that Man was inherently evil – indeed was supposed to uphold the opposite – but Graham had recently come to covet a secret theory which he had never yet dared to express. It was this: that the increasing violence in both Britain and America in recent years was the result of the absence of major global conflicts in which natural masculine violence could be satisfied. Accordingly, that psychosis which had previously been re-labelled Patriotism, and therefore sanitized, was now directed into peace-time domestic violence which was labelled anti-social. People who became national hate figures for killing fourteen people in a hamburger bar would once have been eligible for a medal for doing it to the Vietcong, their insanity interpreted as heroism.

This belief scared him (people might hate you for it, mightn't they?), so he wavered between A and D. In fact, his real feeling was that soccer violence resulted from a combination of social anger and bad planning but it was one box only. So, with the standard bag of misgivings, he selected A. The leap in the screeching around him announced the entrance of the teams, information which he could not receive visually because all the rows in front were now standing. About to rise himself, he was distracted by a bracket:

(If you answered B, C, or D, proceed to Question 16 (the 'right to life') and Question 15 (Negotiation/Warfare); if you answered A, however, please see Supplementary Question 15a).

Bugger, he thought, he always had to do the supplementaries. This time, it was:

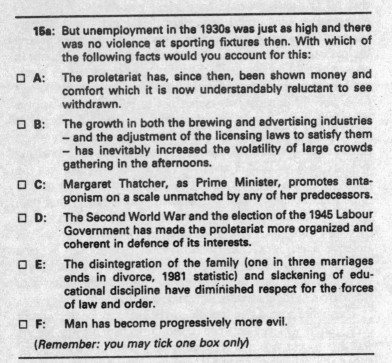

15a: But unemployment in the 1930s was just as high and there was no violence at sporting fixtures then. With which of the following facts would you account for this:

☐ **A:** The proletariat has, since then, been shown money and comfort which it is now understandably reluctant to see withdrawn.

☐ **B:** The growth in both the brewing and advertising industries – and the adjustment of the licensing laws to satisfy them – has inevitably increased the volatility of large crowds gathering in the afternoons.

☐ **C:** Margaret Thatcher, as Prime Minister, promotes antagonism on a scale unmatched by any of her predecessors.

☐ **D:** The Second World War and the election of the 1945 Labour Government has made the proletariat more organized and coherent in defence of its interests.

☐ **E:** The disintegration of the family (one in three marriages ends in divorce, 1981 statistic) and slackening of educational discipline have diminished respect for the forces of law and order.

☐ **F:** Man has become progressively more evil.

(Remember: you may tick one box only)

Six possibilities. Graham shivered. This was clear statistical evidence that the uncertainties were multiplying. It had been bad enough, for a man who didn't know, to have to run the gamut from A-D but now it stretched to F. He quickly dismissed A and D (demographic shifts in the working class) on the basis that Durry would have chosen them and E (the undisciplined young) because his mother would have ticked that. He was therefore left with either F (the devil) or B (the demon drink), both of which were differently linked with Puritanism, so he was forced to opt, decisively by default, for C; the theory that the current government forced its victims and opponents to their own extremes. He savoured the brief, rare, slippery moment of knowing; then it was gone.

Policemen led a few of those involved in the clashes down past the stand in which Graham and Durry sat, towards the tunnel.

'Fuckwits,' said Camel-coat, at Graham's shoulder. 'They wanna bring back conscription.'

The match began. It was what television football commentators called 'real end to end stuff', which meant that the ball was punted from goal to goal, while bunches of players chased after it, usually failing to make contact. Most of the skill was demonstrated by the black players but their efforts were invariably met by jeering from the terraces. Those racist thugs with a crude grasp of metaphor had, during this season, developed the technique of monkey noises or the throwing of bananas but, here, they merely used the boo. The sound rose up now, as a winger whose family had originated in Jamaica pushed the ball between a pair of white legs, evaded a subsequent flailing pale shin and headed for the opposing net. This prowess was greeted by the sounds of derision; the effect was as dislocating as the disparity, in television comedy programmes, between the quality of the gag and the cacophony of response.

'Nice, nice, nice, nice,' growled Durry, unusually close to emotion.

'Jesus!' moaned Camel-coat. 'If they don't close down that black bugger, they're fucking fucked.'

The winger's final shot was soft and easily stopped and closely followed by the whistle for half-time. Graham and Durry walked past the retching kennel stench of urine (even at the larger clubs, the latrines were a steaming, tiled trench in a de-commissioned cowshed) to the refreshments hut where they ate an alleged Frankfurter which a German would have been reluctant to see exiting his body, never mind entering it, and a cardboard cup of the scalded beverage which the club marketed under the names coffee, tea, and Bovril, and which the regulars called Ceabov.

'I, er, love the atmosphere at soccer matches,' Graham ventured.

'Working-class sport,' replied Durry through a splash of Ceabov. 'Can't beat it!'

(What Graham's brain set up for his mouth, which refused to say it, was: 'Though I notice you sit in the stands, John, not stand on the terraces.')

'I thought you'd be at Wembley today,' he said instead.

'Isn't a match, is there?'

This was a joke, in as much as Durry ever sank to them. That afternoon, at the Conference Centre in Wembley, beside the famous football stadium, the Labour Party was holding a Special Conference on the issues which threatened to split MPs and membership.

'I think it is fairly clear that the Angels will win,' Durry continued, his voice obscured by a swab of the impostor-sausage. 'Anyway, each branch can only send so many.'

'Which, er, way is Reginald Fisher voting?'

'Oh, against. Very much against. He's such a reactionary, of course, that even the adjournment for lunch will have been carried with one opposed, I expect. It scarcely matters, though. We've all but swung it now. He'll be out by the next general election.'

'So, John Durry, MP,' said Graham, as lightly as he could.

'Absolutely not. It's a delusion purely of your wife's that I'm interested in power for myself. No, I think we're going to have – I mean, obviously, it's for the Selection Committee to decide – but there's a certain weight of support behind Michael Rowe. Shit-hot operator. From the Anti-Racism League. Of course, Fisher regards him as an uppity nigger . . .'

They dropped their crushed cups as neatly as possible on the rubbish surrounding the few, stuffed bins. The second half restarted with a diagonal dash and perfect, swirling cross by the West Indian (although qualified to play for England) winger.

The crowd hooted its disapproval. Graham's eye caught a yellow boomerang arching high from the far terrace. Others followed and he realized what they were; this club's thugs, too, had discovered the fruits of metaphor.

It struck Graham that here was another aspect of British politics which he did not fully understand. Those whooping jokers throwing fruit, were, predominantly, representatives of the working class whom Durry, a middle-class Marxist, had decided would be better served by a parliamentary representative of the same ethnic origins as the footballer they were abusing. Graham knew – yes, here he would use that treacherous verb – that something was wrong with this arrangement.

'Who won?' asked Eliza, who was watching television, when Graham got home from the match. He told her.

'Oh, good,' she said, with the expert improvised sincerity of the marriage partner. Graham frowned.

'Oh, dear.' She revised her opinion with equal expertise. 'And how was Che Durry?'

'OK. He's not as bla—' The Liberal safety-catch clicked on efficiently. 'He's not as bad as you make out.'

'Oh, I don't make him out to be bad, Graham. It's more that I can't make him out. I mean, to a certain extent, external circumstance must be accepted. I would ideally like a smaller dress size, you would ideally like more hair . . .' Here, Graham reddened and looked away. 'But we are sanguine in the absence of these things. Now, John – John would ideally like not to be white or middle class. The difference is, he really thinks he can rewrite family history, apply some biological over-ride . . .'

Some days later, ruminating on a train, Graham constructed the proper answer to this. It was: 'No, no, no. At least Durry worries about it. That's better, in the end, than what you do, which is to interpret all concern for others, all attempt to identify with other lives, as pretension or pretence. The central problem of all our lives is to have been born rich and white in peacetime England and to have grown up white and richer. It's not ingratitude to look elsewhere, it's emotional maturity. It might be lucky to be what we are but, in the end, we will be judged on how we use that luck . . .'

But, for Graham, remarks perfected after the event – what might be called a late equalizer – were a constant phenomenon. Hours later, in his brain, he trounced all ideological opponents but he knew this had no merit; it was like a satisfied masturbator claiming to be a great lover.

Graham offered his usual response to articulate or lengthy argument, which was silence. Eliza filled it with voices from the television, whose volume she had lowered with the handset when he came in.

Graham saw a florid middle-aged man shouting from a podium. The next shot was of a group of other heads with fat, red faces shaking in dissent; and then a picture of a different pack of unexercised bodies banging their hands together in front of their bellies. It was, Graham quickly appreciated, a report on the Labour Special Conference at Wembley.

Behind the conference chairman – a volcanic, balding Scot – was a banner reading PEACE, JOBS, FREEDOM. In apparent contradiction of the third pledge in the trinity, a commentator observed, smoking had been banned in the hall at the beginning of the day. In further denial of the promise, the photographers – whose clicking was said to be distracting the claques – were banned from in front of the platform until after lunch. 'Stalinist!' someone shouted at the boiling Aberdonian in control.

During scenes like these, the writer is nervously aware that most people are sensibly incurious about the minutiae of politics, but the main decision of the conference needs briefly to be outlined, because of its eventual consequences for the Sterlings and their circle. Against the wishes of the Labour Party leader, the Byronophile Michael Foot, the shares in voting for future leaders of the party – the man the electorate would see on television – were allocated thus: 40 per cent to the trade unions, 30 per cent to the constituency parties and 30 per cent to the MPs. This resulted in an equal influence for, say, John

Durry and Reginald Fisher, MP, but, given that the Durrys were forcing the Fishers out of the party and that the unions were traditionally on the left, the general perception was that the party had tilted away from moderation. It did not help that the popular British press drew little distinction between Socialism and Communism.

This section of the press, therefore, greatly enjoyed the events at Wembley. All day, divided sides yelled from trenches. Tony Benn, MP, formerly Anthony Wedgwood-Benn, a lapsed aristocrat now positioned on the zealous left, accused the centre of the party of defending their stand to 'the last sherry glass'. The politicians of the middle were, he said, 'part of a secretive establishment who hate the creation of democracy'.

The images were disturbing but the Sterlings, like many others, were soon distracted. That Saturday evening, in the week of the death of Marshall McLuhan, who had prophesied the power of television, Graham, Eliza, and a third of the adults in Britain (along with perhaps a third of the adults in the parts of the world which called themselves free), watched the wedding of Lucy Ewing, the diminutive oil heiress, in the soap opera *Dallas*.

International fascination with this marriage may have distracted them from an event which took place the following day in Britain. In Wapping, an area of East London once used for shooting gangster movies, three Labour Party politicians – Dr David Owen, Mrs Shirley Williams, and Bill Rodgers – were joined by Mr Roy Jenkins, the Duke of Burgundy and 1979 Dimbleby Lecturer, for Sunday lunch at the home of Dr Owen.

Perhaps, in retrospect, the venue tarred the party from the start as middle-class. Purchased while he was a penurious medical student, the residence, extended and redecorated, was now both highly desirable and steeply priced. Such property, near the old, closed docks, was now sold for bloated prices to the young rich (Alastair and Hamster Macleod had looked at flats there.)

After lunch – 'What wine?' the reporters all shouted, 'What

wine?' – the politicians issued a statement. The newspapers were calling the quartet the Gang of Four, a topical pun on the Gang of Three (Widow Mao and others), recently put on trial in China. In their statement, the Gang of Four, while stressing that they remained Socialists and members of the Labour Party, said: 'We want to create an open, classless, and more equal society, one which rejects ugly prejudices based upon class, race, or religion.' While seeking to break the 'sterile and rigid framework' of British life, they desired 'radical change in our society but with a greater stability of direction'.

'Can you have radical change and greater stability?' wondered Appleton on the London Underground next morning. 'I mean, at the same time?'

Graham gave an out-of-town try out to three possible replies in his mind: a) 'That's an interesting philosophical question', b) 'I think you can, can't you? I mean, it's a sort of moderate radicalism, isn't it?', c) 'I don't really know.' He rejected the first as pretentious and the second as ridiculous. So he said: 'I don't really know.'

'You're a man of the centre, aren't you, Graham?' asked Appleton with a kind of teasing peal in the voice which was among the repertoire of his effects which Graham envied.

'Yes, I suppose I am in a sort of way,' Graham asserted. If he was sure about anything, it was that he wasn't going to take that cue. The conversation lapsed and the two men read their newspapers. In Graham's, which gave pages to Wembley, the resident Commons clown, sent to the conference, concluded his piece with the line: 'It could be the first step to a one-party state; if so, it will be the Tory Party.' Appleton's paper, which saw the events of the weekend as a blessing for the still tenuous Thatcher government, also reported on the rumbling discussion over whether organ transplant donors were actually dead.

'Would you sign away your bits and pieces for redistribution afterwards?' said Appleton, evenly. Sometimes Graham looked at other people and knew that their life was not hedged around by the questionnaire; that, for them, every dilemma got a quick tick or Not Applicable with no more difficulty than that presented by a hotel registration form. 'For me,' his travelling companion answered his own question, 'even if I had a cast-iron guarantee that I wouldn't know anything, I'd still feel a bit odd about going to the grave – or, in my case, anyway, cremation – incomplete. Like getting home from the swimming pool with the wrong socks. Similarly, about receiving other people's. Although I accept that if death were the alternative . . . but then they usually seem to die anyway. It's a problem.'

His acknowledgment of the moral conundrum was made with all the apparent mental expenditure of someone stuck between two dishes on a menu. Not merely the delivery but also the content shocked Graham who, superstitiously, never referred to his own death out loud. There obviously was not, for Appleton, any A-D (or even F) and tick one box only. Graham was already lost in a dispatch from the possible futures in which a debonair specialist murmured: 'We've located a kidney in Swansea, Mr Sterling, but, frankly, it's a risk.' Appleton, however, had already jumped subjects.

'Did you see *Dallas*? Absolute tosh, of course, but Helen will have it on. One of the critics pointed out – did you see? – that Lucy has no neck. Absolutely true. Nothing to speak of between chin and bust . . . Helen's absolutely bloody hooked. To tell you the truth, I think her brain's gone to Camembert since she got pregnant . . .'

'Oh, I didn't . . .'

'God, yes. Due in March. She conceived – fell pregnant, says her mother in the poor bloody frozen North – in Crete last summer.'

So here was confirmation of what Graham had always suspected: Appleton ejaculated quite naturally. He knew he couldn't ask if it had been an accident or planned.

'We'd barely stopped taking precautions,' came the unembarrassed answer, uninvited. 'It's supposed to be – what? – a year after they ditch the pill, isn't it?'

Whether it was a product of his temperament, or true for everyone of his educated generation Graham didn't know, but there seemed to be a line of Philip Larkin for every occasion of uncertainty. Now it was: 'He must have taken stock / Of what he wanted and been capable / Of ... No that's not the difference: rather, how / Convinced he was he should be added to ...' Capability was, in fact, a difference between him and Appleton, but the shock at another man's insouciant continuation of his traits was apposite.

Accordingly, the Chief Reporter (and *de facto* Features Editor) of *Dentists and Dentistry* was even more than normally thoughtful as he ducked under the skull. When he reached his desk, Napier was sharing an unusually topical but typically insensitive joke with Anne Colledge. 'I'll donate you one of my organs any day, love,' he was offering. 'On condition that I can put it in you myself.' Anne, catching Graham's eye around Napier's gut, made a conspiratorial vomiting charade which lifted his spirits disproportionately.

George Elliott, who had accumulated only two weeks' sick leave during a surprisingly productive 1980, had suffered a relapse over Christmas ('A virus,' claimed his wife on the telephone, unconvincingly) and was not now expected to return, as the office joke had it, until at least Middle March. So Napier was again Acting Editor. ('The kind of Acting you get in *Dallas*,' said Timmy Duvet-Hogg, the office toff, still awaiting better nepotism.)

Graham opened his notebook. Later that day he would need to resume work on a main feature called 'Long in the Tooth' to coincide with an advertising feature on 'the interface between gerontology and orthodontics'. Before that, and more pleasantly, he needed to write up a 'My Teeth' for the next issue. The interviewee had been Anthony Burgess, most recently the author of *Earthly Powers*, a large novel, the narrator of which was the son of a dentist, a profession otherwise significantly under-represented in world literature. The author had been a fluent and amusing talker but had proved to know more dental terminology than Graham, and had expressed it in five European languages, which made transcription problematical.

The Social Democratic Party of Great Britain (SDP) was officially launched on Thursday 26th March, 1981, at 9 a.m. from the Connaught Rooms in Holborn. Although the policies of the new party were as yet unknown, banners outside the building, carried by anti-nuclear campaigners, warned 'Don't join the H-bomb party' and 'SDP – Nato's Poodle'. More personally abusive placards included 'Jenkins the Jerk' and 'Williams the Eurowitch', the latter meaning little to history but probably also a small amount at the time as the divisions on the left were often conducted on closed circuits.

Each journalist attending the press conference, at which all of the Gang of Four were present, was given a pack which included a card setting out ten Tasks and a membership application form. Task One was 'Breaking the Mould'. Others included 'Fair Elections' and 'Society for All'. William Rodgers told the journalists that the four were 'entering a crusade', David Owen that it was their party (he meant the people's, not the press's) rather than his, and Shirley Williams that it would seek to end 'the divisiveness of the class system'. The Duke of Burgundy declared this occurrence 'the biggest break in the pattern of British politics for at least sixty years'. He was a prominent historian, so everyone assumed precision and looked up 1921 in the reference books. The Popular Rates Protest? The Irish Peace Conference? Which of these did the launch of the SDP now dwarf?

Questions about specific policies were met with a certain tetchiness. Next morning, one of the newspaper cartoonists broke the joke about the new group's pan-partisan vacuum of ideas. 'It's very convenient,' drawled a line-drawn middle-class liberal. 'You can join by credit card and, at the same time, write everything they stand for on the back.'

You did, in fact sign up by credit card. That Friday morning, there were large advertisements in the bigger newspapers for the party which hoped to end class divisiveness. 'An Invitation To Join The Social Democrats', they were headed. 'Are You Happy With The Way Things Are?' Announcing the availability of twenty-one phone banks around the nation ('Quote your Amex or Barclaycard number'), the commercials cajoled: 'Nine pounds (or the price of two hundred cigarettes) is not a lot to pay for the new future . . .' The comparison between the cost of tobacco and the price of genuine democracy was probably the advertising agency's idea of cross-class penetration. Presumably fearing that both amount and method might result in class division, the copy reassured readers that they certainly could send less. However, 'the fact is that if you really want a party that's in nobody's pocket, it will mean digging in to your own'. The payoff line was: 'The SDP – the Country's waited long enough.'

Because previous British political parties had been formed through a process of accretion, merger and private funding, and during centuries or decades of less formalized marketing, this was the first vote-seeking organization to announce itself like a forthcoming stage show. The racialist outfit, the National Front, though also quickly increasing its support, was prevented by law from advertising. The novelty, while provoking interest in the SDP, may also have invited satire. It became known as the credit-card party and the dinner-party party.

The Sterlings were, indeed, giving a dinner party on the evening after the appeal for funds was launched. The food was boeuf bourguignon cooked by Graham, uncatastrophically except for some nervousness while searing the meat to be browned, and drunk with a 1980 Bulgarian red.

As Graham raised the first bottle above the glass of John Durry, again accompanied by the taciturn vegan Jenny Cann, Eliza said: 'Bulgarian, John. Is that approved? Just it saves wastage if you could run it through the Amnesty International guide to the world's vineyards now.'

'An uncontentious little vintage,' said Ben Waddle after taking a sip.

Durry responded with an expansive V-sign. This was technically open to interpretation as gently sardonic, just as the tone of Eliza's joke about the wine might have been defended, if challenged, as affectionate; in this way, among this section of society, genuine hostility could be both directed at the target and disguised from bystanders. Also at the table were Ben and Paula Waddle ('Again?' Eliza had said. 'I wonder.' Graham had responded, 'Well, who else?') and, invited to their house for the first time, Timmy Duvet-Hogg and his girlfriend, Rosinia, a tall girl with a mane of black hair which descended to her coccyx and which Timmy, when attempting to intimidate Graham in the office with hints of the vigour of his sexual relationships, liked to refer to as 'grope rope'. As people were told seconds into their friendship with Timmy, she was the daughter of a Conservative junior minister.

The meal got through the first two courses without ideological warfare. The only flashpoint was when Jenny Cann, for whom a vegetarian casserole had been bought, was seen to be eating very little. Timmy Duvet-Hogg made a joke about the Bobby Sands diet (an Irish Republican of that name had just begun a hunger strike against the British government) and Durry tensed. Then, a few minutes later, when Durry praised a particular film, and Rosinia said she thought it had been boring, the Licefinder General (as Eliza privately called him) replied that, for God's sake, it was meant to be boring. It was a common assumption of this period that all art, particularly if found generally lacking, was conducted between invisible quotation marks. Revulsed by a decapitation scene in a horror movie he had been to see with Durry, Graham had been surprised by his companion's defence that these sequences were 'ironic homage to the genre's clichés'.

It was only over the dessert (crème brûlée, which Eliza had agreed to make, not trusting Graham) that Durry detonated the question the host had known would come.

'Oooh! Burnt cream! Delicious!' cooed Rosinia. Where social sophistication had once been suggested by the peppering of the conversation with French, the same effect was now achieved by ironic English translation of foreign phrases.

'Graham!' piped Duvet-Hogg. 'You've surely never drummed up crème brûlée yourself!'

He said something like cwom brohay, for an alternative method of establishing gentility was to deliver extra-Anglo tags in unnervingly official-sounding accents. The motive was much the same as Durry's saying Knee-har-rah-wah – a suggestion of intimacy with the country – although the Licefinder would never have conceded this. It was, perhaps inevitably, their man from Man-ah-wah, otherwise Managua, who said, as the burnt cream or cwom brohay was spooned down, 'I expect you were on the phone this morning, Graham.'

'Er, yes,' admitted Graham, cracking a sudden channel in his caramel and then staring intently at it, waiting for someone else to take up the conversation. He had telephoned one of the London phone banks from his office that morning, elated by the ten minutes it had taken to get through. He had thought: there are others doing this, hundreds maybe.

'I think I'm missing something!' worried Rosinia, sensing that Durry had imposed some kind of short-hand humiliation on Graham.

'Graham has come out of the closet,' Durry explained. 'And joined the SDP!'

'Well, bugger me!' laughed Ben Waddle. 'So have we!' As he spoke, a shard of his dessert squirted from his lips and hit the shirt of Graham who, following what he understood to be the procedure on such occasions, waited a minute or so and then pretended he was brushing away spillage of his own.

'We hadn't nerved ourselves to tell anyone yet,' admitted Paula. 'We ought to have known that Gray . . .'

She smiled. He tried to instruct his brain not to summon an erection, meanwhile marvelling that what seemed to have been for him a major decision and a rare commitment could appear to others as inevitability.

'Anybody else want to confess?' Durry asked. He was relishing this. Graham noticed that the Licefinder was no longer scratching his hair. The inquisitor swung his eyes to the guests he knew least well.

'Timmy?' he said, pronouncing this quintessentially English name as if it were an exotic foreign coinage. This was another of the available strategies in the vocal civil war which most conversations in England still were, even in the 1980s.

'Bugger orff!' Duvet-Hogg countered, a leap in the pitch of his voice. 'I belong to a party – the only party, I may say – which knows what it bloody well believes in.'

The Licefinder-General turned to the recusant's companion.

'And Rosinia . . .' – again, this might have been the name of a bourgeois Mediterranean resort – 'isn't contemplating a rebellion against the father?'

'Hardly,' she insisted. 'Daddy says at Westminster they're calling it the Send Donations Pronto party.'

Durry didn't laugh, but he gave her a look as if to say 'Not bad!' and turned to examine Eliza. It occurred to Graham that an essential weakness of English liberals was the strain of uncertainty and courtesy which led, for example, to the people round this table submitting to the questioning of Durry like small boys cornered in an orchard. He could, however, rely on his wife to fight back.

'Am I now or will I ever be,' she smiled, 'a member of the SDP? Naturally, John, I'd be tempted by any club which wouldn't have you as a member. I don't know. We'll have to wait and see. A good wife, of course, submits to her husband in all things. And my partner – my business partner – was on the phone to enrol this morning . . .'

'Hamster!' spluttered Paula. 'How can Hamster join a party dedicated to ending class divisions?'

'How can any of you?' asked Durry, but was ignored.

'Has she told Alastair?' Paula continued.

101

'She was breaking it to him this weekend. They're in the country, incidentally, Ben and Paula, which is why they can't be here . . .'

Graham panicked that Timmy and Rosinia, seeing that the table could only seat eight, would realize they were only first reserves but their faces gave nothing away. Eliza had gone on to say: 'I mean, I know that Hamster might conceivably have seen this merely as another opportunity to establish to the secretaries that she has a gold American Express Card, but I think that she's a good girl underneath. I think she may actually believe that things are a little bit unfair the way they stand . . .'

'The best way of helping the poor is to encourage wealth creation in society,' Rosinia interjected. She pronounced it as The Paw, just as Graham's mother did. Growing up, he had visualized poverty as the clawed fist of some jungle predator. Even now, during periods of worse than usual professional insecurity, he knew that what he was in fear of was The Paw.

'So the rich will put an extra coin in the charity tins?' sneered Durry, with reference to Rosinia's fiscal wisdom but, as neither of them knew any economics beyond a contempt for what the other had said, it was not an argument which could develop very far. The dinner party was now, anyway, Eliza versus Durry. It was she who resumed the conflict.

'Jenny? How about you? Have you signed up with the sensible people's party or are you siding with John?'

Jenny, who had been throughout the meal a shade of white surprising even for her, now gulped, said 'Excuse me, can I use the loo?' and crouch-ran from the room.

'Oh, dear,' said Eliza. 'I do hope my husband's cooking isn't implicated.'

'She's had viral-type symptoms all week,' Durry reassured them, now at least sounding like a different kind of text-book.

When the girl returned, claiming an improvement in her condition belied by her appearance, Ben Waddle was explaining his decision to enlist with the new party.

'You know Thompson's book *The Making of the English Work-*

ing Class? Well, I'll tell you the book that should be written about our generation: *The Shirking of the English Middle Class.* It's time we stopped thinking that politics was something other people did. It's time we got in there . . .'

'At the coal-face?' Durry sneered.

'Look,' came the reply. 'When you go down with pneumo-coniosis, come and tell us. What are you, if not pampered middle class?'

Durry looked away. Ben and Paula had always been the hardest targets for him, denying him the easy bull's-eyes of wealth and voting Tory. He was soon, however, able to retaliate.

'You're comfortable about the new party supporting nuclear weapons, are you?' he asked.

'Does it?' asked the Waddles simultaneously. They were paci-fists.

'I don't think the policies are fully worked out,' said Ben.

There was a collapse in the conversation. Graham felt he had to volunteer.

'On the radio,' he ventured, 'they were calling us, er it, the Nice People's Party.'

Rosinia grinned. 'I think that was in inverted commas.'

'Even so,' Eliza said, 'it's a perfectly workable sentiment.'

With undiluted loathing in her eyes, she looked at Durry, raised her glass of Bulgarian red, and proposed a toast.

'To the Nice People's Party!'

On the Monday of the following week, Graham made his weekly telephone call to his mother in Somerset. Unlike those of most of his contemporaries, his parents had remained married, appar-ently happily, throughout their son's first two decades until his father had died suddenly, aged forty-seven, when Graham was twenty. This meant that, again against the pattern of his gener-ation, Graham had experienced a tranquil childhood but incremental terror would possess him throughout his twenties and thirties as he approached his probable genetic destination.

Sometimes, now, he would try to remember the conversations

which had taken place between his mother and himself during his youth. His recollection was of a close relationship, of hours in her company. So what had they spoken about? He sought the information now because their present dialogues were halting and inconsequential to an extent which could not be blamed on electronic separation alone. This week, as usual, they did a burst on their respective local climates, then moved on to his mother's visit to see an Alan Ayckbourn play in Exeter.

'Very clever. But then he always is. You wonder how he dreams them up. They toss a coin in the middle to decide what happens next. If it's heads, they tell you when there's a tails night. Or you can take pot luck. Mrs Florett, you remember her, she lost her husband about the time your dad died, she went twice and got the same ending both times. Asked for her money back – well, you remember what she's like – and they said pot luck is pot luck. She's written to the paper . . .'

Graham tried to force into coherence a perception which often stalked him during these calls. It concerned the stages in communication between a mother and her child. 1) She speaks to it, unhearing, gently through a swell of flesh. 2) Hearing her, it reproduces her vocabulary and accent. 3) Chiding, she speaks to it, unhearing, tearful, resentful. 4) From convention, she recounts her life to it, unhearing, impatient. 5) Dying, she is spoken to, unhearing, by it, through folds of her own skin.

'How's Eliza?'

'Fine.'

'How's work?'

'Fine.'

These six words, in this same sequence, featured every week. He was reluctant to say more, for he suspected that, in both his professional and personal arrangements, he had disappointed his mother.

'Oh,' his mother afterthought. 'I've joined that new party they're starting up . . .'

'Mother!' said Graham, now genuinely engaged. 'I thought you were a Tory!'

'I've never particularly been anything, dear. I never, in twenty-two years, told your father which way I voted, so I think he called me a Tory to smoke me out. He said he was a Socialist, of course. But I could never quite see how, with our lifestyle. Granny's joined as well. She's terribly excited, particularly when they call it the Nice People's Party, although she was a bit put out when she discovered that the couple who run the butcher's now are in it too. Of course, Granny's been leaning away from the Liberals ever since that business with the dog . . .'

Two days later, Graham discovered that a party which already contained, improbably enough, his grandmother (seventy-four, Liberal), his mother (fifty, uncommitted Tory), himself (twenty-six, Liberal Humanist), would also be required to accommodate his wife (twenty-five, Cynic).

'Oh, by the way,' she said one evening after dinner, looking up from the first few pages of a novel she was reading, 'I've decided to join that party of yours.'

Graham feared that the choice of this form of words was deliberately calculated to allow the possibility of blaming him if there should be failure or rancour later. But, at about this time, he read that one of the party's founders had received a thousand letters of support on a single day, so the fear of embarrassing isolation, which attended every decision he made, probably did not apply here. On another day, volunteers were pictured surrounded by stacks of mail from intended members. The images were reminiscent of those charitable appeals in which the British middle classes accumulated their detritus to be recycled or resold for Africa, the refugee boat people or another limb of The Paw.

This analogy had apparently also occurred to Durry who, calling to make football arrangements one night, remarked: 'I see the appeal to save the refugee car people of middle England is going well.'

'The Labour Party must be getting worried, isn't it, John?'

'There is a view – with which my own essentially coincides

– that it is better that those who are not true Socialists go, leaving those who are constant to proceed without the distraction of the dissemblers ...'

There were a couple of volumes of this treatise, with footnotes, appendix, and suggested reading list, before a gap, in which Graham said: 'How's Jenny?'

Instead of the approved and required reply – the brisk, unspecifying, if necessary lying 'Fine' – he got: 'Oh, Jen? Jen, in fact, has set me something of a dilemma, having, you see, announced that my genealogical line is to be extended. Or will be, unless diversionary tactics are employed, this being my inclination but not, despite intense debate, yet hers ...'

Graham's brain, with commendable speed, drained this speech of the concealed message that Jenny Cann had conceived.

'She's pregnant?' he double-checked.

'We are having a baby,' Durry confirmed, in a voice of exaggerated unenthusiasm. 'Or, rather, Jenny says we are, choosing to see this as a communication from God or fate or nature, where I take the more prosaic view that it was a mechanical breakdown in rubber production ...'

('John, of course,' smiled Ben Waddle, when Graham relayed this to him, 'needs to see everything in terms of the decline of British manufacturing industry ...')

Durry related that Jenny was refusing to have an abortion, which he called a termination. He had told her, he said, that, if that were the case, he could not be responsible for what happened. Reflecting on this, Graham had two immediate – well, not-too-long chewed – thoughts. The first was relief at explanation of Jenny's flight from the table the previous week. It was Graham's muffled assumption that sudden illness, of himself or others, presaged at best a failure of his cooking and, at worst, the first signs of a fatal illness. His subsequent reflection was merely the arrogant calculation of any human being permitted to witness the insensitivity of another; pride that he was nicer. He quietly moved himself ahead of Durry in the secret League of Decency he ran.

But judgement was difficult. Durry was clearly to be charged with selfishness, but against which other rules had he offended? Graham tried to blink away the questionnaire, but in vain.

16: Do you believe that the entity [*NB: this word is chosen to have no emotive status*] in Jenny Cann's womb is:

☐ **A:** A human being, sacred of God.

☐ **B:** A cell cluster, with the potential to develop into a human being.

☐ **C:** A human being, not sacred of God, but already under the protection of those civil rights – contained in both Conventions and convention – which it is formally awarded at birth.

☐ **D:** A piece of tissue, its destiny as much within the control of the host organism [*NB: this word is chosen to have no emotive status*] as is a tooth, a kidney, a tumour.

☐ **E:** As D, but in this special circumstance, its destiny to be shared between the host organism and the co-generating organism.

☐ **F:** A cell cluster with no rights or special legal or moral status until it is quite a bit bigger and looks like a proper baby without an electron microscope.

(*Remember: you may tick one box only*)

Graham detected in certain of the alternatives (six again: doubt was really spouting in this decade) a tendency to mock the rhetoric of the standard moral accommodations. He soon dispensed with A, which you needed to be a Catholic to agree with, although Graham's secret fear was that his true belief was that abortion was morally wrong but that the material circumstances of his class and generation had rendered births frequently inconvenient. He was not, however, going to say that in front of Durry. He also concluded that options C and D (the decision left to the entity or to Jenny) were equally inconvenient for Durry. The most equivocal was E (choice between Jenny and Durry) and B the easiest but he opted for F, on much the same moral grounds that he would eat, in a restaurant, pieces of fish in a sauce but not, say, a whole trout staring up from the plate with glazed eyes. The words with which he conveyed his maintenance of this moral position to Durry qualified it still further.

'I think it's entirely up to you,' he said, leaving his friend to conclude whether a singular or plural pronoun was intended.

Graham told Eliza, who said: 'Poor her. But I would have thought that carrying an embryonic Durry would be incontestable grounds for an abortion.'

Then, Graham switched on the evening news and learned that President Ronald Reagan had been shot. A blanched newscaster – his pastiness almost certainly due more to a hastily reordered bulletin than to personal distress – reported that the President was in no danger in hospital, but kept repeating that Reagan was a man of seventy.

'Do you think,' asked Appleton next morning, 'that he actually did say "Gee, hon, I forget to duck!", when his wife arrived at the hospital? Or do you reckon there's a gag-writer in a side ward, knocking out this stuff and feeding it straight to the press? I mean, look at this . . .'

Appleton indicated a phrase in the newspaper on his knee. Curiously, after months of never coinciding, they had met four times in the last fortnight. They were currently stalled in a tunnel for reasons not revealed to the passengers. Appleton waved the front page in Graham's direction.

'While they were still wheeling him down for the operation, he's supposed to have said "All in all, I'd rather be in Philadelphia." But that's wrong. I mean, that's a line about death, isn't it? Do you think, then, that Ronnie thought he was on the way out or that a really hack gag-writer was doing that shift? It makes you wonder whether they had a team working on his last words while he was in surgery . . . '

The press that morning was delirious with the pre- and post-operative jokes allegedly cracked by the septuagenarian President, while he waited for the removal of the bullet fired from a .33 revolver by John Hinckley III, who had done it to impress a movie actress, and about whom books, film scripts, and musicals were already being written. All of the contemporary media accounts insisted that Reagan's life had never been under threat. Nearly a decade later, however, the memoirs of sacked or disgruntled aides suggested that the President had nearly bled to death. There were even rumours – although this may have been merely Washington gossip – that, far from the routine of lie-down comedy reported at the time, he had, in fact, incoherently mumbled 'Mommy, Mommy'. The original witticisms have, in the way of history, tended to stay on the journalistic record.

'I mean, one starts to get into school debating territory,' said Appleton. 'Would it have been morally permissible to assassinate Adolf Hitler and so on. But, even from my side of the fence, one found it hard to be too desolate about Ronnie being knocked out of action . . . '

'I know what you mean,' Graham replied. Appleton's admission was a relief to him. The secret he was carrying this morning was that he had hoped, on first hearing the Reagan headlines, that 'shot' meant shot dead. Even now, he was quietly banking on the possibility of complications setting in – what a jolt the bullet must have been to a system nearly seventy years old – and forestalling what he still believed to be the serious prospect of Reagan ending the world.

The conversation had halted. Both men flicked through their newspapers, away from the frame-by-frame presentations of the assassination attempt. There was a picture on an inside page of Appleton's edition of the latest progress in the appeal for the political refugees of middle England: a Nice People's Party volunteer posed with a dizzied expression amid alps of packets and envelopes. Graham feared that the other man would make some comment but Appleton closed his newspaper, tilted back his head and shut his eyes.

'Is it the baby keeping you awake?'

'Is what the baby keeping me awake?'

'You're, er, looking a bit pale.'

Like most of the unbeautiful, Graham had the habit of monitoring his more attractive acquaintances for signs of equalizing decay. Appleton, even allowing for the effects of the early-morning motion of ancient railway stock (when, that was, it moved at all) had a drained face, careless hair, and lustreless eyes.

'Oh, that,' explained Appleton. 'I've had some kind of bug. Was off, actually, for a couple of weeks. Well, working from home. Got some firewater from the witch-doctor and I'll be . . . no, Jack's a good little sleeper. Splendid chap all round, in fact. You don't have any, do you?'

'Er, no.'

Somehow, he felt that the intention of the question had been to switch the conversation to attack or, anyway, distraction. Appleton examined him closely. Graham wondered if retained semen – children wilfully unspent – produced physical effects which others might detect.

During the following year, the momentum of the new political party accelerated to the point where it received one of the most sincere compliments in politics: the established parties held feverish meetings to decide how it might be neutralized.

Membership was flourishing. In May 1981, Graham Sterling, reluctantly standing in the elections for Secretary of his West London branch, received eight votes (how he blushed when the result was read out), behind a special-needs teacher and a BBC producer, whose 'media contacts' were much gloated over.

The national party's first electoral results were also encouraging. In July 1981, the Duke of Burgundy stood in a by-election in Warrington – one of the few places in Britain whose name he could pronounce with impunity – and was a hair's-breadth second. In November, Mrs Shirley Williams, SDP candidate in Crosby, won, giving the party its first MP by over-turning a 19,272 Conservative majority. It seemed that the nice people of England were getting serious.

'It's just a fad, the political equivalent of paper knickers,' said Alastair Macleod at breakfast to Hamster, who had narrowly failed to be appointed treasurer of her local party branch, despite having carefully referred, in her speech to the members, to 'my other half, who works in the city, and can help me with the numbers if I get stuck!'

The only set-back for some of the excited moderates during this period had occurred in June when, kneeling on the grass at Westminster, the leaders of the SDP and the Liberal Party announced that they would combine to fight elections as the Alliance, presenting a joint candidate for each seat. This move caused some distress to Ben and Paula Waddle, who had left the other party, amid agonies of conscience, and now found themselves effectively back in it. 'Bloody hell!' Ben complained. 'It's like trying to storm out of a room through revolving doors!'

A more positive view – towards which Graham, on balance, inclined – was that the Alliance was a pragmatic decision which increased the possibility of power. It was hard for the Sterlings and their like-minded friends not to shiver with anticipation when, in September 1981, the Liberal leader, David Steel, exhorted delegates to his party's annual conference to 'go back to your constituencies and prepare for government'.

Curiously – or, perhaps, logically – the rise of moderation coincided with a time of exceptional violence and social division. During 1981, Bobby Sands became the first British MP to die while on hunger strike in prison. 'Most British MPs,' observed John Durry at a dinner party, 'are more likely to die while eating in restaurants. Which makes this a kind of poetic irony. Yeatsian, precisely.'

Any Irish Catholics praying for Bobby Sands were required, in May 1981, to split their petitions when their Pope, John Paul

111

II, was shot, allegedly by the KGB, who feared his influence on stirrings of democracy in Poland, where, by December 1981, martial law had been imposed.

One sentence, forty-seven words, three countries: Ireland-Italy-Poland. Three distinct creeds – Republicanism, Catholicism, Communism – linked in one sentence by commas. History permits to the hindseer shapes sometimes denied to the journalist by proximity. From a longer perspective, the dominant themes of Britain in 1981 seem to have been racial violence and monarchist triumphalism, at best an odd couple, though perhaps in some way related. In Birmingham, London, and Liverpool, riots erupted, those in the capital occurring barely two weeks before, merely a few postal districts west of the flames, Lady Diana Spencer – a shy young daughter of the aristocracy, publicly proclaimed by her uncle on national television to be a virgin – walked down the aisle of St Paul's Cathedral, in a dress already being copied and rushed into the shops, to marry Prince Charles Philip Arthur George Windsor, heir to the throne of the United Kingdom of Great Britain and Northern Ireland and to the Commonwealth.

It was, perhaps predictably, Durry who made the link between these simultaneous manifestations of ancient and modern Britain. 'Suppose,' he said, 'you were a West Indian, living in racist Britain. You switch on the television and there's Lady Di in her dress, yards of pure silk. What is she but a white power salute?'

Her future kingdom included – although little mention was made of it at the time of the ceremony – the Falkland Islands. In April of 1982, the Argentinian Navy invaded that parched inhabitation of sheep and British passport holders which the generals in Buenos Aires liked to call, particularly at times of high inflation and gathering opposition, the Malvinas, and to which they staked an ancient claim.

Depicted by cartoonists in the popular – and now patriotic – press as Britannia, Margaret Thatcher, who was herself suffering serious domestic unpopularity, sent battleships from Portsmouth.

It was the flags and the chanting which first disturbed him. Graham watched the departure of what television and the press had already learned to call the Task Force with dismay. It was like seeing old war-time newsreels somehow enhanced to have the clean colour of contemporary footage.

The dock was like a football terrace on which all the family could feel safe. No bananas were hurled but this crowd also had its food metaphor. Tins of Argentinian corned beef were dropped off the quay or fed to slavering symbolic British bulldogs. Theatrically stabbing hankies at eyes equidistant between Union Jack hats and scarves of like design, grandmothers seized the unexpected opportunity to wave another generation of their family's men away to death.

Except that, if the lachrymose grannies had read the small, square, screeching newspapers in which England specialized, they would not have feared for their grandsons. Chortling distinction was drawn between the Argentinian conscripted Army – one forced by law to kill other people – and the British forces, in which men volunteered to do so. The popular prediction of the result of a meeting between these two teams was voiced by Napier in Graham's office: 'As soon as HMS *Hermes* comes round the corner, the Argies will shit themselves. The only blood spilled will be General Fucking Galtieri's when he has to wave the white flag.'

Napier's analysis was to prove over-optimistic. When, in the third week of the conflict, John Durry issued invitations to 'a meal' (he refused to use the term dinner party) many men were already dead and senior British Naval officers giving interviews on deck – footage which, presumably for technical reasons, reached home ahead of pictures of blazing ships – spoke of the unexpected strength and organization of the Argentinian Army. It now seems likely that these compliments were deliberate preparation for the possibility of defeat or a fudged peace settlement.

Perhaps because of this, it was obvious to the Sterlings, at the meal in June 1982, that John Durry was having a good war. His guests were Graham and Eliza, the Waddles, the Macleods, and Ian and Tony, friends of Durry whom, Graham soon surmised, were a couple. He consciously adopted the air of studied calm – not unlike the nonchalant whistling of the urchin standing by the broken shop window in old comic books – which he tended to employ in the presence of nudists, blacks, and homosexuals. This carefully advertised ease in the presence of Ian and Tony did not extend to speech and he was glad when Durry returned with drinks and said: 'Do feel free to switch on the television if you want to see the latest casualty figures . . .'

'That. . . . is. . . . very. . . . good. . . . of. . . . you,' said Ian, pausing laboriously between words. Everybody chuckled. All wars spawn jokes among civilians and a source of humour in this conflict was the official Ministry of Defence spokesman, a man who spoke at quarter-dictation speed.

Eliza was about to be rude to Durry but the doorbell prevented her. It was the arrival of the Macleods. Hamster was first, trilling and kissing. Alastair slumped into an armchair, sighing as if he had crossed the Arctic on dog-sled to be there.

'Bloody hell! I don't think I've ever been to Brixton!' he gasped. 'Quite a sodding yomp to get here!'

As well as their humour, all wars have their own vocabulary. Part of the language of the Falklands campaign was that it was never officially called a war, but remained a conflict. Another usage which the conflict had promoted was 'yomp', which, the newspapers explained, was the Army's term for a long march.

'I do hope,' said Durry, 'that the taxi-driver showed you the Brixton sights. We're particularly fond of the massed riot shields and police barriers on the outskirts of town. On a clear day, you can see the tear gas . . .'

'I expect, John,' Eliza interrupted, 'that you're one of the very few people who would be glad to have riots near by – as long as they stopped short of your own property – because it supports your claims to live nearer to real life than the rest of us . . .'

But Durry merely smiled politely, as relaxed as might be a man of political certainties who had invited four (at least) known liberals to eat with him during the first serious armed conflict involving his country for twenty-six years. The arrival of Ben and Paula Waddle merely consolidated his *bonhomie* and, soon, Jenny Cann entered timidly from the kitchen to suggest that they might start eating.

'Jenny!' Eliza called across the room. 'How is he?'

This was a reference to Frederick Thomas Durry, born the previous August. 'A boy,' Eliza had been baldly told, taking the phone call in the absence of Graham, who was delayed working on a major feature about fluoride. 'That's nice,' she had improvised weakly. 'Not really,' Durry had replied. 'Why?' she had said. 'Did you want a girl?' 'No,' he drawled, 'I wanted an abortion.' When this conversation had been reported to Graham, he had quietly awarded himself another four points in the league of Comparative Decency.

Now, as was his habit, Durry looked away when the baby was mentioned, like a prude who had heard youths swearing on the train. He remained subdued while the women discussed little Freddy's eating, sleeping, and defecation, and only really recovered his aggressiveness when Jenny carried in the covered earthenware serving dishes and plates. Because of the numbers, and the size of Durry's flat, they were to eat on their knees.

'Camp fashion!' joked Tony, with a pout at Ian. Graham's guffaw of support for their chosen lifestyle sounded more loudly than he had hoped, perhaps because it was backed only by quiet smiles from the Waddles. Eliza and the Macleods had inclined heads and eyebrows in a code which might have been broken as: 'Are they? . . .', 'Mmmm', 'God!'

Durry uncovered the largest dish with a gesture like a children's magician.

'I don't know what it is, John, but it smells pretty scrummy,' sang Hamster.

'Corned beef hash!' announced Durry with deliberation.

'Typical,' giggled Ben Waddle.

'Oh, fuck,' groaned Alastair Macleod.

'You would,' added Eliza.

Graham's first reaction was that this was an American recipe, so he failed to understand the fuss until he spotted the Latin American connection. This delay ensured that any response he might have intended was prevented by Alastair saying: 'I mean, look, John, very funny joke and all that, but I'm not convinced it's right to put guests in this position at this time . . .'

'Ah,' Durry cut in. 'A new social *faux pas*, you mean. Like serving pork to Jews or beef to vegans. Giving corned beef during the Falklands War, excuse me, Conflict, to patriots . . .'

He spat the final word. Alastair was equally vehement in reply. 'It's just a very clever little middle-class—' Durry flinched – 'yes, middle-class, joke, when the actual point is that people have died, actually . . .'

Jenny Cann had quietly begun to spoon out the ruddy stew and pass it round, beginning, shrewdly, with Ian and Tony and the Waddles. Durry was replying to Alastair: 'Oh, actually, I'd agree with you that the actual point is that people have actually died. But tell me why declining to eat tinned meat is actually an appropriate response. . . .'

'It's a form of economic sanction,' protested Alastair.

'Oh, great, I mean, I'm sure that the staff canteen at Hanratty Forest Podge – and perhaps even the directors' dining-room – stopped serving Corned Beef Fritters before the fleet slipped anchor but it's a pretty infantile response, isn't it?'

'Well, so is serving this,' contributed Eliza.

Graham, silent, was admiring again, although he did not necessarily approve of it, the way in which Durry used details about his opponents – the carefully filed, faintly ludicrous name of Alastair's employers, for example – to broaden the attack.

'I've heard that not all corned beef is Argentinian, anyway,' chirped Hamster.

'Don't worry, this is,' said Durry. 'The shopkeepers round

these parts tend to take a cool view of the prejudices of the mother country. The point is, Eliza, that, yes, it might be silly to force enemy provender down the throats of patriotic British bankers, but it's equally immature to ban a particular sandwich filling as some misguided contribution to the war, forgive me conflict, effort. Have you read about the lady who, according to one of our more sought-after morning newspapers, is dialling random telephone numbers in Buenos Aires and singing 'Land of Hope and Glory' down the phone? I mean, really. . . .'

Bween-ez Are-ess, Durry said it. Ben's gentle voice was the next to be heard: 'As a matter of interest, how would you have viewed, assuming that telecommunications made it possible, the actions of a British granny in 1939, dialling Munich and belting out the National Anthem to random Nazis?'

Durry nodded, with the respect he always extended to Ben. 'Yeah. I see the trap you're setting me. The Great British War Spirit, without which Graham here would be writing features about the use of dentistry in the interrogation of non-Aryans. Well, yes, I think it's true that Hitler represents a difficulty for pacifists . . .'

'Too damn right,' interjected Alastair.

'But I do think there's a difference,' continued Durry, 'between protection of the land which is your national territory and stray islands left over from a time when the big bully countries of the world could get away with more . . .'

'They're British citizens . . .' insisted Alastair.

'Oh dear. I think we should agree not to talk about politics when we meet!'

That was Hamster. Now Ian tried to soften the tone with: 'It's the sheep I feel sorry for. I hope supplies of vaseline are getting through.'

Eliza reflected that homosexuals were irredeemably frivolous people. Accordingly, she was surprised, though not sufficiently to retract her opinion, when Tony looked suddenly thoughtful and said: 'What I think is. . . . and I'm not a political animal like some of you. . . . I only belong to a party – John's party –

because, on balance, I think it's less likely than the others to put a pink triangle on my forehead and confine me behind barbed wire on the Isle of Wight, purely because of where I choose to stick my prick . . .'

Hamster, Alastair, and Eliza all frowned slightly at that noun. Durry interrupted with: 'Well, that's an interesting point, Tone. What's the policy of our newest party on homosexuals?'

An outside observer watching Hamster, Ben, Paula, Graham, and Eliza would have thought that an irritating insect was circling above their heads and they were following its progress. As the pause continued, it was Graham who rashly made the sacrifice.

'I think the point is,' he said. 'I mean, I don't mean . . . I mean, the idea is that everyone will be treated exactly the same . . .'

'So we'll be able to marry and have children?' asked Ian excitedly.

'I, er, I'm not . . .'

Ben rescued Graham from the general merriment, saying: 'As you know quite well, John, policies haven't been finalized yet . . .'

'Let me think,' said Durry. 'The policy would favour bi-sexuals, wouldn't it? The middle way.'

'The point I was going to make,' resumed Tony, 'is that my view on this Falklands business, which you may mock as you like, is that the time has passed for dispatching armadas to get the ball back from the grumpy sod next door. The world's too dangerous now – with the weapons we have – to risk it for a few tons of mutton and a couple of plumbers who could live somewhere else. Give them till, oh, I don't know, 1992, to get out, something like Hong Kong. Then, everybody shuts up shop, has their own patch of ground, no empires, no dependencies. . . .'

Graham was impressed. So, apparently, was Ben, who said: 'Mmm. I think you're right. A kind of closet diplomacy, you mean? Oh, Lord, when I said closet. I didn't . . .'

'No, really, no problem,' Tony reassured him. 'Do you know? I think being gay – or black, I suppose – in a room full of English liberals, or mainly liberals, you realize what it must be like to be a nun or a vicar or one of the Royals. Everyone watching their language all the time . . .'

'Your theory's all very well,' said Alastair Macleod, impatient to resume the row. 'But what if somebody doesn't stay within their neat little borders . . .'

Ben and Graham looked at each other. 'Er, economic sanctions,' said Ben.

As if this reminded her of the food problem, Jenny stood up decisively. Everyone had eaten Corned Beef Hash – in fact, Graham and Ben were on second helpings – except for the Macleods, and Jenny, who had eaten nothing for reasons which were probably to do with her own expanding borders rather than Argentina's.

'Look,' she said, very quietly, as if hoping that Durry might not hear. 'I'll get you something else. It'll have to be cheese salad I'm afraid. . . .'

Alastair said that would do very well and Hamster nodded. Durry, however, was not yet prepared to surrender the issue.

'I hope you realize it's Gruyère, Alastair. Bloody Swiss wimps, sat out two world wars. Each bite of that salad is an endorsement of neutrality. . . .'

'What about South Africa, John?' said Eliza.

'Yeah?'

'You believe in the boycotting of South African produce – when you come to our house, we can't pass round the fruit bowl without you wanting a birth certificate for the bananas – so what's the difference with economic sanctions against Argentina?'

'Oh, that one. That's easy. Apartheid is an evil system which must, as far as possible, be starved to death. Hit them where it hurts. In the krugerrands. This little scrap over the Malvinas is just banal . . .'

Alastair had been becoming increasingly agitated. Durry's

use of the word Malvinas – which he pronounced Marl-feen-hars – was the final goad. He rose to his feet, catching hold of Hamster's hand as he did so, causing her to spill her drink.

'Fiddlesticks!' squeaked Hamster.

'Look,' began Alastair, his hands on his lapels like an old-fashioned politician. 'I don't want to seem like a silly arse, but there is a war on . . .'

'A conflict,' pointed out Durry.

'A war, in which people are dying. Dying, in the end, so that people like you, Mr Durry . . .'

'Mister!' shouted Ian, throwing up his hands as if a stone had landed in his lap.

'So that people like you can make smart remarks at dinner parties about "the Malvinas", I think it's better if we go . . .'

As he led Hamster to the door, past the surprised faces of most of the guests and the grinning ones of Durry and Ian, Hamster soundlessly mouthed 'Sorry.' There was the slither and hiss of coats being found from the pile in the hall, then the slap of the front door, which coincided with the opening of the one from the kitchen to reveal Jenny Cann carrying two cheese salads.

'Oh God, John, not again,' she said but Durry narrowed his eyes at her and she fell silent.

'Strange days,' remarked Ben Waddle. 'It's that subject. I've never known such disagreements in England, except over jazz and abortion. I mean, it's such a bloody tricky one, the Falklands. The truth is that, of all generations in recorded English history, ours is probably one of the first to get to our late twenties without a war somewhere. But we've come to believe that peace is our right . . .'

'I'll tell you something scary,' said Ian. 'A friend of mine, he works for a theatre company. Anyway, because of what's going on, they decided to drop the play they had planned and do a thing about Wilfred Owen and the war poets. So, they need a new poster and leaflets. Then he – my friend – rings up their usual printer and says "Can you do us a favour, mate? Rush job." And the printer says, "Wish I could, but it's all hands on deck here already, doing a quick print for the Ministry Of Defence." ' he paused for effect. ' "Call-up papers." '

'Oh, Jesus,' said Paula.

'How fascinating,' said Ben. 'That story always crops up. Suez, even Cyprus. Always the phone call to the printer, the chance remark . . . It's an urban myth . . .'

'It's true,' snapped Ian. 'The printer showed him.'

'I'm not saying I don't believe you,' said Ben, although he clearly was saying that. 'The point I was making was that our generation has been able to behave – we didn't even do National Service – as if there aren't wars any more, as if we're somehow more mature, like an adult not getting measles. Well, why should we be so arrogant? Why should we be so lucky? The ironic thing is that nuclear weapons – which most of us don't believe in – were going to spare us ever making the decision whether to go and fight. The next war was supposed to be over before they had time to print call-up papers. But, here's a question. Suppose this goes on and on or finishes and a government, to defend the bloody thing, brings in conscription, would we fight?'

On the first ballot, there was unexpected uniformity. Ian began with a joke about all those boys away from home but Tony frowned at him – a wife's look, Eliza reflected to herself – and he voted No, closely followed by Tony, Ben, Durry and, after a fractional further hesitation, Graham. Jenny Cann announced that she would never, ever, let Freddie go to war. Durry told her that was irrelevant and asked whether – in these times of feminism – the girls would serve in the armed forces. He thought that Lizzie (Eliza), for example, would be more frightening than five men, if she – oh, blissful fantasy – were to come out of a trench, running at him in combat gear. Eliza replied with a V-sign, before revealing that she would ignore the call to recover or secure the Falklands. Paula and Jenny concurred.

'Well, well,' said Durry. 'Equanimity.'

Ben said he was worried that it was not the whole answer. Suppose that Galtieri – or some basket-case like Gaddafi or one of the mad Mullahs – launched an invasion force – à la Adolf – towards these shores, would that be different?

The second ballot was a revelation. Durry, arguing that only a corrupt government would allow the situation to reach the point of invasion, still declined to fight but Tony, to a not particularly playful push from Ian, and Ben, to a gasp from Paula, both declared that they, in those circumstances, would join up. Ben said that he didn't want to be pompous about this but one of the things their generation, if he could grandly call it that, must not do was ever to forget that – this sounded corny but how else could he put it – men had been gassed and slit and drowned and blown apart for what they now had.

'For Gruppenführer Thatcher's police state, you mean,' said Durry.

'There are some who would consider that remark banal,' responded Ben, moderate even in contempt.

Graham had still not voted in the second ballot. To his dread, he could hear in his head the unrolling of the questionnaire. He reflected that his answer to Question 16 ('The Right to Life') lay wet and fleshy in the next room: Frederick Thomas Durry. By logical extension, his response to the next one, if it were to taunt him in similar form, would be his body rotting on a foreign field or buggered in a prison for conscientious objectors. Here it was:

17: If required by Her (or His) Majesty's Government to fight in defence of the British Isles [*the words are chosen to have maximum emotive status*], would you?

☐ **A:** Yes, I would.

☐ **B:** No, I wouldn't.

It was becoming a bit blunt, he thought. But with the bolt-holes reduced to two, his certainties cemented; or, anyway, as

all jellies eventually must, began to set. He was clear that it had
to be B.

'No,' he said in the main room at Durry's flat. 'I wouldn't
fight. Even then.'

For the rest of the evening, he attracted something like
respect. He was struck by the paradox that, among this grouping
of human beings, pacifism was regarded as courageous,
whereas, among most others, the same declaration was registered as cowardice. His pleasure in his new status among his
friends – as the talk wound down to football, babies, summer
holidays and the yawning departure to cars – was lessened only
by the unexpected arrival of a supplementary:

17a: Which of the following statements is closest to your personal justification for declining to defend the British Isles
for Her (or His) Majesty?

☐ **A:** I eat the right foods, jog, don't smoke, and avoid strong
sun in order to live longer and I am not going to live shorter
because of some bloody politician.

☐ **B:** I am a coward.

☐ **C:** I believe that war is unjustifiable in the present day.

☐ **D:** I accept that war is inevitable – and unavoidable, given
acquisitive tyrants – but I hope to get through my life
without one.

☐ **E:** I believe that I am a person of special intelligence and
potential achievement and accordingly recommend that a
centre should be established in Switzerland (if necessary,
underground) for those like me.

He was relieved that the multiple choices were back but
against this had to be placed the fact that so was the sarcasm
of the setter. He had thought that his reasoning was C (war
morally wrong) but, as D pointed out, foreign (and, indeed,
domestic) politicians might not observe morality. Clearly, E (the
Basle bunker) was a category, though tempting, intended for

novelists, film stars, and politicians, although, if Britain was involved in the selection, judges and civil servants would probably be admitted as well. He was left only with A – the burrowing terror of personal extinction – which he chose.

He was unsettled by the evening – a night of being caught up in the coil of choices – and took the rare risk of not really listening to Eliza as she drove home. She was talking about the Gay Couple ('I don't mind – but they made such a thing of it') and asking herself why bloody Durry had asked the Macleods. She answered herself that it was because he enjoyed manipulating people.

So Graham wasn't really ready for the, quite unprecedented, second supplementary when it came.

17b: 'Response to military aggression is one of the problems which liberalism has most conspicuously failed to solve.' Do you:

☐ **A:** Strongly agree.

☐ **B:** Fairly strongly agree.

☐ **C:** Strongly disagree.

☐ **D:** Fairly strongly disagree.

Screaming for peace, Graham closed his eyes and fairly strongly agreed.

5

The Last Temptation of Graham

IN MAY 1983, Margaret Thatcher, victorious in the Falklands though furious with her senior archbishop for what she saw as liberal equivocation at the victory service, announced her intention to hold a poll on June 9 ('Well, at least she still believes in them,' said John Durry.)

It was also during 1983 that Graham Sterling, like Christ in the desert – although he was not, you must understand, inviting a direct comparison – faced a series of temptations. The tests might have been designed to question whatever convictions he held.

The first temptation was power. It began at an editorial meeting of *Dentists and Dentistry* in early May of that year.

'Graham,' said George Elliott. 'Yesterday, I asked you to think about ways in which we might r-r-r-reflect the election . . .'

'Er, yes, I've been . . .'

'On re, re, re – I've just used reflection, haven't I? I need subbing, Graham, don't I?'

The laugh which rose from the four people in Elliott's office was too loud. Furthermore, all four chucklers ended neatly on the same beat, as if watching an invisible baton. It was the kind of response awarded to the wisecracks of geriatric judges or by studio executives at the first screening of comedies which had been troubled in production. Elliott had been back three months from his latest breakdown and it was widely said – first, and most frequently since, by Napier – that the board had warned him that his next sick leave would activate his invalid pension. Certainly, Napier was behaving like an eldest prince who has seen the king's physicians huddled worriedly in a corner.

'On second thoughts,' continued the editor. 'I think we should clear steer, steer clear, of p-p-p-politics. I mean, I think our readers are getting enough of that elsewhere. You look distressed, Graham . . .'

'He always looks distressed!' Timmy Duvet-Hogg cut in. Disconcertingly, as was his habit when making such pronouncements, he jerked up his chin and tweaked his lips in the manner attributed to Oscar Wilde when delivering quips. This unearned echo was almost certainly intended by the speaker.

'No, it's just that I, er,' Graham replied. 'It's just that I've lined up M-M-Margaret Thatcher for "My Teeth".'

'Waaa-loppp!' said Duvet-Hogg.

'Fuck me with a lawnmower,' said Napier.

'Well done!' said Anne Colledge.

George Elliott said nothing for some time. When his words did emerge, they were not necessarily the better for the preparation.

'That's really very good,' he commented.

The meeting rapidly agreed that the ban on political coverage in *Dentists and Dentistry* should not extend to the Prime Ministerial teeth.

'Put in a good word for me!' screeched Duvet-Hogg. He had been seeking adoption as a Conservative candidate for nearly eighteen months, driving on Fridays, Rosinia at his side, in the Alfa sports car he called Luigi, to flash his accent and background at Tories in towns in Northern Britain where it was an event if the Socialists won by less than 15,000 votes and Conservatives were regarded as dissidents. This process of losing heavily in a constituency where the locals either hurried away from you, or failed to understand a word you said, was known in the Conservative Party as 'blooding'.

'Generally,' Duvet-Hogg explained to Graham, 'it's two absolute bummers and then you might just get a marginal or even a sinecure, if deaths and resignations fall out right. And, of course, Rosinia's very bankable. In the North, they consider her pa a bit wet on Immigration, but I make all the right noises on that one . . .'

Gorilla and baboon noises, probably, thought Graham. The revelation of his colleague's political ambitions had been a shock for him. Like most people who have visited the House of Commons once or not at all, Graham still believed that politicians were people with some kind of special yeast: leavened men, enabled to rise through society by this rare ingredient. And yet Ben Waddle, a gentle and articulate man whom Graham admired more than anyone else he knew, was being paid per annum around the total price of a medium-smart car to interest in literature children whose lives were, predominantly, already doomed, while Duvet-Hogg would doubtless end up as Education Minister, telling Ben the country could not afford to give him any more money. It was the logic of politics but it was still sick. Well, sick was too strong a word. It was unfortunate.

'Timmy,' said George Elliott, 'in fact, has s-s-s-something he wants to tell us.'

Oh God, thought Graham, he's been adopted. And, then, an afterthought: what a ridiculous language it is which uses the same word for a wretched orphan finding a family and a power-crazed maniac being offered a political constituency. Graham braved a glance at Duvet-Hogg, which was unhelpful as the level of self-satisfaction on his face could only have been accounted for by an unprecedented election waiver and immediate elevation to the cabinet.

'I'm off, chaps and chapesses,' he began, seemingly confirming the worst predictions. 'I've been offered a job . . .'

Graham raised a secret cheer. He had been bested only professionally, which was the kind of reversal for which he was always prepared. He listened to Duvet-Hogg outlining his duties, doubtless grander than in fact, on the gossip column of a tabloid newspaper. He omitted to add that it was the one his uncle edited, but Graham reflected: nepotism, even better.

'Well done!' said Anne Colledge, managing a glance at Graham which worked like a maliciously translated subtitle reversing the meaning of the original sentence.

'If I can give ye any advice on The Street,' rasped Napier, whose accent became indisputably Glaswegian only when he was filling the role of newspaper sage. It seemed to be sacramental, like the way in which priests had spoken Latin for the solemn parts of the mass.

'That's really very good,' remarked George Elliott. It seemed to be expected that Graham should now mount the merry-go-round of insincerity.

'You must be thrilled,' he told Duvet-Hogg, neatly avoiding deceit but then falling into the theologically grimmer sin of pride at having done so. Elliott, dismissing the meeting, asked Graham to stay behind. From habit, he calculated whether there were any outstanding grounds for being sacked: fumbled quotes, mashed facts, fudged expenses. The editor waited for the door to close, which took fully half a minute, as Napier was pulling it slowly, hoping for eavesdroppings.

Graham looked at Elliott's desk, which was in a corner of the room, two of its edges flush with the walls. It was as if he feared even the possibility of facing his staff, as the traditional body-language of office domination demanded, across it. Next to the telephone – there was only one, a grubby colour and old-style dial type – were two phials of orange plastic with grey caps. They stood beside a cup, muddy undrunk liquid half-way up, and, on the saucer, a slug's trail of a colour like old blood, where he had clearly balanced the pills before swilling them down. Whatever recovery and return to work he had accomplished was obviously heavily underwritten by pharmacology. There was a photograph in a cheap frame of Elliott with a startled-looking woman and two scrawny, sullen teenage boys beside some windswept harbour wall.

'When are you seeing the Prime Minister?' Elliott asked. It was typical that he should use the official title, risking no colloquial diminutives, still less abusive ones. Elliott always spoke of his superiors and public figures as if they might be listening. Graham gave him the date, which was ten days thence, and mumbled something about how he thought they gave a lot of interviews around election time. His editor stammered back that he was sure that was being too modest.

The non-aggressive positioning of his desk dictated that both men were sitting close together in chairs which were turned round from its leading edge. As Elliott played with the papers in front of him, Graham caught sight of a dark smear on one of the restless hands. He charitably tried mud and chocolate as alternatives to the excrement he was rapidly forced to accept the substance was. He realized that Elliott's hands must shake too much for him to wipe himself neatly or steady his hands under a tap. He tried not to gaze at the stain.

'Timmy was never a sticker,' Elliott was saying. Sticker-sticky-stain-shit. Graham's brain absently made these connections: it was the mind's equivalent of running on the spot, to keep warm. 'And with his contacts ... Do you think that was where we went wrong, Graham? Not having c-c-c-contacts?'

We. We? Graham felt an inner tremor. He had been claimed as kin by a man he pitied. It was a moment psychologically as shocking as a kindly teacher, giving extra tuition after class, resting his hand on your knee, his thumb directed towards your thigh.

'I mean, I don't know about your family, Graham, but mine was nothing. Solid Northern nothing. Never in debt, but never much to leave behind, if you see what I mean. Starriest trade they ever aspired to was local government. There was a brief flurry of excitement when an uncle got to read out a by-election result on nationwide television – three in the morning, if I remember, but nationwide – the proper returning officer having dined too well, but otherwise sod all. Would you credit it, I'm a kind of celebrity in our family? Mainly on account of how I was once interviewed on the radio because of a threatened general strike by Britain's dentists. That was before your time, I think, quite a yarn. Industrial action was prevented at the eleventh hour by arbitration but it was a close run thing . . .'

The editor paused. He had been looking at the wall, as he spoke, as if it were the kind of electronic prompter from which television presenters and modern politicians cribbed their ad-libs. Graham had never heard such a long speech from Elliott. It was noticeable that the stammer had ceased.

'Graham, I . . . men, and English men more so, are bad at saying these things, and me more than most . . . I'm very fond of you . . .'

Oh God, thought Graham, he's a closet homosexual. They quite often have stammers, he reflected. And mental problems, if they marry. But his next thought was: Jesus, what a small-minded, offensive thing to think. What does it matter if he's gay, not of course that I am but wouldn't it be a kind of flattery for him to offer, mistaken though his interest is? Despite this anguished rationalization, it was still with some relief that Graham discovered the other man's declaration of affection to be nothing more sinister than a middle-class Englishman attempting to offer a compliment.

'I mean, Graham, to be honest, Timmy never had his heart in teeth . . . as, as it were. His heart in his teeth? I'm supposed to be a writer, of a kind, and listen to me. Whereas you, you have a real feel for the subject . . .'

Graham's mind, which had been jogging through this conversation, was now seriously running. He could see, with terrible vividness, a small piece headed Obituary towards the back of some future edition of the magazine. 'Graham Sterling, perhaps one of the most dedicated dental journalists of his generation, died this week, aged six, no seven, no, eight, no, no, no, fort, thirt . . .' He superstitiously refused to complete the sentence. He felt a deep hopelessness approaching. George Elliott, by common consent of the office an object of contempt, had elected Graham his equal. It was as if a man, toppling backwards, from accident or malice, off a cliff or building, catches the leg of another. Who would ever know if he had done so as to save his own life or, in final spite, to take a second with his own?

'I think, Graham, what I'm saying is . . . I think it's widely known my nerves are . . . well, in a war, I could call it shell-shock but I was never a soldier. I've got, well, whatever the peacetime equivalent is, and there's generally felt to be less excuse. The company's been absolutely splendid to me. Away more often than not. But – I'm speaking just between us now – the word is that Lord Jarrow is looking around for a buyer for the specialist arm. Leaner, fitter, rationalized. Do you read the business pages? These are the kind of words being used. And the print unions have got a gun to his head which, for a man who began as a kind of gentleman publisher . . . What I'm saying is, if we're sold, I'd be a fool not to go. Or do I mean they'd be a fool to keep me? I think there's a strong chance the new people might be less, er, er, liberal about sick leave. What I'm getting at is . . . I'd rather you said nothing to anyone else yet, but, I'd recommend to the new management, assuming they'd even listen to me, that you take over . . .'

And so this was the first temptation. Graham tried to pretend that the editorship of *Dentists and Dentistry* was not really power but the principles remained the same.

'But what about Nap, er, Mr Napier?'

'Ah. He expects it. But – I'm being perfectly frank with you now, Graham – one of the duties of this job, such as it is, and I'm not knocking it, is attendance at the annual dinner-dance of the British Dental Association. Tell me, can you see Ernest Napier, in all honesty, there?'

And, for the first time in Graham's experience, Elliott laughed. His teeth were revealed to be broken and deeply yellowed. The rare rictus also expelled a gale of stale breath towards Graham, who, flinching as discreetly as he could, reflected that this made Elliott dental journalism's equivalent of a spoiled priest.

The interview with the Prime Minister served as an interlude between the temptations, although its theme was also power.

On the appointed morning, Graham was amazed that the policemen at the end of Downing Street and inside the door seemed to be expecting him. Inside Number 10, a sort of dun-coloured over-felt covered a red carpet which stretched from the front door. It was unclear whether the red carpet was for visiting celebrities or the daily use of Mrs Thatcher herself. To the right of the door, an antique writing bureau now had two security monitors set into it.

A bustling man with ginger eyebrows which resembled entrants for Cruft's, who introduced himself as the Chief Press Secretary, came to collect Graham and guided him through thick doors into a room where the Prime Minister waited.

'Mr Sterling,' she said, in a voice which he always associated with dentists' drills. Graham began to bow, but remembered that was intended for Royalty, and snapped back upright.

'We don't take *The Dentist*, I'm afraid,' joked the Prime Minister.

'Er, actually, it's er, called . . .'

'You 'ave twenty minutes,' cut in the man with the lavish eyebrows, hurtling out of the room.

'Do you know Bernard? Bernard's terrific,' said the Prime Minister with the husky come-on lisp familiar from television. She gathered her hands on her lap, and leaned forward, fanning her eyelashes at him. Graham was surprised by the flirtatiousness of her style. He was, however, pleased he did not develop an erection.

'Er, do you, er, remember your first visit to the dentist as a, er, little girl?' asked Graham.

'The Health Service has one million employees,' she began. 'It is the largest employer in Europe. It really is our job to see that it is managed properly. I pay tribute, as we all do, to those doctors, nurses, and others who work so hard to keep up the standards of care. We are all thankful for the. . . .'

Graham began to panic. Durry had bet him in advance that the Prime Minister would not directly answer any of his questions. It seemed that there might be some truth in this view. As her answer continued, Graham tried rocking forward, with his mouth slightly open, as if about to speak, but the Prime Minister responded with a mirthless smile and rapid flash of eyelashes. Finally she concluded: 'But, and this is the point, every human institution can be improved. I reject totally the Socialist view that the most efficient organization is one that employs the largest number . . .'

'Yes. Did, er, your parents stress the importance of regular brushing?'

'Our opponents would spend, spend, and spend before they'd even filled in the coupon, let alone won the pools. You may remember that, at our conference last year, I said: "The NHS is safe with us." I will go further. The NHS is only safe with us, because only this government will see that it is prudently managed and financed, and that care is concentrated on the patient, rather than on the bureaucrat. That is the true and genuine caring . . .'

'It's been suggested that you might have had some, er, cosmetic dentistry yourself. Is there any truth in . . . ?'

'I hadn't quite finished what I was saying, Mr Sterling, so you'll forgive me if I just go back to this. We have a duty – yes, a duty – to make sure that every penny piece we raise in taxation is spent wisely and well. People talk about a free Health Service. It is not free. You have to pay for it . . .'

Graham could sense that his twenty minutes were disappearing. He realized that either the Prime Minister completely misunderstood the point of the 'My Teeth' feature, which he had carefully explained in a lengthy letter to Number 10, or she had agreed to the interview purely in order to put her view about the National Health Service.

When Graham transcribed his tape of the meeting, he discovered that the Prime Minister had mentioned teeth only once, and then metaphorically. 'There must be quite a lot right about a country that can sell 30 per cent of its output in the teeth of fierce competition.' Margaret Thatcher's 'My Teeth' never appeared.

The second temptation was despair, although this vision, confusingly, first presented itself as a further illusion of power. At evenings and weekends throughout May 1983, Graham and Eliza worked for their constituency branch of the Nice People's Party, canvassing for the general election.

The party headquarters was an abandoned unit in the vicinity's largest shopping mall. The site was available because of a bankruptcy resulting from the recent recession. Party volunteers were encouraged to make this point – 'Ironically, if they'd run the economy properly, we wouldn't have such a prime site for HQ!' – to any hovering journalists. However, the Briefing Notes issued by the Campaign Manager, a somewhat bossy BBC Education Producer, urged workers to describe the previous occupancy as a haberdashery store. In fact, it had been a wool shop but the party organizers were nervous about sarcastic references by the press to the tradition of woolliness continuing at this address, despite the demise of the knitting emporium.

A scrap of paper on the wall bore the latest betting-shop odds on the outcome of the election. On the day that the Tucks first presented themselves for service, accompanied by Hamster Macleod, the notice disclosed: Conservative 2–9, Labour 3–1, Alliance 33–1. Underneath, some true believer, or courageous cynic, had scrawled in red ink: 'Your chance to get rich quick!' Most newspaper commentators agreed that the result was unlikely to be other than a second term for Margaret Thatcher, but the leaders of Graham's party were encouraging the idea of a 'hung parliament', in which the election produced no overall majority. Dusty peers discussed on television the options available to the monarch in such an event. Some volunteers, even more optimistic, earnestly discussed which of the joint leaders of the Alliance should serve as Prime Minister.

The peeled walls and whitewashed windows of the converted wool shop were thick with pictures of the party's candidate. He was a dark-haired, blue-suited, thirty-three-year-old personnel manager in a local electronics firm. There was considerable antipathy towards the candidate from those campaigning for him. As is almost inevitable in new ventures, there had been an early heady atmosphere of co-operative equality. This probably resulted from the fact that, in the absence of established hierarchies, everybody involved expected their ambitions to be swiftly satisfied. Many had joined from the better-known parties, in which they had felt their talents to be blocked by nepotism or cronyism. Once preferment had begun, with elections for branch officers and then for the parliamentary candidate, rebuffs, with their pay-off of bitterness, had begun. The candidate, hesitant and unmarried, was now widely said, mainly by his disappointed rivals for the nomination, to be a homosexual. 'It's not that I'm against them,' explained one whisperer. 'It's just that his, er, preference is the kind of thing which our less scrupulous opponents might make hay with.'

Poppy, the BBC Education Producer, briefed the groups of canvassers before they went out. 'OK. You've all been given an Action Pack. That's got in it badges, stickers – give 'em to the kids, if they come to the door with mum, OK? – and policy leaflets. People are putting it about that we haven't actually worked out what our policies are, so I want you to play hardball with the pamphlets. There are two fundamental messages we have got to get across. One, we're here to put an end to the idea that politics has to be about bickering and point-scoring. We are the party of conciliation and moderation. Two, this election offers, at national level, a stark choice between a fanatic and a geriatric . . .'

The fanatic was the Prime Minister; the geriatric was the Leader of the Opposition.

Poppy had divided the canvassers into packs of four, two to

each side of a series of streets, which were picked out in vivid yellow on a map. 'I'm afraid I've done it like a dinner party,' Poppy explained. 'Boy, girl, boy, girl.' In the selection process, the Sterlings had somehow become separated, although many couples seemed to have stuck together. Graham conducted his usual fretful inspection of the two men in Eliza's quartet, identifying their potential as cuckolders. One of the two was encouragingly balding but the other had a waist like Graham's wrist. The Pentagon of his ego saw no reason for more than a level one alert (level three was a serious conversation with his wife, and level five the appointment of a private detective, although neither of these options had ever been used).

His own group included Hamster and a hand-holding, softly-spoken married couple, both teachers, called Barry and Sue. Poppy asked the foursomes each to choose a 'nominal organizer', who would be called 'Campaign Group Co-ordinator'.

Barry and Sue looked bashfully at each other before Barry said: 'I don't think we're really, you know . . .'

'No. Well, I . . .' Graham concurred.

'Well, if you absolutely and utterly insist,' Hamster conceded. She, and the other elect (in some groups, the discussion had been noisy and prolonged), were called up to Poppy to be given a red, white, and blue badge (the party colours) saying: Campaign Group Co-ordinator.

'See you later, my love,' said Eliza, leaving, already in conversation with the level one suspect.

Hamster's team was driven to the designated area by Barry, in a juddery, rusted family saloon. The couple apologized for both its condition and the discomfort caused by what seemed to be several baby seats. 'Do you have kids?' asked Barry. Hamster and Graham shook their heads, the latter looking guilty while he did so. 'Well, don't have four!' advised this thin, cowed over-populator. It was the kind of mock-regretful remark which was obviously intended to make you feel pretty small about not having done your bit for the species in the selfless manner of this couple. The clear subtext was: We could have put ourselves first too.

Baby-seat straps gouging weals in their backs, Graham and Hamster chatted.

'I'm amazed Lizzy joined – Lizzy is Gray's wife, Eliza, incidentally, Bob and Sue,' Hamster said. 'I mean, she was always going on in the office about how she admired Mrs Thatcher . . .'

'I'm not sure you should be telling me this,' Graham protested. The other three all giggled. He had always seemed to possess this ability to make jokes without intending to.

'How's Alastair?'

'Oh. Busy, busy, busy. Now he's a partner – well, a junior partner – sometimes I have to iron two shirts, so that he has one to change into for the evening. Last month, I was late. He said, "You're not pregnant, are you?" I said, well if I am, you ought to be worried, because it couldn't be yours. I don't know when we last . . .'

In the front of the car, Sue and Barry coughed in unison, as if expectoration were some new form of musical duet. Graham had noticed that it was a characteristic of his generation to reflect ruefully on how little sex they now found time for. Was it from a latent Puritanism? A way of saying: we're not actually very interested in it, this silly, sticky game? Or was it that to be too distracted or drained for intercourse – because of making money – had become the '80s equivalent of erotic boasting? So that, for them, the notch on the bedpost was the zero on a cheque and for a man to have a big one meant his salary?

The first street to be canvassed was a leafy stretch of Victorian town houses. There were two cars in most driveways; usually a solid German or Sweden gasaholic beside the kind of bright, compact, less reliable British makes which men thought fitting for their wives. The first two doorbells produced no answer on this Sunday afternoon.

'Of course, the problem with an area like this is that absolutely everyone has weekend cottages,' Hamster complained.

137

'Ally and I are thinking of looking in Devon, now he's a partner, well, junior partner . . .'

Graham noticed that she had now drawn attention to her husband's promotion twice in thirty minutes.

'Do you use yours much?' she asked.

'Well, it's Eliza's, really. I mean, she bought it. She goes more than I do. Exmoor's not very good for my allergies . . .'

With a shiver, he realized that he sounded like a politician justifying some departure from party principles.

The third house they approached was bright and noisy, betraying occupancy. It had been agreed that, for the moment, Hamster would do the talking. The door was answered by a grey-haired woman in her fifties, her ageing neck concealed, from vanity, behind several strata of pearl necklaces.

'Hello. I wonder if you've thought about which way you'll be voting in the General Election . . .'

'Mmmm. Well, we voted Tory last time but we haven't finally made up our minds this time . . .'

'We're finding so many people are saying that. Aren't we, Graham?'

Hamster turned to her co-canvasser with the urgent chirpiness of a children's television presenter. Graham nodded emphatically.

'Can we give you these?' asked Hamster, handing a wedge of leaflets across the step. 'They explain how a vote for us can start to replace dogma and division with partnership and progress . . .'

The party's leaflets and manifesto were riddled with alliteration of this kind. This irritated Graham, who remembered from school the sterile exercise of underlining all the alliterated phrases in poems. 'What's the point of alliteration, sir?' a more forward boy had asked. 'It's a device,' the teacher had revealed. 'But what does it do?' the student had persisted. The master had muttered something about assisting the rhythm but Graham had always felt self-advertising alliteration to be the refuge of a vulgar versifier. This prejudice extended to the frenzied letter-repetition favoured by his party's politicians.

He had studied the manifesto intently, ready to be tested by a hostile doorstep ideologue. There was rather more about the importance of nuclear weapons than Graham would ideally have liked but this was apparently a part of the 'tough but tender' stance which the Alliance was promoting, Graham discovered from his reading that his party believed in 'Sustained Policies For Growth'. These included 'capital investment in the water and sewerage system', 'electrification of the railways' and 'building and repairing roads'. ('We mustn't be ashamed to be crazy, no pun intended, about cracked paving stones,' Poppy had rallied her canvassers.)

If Graham had an argument with the manifesto, it was that the eschewal of dogma had perhaps gone too far. The document essentially consisted of generalized promises to make this better or to do something about that. For example, turning with – well, excitement was too strong a word but interest, certainly – to a paragraph headlined 'Agriculture and Fisheries', Graham had discovered the pledge: 'To encourage the development of agriculture and fisheries.' He nervously speculated about whether he would be adequately briefed if he were to meet a real farmer or seaman while campaigning.

Hamster, as she took the lead in speaking to those electors who answered their doorbells on the Sunday afternoon, seemed less troubled by the absence of specifics. When a red-faced ranter in a blazer, who claimed to be a Don't-Know, spoke at some length about his reluctance to see 'the tax-payer bankrolling wasters who don't want to work', Hamster brightly informed him: 'Absolutely, Mr, er, Arnold.' She plucked his surname from the sheets of the electoral register fixed to her clipboard. 'We believe very strongly in people standing on their own two feet.' Mr Arnold had smiled and said that, well, the chaps in power at the moment hadn't cracked down hard enough and if they (Graham and Hamster) were talking about really giving them the whip, he might very well be for them. When he closed the door, Mr Arnold was gazing at the pamphlets as if they were banknotes.

As they scuffed down the drive, Graham worried aloud: 'Um, do we believe in people standing on their own two feet? I mean . . .'

'I don't know. You tell me, Gray. I think we pretty much believe in whatever we want, until they specifically tell us not to. That's the beauty of this party. Tough but tender might mean people standing on their own two feet just as easily as it might mean anything else. Oh, there's no good to look like Thomas More. It's just words. All we're actually promising, if you think about it, is that we won't pass legislation requiring people to remain permanently seated . . . The trick is not to say anything that can't mean something else later if it needs to.'

'Well, yes. I suppose . . .'

Graham was forced to admit that Hamster compensated with fluency for her debt to integrity. Whether the person who answered the door was serious about forcible repatriation or intent on the outlawing of abortion, she would insist: 'I think you'll find that this is a party that's talking your language.'

By the end of the afternoon, in the various ethical ghettos encompassed by a single London postal district, she had posited a politics which embraced simultaneously genocide, privatization, state investment, the legalization of cannabis and prostitution, imprisonment for pimps and pushers, a statutory requirement for the teaching of both Latin and Computer Studies, the abandonment of nuclear weapons, and the immediate destruction of Moscow.

Many doors went unanswered and some which opened were quickly shut with a tight smile and a pledge of allegiance to one of the major parties. At another address, a frail old lady leaned close, glanced beadily both ways for the presence of hostile agents, and confided that the War Office had put a listening device in her wardrobe and a camera which filmed her when she undressed at night. After carrying out another 360-degree surveillance of the surrounding territory, she confided that this was because she was having an affair with Winston Churchill. As the canvassers backed away, she announced that she would be voting for Sir Alec Douglas-Home, whose smile she had always liked.

In most places, however, Hamster and Graham were the beneficiaries of English politeness, too disengaged for either rudeness or real curiosity. Only two encounters were disturbing; the first politically, the second personally.

The ideological unsettling came from an agitated home-owner, in a part of the constituency where houses big enough once to have had servants' quarters were divided into flats. He seized the leaflets and the poster bearing the face of the bemused, besuited candidate and crumpled them into a cab-bage-shape of glossy paper. 'You don't understand,' he spat. 'You can't actually change anything. I'm not saying you're per-sonally to blame, don't get me wrong. You're not evil people. But you can make your speeches and find men with decent teeth to go on television and be sincere . . .' Here, he gestured at the leaf of the cabbage which showed a part of the candidate's face. 'But in the end, you won't actually change anything. What happens, happens. It is in other hands.'

'I see,' said Hamster. 'Are you religious?'

'No. I'm a historian,' he hissed, handing back the cabbage to Hamster and slamming the door.

The psychological blow, to Graham at least, was effected when, ringing a doorbell twice and producing no response, Hamster, hearing rock music from an upstairs room, suggested that they should be persistent. Eventually, the door was answered by a teenage girl in a bathrobe, which she kept closed by embracing herself. She had a cascade of hair, from which water was dripping. Looking carefully, however, Graham saw that there was only a small dark patch of dampness on one side of an otherwise dry mane. Graham, whose insecurity had given him good antennae for deceit, thought: she was screwing her boyfriend upstairs. The bell went on so long that she dared not ignore it, so decided to pretend she'd been washing her hair.

He visualized the boy, tumbling into his underwear and jeans upstairs. Graham thought that he could smell semen on her breath – how amazing, she was sucking him off! – but he accepted that this might have been a hallucination, like a man in a famine taking a stone for a loaf.

'Oh, God,' said the girl, realizing for what she had been interrupted.

'Have you decided which way you'll vote?' asked Hamster, seemingly untroubled by the situation.

'I'm not old enough yet. Ma and Pa vote Tory. They're very big on Family Values.' She widened her eyes ironically. 'Look, I've really got to . . .'

They handed her a leaflet and retreated. Graham had to accept that it was probably the wrong time to stress their party's interest in encouraging the development of agriculture and fisheries. The voyeurism of canvassing – these brief scenes from days preoccupied with seething personal obsessions, sexual encounters and forty-year-old paranoid fantasies – had made him even more equivocal than before about the claim of politicians to change or shape these lives.

Graham had read in a magazine article that, in Indian elections, where the bulk of the voters were illiterate, the candidates handed out sweets and stickers with a symbol on them. They hoped that, on polling day, the villager would remember the star or the wheel on the campaign confectionery, and tick the equivalent picture on the ballot sheet. It was easy for an Englishman like Graham to chuckle at this but how much more sophisticated were their own campaign practices? It was a system apparently constructed on the theory that a shake of a hand could convince a man, that a yell from a van speeding down his street could secure his allegiance. Was it really more complex than the lollipop politics of the Calcutta slums? And yet English writers, in papers like the one that Graham read, moralized about vote-buying in India, while ignoring the ancient British tradition of cutting taxes and interest rates just before an election.

Graham felt the approach of the questionnaire. He composed himself:

18: In your opinion, which of the following factors most affects the way in which those in Western democracies vote?

☐ A: The greatest happiness of the greatest number.

☐ B: The amount of money they personally have to spend.

☐ C: The provision made by politicians for the weakest in the community.

☐ D: The possession of the means to deter or resist other countries with designs on your own.

☐ E: The possession of the means to invade other, smaller countries, if they get uppity.

☐ F: Some personal obsession with a single issue (abortion/ecology/radio reception/immigration).

(NB: The answer that some do it for some reasons and some for others is not applicable. We are asking you why most people vote.)

It would have pleased him if this had been the hardest of all the questions. In fact, it was the easiest. His heart said A (altruism), his head B (cash). He ticked B, with the silent proviso that, in Britain, it was probably a combination of B and D and, in America, a combination of B, D, and E.

The interrupted lover had been their last call of the day. They met up with Barry and Sue, who were bubbling in a low-key way.

'We've had a very very promising response,' announced Barry. 'Haven't we, darling?' His wife smiled. 'Three definite yeses before we'd even opened our mouths. More than half took a leaflet. One chap actually admitted that we'd changed his mind on the structuring of local government! We only had one who was downright nasty and that was on the estate. He actually answered the door in a vest. He said he was a Don't-Know, but we put him down as Socialist. I'd say, by and by, we're looking at a hung parliament at the very least. Nice people of the world unite! You know what I think we're involved in here? The world's first protest movement in which you don't have to break any laws!'

'And we don't all have to sleep with each other...' added Hamster. Barry and Sue coughed.

This vaulting optimism about the likely outcome of the result continued until near to polling day. The Nice People's Party had been campaigning under the slogan The Time Has Come. Regrettably, on election night, they were proved to have set their watches wrongly. Margaret Thatcher won her second electoral victory, while the Alliance, despite polling 25 per cent of the vote, received only 4 per cent of the seats. The Labour Party gained 30 per cent of the seats for only 27 per cent of the vote. This was how Britain's constituency system worked, so that the vote of a committed supporter of one party might count for less than that of an apathetic member of another purely because of the accident of where they lived. As a result, power would not yet be a problem for Graham and his friends.

The third temptation was lust. There was, however, a complication in this test of the spirit too. The opportunity for sexual misbehaviour first revealed itself as an occasion for compassion.

In August 1983, John Durry telephoned and, in the manner of a suddenly notorious public figure reading a statement on which they hope to take no questions, told Graham that he had left Jenny Cann. Balancing the training of a journalist against the discretion of a friend, Graham did not ask 'Why?' but, rather, 'Really?'

'I'm well aware,' said Durry, expanding on his short announcement, 'that this action will have accorded me the status of a fugitive Nazi war criminal among my acquaintances – with your wife, I expect, as Chief Nuremberg Prosecutor – but the point is, Graham, that I refused ever to issue guarantees about my likely conduct if she persisted in taking the pregnancy to full term...'

Graham had noticed before his friend's tendency to talk about Frederick Thomas Durry in the abstract, so that he sounded more like a court case than a baby.

'Do you know what I think the last circle of hell will be, Graham?' Durry went on. 'A crèche. In which the doomed will burp and change grotesquely bloated infants until eternity. And there will be no fire but only crying. And – this is the point, Graham – the damned will not have chains but commissions to complete books. But every time they hit the keys the little bastards will start howling . . .'

Durry was writing a history of the welfare state for a left-wing publisher. 'The chapter on single-mother benefits should be particularly fascinating,' remarked Eliza when her husband reported the contents of the phone call.

For Eliza, the act was confirmation of Durry's general venality. With reference to Jenny Cann, she composed an instant social epitaph: 'Poor little silent Jenny. I think she's probably quite sweet, although, as she never spoke, it's hard actually to know. I wonder what it was that drew her to him. Anyway, her life is ruined now.'

Graham reflected on how similar this comment from a supposedly liberated, post-Christian woman in the 1980s was to what might have been expected from a God-fearing village matriarch a century earlier, discussing the wronged farm girl over the parish pump. The only difference was that, now, Man (or, specifically, Men) was held responsible instead of the deity.

For his own part, Graham again felt, and tried to repress, elation at the contravention by another of the loosely agreed rules of the community. Durry, it had to be faced, was now hovering in the relegation zone of the league of decent people, while Graham, surely deserving another two points from this skirmish, might even be within reach of the championship. Eliza, who had two older brothers, had once told Graham of the special glow of love and security she had felt at the family table when one of her siblings was in disgrace over an earlier incident. Graham, the only product of his parents' marriage, had never been exposed to this emotion but he understood it now. Just as the young Eliza, smug at supper, had been Mummy's Good Little Girl, so he was Liberal Humanism's Good Little Man.

'What are they doing about houses?' Eliza asked.

'Oh. John's moved in with some friend. From the party...'

'A lady comrade...?'

'He didn't say...'

'I bet. And Jenny?'

'He said she'd found some place in... you know what I'm like about places... South London, I think... A council flat...'

'Oh, very nice. At least John's principles remain intact.'

It was, indeed, South London. As Graham approached the block of flats – a week after the phone call from Durry – a gross, morose dog barred the shared entrance. The animal was connected by a chain, with the approximate width of those more usually used to secure a ship, to a youth, who wore a T-shirt with the slogan FUCK, a pair of cheap jeans so torn that they seemed to be spontaneously evolving into beach shorts, and the kind of huge boots which looked as if they might be orthopaedic but were not, although they may have been implicated in creating work for orthopaedic wards. Graham looked from man to dog and it was clear that they had done a deal to meet somewhere in the middle of their species. Each had a tightly cut fuzz of hair, a long, nearly conical chin and big square teeth arranged like yellow storm fences, although it was apparent that it was the dog who had the better dentist.

It occurred to Graham that the pair might be a security measure imposed by the local council but he soon realized that these were more likely to be insecurity guards. He tried not to make either human or canine eye-contact as he approached the entryphone. He felt a sting on his shin and stumbled, needing to steady himself against the graffitied wall. He tensed himself for a mugging, instinctively moving his hand towards his thudding heart, where his wallet was, ready to hand it over when asked. But there were no further blows. On this occasion at least, the sentinel was getting his kicks from trips or, Graham's mind punned triumphantly in celebration at escaping pain, his trip from kicks. He buzzed Jenny's number.

'Yes?' A frightened voice, he felt.

'It's G-G-G-Graham.'

'Hi.'

With an electronic belch, the latch eased back. It was five floors up to Jenny's flat, exactly half the reach of a tower-block relatively stunted by the standards of the period. This estate had clearly been built at a time when politicians were beginning to be afflicted with guilt about vertigo housing. Graham was grateful that they had, as the handle of the lift door wore a white collar on which OUT OF ORDER, in the black type of officialdom, had been scratched out and replaced with FUCKED. Presumably one of the very few job openings locally was that of simultaneous translator.

Graffiti on the stairwell walls suggested various ways in which the writers would like to inflict pain or painful sex on Margaret Thatcher or more obscure methods, involving beasts, machines, and hermaphroditism, by which she might give pleasure to herself.

At the fifth-floor door, which Graham reached appearing more breathless than he would have wished, Jenny Cann was waiting. Her fringe was lower and thicker than he had ever seen it, so that her eyes were really only visible when she exhaled with particular force or nodded in fierce agreement. This, apart from her tendency towards silence in company, contributed towards her enigma because, once the eyes of the person being addressed were removed from the equation, all conversation was subject to a kind of emotional Braille. Graham tried not to be surprised by the hug Jenny now gave him. He assumed it to be the solidarity of the wronged with the good.

'You found it all right?'

'Er, yes . . .'

This was an imprecision. The Deep South was one of the

147

areas of London blacked by taxi-drivers since the riots. In fact, there had been no trouble in this vicinity, although the streets down which Graham walked from the Tube station held no particular sense of having been spared anything. All the shop windows had thick grilles, like those worn by ice-hockey goalkeepers. In the window of an off-licence were stacked the big tins of beer which had been known at Graham's university as gang-bang packs and dusty bottles of a viscous red wine which, Graham thought with a shiver, he and Eliza would use only for cooking and, he further qualified the concession, only then when only cooking for themselves.

He quietly commended his good sense in buying a '77 red as a visiting gift for Jenny before leaving the centre of the capital. An additional source of unease for Graham had been the gang of black – he was sorry, of Afro-Caribbean – youths on most corners. He had tensed each time he passed them. It was not, you understand, that he felt any resentment towards them: it was that they might mistakenly interpret him as a representative of a class which oppressed them and that they might express their frustration against Graham.

But he had survived and here he was, chinking his tumbler ('John got the wine glasses. I'm sorry') of Burgundy against Jenny's and offering her a toast of 'Er, better times.'

Because both participants habitually let others lead the conversation, the initial encounter between Graham and Jenny had the awkwardness of a comic double-act consisting of two straight men. The male half of the duo fed the female half the fact that it was a nice flat. She riposte that it wasn't, really.

This exchange at least provided the excuse for them to look around the kitchen. The walls showed the eczema of recent damp combined with ancient painting. Perhaps in an attempt to distract from this, large posters had been liberally deployed. One was for a rock group whose name Graham had heard while trying to find the cricket on the radio; another advertised a rally for Nicaragua. Knee-har-rah-wah. That, Graham assumed, was the taste of the Samaritan who had given her space here, rather than of Jenny herself.

Subsequently, there was a lengthy spell of sipping wine and smacking lips appreciatively (Graham) and running an index finger round the edge of the glass (Jenny).

'It was nice of you to come,' Jenny said eventually.

'I just . . . I got your number from the party . . . I mean, I hoped . . . John's a . . . but even so . . .'

Like an archaeologist with the shards of a Roman bowl, Jenny pieced together something like: 'I hoped you wouldn't mind. John's a friend but even so, we worried about you.' In response, the areas of her face available to daylight smiled. She explained that the flat was a council property, in which an old school friend of hers was now living. Tony (a girl, Antonia presumably) was currently out.

A further epigrammatic impasse occurred before Graham asked: 'How's Freddy?'

'Oh, Freddy's great, Graham. I mean, I think he knows there's been a bit of a heave-ho going on but if I didn't have him, I'd be . . .'

They both took refuge in another gulp of Burgundy. Graham wondered if Jenny had shrunk from the momentum of the sentence she had begun: if she hadn't had Freddy, there would not have been a problem with Durry. He noticed that the edges of some of the strands of her fringe were glistening. Was she crying? She had not yet said anything long enough to listen for the sob in her voice.

The kitchen was crammed with the cardboard packets and plastic tools which apparently went with being a baby. It was a small room and two sides of the table were flush with a wall and a fridge, so that Graham and Jenny were sitting in much the same formation as the day in the editor's office when the wreck had designated Graham his successor. Accordingly, Graham could smell the wine on her breath when she moved sharply towards him and began the longest speech he had ever heard from her.

'Oh, Graham, there are all these questions you're too polite to ask. About me and John. Or Durry. Did you call him that? Everyone seemed to. I always found it a bit odd, not being on first-name terms with your lover. Anyway, I probably flatter myself but I used to think that everyone – you, Ben, Paula, Lizzy – was thinking: what's *she* doing with *him*? Oh, you sweet thing, you're nodding. Well, it's too too simple, really. I'm only grown up enough to admit it now but it was that terribly, terribly boring English thing: Upsetting Mummy. Choose the specimen most likely to cause apoplexy at the manor and, you know, fuck it . . .'

The genetic shred in Graham which held that women should not swear recoiled briefly here but he was nodding sympathetically at the rest of the account. His own experience, most notably at university, had been that the kind of sweet, middle-class girls he felt to be his birthright had told him, over supposedly pre-coital drinks in the college bar, how nice he was, before surrendering their virginities to a proletarian nose-picker. He was also finding himself fascinated by Jenny's voice. Now released in quantity, it was revealed as firm, elocuted but faintly bashful: a Head Girl's Speech delivery.

'We're Army and County, you see,' the voice went on. 'A two-Brigadier family. My father and his brother. Small parts of various cousins and uncles scattered over the poppy fields of France. You know, impeccable. Daddy called Durry John the Marxist. The reference being to his head on a plate, I suppose. I liked that. I loved the way Durry infuriated them, didn't play by the rules. You know how it is. If a dinner guest says that, oh, it's time they shipped the niggers home, and have you, incidentally, tried Pretoria claret, the convention is that you don't Make An Issue Of It At Dinner. John used to say that, if it was impolite for him to challenge them, it was impolite of them to have said Fascist things in the first place. So he'd go for them. Statistics, graphs, quotations from jailed Turkish playwrights. You know how he is. He fed my guilt – and it is guilt – about what I am. I was his prize exhibit: the Brigadier's

Daughter – Fallen. I admit the fascination palled. I used to cry after those frightful dinner parties. In the end, I think what happened is. . . . did you ever see that documentary – they're all I watch really – about the hermit in some French village, whose vocal cords actually, you know, closed up? . . . In fact, I was at Cambridge with a girl who thought that the sides of your, you know, isn't vagina such a prissy word? stuck together – the skin actually grew over – if you didn't do it for a month. . . . Anyway, living with John, I think my mind healed up. Redundancy. There was actually no point in beginning a conversation in which he had the last word. The mandated last word, he would have said. The point is, Graham, feminism I can take or leave but I do sometimes find it a little odd that, after all those degrees and Daddy's school fees, we can still end up as a kind of sexual lavatory for, nice old-fashioned word, rotters . . .'

She gave the last word the full round r-sound of the English upper-classes; an inflexion which, ironically, made them sound briefly Mittel European. Graham wondered if this was a relic of the British monarchy being foreign. He was vaguely aware that he might have been gazing, for quite some time, at the co-ordinates on her fringe which he believed might mark her eyes. He adjusted his eyes to a lump of butter, probably from a breakfast twelve hours earlier, now retreating to its constituent greases on a cracked floral saucer which someone (surely not Jenny, Graham proprietorially thought) had employed as an emergency ash-tray.

Jenny was saying: '. . . It wasn't just that John jammed all other wavelengths conversationally, as it were. There was this baby business, about which he's doubtless given you the Authorised Version. Don't blush, Graham. I'm not going to ask. But the actual point is that he went so absolutely AWOL – now literally, of course – about the damn thing. "I didn't know you were religious, Jen," he'd say in that, you know, Spanish Inquisition voice of his. Well, hell, I'm not. I mean, no more than Church of England sort of thing. I just think that, if I may put it so pompously, For A Woman, it's a bit different, actually, in the end, than your granny going to get her bunions done. Should we try another bottle?'

He had obviously nodded, or she had made the decision for them, because she took the five steps which the kitchen permitted you – why hadn't he noticed before that her feet were bare? – to a wine rack, from which she pulled a white with a supermarket label. She fumbled for a corkscrew near the cooker and had the plug half out by the time she sat down again and continued: 'It's not chilled. Is that too sordid? Good. I mean, what was he so frightened of, Graham? You would think that, given the general drift of his psyche, he'd welcome little replicas. In fact, that he would have started as early as possible on the creation of a master race. Racks of red-blooded women in stirrups awaiting impregnation. Actually, he did have that kind of arrangement, I discovered, with the party girls. Well, for sex, not babies . . . That was the low blow, Graham. I mean we'd never discussed it as such but I'd sort of assumed it was forsaking all others . . .'

Although it was sometimes a problem for him that almost everyone he knew spoke in code almost all the time, Graham had translated from the previous sentences that Durry had been an adulterer. A technical adulterer, it was true, given that he had not been married, but still enough to give a faithful husband another boost in the league of decency. A line from a nursery rhyme entered his head: Oh, what a good boy am I! Immediately, however, one of the strange little magnets in the brain reached out and brought back a snatch from a playyard parody: 'He put in his thumb and she started to come/ And said, what a good boy are you.' He felt a blush arriving and raised the tumbler, now filled with the first of the second bottle.

'Oh, Lord, am I embarrassing you?' asked Jenny.

'No, I just never knew that Dur . . . that John had . . .'

'Well, neither did I, until one of the recipients of the Heroic Copulation Medal, or whatever the party calls it . . .'

Graham felt this to be unfair. The party to which Durry belonged had no connection with monolithic Communism of the kind which Jenny was satirizing, but he reflected that she had been under a great deal of stress recently, so did not challenge her. Instead, he found himself wondering: what is she doing for sex now? Is she masturbating?

She was continuing: '. . . arrived one night, when John was at a branch meeting, to confess to four months of passion over the canvass returns. I, please note, have just given birth at this point. What is it with men, Graham? Is it that they actually can't bring themselves to go without for that bit when – don't worry, I'm not going to go all gynee on you – they have to? I mean, it can't actually be true, can it, that thing I read in a book, a novel admittedly, that what they're really scared of is that, afterwards, you go all, you know, baggy down below? I did my exercises, breathing in deeply on the loo and so on, religiously . . . oh, fuck it . . .'

'Oh, dear. Had you better . . . ?'

This exchange was prompted by the sudden activation of Frederick Thomas Durry, whose bawling could be heard through the wall. Jenny was instantly up and busy.

'I'd better go and glance at him. I hope he's not hungry because I'll have to make up a bottle. I'm not breast-feeding now. Pour yourself some more . . .'

'Do you want me to . . . ?'

'Thanks, but you'd probably rather not. No, no, that's not a criticism . . . you've been an absolute darling so far . . .'

She kissed him lightly at the side of the head, where he hoped he wasn't as bald as he feared was probably the case.

'Oh, shut up, Freddy, I'm coming . . .'

Within a minute, the child's cries became more subdued, now presumably muffled by Jenny's bosom as well as the wall. Graham, in the kitchen, had found one more worry in addition to those he normally carried round. Was this a seduction, he was wondering.

The special session internal inquiry into this matter heard three submissions.

His libido put in the first bid. Its case was mainly based on detailed textual analysis of Jenny's speeches. The way in which she had talked raunchy [counsel argued], and from which Graham had first shrunk, was now revealed to have been a deliberate tactic. It was, if the jury would permit a vernacular inflexion, her cunt talking. The libido rested its case on two pieces of evidence: the reference to her vaginal exercising and the declaration that she was no longer breast-feeding, clearly suggesting a readiness for sex. The libido wished to enter a plea of hot for it.

His intellect was next on its feet, speaking in scornful tones. Surely no rational and balanced man [counsel argued] could construe from the evidence cited by the libido that sexual intercourse was demanded. It was now common for young women of good social standing to speak frankly of their sexuality in the presence of men. The intellect would rest its deposition on one central point: the entire thrust of Jenny Cann's conversation had been against the sexual avariciousness of men and in support of physical fidelity. In this respect, Ms Cann had drawn a clear contrast between the morality of Mr Durry and what she clearly imagined to be that of Mr Sterling. The intellect entered a plea of don't flatter yourself and don't be so bloody silly.

The final submission was from his conscience, which chose to put a written document into court:

19: In your opinion, is the concept of sexual fidelity between two established partners:

☐ **A:** A killjoy device of sex-fearing Christianity, irrelevant in a secular age.

☐ **B:** A necessary limitation of an act, which, if randomly exercised, can be physically and psychologically damaging.

☐ **C:** A denial of Man's (or Men's) genetic instinct to impregnate as generally as possible.

☐ **D:** Morally correct.

[NB: Those selecting B and D, move on to question 20 (Death/ Afterlife). Otherwise, please answer supplementary question 19a.]

Graham was shocked by the narrow solidity of the fourth option. He dreaded the supplementary, which was almost certainly about spouses or venereal diseases, but was able to abandon the questionnaire – a heady feeling – when Jenny reentered the room and seemed, he felt, to take the decision for him.

'He's gone off again,' she said, quieter, breathier, it seemed, out of consideration for either Freddy or Graham. She was washing her hands (burp or worse?) at the sink.

'Oh, Graham, you're such a ... I was going to say nice ... but nice is somehow so ... John used to – his highest accolade – call people good blokes. I suppose that's what you are, is it Graham, a good bloke ... ?'

She had turned back towards him now. There was a new quality in her voice, a liquidity, from either alcohol or emotion. The special session internal inquiry, if only it had still been in session, might have pointed out that the timbre could have designated a general teary resignation towards males, from which category she clearly excluded Graham (cf, 'What is it with men, Graham?') quite as well as it might have designated sexual desire. But Graham chose to stand and, an erection denting his trousers, to cross the kitchen.

'Oh,' Jenny said.

A distinct snuffling beneath the fringe, like a small bird in a hedge, established that she was weeping. Graham drove a valley in the curtain of hair (Moses was the analogy his brain distantly, chortlingly, made) and exposed her flooding eyes.

'Oh,' she said again.

Jenny raised her head. The libido jumped to its feet in what was now an otherwise abandoned courtroom and claimed this twitch as prima-facie evidence of a deliberate manoeuvring of the lips. Graham, still vaguely intending to contest the contact as accidental if challenged, and inwardly yelling for her to make the decision for him, met the lifted mouth with his. The suction was brief, like an arrow in a junior archery set failing to adhere to its target.

'What about Lizzy?' asked Jenny, still weeping, looking away.

All of Graham's theoretical projections of infidelity had depended on this question being impolite. He struggled to construct an answer.

'I'm sorry. I'm not supposed to ask that question, am I?' asked Jenny, perhaps still more liquidly than before. Graham was grateful to her and tried to turn her head towards him, but wordlessly, she dropped to her knees and began – he was already imagining her afterwards, on his shoulder, the sobbing over – to unzip and unbuckle his trousers. He hoped that there was not too obvious a stench of urine on these, or his briefs, or, indeed, on his penis, now free and (well done, well done, steady on parade) firm and, surely, not disgracefully small, allowing for foreshortening from this angle, and to which she now cupped her lips.

For a dizzying millisecond, he realized that his debut ejaculation in the presence of another, which could not now be much longer delayed, would be in the mouth of a woman not his wife. There was an almost totemic defiance about it. What greater refusal of the separate claims of morality and nature could there be? This act said no, simultaneously, to A,B,C, and D on the questionnaire.

And then, not hard, but with definite purpose, Jenny Cann bit him, just above the ridge which separated standard skin from special, sexual cortex.

'For God's sake, Graham,' she was saying, anger clearing her speech, as she sat on the kitchen floor, hugging her huddled knees. 'Even you. Even you. I never ever believed that feminist thing about all men being rapists. It was so crass. But I do know something else. All men are conmen . . .'

And so it was that, without anything ever being committed to paper or speech, Jenny Cann was excommunicated from the dinner party lists of the Sterlings and the Waddles and their circle, while John Durry remained as friend or tolerated irritant.

Graham's penis escaped with a surface abrasion. Jenny Cann had used the pressure necessary to bite, say, a chip, rather than, say, a stick of celery and Graham had been stiffer than a chip. Eliza, who tended to avoid visual or tactile contact with that part of Graham, never found the graze. So, outwardly, there was not a problem. But Graham knew that the rubric of the questionnaire stated clearly [NB – *all* questions must be answered] and he expected at any moment the firm tread of the invigilator stalking up the aisle to denounce, to encourage the others, a cheat.

The fourth temptation was desolation. The Roman Catholic Church – of which Graham was not a member and never would be – would have called it Spiritual Despair and ranked it in the highest category of sin. A secular definition would be hopelessness; a loss of the future tense.

It began at breakfast in October 1983. Having forced himself through the news pages – Mrs Thatcher's trade minister had made his secretary pregnant and, with some reluctance, resigned – Graham braced himself before braving the obituaries. He always read them alphabetically, so had been awarded the consolation of only Adams, Dorothy, 81, at home, when he saw:

'APPLETON, Richard Anthony, aged 32. Beloved husband of Helen and loving father of little Jack. Loving son of Clement and Marjorie. Funeral service on Wednesday 20th, St Godolph's, Guildford, 11.30 a.m. All friends and colleagues welcome. Family flowers only, please. Donations, if desired, to. . . .'

To a Fund, at the research unit of a hospital. So Appleton had known. It had been one of those, not a car crash or a freak internal blow-out playing squash. Graham read the announcement through again, beginning the tortuous process of literary criticism. Neither Clement or Marjorie was described as late, so both of Appleton's parents had outlived their child; one of the harshest accidents that can befall a family. Also to be noted was the one individual flourish within the consensus sentences, the newspaper's style for death. That was the adjective 'little', applied to Jack. The author – some relatively unaffected

157

nephew, perhaps, for surely Helen, Clement and Marjorie would all have been incapable of making the phone call – had clearly decided to impress upon the reader the wretchedness, the tragedy within the tragedy, of Jack. In this context, 'little' meant: the daddy he hardly knew.

'Have you got the squits?' asked Eliza.

'Sorry?'

'You went a funny colour after that grapefruit. I wondered if you'd been ...'

'No. It's Apple ... someone I travel with sometimes on the tube. He's died.'

'Ah. Old?'

'Four years older than me. Little boy ...'

'It makes you. ...'

Eliza swallowed what was clearly going to be the observation that Appleton's death made you think. Graham reflected that one of the toughest punishments ever inflicted on the middle classes had been their teachers alerting them to what a cliché was, so that, incapable of finding fresh sentiment for every thought, they littered their conversation with abandoned platitudes. Originally phrased compassion failing her, Eliza took refuge in practicality, saying: 'I hope he was well insured.'

Graham blinked, the reflex feeling, as he had feared, better lubricated than was usual. The reference to insurance had alarmed him. Occasionally, he would panic because his domestic circumstances seemed too closely to resemble a television commercial for breakfast cereal or fruit juice but he had never, until now, felt trapped inside an advertisement for financial services.

Donne's Syndrome, complicated by acquaintance, shallow but frequent, with the one who heard the bell, descended then and remained with Graham throughout the Monday and Tuesday, making completion of a feature on an antiseptic mouthwash price war almost impossible.

In reality's version of a phenomenon which cinema had popularized, Graham kept flashing back to himself and Appleton on the train a few months earlier.

'You're looking a bit pale . . .'

'Oh, that. I've had some kind of bug . . .'

But there was also a gap in the narrative which he was desperate to fill. He needed to visualize Appleton's final moments. In his mind, he located the scene at home, finding hospital too horrible to contemplate, and quickly sketched in the narrow body in the double bed, the invalid's half-light behind the drawn curtains which, in daytime, spoke of sex or sickness. He cast it with Helen, a haunted beauty, holding her uncomprehending child tight against her to spare him too much detail in the memories which would be all of his father he had.

What Graham could not easily provide was the dialogue. The problem with the forewarned death, as he saw it, was how your last words could ever live up to the billing of being such. So many of the best – those ones along the lines of 'Ho! They couldn't hit an elephant from th–', which they laughed about on radio talk shows – were retrospectively elected. Through several drafts, all Graham could write for Appleton was a croaked 'I love you', variously amended to 'I'll love you always', which was no less black-and-white Saturday afternoon matinée, and opened up new streets of fear.

Surely, even as you said it, you would be sullenly wondering which of your friends or relatives, or her former consorts, would be your replacement. If there was an afterlife, Graham wondered, did your soul watch human life continuing – enemies' successes, your widow's first sexual encounter with someone else – as if on television? But, if so, how could that be paradise? Or was news from earth censored, with angels bringing discreet reports like nurses in intensive care: 'Your wife's doing just fine, Mr Appleton. She's getting over your, um, demise, beginning to see a few people. . . .' 'Men?' 'It, er, doesn't say, I'm afraid . . .'

Or perhaps part of the relief of ceasing to be visceral was that envy and competitiveness went and you viewed future storylines without rancour: 'Hey, she's doing it with *him*! And they'd been having an affair for five years before I died? Well, good luck to them!' The problem was that, if this were the case, then the quality which made us truly human was the ability to despise others, which presupposed a deity other than the one worshipped in thousands of churches, including St Godolph's, Guildford, where the mortal remains of Appleton were to be spoken and wept over, either because he himself had believed in a bodily resurrection, or because some of his family did, or, alternatively, simply because they had been social church-goers.

It was easier for a camel to get through the eye of a needle than for Graham to find the church when, on the Wednesday morning, having claimed a dental appointment ('Fucking busman's holiday, eh?' snarled Napier in sympathy), he set out from Guildford station with a *Surrey Streetfinder*, a new work for his atlas archives. With this, and with no more than three sets of supplementary instructions solicited in the street, he found first one church, which was derelict, and then another, which was a synagogue. His watch told him that it was 11.25 a.m., five minutes before the beginning of the end of the late Appleton. Sensing that unpunctuality in these circumstances would be literally the ultimate impoliteness, Graham hailed a cab, which ignored him, as did a subsequent two, before a third acknowledged his existence. Fumbling with the crumpled cutting from the Births, Deaths, and Marriages page (an interesting order of priorities, he had often reflected during his morning doomwatch), he asked for 'St G-G-G Godolph's,' adding, he hoped helpfully, 'it's a church.'

The taxi-driver did the kind of vigorous lip-twist which telegraphs examination of conscience and said: 'There are thousands as would take your money without a word but I'm gonna be kind to you because I like your face. You're practically standing on top of St G's. Left at the end of 'ere, third right on Maybury, and across the mini-roundabout. Bleedin' great steeple. You'd 'ave to be blind to miss it and, if you've got a white stick, I'm blind myself . . .'

Graham stared at the taxi-driver. Four years of Margaret

Thatcher's self-help, help-yourself policies and capitalism still tolerated Samaritans.

'I'm very late,' he pleaded.

'Two minutes max,' countered the driver.

There are moments when the socially hopeless must expose themselves in front of some uncomprehending competent and this Graham now did.

'Look, I'm just very bad at finding places. I haven't got my glasses. I've been trying to find it for half an hour. If you take me there, I'll make it worth your while . . .'

The combination of pathos and implied financial gain was successful and the driver started the clock.

As they began the short haul to St Godolph's, he grumbled to his profusely sweating passenger: 'Ah, well, it's your funeral.'

Graham, having handed over a tip which was double the fare, was just in time for Appleton's. St Godolph's was a small, sandstone building. One of the consequences of Graham's tendency towards agonizing internal assessment was that he had little feeling for the external pleasures of landscape or architecture. Accordingly, he was unable to date the church but thought its general dilapidation and unfashionable name (he had never met anyone called Godolph) made it old enough to have been one of King Henry VIII's wedding presents to himself.

The first hymn had begun. As Graham found a seat, the congregation was singing: 'The Lord's my shepherd I'll not want.' He remembered, as he had when the same psalm had started his father's funeral, a moment during a service at school when he had been struck by the inappropriate sentiments of the words. To his '70s ear, the famous first line had translated as 'The Lord's a shepherd who I could do without' rather than the historically intended 'If the Lord is my shepherd, then I shall lack nothing'. It was true that there was a comma on the song-sheet, indicating the conditional, but in most renditions, the punctuation was not sung. A linguistic shift had made an expression of religious acceptance sound like one of secular rejection. The unquestioning survival of the original was per-

161

haps an indication of how little notice worshippers took of the words they mouthed. Certainly, the tuneless, fractured stress given to the phrase by those attending Appleton's funeral held the inadvertent modern message. The Lord was the shepherd they didn't want.

The first two rows on either side of the aisle were not contributing to the heretical rendition or to any other, although they held their hymn books open in front of them with solemn correctitude, like Japanese fans. This was evidently the family. Graham examined their backs and profiles. The long, blonde hair, its sheen assisted by the requisite black of a coat, must be Helen. A huddle of bald head, blood-pressure red, stooped close towards an old-fashioned hat of dark blue waxed lattice, he took for Clement and Marjorie. The uncomprehending Jack seemed to have been spared the occasion.

Between those in the front rows, closest to the box holding Appleton, and the rest of the congregation, there was a clear visual division. Up front, the faces – red, wet, snuffling, twisted, baffled – were how they came out, without rehearsal. Those wearing the expressions had no control over them. From approximately the third row back, the faces had needed to be arranged. For these mourners, the visages of respect, dismay, reflection were decisions as conscious as the clothes they had put on.

This was particularly apparent among the tight pack of black and dark grey ready-to-wear suits, contributing intermittent snatches of the 13th Psalm in the manner of a rugby song. These were, presumably, the dead man's office colleagues. Alone in the rearmost row on the right – St Godolph's was not quite filled – was a tall blonde weeping so strongly that she had abandoned the damming dabs of handkerchief. It was hard not to wonder, suspiciously, if she had been the corpse's mistress.

When the singing stopped, to be replaced by an involuntary coughing, the eyes of the entire congregation moved to the altar, where the vicar was shuffling his notes like an after-dinner joker. The cleric was significantly overweight – fatter, far fatter, than me, thought Graham with satisfaction – and, as the priest bowed his head in either reverence or inspection of his papers, a few dank strands of his remaining ginger hair were laid across his scalp in wavy lines, like those on a postmark.

'Let us pray,' the vicar began. 'We are here today for the solemn duty of commending our brother Dick to the care of his Almighty Father.' Our brother Dick. It sounded wrong, and not just because of the weight of innuendo which that abbreviated name was forced to carry. He had been Appleton to Graham, Richard in his obituary but, apparently, Dick to those who loved him. 'I'm Father Tony and you are all most welcome to St Godolph's,' the welcome went on. 'I know that some have come from as far, er, distant as Canada . . .'

At this, the cleric turned and nodded to the far end of the pew containing Helen, Clement, and Marjorie. A tall girl with short, dark hair suddenly busied herself with the wrappings of the infant she was holding. His sister, Graham thought. Graham's unfailing class radar had now reported on the clergyman: public school, probably Oxbridge. The moulded tones now announced that Dick's brother, Henry, would read the lesson.

In addition of adipose tissue and exposure of forehead, Henry looked about ten years older than Appleton; a fact which was particularly cruel, as he would surely always be to Helen a reminder of how her husband might have looked in time. This was the harsh side of the way in which genes teased, the recompense being that Jack, as he grew up, would become a shadow-Appleton of a kind more comforting to his mother.

'O death, where is thy sting? O grave, where is thy victory?' boomed Henry. Graham had almost as much trouble with these words as he did with the Lord being the shepherd no one wanted. When this thundering taunt to mortality was read, as it had been at his father's funeral too (did all the English dead go out to the same hymn and lesson?), Graham always had an image of a deluded playyard weakling offering to take on the sixth form extortionist and bully. 'C'mon, death, c'mon,' taunts the bobbing contender, 'where's ya sting?' In haughty answer,

163

the bully flattens him with a single blow. Or, if you wanted another analogy, it was as if Britain, in 1982, had taken on Russia instead of Argentina. The truth, as Graham saw it, was that anyone seeking the location of death's victory and/or its sting had only to look at the box of stripped pine – once just Appleton's kitchen, now his whole home – containing the man with whom he had passed time on trains.

As Henry came off the ropes for another rhetorical round with death, Graham's eyes wandered to the three large stained-glass panels above the altar. The first was Jesus with a sheep, the animal an opaque patch of glass, through which the bright cold light produced an incandescent lamb. Then there was Mother Mary in a cloak of light-refusing blue, clutching blooms in all the primary colours. The last panel contained an all-purpose Old Testament beardie, with bloody robes and unkind eyes, giving an admonitory flick of his staff. Was that God?

Henry, having set out the terms on which extinction would be met, returned to his seat. Graham looked around the congregation. It was a bitter morning and from every mouth came a small smoky cloud, like a baby dragon in a comic book practising tantrums. It was as if, on this occasion, everyone present was defiantly drawing attention to the fact that they were still breathing.

The vicar took Henry's place in the pulpit. Graham, fascinated to discover the line which Father Tony would take, listened intently. The vicar coughed; a dry sound, required by the mind rather than the lungs.

'As I was walking across from the rectory this morning,' he began, 'I looked around and it was one of those inbetweeny kind of mornings. You know, the sky bright enough for it to be summer but a kind of sharpness in the air which would make you think it was winter. It's my favourite kind of weather, really. And, perhaps because that kind of inbetweeny day gives you such a strong sense of the passing of the seasons – that particular wonder of, er, Creation – mornings like this always, when I was a theological student – more years ago than I care to remember! – made me feel particularly close to, er, the provider of this sight . . .'

Whether or not they had expected the official explanation of their son/husband/brother's brutally early death to begin with a weather forecast, the Appleton family gazed up politely at the clergyman. Graham, a more dispassionate critic of the homily, had noticed both the reluctance to mention the name of God – the occasion's sponsor, after all – and a joke about getting old ('More years ago than I care to remember!'), which, in the circumstances, was worse than tactless.

Father Tony continued: 'And I still feel the same on those mornings. But, if life is full of those little signs, those little "hello theres" from God, as I like to think of them, then it is also, we have to accept, full of little – and even big – temptations to think that there is no God. That we are alone on this spinning globe. I would not blame any of you if the occasion for one of those temptations had been offered by the awful, terrible, inexplicable, cruel, unfair death of, er, Dick.'

The priest paused slightly here, clearly unsettled by the clergyman's occupational dread of forgetting the name of corpse, bride or infant. Graham was enthralled by the sermon's development. Having reached the atheism-would-be-under-standable phase, what would Father Tony do to swing the balance back to the position which, after all, he was profession-ally required to promote?

What he offered was: 'However, I want you to think of when you were young. No matter how much we try, we can't remember what it was like to know nothing, to be completely uncomprehending. The point I'm making is that there was a time when we actually didn't know that two plus two equals four. There was a time in our human lives before knowing even that small thing. Oh, now, we can manage seven times seven or even twelve times twelve divided by two or even more compli-cated sums. Personally, I was never very good at Maths – I was an Arts man, I suppose – so my progress through the subject stopped at what we called School Certificate. One of my daughters is taking her Maths O-Level, as it has become, now. But others go on to A-Level, or to university, gradually learning more of Maths. And yet even those who give their whole lives to the subject of Maths cannot expect to understand everything. There's a particular sum – I saw a documentary on television recently – the sum is called, I think, Fermat's Last Theorem and it has never, ever been solved.'

Father Tony, who had been addressing the congregation generally, now focused his vision and delivery tightly on the family of the dead man.

'Do you begin to see what I'm getting at, er, Helen, er, Marjorie, er, Clement?' he asked. 'In general terms, life is about knowing more and more as we get older . . . understanding more and more . . .'

Speak for yourself, thought Graham, beginning to fear that he really was the only person in the world for whom life was not an incremental progress towards certainty.

The vicar's voice rose, signalling the peroration: 'And yet we cannot expect to understand everything. There are things which we will never know. That is the similarity with Maths. All of us who call ourselves believers are, as it were, signing up for the course. We can all do the simple sums: like God equals Love. Some, of course, will always understand more than others. But no one, not even the great theologians – who are, in this analogy, the Professors of Mathematics – have solved the question of premature, painful death. In this regard, we are all kindergarten students of God's plan. We can only get our BAs, MAs and Ph.Ds in the next world. Of course, nobody knows either which grades we need to enter that academy. But we need have few worries on that score. Dick was well-qualified for admission. A loving husband, a good father during his too-short time with little Jack, a devoted son and – some of you told me as you arrived this morning – a first-class work-mate, who would, one among you said, have risen to the very top of chartered accountancy. Now Dick has entered into a full understanding of God's love. We who remain must accept, tough as it sometimes is, that life is not about answers, it is about questions. And yet a certainty which you can have, er, Helen, er, Clement, er, Marjorie, is the love and prayers of all of us at this profoundly difficult time.'

Graham blinked, and felt an unbidden wetness. His mood, as the vicar commenced the final prayers over the coffin, was one of total hopelessness. As an outsider, he had always regarded religion and church-going, activities which he vaguely expected to resume when older, as a source of comfort and support to those who turned to them. It now seemed clear that, on the big ones, the licensed believers were no better off than him. 'Life is not about answers, it is about questions,' Father Tony had insisted. He already got enough of that sort of thing at home.

20: In your opinion, is Appleton, whom you occasionally met on the train and engaged in conversation, at this moment:

☐ **A:** Nothing more than a sophisticated form of fertilizer for the earth.

☐ **B:** A ghost [cf Shakespeare's *Hamlet* or Coward's *Blithe Spirit*] who can walk through walls and see you without you seeing 'him'.

☐ **C:** An 'angel' or other entity in the spirit-world which Christian believers call 'heaven'. [*Those of other faiths may substitute cultural equivalent.*]

☐ **D:** About to return to earth as an insect, dog, or other animal as a stage in a cycle of reincarnation.

Graham had long felt that the most credible answer of all was reincarnation. He was uncertain about some of the details, like the fact that swatting a fly might be parricide, for example. Perhaps the most comforting thought was human recycling, so that Appleton's low score this time had to balance against a previous or future septuagenarian existence, in the manner of batting averages. Under such a scheme of compensation, maybe

Graham, in a previous life, had possessed firm opinions. It was an attractive theory. Graham would probably have become a Buddhist already if he had not feared the disapproval of his mother and the sarcasm of Durry. He refused to believe that Appleton was just manure and found the Hallowe'en option a little too Walt Disney, so, quietly, and on the basis that this was a private survey of which the results would not be published, he opted for a heaven, though unsure of its precise dimensions.

His decision did not, however, lift his depression and he had ceased even to try to appear not to be crying by the time Appleton was carried back down the aisle. He noticed that Clement, following the coffin, was limping heavily. Was it a result of some old and innocent injury or the indication of some new malaise which would shortly bring the family together again in this way? Graham fantasized about distributing No. 20 on the questionnaire to everyone as they left the church. Were they burying Appleton in this way from conviction or convention? Did the majority, as they shuffled out, visualize him with wings, in the style of Christian and Hollywood iconography? Or did they all, really, secretly subscribe to the fertilizer theory of the after-life?

It was on the train back to London that Graham, gloomily inspecting the progress of his hairline in the window-reflection, received a kind of revelation. In a sense, it was mathematical, and therefore perhaps a subconscious product of the morning's homily, but, whatever its origins, the effect was to restore his hopefulness, his forward motion. The equation which came to Graham was this: 1. It is unusual for a man to die as young as Appleton. 2. Therefore, in any chosen group of peers, few will do so. 3. Consequently, by having known one of those few, I have reduced my chance of being another.

It was the same kind of statistical Darwinism which had always led Graham to feel secretly pleased if there was a major aviation accident shortly before he was due to fly: if x planes crash per year, then y has just been removed from the reckoning.

He wondered how many of Appleton's colleagues and relatives had done the same guilty sum during the funeral.

'Not too terrible, I hope,' said Anne Colledge, when Graham reached the office shortly after lunch. He stared at her, which was not an opportunity he regretted. She giggled. 'I hope they didn't give you any of the things you write about!'

He remembered he was supposed to have been at the dentist's.

'Not too bad. I mean, funnily enough, knowing about it doesn't make it, you know . . .'

'Well, no. If that were the case, we'd all be going out with gynaecologists . . .'

He was developing an erection. Did she always talk about sex? Graham was going to ask her whether she ever had been out with a gynaecologist – and who, in fact, if anyone, she went out with now – but then he remembered that he was married, and the faint scar of Jenny Cann's teeth on his penis, and, anyway, the Napier Ape stormed into the newsroom and bawled: 'Can you gather round? There's to be an announcement.'

And so the last temptation, being essentially an extension of the first, was power. When Napier had assembled the staff – including the rarely seen advertising department, who proved mainly to be big-boned girls whose names ended with the letter a – in Elliott's office, he said: 'As even the least attentive among you will have sussed, Emily Brontë, our glorious leader, is off sick again. However, the statement which I am about to read has been conveyed to his sanatorium . . .'

Napier altered the pitch of his voice to something probably copied from politicians' press conferences on television and said: 'To All Staff. Embargoed until 14.30 hours. Lord Jarrow, chairman of North-West Publications Ltd, today announced the sale of the subsidiary NW Magazines Ltd to Mushroom Publications Ltd. Lord Jarrow said in a statement that the company had decided to streamline its publishing interests in order to concentrate on consolidating the profitability of its national and regional newspapers.'

Napier, still apparently aping scenes from television news programmes, laboriously transported his half-moon glasses from the bridge of his nose to the inside pocket of his jacket, and looked round slowly at his colleagues. 'OK. Providing subtitles for the slow – don't blush, Bob, it wasnae personal – we have been sold. As part of a job lot involving our friends *Which Lightbulb?* and *You And Your Vacuum* and other such specialist organs. Let me reassure you that the new management has said there will be no redundancies . . .'

Some theatrical 'phews' were exhaled. Then Napier said: 'Except through natural wastage.' Some equally stagey 'aaahs' were let out. Napier's statement was not, however, yet completed: 'I am also instructed to tell you that the present editor of *Dentists and Dentistry*, Mr George Elliott, has shown the sense and indeed the sensibility to take early retirement on the grounds of ill health. Lord Jarrow wishes to put on record his gratitude to Mr Elliott for establishing this magazine as the market leader in dental journalism, although some of this headway was lost in more competitive recent markets . . .'

Anne Colledge looked across at Graham and raised her eyebrows. The hunched and blenched Eric Foster-Thomas, who was rumoured to have impregnated another of the elements in his domestic chain, asked if the staff would be staying in the same building. This was possibly because even a slight relocation could have affected his complicated timetable of loyalties. Napier said that Mushroom had taken over the lease. It was Anne who asked the question which Graham instantly realized he should, as the senior journalist, have been the first to raise.

'What do we know about Mushroom?' she said.

In as much as the adjustment registered, Napier began to look shifty. 'Ah, yes, Annie, you've got your finger on the, er, er, er, er, pulse. And more's the pity it's not mine . . .'

'The union's increasingly keen on sexual harassment,' warned Anne.

'Is that so? Well remember I asked ye first,' Napier leered.

'Mushroom?' Anne prompted.

'Aye. Our new proprietor is, I'm not sure how many bells he'll ring, Garry McKenzie . . .'

'Fuck,' said one of the Arabellas and Susannas from Advertising.

'He's been generally known up to now for leisure publishing,' Napier explained.

'Meaning pornography,' whispered Anne to Graham, who realized that he had recently read an article about Garry McKenzie in his impeccably fretful liberal morning newspaper. He vaguely remembered McKenzie telling the interviewer that his ultimate ambition in journalism was to run a full-frontal nude shot of Margaret Thatcher, to whose policies he attributed his commercial success. Anne now asked the question which Graham realized should have been his second.

'Has a new editor been appointed?' she said. Graham noticed that her fingers were crossed against her thigh, out of view of the deputy editor.

'I understand the job is to be advertised,' Napier replied briskly. 'And now I'd be glad if we got back to this week's issue. Let's make it a good one – for Lord Jarrow and Emily Brontë, eh?'

When they had all left the office, the staff, with the camaraderie of shock, gathered next to the news desk television.

'What would he want with this rag?' asked Bernadette, the office secretary.

'I doubt that he even thought about us,' argued Anne. 'He wanted the computer title. That's where the money is. Didn't all your little brothers want software for Christmas? We're a makeweight. Hopefully, that means he'll leave us alone . . .'

'Apart from appointing an editor . . .' an Arabella interrupted.

There was a nervous consensus that McKenzie and the Ape was an all too plausible alliance. Graham noticed that, to his public shame and private fascination, Anne seemed to be regarded as the leader of the group. He wandered away to the

171

small storeroom called the Library, which was an ambitious description for haphazard stacks of old national newspapers. He found the profile of McKenzie he remembered.

Leaning against a filing cabinet, Graham read that their new proprietor was an East Ender who had built up a successful string of mildly pornographic magazine titles, skilfully directed at what were now called market-sectors (bondage, leather, school uniforms) but insufficiently explicit to worry HM Customs. He had recently received much media attention after the launch of a new magazine called *Whopper!*, which combined colour toplessness ('No pubes!', an anonymous source alleged he had instructed his editor) with wild stories, usually from uncheckably distant regions of the globe or of history, along the lines of Half-Man Half-Donkey Wow With Local Senoritas and Churchill Was German Agent.

'I suppose that means you'll become a "tit and gum" magazine,' joked John Durry when, that night on the telephone, Graham told him about the takeover. Durry suggested that the staff called in their union. Graham replied that not enough people were members and Durry said, slowly and gloatingly, 'Ah!' Durry's last remark was, however, the most alarming. 'Jen mentioned you'd been round to see her,' he volunteered, but refused to reveal how much he knew. Graham was aware that the balance of power in his relationship with Durry had shifted even further towards the other man.

Eliza, when told over supper, asked, at once: 'So, has the Ape got Gormless George's job?'

'Everybody thinks he will. But they're, er, er, advertising . . .'

'Good. Well, I hope you'll be applying . . .'

'Well, I, er . . .'

'You must, my love . . .'

Involuntarily, Graham thought of the scene in *Macbeth* which begins with the line 'The King comes here tonight' but then decided that, on balance, the comparison was a little strong. It was, however, to occur to him again when, later that night, Eliza initiated love-making, in what was clearly a spirit of reward.

Their passion followed the standard pattern. After ten minutes of unproductive rhythm (for him but not, apparently, for her), Eliza said 'Can we stop now?' and he withdrew, sticky only from her moisture. Before she fell asleep, she said: 'That was jolly nice. I'll coach you before the interview, if you want . . .'

In fact, her contribution was more substantial. Eliza composed her husband's application and commandeered her secretary at Dazzlem to word-process it. One week after the closing date, it was announced that a shortlist of four – Napier, Graham, and two outside applicants, both rumoured to be dentists – would be seen by McKenzie himself on the following Thursday. On the Wednesday evening, over a Thai takeaway and a supermarket claret, Eliza faced Graham sternly from one end of the sofa to the other.

'Essentially,' she began, 'you have to remember three things: one, finish your sentences . . .'

'You mean I . . .'

'Almost never. I find it quite endearing. The Porn King wouldn't. Two, do not begin any of the sentences you finish with the formula "As a liberal . . ." It's a dirty word in business nowadays . . .'

'Do I say that a lot?'

'Invariably. Particularly if you're about to say something with which you fear the other person might disagree. Three, if he asks how you'd feel about having nude dental hygienists on page three, stall him for the moment by saying you'll certainly be seeking to make the publication more accessible . . . oh, and if he asks what you think of *Whopper!*, don't, for Christ's sake, get involved in value judgements. Say something like, you understand it's been the most amazing success . . .'

And there was sex again that night, employed, Graham assumed, as a charm or potion.

The following afternoon, he knocked timidly on the door of the part of the *Dentists and Dentistry* office which was called the boardroom, where a stone bowl of dulled plastic fruit rested on a scraped and faded table, which looked like imitation-imitation mahogany, at least two removes from the effect it intended. McKenzie was sitting at the far end, with papers and magazines scattered across most of the surface, as if it were some comically out-sized desk, planned as a status symbol.

'Graham? Garry McKenzie. How's tricks?' said the new proprietor, half-standing to shake hands. 'Park your arse there, all right?' he added, indicating a chair to his left. McKenzie had the chest and belly of a rugby player out of training. His hair was a high pile of dirty-blonde curls. The newspaper profile Graham had read revealed that, because of this, the young McKenzie had been known at school as 'Bubbles'. The journalist had also quoted a famous rival media mogul as having supposedly said: 'I can't do business with a man who has his hair permed.'

'OK. Tell me what you think of this, all right?' McKenzie began. He skimmed a thick, shiny magazine towards Graham, who saw that it was a copy of *Whopper!*. The lead story carried the headline: Transplant Joy Of "Wee Willie Winkie". There was a large colour picture of a diminutive, sun-tanned man in late middle age, grinning saucily upwards beneath the promontory of a blonde, bronzed model's statuesque chest.

'Take your time. As the tart said to the teenager,' McKenzie interjected encouragingly. Graham glanced at the first few lines of the front page lead. They were: 'Brazilian ice-cream salesman Ray De Janiero, 54, had a problem! The lovely beach senoritas wanted his cones but not his (sorry, ladies!) cojones.' An asterisk on the final word directed monolingual readers to a footnote at the base of the page, which explained 'Spanish for b**ls'.

The story continued: 'Sad Ray had stopped growing at 4 feet 6 inches. And, whatever the agony aunts say, girls tend to think shortness is a clue to a fella's other measurements. Ray took to seeing a shrink. Although, as he told us: "I couldn't have afforded to shrink any more." Then doctors at Brazil's posh Santa Christoffa clinic heard of his plight. And, when local gigolo, six-footer Coco Cabana, 21, died in a tragic surfing accident, surgeons sprang into action for the world's first naughty-bit switch . . .'

'What do you reckon?' the proprietor pressed him. 'Give it me between the eyes, Graham. I can take it.'

'I, er, understand it's been enormously successful,' Graham answered.

'The transplant or the paper?' shouted McKenzie, rocking backwards on his chair.

'The magazine,' the applicant clarified his answer.

'Tasty story, eh?' McKenzie was tapping the front cover. His finger, Graham noticed, was hitting the breasts of the girl in the photograph.

'Er, yes. Is it true?'

There was an explosion of spluttering, as if the proprietor were choking on a piece of meat. In his open mouth, a large number of gold teeth were visible. His face reddened, as, co-incidentally, did Graham's, from a different emotion.

'That's nice. I like that!' gasped the interviewer. The interviewee wondered whether the other man was being ironic but then realized that McKenzie had wrongly detected irony in Graham's reply. The proprietor recollected himself.

'You see, Graham, I mention this at the commencement, because I have been the victim of a certain amount of snobbery. From the English, middle-class liberal types, mainly . . .' The three adjectives were delivered with escalating aggression, like a witch's curse. 'So, what I'm saying, Graham, is, if you happen to be an English middle-class liberal, I am giving you an opportunity to leave the room now.' McKenzie began to choke again, as he added: 'Are you now or have you ever been, eh?'

This eventuality had not been covered by Eliza's notes. Graham sat still, hoping that silence would be taken for tacit denial of the charge.

'All right,' McKenzie said. Graham expected to hear a cock crowing. 'You see, Graham, I'm not a political animal, funda-mentally, but the reason I have voted twice for Margaret is that Margaret has give a chance to people like me. I don't agree with all she's done but Margaret gave two-fingers to old sick England with its which fucking school did you go to and its ooops, darling, he's fucking passed the fucking sherry to the vicar not the colonel. Where Margaret's all about choice. It's like teeth, isn't it? If you can pay for gold fillings, then you get them. If you can't, then, no question, a man-made substance should be available to those of the work-shy who are in genuinely life-threatening pain. I'm jesting, of course. But the fact of the matter is that *Whopper!* could never have existed without Margaret. Actually, she sent us a good-on-you note for our first anniversary last year. We put it on the front page. I don't expect she wrote it but it's the thought. I like that about Margaret. The Archbishop of Canterbury told us to fuck off, don't you know? You see, frankly, Graham, when I bought the whole bloody joke-shop off "Bertie" Jarrow, it was the microchip stuff I was after. You boys just came along for the ride. But there aren't going to be any passengers. This magazine makes a small profit and there's no reason why it shouldn't make a large one. I can help you by kicking the print unions' butts, which I plan to do royally, but certain editorial concepts are going to have to be taken on board. Tell me what you would do, if you were lucky enough to become editor, and there was one of these tasty little stories about a dentist putting his hand up a patient's skirt – or, I'm not fussy, down her blouse – while she was under. All right?'

Graham had become depressed by the direction of the conversation. Pragmatically, he knew that he should use Eliza's formula of being prepared to consider a whole range of editorial innovations, but his instinct was different. 'I'd, er, think that would get enough coverage in other places,' he replied.

'All right,' said McKenzie. 'All right.'

His tone had changed. It was clear that the interview was almost over.

That night, Graham told Eliza that the meeting had been 'all right' (the accidental echo of the proprietor's favourite phrase made him shiver) but he knew that he needed to speak in detail about it to someone. Durry would be too judgemental, so he phoned Ben Waddle. Apologizing that 'I can't actually do his voice,' Graham gave an account of the conversation with McKenzie.

'I, er, sort of feel that the honourable thing to do would be to resign,' he concluded. 'But there aren't, well, all that many jobs and, even if there were, I wouldn't . . .'

'It's a problem,' Ben cut in. 'I mean, in a sense, in our society, the possibility of intellectual integrity stops at about twenty-five. After that, we're all, in the end, caught between our principles and the building society. Do you know, this term I'm teaching *King Lear* with fifteen copies for a class of thirty-four? And in about half of those, the storm scene, among others, has fallen out. So, at the top, you have the children of the rich socialists and liberals, whose folks just order from Hatchards all the available paperback versions for comparison, and then you have the rest, for whom the state system was actually intended, making do on school copies inadvertently bowdlerized by neglect and rough handling. So what do we do? If we strike, it just gives them an excuse for treating us as badly as they already are. I complained to my MP once, told him some of what I've just told you. You know what he said? "You're a teacher. So you would say that. This government is going to listen to the parents." But if I resign on principle, what do I do to pay the bills? Live off Paula? Bad karma, one way. Become a salesman? Bad karma, another. So I carry on, the theory being that I am an irritant within the system . . .'

These remarks had given some comfort to Graham, who reflected that, by remaining on the staff, he might be able to uphold the editorial traditions of *Dentists and Dentistry*. Then, a more alarming thought occurred: suppose the new editor, whoever it was, sacked him. Graham's skill of vivid empathy, which made reading an obituaries column or walking past an undertakers' so treacherous an activity, also afflicted him when he walked past a Job Centre or read in the newspaper of a factory closing down.

Such stories had been increasingly prevalent in the last two years, so the cumulative effect had become more disturbing. Sometimes, on the train, Graham would say inside his head the words 'my job', with the kind of soppy, possessive intonation usually reserved for a person or a place. He sometimes thought that 'job' and 'health' and 'love' were the three most emotive words in the English language, for it was never clear where they came from or when they might go.

Two days later, a press release from Mushroom Publications announced that 'Ernest Napier, 59, a national newspaper journalist of wide experience' had become the new editor of *Dentists and Dentistry*. One week after that, a further notice on the office cork-board revealed that Graham Sterling had accepted the position of Features Editor. In November 1983, the magazine officially changed its name to *Oral*. The gossip column 'Mouthing Off' was renamed 'Deep Throat' and it was decided that 'My Teeth', the column still written by Graham, would subsequently be called 'Mouth-to-Mouth'.

6

The Dentist In World Literature

IN EARLY 1987, the liberal newspaper columnist who most decisively – if that word could be used in this context – moulded Graham Sterling's thoughts adopted a new coinage: 'The Worrying Classes.' This was the journalist's riposte to the fashionable sneer of the right-wing writers of the time: 'The Chattering Classes'. The latter tag was intended to suggest a social compassion ('Those poor, poor people, sleeping on the streets') expressed over drinks and dinner in London houses whose values were escalating like great paintings, but not translated into action.

The liberal columnist said that, a few years before, his suggested alternative would have been 'The Compassionate (or Caring) Classes', but that the politics of the '80s had regrettably succeeded in smearing the words 'compassion' and 'caring' with the inference of insincerity. 'By falsely rendering compassion suspect,' the pundit wrote, 'they have somehow made the lack of it seem admirable. It is as if a teacher, by consistently delivering the word "politeness" with an ironic sneer, encouraged his students to believe that rudeness were a virtue.' (Graham was impressed by this point and rather regretted that the only comeback on the paper's letters page was from a female reader bemoaning the writer's assumption – 'his students' – that the teacher in the metaphor was male.)

179

The columnist went on to say that the label for the attacked chatterers which he now proposed was 'The Worrying Classes'. He accepted that the word 'Worry' had itself become debased – it was certainly true that 'no worries', an import from Australia, had become the topical insincere felicitation to replace 'Have a nice day!', imported from America – but worry, about the conditions of your fellow human beings, was an honourable thing.

The article's last paragraph was: 'It would be a pity, and indeed a betrayal of the principles of debate and advocacy in democratic politics, if the criteria were to be established that only the penniless can speak of poverty, only the convicted of the condition of prisons and, presumably, only the dead of the inadequacy of hospital funding. Equivalence of circumstance matters less than the ability to empathize. This is particularly the case because – and here is the cunning double-bind in the argument of those on the right who damn the so-called chatterers – the penniless and the dead have, of course, no voice in the debates on poverty and hospitals and, if a convict criticizes his prison, well, we are told, he would, wouldn't he? By these means, half the dissenting voices are disqualified by lack of involvement and the other half by involvement. Perhaps the most quietly pernicious aspect of '80s politics, in both Britain and America, has been the desire of democratically elected politicians to rule in an echo chamber, in which the only answering shouts are repetitions of their own. Long, then, may the chatter irritate them.'

The worrying classes. As an habitual ideological window shopper, Graham liked the label as soon as he saw it; he was sure it would fit. His first reaction was ironic. Worrying Classes, he thought, sounded like an adult education course: lessons in fretting. He reflected that he could teach such a subject with ease. He had the potential to be a professor of distress, a wreck emeritus. On more sombre reflection, however, he saw that the phrase had useful applications for him. By suggesting that worrying was a symptom of intellectual maturity, it legitimized his indecision, made useful his insecurity. The columnist almost convinced him, at least briefly, that his weaknesses could be harnessed to a purpose, like the invention of a car that ran on water.

This was encouraging because, in the four years that passed between this chapter and the last, there was much for Graham to worry about. Late in 1983, the shooting down by the USSR of a Korean civilian airliner briefly seemed, to tender breakfast ears hearing the excited voices on the radio, another potential trigger for the final war. (Many years later, Graham would watch a television documentary which revealed that some employees of the Pentagon had taken the same view.) Thankfully, the Soviet action was accepted as an accident and subsequently an American warship erroneously exploded an Iranian passenger plane, making it one-all between the superpowers, a moral score-draw.

But the virus of accidental death seemed to have entered the computer program of the times. The world record for fatalities in aircraft disasters in a single year was broken: nearly eight hundred, none of them the result of regrettable mistakes by superpowers – it was always, somehow, better to have a solid excuse for mass extinction – but just dumb chance. America's Challenger spacecraft popped like a party balloon, turning Christa McAuliffe, the first female-teacher-astronaut, into stratospheric confetti live on network television. A British car ferry leaving Belgium overturned, killing two hundred passengers, many of them enticed by a £1 shop-on-the-continong ticket offer run by one of the patriotic-indignant newspapers. (Napier, to the discomfort of his staff, joked about the 'drown for a pound' promotion. None of the dead were dentists.)

In the comfortable world, sex, which, for Graham's generation had blessedly been stripped of its associations with guilt and babies, was shown to have another complication: death, as Acquired Immune Deficiency Syndrome (Aids) spread from – if you believed the patriotic-indignant newspapers – monkeys in Africa to homosexuals in San Francisco to – if you believed the liberal press – heterosexuals in London. Ben Waddle said:

'I've never, ever found myself thinking it was a judgement on gays. I'm clean on that one, I hope. But, I know this is awful, but don't you find yourself secretly gloating about those of your colleagues and friends who have been getting more sex than you have? Don't you catch yourself thinking *serves you right* . . .'

In the uncomfortable world, famine ravaged Africa. Graham sent his old socks to television programmes, never passed a rattling Saturday morning tin without contributing and bought, and even played, a pop record, called 'Do They Know It's Christmas?', by a consortium of those new figures of the mid-'80s, rock millionaires with a conscience. Graham's decisive actions against famine were partly a result of a belief that this was a cause which surely no one could oppose, but, in this, he again proved naïve.

'What the people of the Third World actually could do without is the crumbs from the pockets of the fat cats of the First World,' said John Durry. He referred to the record Graham had bought as a 'Western guilt-ditty'. Alastair Macleod insisted: 'Any money I give will, in all probability, go into the Swiss bank accounts of the tin-pot Marxists who run these basket-case economies.' Hamster, however, rummaged in her cupboards. 'I've given our local Oxfam Shop labels it has never seen before,' she boasted. It was Ben Waddle who voiced the view which Graham would most like to have owned: 'Look, if the money gets through and saves one sick kid, that's fine. If it doesn't, we've still got our stereos and Volvos. If money from the rich is guilt money, and money from governments comes with strings, then the only people qualified to give money are those that haven't got it.' Alastair Macleod, trying to catch the eye of a waitress in a crowded wine bar, riposted that Ben was 'a typical '60s liberal, tragically born out of time'.

Death was relentless. Even sport began to fill the morgues. In England, forty football supporters died in a fire at Bradford, and, nineteen days later in Belgium, forty-one spectators perished when English fans rioted at the European Cup Final. Durry attributed the former fatalities to the failure of the British government to enforce safety standards at grounds and the latter to the social consequences of high unemployment. Graham, far less certain of whom to blame, fell into a general gloom. In this mood, he read a lot of Philip Larkin, for company rather than comfort, but soon the poet was dead too, of throat cancer.

As the toughest human truth – of individual fragility – was so often underlined, a new welfare profession developed: Bereavement Counsellors. And these were difficult years too for a sufferer from Donne's Syndrome. The profligacy of destruction made impossible personal identification with each, or even many, of the dead, thus triggering the Syndrome's most dangerous complication: worry about not worrying. Graham's worst bout of the condition occurred in August 1986, when his newspaper reported (does anyone remember this?) that one thousand five hundred and forty-three people had died in the region of Wum in the Cameroons after a leak of naturally produced poison gas from a fissure beside a lake. The odourless cloud, the newspaper said, had crept along the ground, undetected. At the same time, the normally clear water of the lake had stained bright red. President Paul Biya had appealed for international aid. Graham thought: Will they blame the politicians? If they did, it was further proof that a successful career in politics depended as much on what you coincided with as on what you did.

And then he wondered about the effect on the religious beliefs of those in surrounding villages. The size of the demise, and its invulnerability to personal free will (the people were asleep), seemed to support the idea of a godless lottery of fate. And yet there was a case for seeing the hand of a vengeful deity in the hideously biblical detail of the blood-coloured lake, which scientists rationalized as oxidization caused by subterranean volcanic activity. Was Wum a modern Sodom? What religion had these people been? Moslems? Christians? Next day, in its last article before the story was forgotten, his newspaper settled this point. Much of the population of Wum was, apparently, Animists, a faith which, the agency reporter claimed, 'attaches religious significance to natural disasters'. Graham vaguely remembered from a television programme a tribe which believed that trees had souls. He thought about investigating the faith, with a view to possible conversion, but his local bookshop had nothing on it.

So Graham remained a liberal humanist. Politically, the years between the two chapters saw the first democratic elections in Turkey, Portugal's first civilian president for sixty years, and also the first for Brazil, who unfortunately died the night before his installation, though not apparently, as some first feared, a victim of a murder by the disgruntled military. Mikhail Gorbachov, a rumoured reformer with a full hand of faculties, followed the USSR's recent trinity of hardline near-stiffs, Brezhnev, Andropov, and Chernenko. 'It's the global march of moderation. And we're a part of it!' said the chairperson – the bossy BBC Education Producer – of Graham's local branch of the Nice People's Party.

Visiting Poland, Pope John Paul II supported man's 'God-given' right to form trade unions. 'An interesting endorsement, no?' asked John Durry. 'I thought you didn't believe in God,' objected Ben Waddle. 'That isn't the issue,' insisted Durry. The Pope had met Lech Walesa, the leader of the Polish free trade union Solidarity, who was soon to receive the Nobel Peace Prize. In a tentative way, about which he would never have spoken, Graham identified with Walesa. Shabby, tubby, apparently bashful, he was the single world political player who might be a plausible role model for a nervous dental journalist.

Even without such an *alter ego* for the ordinary, a political moderate like Graham could easily be tempted to feel positive during this period. Admittedly, the army took over in Nigeria, but the dictators Jean-Claude Duvalier ('Baby Doc') of Haiti and husband-and-wife team Ferdinand and Imelda Marcos of the Philippines were forced to flee. Mrs Marcos was revealed to have three thousand pairs of shoes. 'Nearly as many as my wife, what?' was Alastair Macleod's only recorded remark on the events in the Philippines. In exile in Miami, Madame

Marcos would later tell interviewers that her footwear collection had been an attempt to encourage the country's leatherware industry. She also revealed that the Marcoses had believed, when the American helicopters arrived, that they were being moved to their summer residence, not out of the country. They regarded this as American duplicity.

By contrast, John Durry viewed the removal of the Marcoses as rare American commonsense, if belated, but saw almost all other USA foreign policy of the '80s as duplicity. He was particularly opposed to the bombing of Libya, from US bases in Britain, against which he marched with a banner saying YANKS GO HOME. He also frequently addressed dinner parties on the subject of President Reagan's support for the rebel Contras in Nicaragua. Knee-har-rah-wah, he still said. And Car-hoont-rahs. 'Oh. Is that how you say it?' asked Hamster. 'Like Cointreau?' Durry had been ridiculing Reagan for comparing the right-wing Car-hoont-rahs or Cointreaus to the Founding Fathers of the United States. Eventually, the American President was censured by the European Court of Human Rights for his behaviour with regard to Nicaragua. The American electorate seemed less concerned, returning the seventy-four-year-old for a second term in 1984 with 59 per cent of the poll.

In British politics, the Labour leader, Michael Foot, and the leader of Graham's party, Roy Jenkins, the Duke of Burgundy, both resigned after the 1983 election defeat. The Socialists chose Neil Kinnock, a young Welshman who had once sung the Red Flag in the chamber of the House of Commons but had since tempered his convictions to the possibilities of office. The Nice People voted in Dr David Owen, a dashing but arrogant former Labour Foreign Secretary, although Graham had personally favoured someone called Ian Wrigglesworth. Margaret Thatcher's second administration announced that it would sell off the state interest in first telephones, then aeroplanes, then water. 'It'll be air next,' said John Durry.

Durry had an arm in plaster when he said this, having been

injured in a clash with police during the Miners' Strike of 1984, victory in which ensured Margaret Thatcher's canonization by the patriotic-indignant press. He began extensive litigation for personal injuries against the police, which was still unresolved by 1987 and had been joined by separate claims relating to a shoulder broken during the Brixton Riots of 1985, which followed the shooting of a black resident during police raids. Wearing his second plaster cast in eighteen months, Durry told Graham: 'I'd rather have been gashed. I'd have liked to have a scar, to teach my grandchildren about the police. Bones heal over.' Eliza told Graham to send round a bunch of South African grapes to his injured friend.

Cradle To Guillotine, Durry's book on the Welfare State in Britain, was published in early 1987, earning unexpected attention because of a widespread belief that the current government intended to retreat from the ideal of free health care. A review in Graham's morning newspaper by a well-known feminist author found the work 'somewhat earnestly written' but 'commendably alert to society's cruelties to women'. Eliza smiled when she read this and said: 'Tell that to Jenny Cann,' and, then, 'You don't have to blush when I'm rude about Durry, my love. I'm not using him to get at you. I'm using him to get at him.'

As a result of the book, Durry received more commissions from the left-wing and liberal press but his income never leapt like those of others in the Sterlings' circle. It was a good time for making money. Indeed, the area of industry in which to operate, in which to be apprenticed straight from school, seemed to be the manufacture of cash: the smelting and moulding and hammering out of vast intangible profits from selling stocks and currency. And those who sweated in the pound foundry, the dollar factory, were more amply rewarded than their equivalents in older industries. Graham's liberal newspaper reported disapprovingly a New Year party in the City – 1986 into 1987 – at which the plumbing system of the selected venue had been filled up with champagne instead of water. He thought, with a kind of dulled wonder, of people pissing and shitting in Moët et Chandon.

And, whether or not his own cisterns swilled with fizz, Alastair Macleod was a beneficiary of this spirit. Details of some of his accumulating gains were recounted to Graham by Hamster at party branch meetings and others were reported to him in the evenings, with what he took to be accusatory intent, by Eliza, to whom Hamster had presumably been boasting at work. In the mid–1980s, Alastair had become a partner at Hanratty Forest Podge. It was at this stage that he began to refer to the Prime Minister as 'Maggie', usually in sentences along the lines of 'I:'s Maggie we have to thank for this country not becoming a bloody Third World dump', or 'The Japs would never have come in so big, if it wasn't for Maggie. No way.'

Alastair began to drive a Porsche and Hamster started to tell complete strangers where her husband bought his suits, in the way that she had once reported on where they took their summer holidays. 'Ally's in Tokyo' became her favourite excuse for the refusal of a dinner party invitation. Early in 1987, Hanratty Forest Podge was taken over by Potomac Johnson (US), a Boston conglomerate, to became Potomac Johnson Hodge. This move was possible because of the impending deregulation of the London financial establishments: a process popularly known as Big Bang, a coinage which encouraged much smutty rugby-team punning from brokers.

In his ceaseless, but usually futile, attempt to comprehend how the world worked, Graham began to read the City pages of his newspaper in the hope of finding out what Big Bang meant, but, as with most of the knowledge owned by the media, the details seemed to be on sale only to those who already understood. Graham was again forced to rely on the summary of Durry, at a football match: 'Ah, yes. Big Bang. It's called Bringing the City Into the Twentieth Century. What it means is they stop using quills and wing-collars and switch to computers and white socks. Also, anyone can do anything, without this historical division into Buggers and Fuckers, or Brokers and Jobbers, or whatever. What it essentially means is that it is no longer true that only very very stupid, vulgar people who went to public school can make money. Now, very very stupid vulgar people who left state schools at sixteen can do so too. As a sort of general working principle, it's about making this country more and more like America.'

Graham had noticed before that Durry, who generally affected to detest patriotism and national self-pride, as well as fusty British institutions like the Stock Exchange, became indignantly defensive of the status quo whenever a practice or idea was imported from America. If he had possessed more intellectual self-assurance – or, perhaps more accurately, any at all – he would have wanted to ask whether Durry ought perhaps not theoretically to believe in those products of the state education system who were now driving Porsches and crapping in champagne. But this thought, like so many of Graham's, was aborted.

And, although Hamster reported that her husband had been given a 'big hunk of equity' by his new American employers, and the Macleods now spoke of buying a summer villa in Tuscany, Alastair would mutter in increasingly expensive restaurants, in which Graham became ever more guilty about the bill, on the subject of his new colleagues: 'Chaps with crew-cuts called Chuck and Hank, who come into the office at 7 a.m. and say stuff like "Shitsville" if the Bank of England intervenes, and think that belonging to a club means having somewhere local to play squash at lunchtimes.'

But, if the '80s was a rewarding period for selling money in order to make more money, it was also an age which put a premium on selling yourself. Hamster and Eliza's public relations company Dazzlem was well placed to assist in these transactions. Increasingly, Eliza would be away until late in the evening, having escorted, for example, a party of technical journalists to a lunch in Paris, intended to assist their research into a new micro-computer. 'Is it a French company?' asked Graham. 'Not a franc in it,' admitted Eliza. 'But lunch in

London wouldn't sound very sexy, would it?' (The word 'sexy' was now generally used to mean vaguely interesting, enticing or even professionally useful. Napier even described a plane crash, with mass fatalities, as 'a sexy little disaster', though, regrettably, one erotic for the general press rather than for *Oral*, there being no dentists among the dead.)

But Dazzlem's greatest coup, in the opinions of both its co-founders, was what they called the Black Pudding Promo. When one of Eliza and Hamster's biggest clients, a Swiss-based food consortium, took over a family-owned pie and sausage manufacturer based in the North of England, Dazzlem arranged for the elderly chief sausage-maker to construct the longest black pudding in the history of offal cuisine. 'I hope no pig in Britain needs a blood transplant tonight,' muttered Eliza, as she watched the massive, brimming vat of porcine plasma, the main ingredient of this traditional delicacy. The resulting pudding, thick as a juggernaut tyre and said to be equivalent in length to two circuits of an Olympic athletics track, was then cooked and served at the official opening of the new high-technology factory built by the Swiss buyers.

The first link was cut and tasted by an actress who played the owner of a corner shop in a popular television soap opera set in the region in which the company was situated. The star's participation, for a fee of about half the annual wage of a pudding-packer at the factory, ensured extensive tabloid newspaper interest, as did the attendance of a judge from the Food Records section of *The Guinness Book of Records*, to measure the pudding. Attention was also generated through the strategic leaking by Eliza to a reporter from a particularly patriotic-indignant tabloid that impending Common Market legislation might result in the outlawing of the name 'black pudding'. In future, according to the rumour Eliza spread, the term 'blood sausage' might be legally enforced throughout western Europe. The newspaper ran an intemperate story under the headline Bloody Cheek, inviting readers to send postcards to the President of the European Commission, calling him a 'daft pudding' for the decision.

Ben Waddle, telling the story at a dinner party, said: 'It's a bit ironic, isn't it, getting in a patriotic lather? I mean, correct me if I'm wrong, but the whole point was that Old Sid's Piggery had been taken over by the Europeans, wasn't it?' Eliza smiled and said: 'Don't read it. Measure it!' Hamster, nodding vigorously, added: 'It was just an absolutely brillo photo-opportunity, OK?' Alastair Macleod commented gloomily that the old Hanratty Forest Podge crest, all sovereigns and castle doors, had been replaced by 'some bloody big golden eagle' which the Chucks and Hanks called a 'corporate logo'. Shivering as he fingered the solid old school stripes he wore at his neck, even socially, like garlic against vampires, he complained: 'They even want me to wear it on my damn tie!'

But, if Alastair and Hamster and Eliza all prospered in their jobs during this time, Graham achieved, for most of the period, at best stasis. His discomfiture was increased by the fact that he now faced the additional social awkwardness of telling people that he was employed by a specialist magazine called *Oral*. The change of title, and Napier's other editorial innovations in the McKenzie mould, had failed to increase the circulation of the magazine. In fact, throughout the period between 1983 and 1987, it showed a small year-on-year decline. Napier, having finally achieved power, seemed dissatisfied by its manifestations, falling into listlessness, and, after a limited early burst of bullying ('Ya not working for Emily Brontë now!'), leaving the staff alone.

The editorial interference of Garry McKenzie himself also proved to be less than had been feared. The proprietor had been variously distracted by the rocketing profits of his computer magazines, his attempt to take over a local radio network, and the general euphoria caused among publishing tycoons by their colleague Rupert Murdoch's midnight flight to Wapping, East London, in 1985, locking out his obstructive and expensive print unions and ensuring, after a brief period of barbed wire fencing, riot shields and liberal indignation, that newspapers would in future be produced at considerably greater profit to those who owned them.

Amid these developments, the fate of *Oral* (formerly *Dentists and Dentistry*) was further relegated from its already low priority among McKenzie's obsessions and it was not until early 1987, just before the general election, that Napier caught his proprietor's attention with a miscalculated front page story about the concern caused to the dental profession by Aids. By now, Government ministers were to be seen on television unfurling contraceptive sheaths, the best protection against infection, on chubby fingers held up as a simulacrum of a phallus.

Media hysteria in the patriotic-indignant-heterosexual press encouraged theories about the possibility of diners dying after food prepared by 'bent chefs' or swimmers becoming infected by other pool users. Medical experts insisted that danger occurred only in 'direct exchange of body fluids' (a reference to the process which had been known to previous generations as sex), but this did little to reassure Britain's dentists, who, they pointed out, were potentially exposed to the blood and saliva of their patients seeping into cuts or abrasions on their own hands.

A circular from the British Dental Society instructed its members to wear thick rubber gloves. Napier, who liked to refer to homosexuals as 'turd burglars' or 'chocolate packers', which Graham assumed to be vernacular descriptions of anal intercourse, seized the press release and wrote a front-page story headlined Gay Dentists Threat to Patients, neatly reversing the circular's warning. 'Are many dentists gay?' Anne Colledge had asked, when the editor handed her his copy. 'In my experience, they're mainly Australian,' replied Napier darkly. 'Are many Australians gay?' Anne had persisted. 'Do bears shit in the woods?' the editor had bellowed, following his stomach back to his office. Graham was unsure whether to believe Napier but he was subsequently careful never to be too friendly to Australians.

Following threats of cancelled subscriptions and representations to the Press Council, Napier grumpily informed his staff that he had been 'moved upstairs' to the position of Managing Editor of *Whopper!*, which had become one of the outstanding publishing successes of recent times, with front page stories like the December seasonal reincarnation exclusive Dead Hubby Came Back As Turkey (Widow Stuffed Him for Xmas!) On this occasion, the only two applicants for the editorship of *Oral* were Graham and a semi-retired dentist living in Jersey.

After a desultory interview with McKenzie, Graham was appointed. Eliza, in the manner of a presidential speechwriter, had given him a series of prepared answers, including 'I think it's time for a dental magazine with teeth', but the proprietor seemed more concerned to offer anecdotes about the improvements effected to the country and to publishing by 'Margaret' and 'Rupert', and Graham's takeaway phrases were not needed. 'Look, *Oral*'s never going to be another *Whopper!*,' McKenzie generously conceded. 'Frankly, Graham, I generally like my editors with a bit more spunk, but perhaps you're gonna surprise me.'

It was not, perhaps, the most unqualified endorsement ever offered by an employer to a promoted employee – Graham was particularly troubled by the (shrewd?) use of the vernacular for semen – but the appointment seemed to satisfy Eliza and Graham's social stock rose perceptibly. His mother said, on the telephone, 'Good boy!' and her son had a brief sense of how a puppy must feel when it receives the same endearment. The Waddles were characteristically enthusiastic and even Durry muttered: 'An editor's an editor. You must be pleased,' which was as close as he was likely to come to 'Well done!'. On his first day at the desk from behind which George Elliott had first tentatively elected him his successor, Graham pledged quietly and hesitantly to himself that his editorship would be – in, you understood, a small way – a test-case, an exemplum of liberalism exercising power. He would become neither the flaccid wreck which Elliott had been nor the vulgar bully represented by Napier. There surely had to be a middle way.

This spell of professional fruitfulness for the Sterlings and their closest friends was also, for their acquaintances at least, productive in another sense. Just as weekends in the middle '70s had become associated with driving to old stone English churches for the weddings of their work and college friends, so weekends in the middle '80s were increasingly built around a hospital visit to a flushed mother, with her proud, damp bundle held up triumphantly like a sports trophy, or a return visit to the same ancient places of worship for christenings, a tradition on which their predominantly agnostic circle still insisted.

By the beginning of 1987, Ben and Paula Waddle were the parents of Sarah, aged three, and the two-year-old twins Russell and Emily. Alastair and Hamster Macleod had already put down for his father's public school the still speechless and incontinent Christopher Dibdin Alastair Bartholomew. And Timmy Duvet-Hogg, now deputy editor of the gossip column he had joined and prospective parliamentary candidate for a safe Tory seat in the South-East, was the father of young Jessica-Rose, born less than six months, although a healthy weight, after his sudden marriage in Venice to Rosinia, the Minister's daughter. It was John Durry who pointed out that Jessica-Rose Duvet-Hogg would have the distinction, rare even in England, of a hyphenated Christian name and surname.

For Graham and Eliza, the inevitable social goading towards procreation was now intensified by precedent. In early 1985, Eliza wondered out loud to Graham whether, with the business well established and Hamster already pregnant, it was not time for her to leave her diaphragm in the bathroom one night. The much braver human being who lived silently inside Graham's head cackled fiendishly and shouted that it wouldn't make much difference either way, given that nothing much was going to trouble her ovaries, but the Graham who was on public display merely blushed and nodded and said it all seemed terribly grown-up but, yes, perhaps they ought to see what happened.

Eliza treated the attempt at conception much as if Dazzlem had secured a new client: a campaign to put a new human being on the market. Key dates for intercourse were marked, like meetings, in Graham's diary. Because of an article which Eliza had read about foetal alcoholism among Aboriginal children, Graham was required to drink mineral water rather than wine with his evening meal for two days before each coupling. He was also denied red meat, this restriction resulting from American research on the alleged tendency towards aggression of the progeny of dedicated carnivores. 'I want high-quality stuff coming out of you,' said Eliza coquettishly as they ate a vegetable curry.

This, of course, was his difficulty. At some point, surely, Eliza, sexually self-preoccupied as she was, would realize that his body did not meet its half of the bargain during their encounters. The problem was that Graham – who, as the ghostly biography and questionnaire still regularly testified, was a man whose life was circumscribed by writing – was faced with a human problem for which there seemed to exist no literature.

There were entire shelves of novels about men who couldn't get it up and several priapic comedies about blokes who couldn't get it down, but he could discover no fiction about a lover who was unable, as it were, to get it out. Tales of premature ejaculation were virtually a genre in themselves, and there were easily enough fictional masturbators for an *Oxford Anthology of Literary Wankers*, but no lurid chapters about eternally deferred ejaculation were to be found. Great American Novelists had devoted half their *œuvres* to fretting about fellatio (girls who 'blew' and girls who refused), but none had been moved by their muse to a meditation on Graham's own urethral peculiarity.

Failed by fiction, Graham found no more enlightenment in fact. He would idly scan the health pages and the agony columns of newspapers and magazines, but, while there was always much discussion of the female climax (mythology, sensation, and technique), there was never any equivalent information about the male orgasm. Graham was eventually forced to concede that this was because the latter was a given. It was, he supposed, like expecting to find articles summarizing the arguments for and against the wheel. And even the more reactionary right-wing journals of the 1980s did not print those.

In early 1987, after two years of unrewarded intercourse to Eliza's meticulous schedule, the Sterlings' doctor decided to send them for tests. 'It's just as likely to be me as to be you,' Eliza reassured him, but he thought, when she said it, of those students who, after exams, solemnly, from democratic convention, agree with their peers about the difficulty of the paper, although everybody knows that they will later claim top grades. He assumed that both Eliza and the gynaecologists shared the conviction that the fallibility was Graham's. His gloom was only reduced by the realization that the medical profession would almost certainly not suspect that, in this case, the sterility was technical rather than chemical. Soon, however, this calm was succeeded by a new alarm: suppose he should be unable to produce a sample.

The test, in two senses, took place one winter morning in a draughty side room of a West London hospital. On arrival, Graham had walked through a demonstration by doctors and nurses against National Health Service cuts and, as he gave his name to a receptionist whom he thought he caught smirking, he felt guilty about wasting NHS resources on an unnecessary test. But then it occurred to him that there was no reason why he might not be barren as well as non-ejaculatory, and he felt better. He was given a scuffed grey plastic receptacle, tactlessly reminiscent of an infant's drinking cup. 'There are, er, magazines in the rack if you want something to read while you're, er, waiting,' said a nurse. Later, he realized that this was agreed code for the mildly pornographic battered magazines which were provided for the inspiration of those men who carried no erotic fantasies in their heads. When he first heard what the nurse was saying, however, Graham, assuming that she somehow knew his occupation of the room was likely to be prolonged, lowered his head in humiliation.

The (thankfully) windowless room he was allocated for his solo performance contained two torn posters: one demonstrating breast self-examination for women, the cartoon bosom the vivid pink of children's party blancmange, and the other advising of the health-giving properties of citrus fruit. Neither image inspired him to an erection and, although one close-up of spread female legs in the state-provided porn mags produced the necessary rush of blood, the next stage in the process proved typically elusive. Trousers and pants around his ankles, as if for defecating, and jumper and shirt bunched up towards his chest in case of splashing, he sat on the cheap tin-and-wood chair and suddenly identified, in a lesser but still distressing variant of Donne's Syndrome, with those couples who submitted to this indignity because of the desperation to replicate themselves. Awful as his present experience was, he had the consolation of being a fraud.

Then, after nearly twenty minutes of self-manipulation without a tremor of pleasure, pictures arrived unbidden in his mind of the evening in Jenny Cann's kitchen four years before. In flashback, Jenny, in technicolour replay, kneeled towards his suddenly right-angled slacks and slipped the zip. In real time, Graham, eyes tight against reality, felt an unfamiliar warm wet slap on one of his folds of belly fat. Scraping the pitted rim of the clammy plastic cup across his flesh, he collected the congealing gobbets, cleaned himself with paper handkerchiefs and left.

A week later, the specialist told them, with a patronizing smile, that they 'had both passed their exam with flying colours'. 'In fact, Mr Sterling,' said the doctor, turning towards Graham, 'you scored very high indeed. *Cumma sum laude*, as it were.' Graham guessed that a 'surprisingly' had been censored from the sentence.

'So,' the specialist concluded, 'there's absolutely no physical problem. Just keep trying.'

*

However, to Graham's relief, the Sterlings' efforts towards conception were interrupted by the general election of June 1987. Frequently, what the thermometer called for, the canvassing roster would prevent.

Shortly before the campaign began, there had been a curious illustration, from America, of the peculiarities of politicians. It was provided by Senator Gary Hart, widely regarded as the only Democrat with the looks, phrases, and Wasp genes necessary to defeat Vice-President George Bush, the political son of Reagan, in the following year's election. Hart, however, was rumoured to have a mistress, a sure vote-loser, given the surface puritanism of America.

But Hart pulled a publicity masterstroke: listen, fellas, he told the press, if you don't believe I'm clean, follow me around this weekend and see if you catch me with anyone who isn't Mrs Hart. A kind of macho innocence, perfectly pitched to impress both cheating husbands and hurt wives among the electorate, it was an expert defence. Except that the invited media snoopers saw, early in their watch, Senator Hart's girlfriend, Donna Rice. The story fascinated Graham, for it was impossible to see it as other than a political death-wish. Or had Hart calculated that the invitation to reporters, clearly madness from any man possessed of secrets, would be enough to end the speculation?

The incident did not help Graham's comprehension of politics, which was already further diminishing, along with his appetite for its procedures. Once again, he carefully studied the manifesto of the Alliance, which the Nice People's Party again formed with the Liberal Party. It was not that he disagreed with any of it – although he had not yet lost his inability seriously to adhere to any belief – but that, in a commendable effort to avoid the rhetoric of division, the party seemed to have been drawn to pettinesses – the state of Britain's phone boxes was treated as a *cause célèbre* – or self-cancelling sops to two sides: 'We will strengthen the police BUT increase their accountability.'

The cover of the manifesto showed the joint leaders of the Alliance, David Steel and David Owen, shoulder to shoulder in hand-knitted Aran sweaters. Their physical closeness was intended to suggest ideological like-mindedness but was open to more ribald interpretation. 'It looks like the brochure for a gay dating agency,' said John Durry over take-away pizzas at the Sterlings' house in the first week of the campaign. 'Isn't that joke homophobic, no?' asked Eliza, in what Graham had to admit was a decent impression of Durry's sternness.

Sometimes even Graham worried that his friend and political mentor was the ideological equivalent of a bent policeman, pouncing on conversational transgressions of a kind which he permitted himself. For example, at their nearest trattoria, Graham always ordered a particular pizza from which a small percentage of money was given towards the restoration of Venice. Every time, Durry smiled and said 'Keeping the Doge afloat, yes?' when the cause was surely one he would normally have supported.

Durry had less personal involvement in this election than in the previous two, having been expelled from the Labour Party for membership of a proscribed far-left organization. This had left him both more bitter – 'And yet we dare to talk about the one-party states of Eastern Europe' – and, unfortunately, with more time to mock the involvement of Graham, Eliza, Hamster, Ben, and Paula in the revolution of the Nice People. Particularly fertile material for him was an Alliance poster with the slogan: 'The Only Fresh Thing On The Menu.' Durry seemed to find an inexhaustible stock of culinary puns: 'Yes, but what's the sell-by date?' he would snarl, or, 'Fresh, but a bit, well, nouvelle cuisine, no? Where's the beef?'

For all of these reasons, Graham found the round of canvassing dispiriting in a way which it had not been four years earlier. His temper was not helped by realizing one evening, when the manner of a courteous life-long Conservative at a mock-Georgian front door suddenly reminded him of Appleton, that he probably now thought perhaps once a year of someone whose death had, at the time, obsessed him. The rapidity of the average person's recovery from bereavement was a form of natural human ruthlessness which was both necessary and yet somehow unpleasant. Graham reflected that Helen was probably remarried by now. Soon, Appleton would have left no dent at all.

The sense of depression which Graham felt seemed to be reflected in the mood of the party headquarters. Photocopying, stapling, and canvassing were frenetically conducted but there seemed always to be a feeling that the best chance had been last time. Then, the Labour Party's candidate in Graham's constituency had been a lesbian who spoke of 'the army of occupation in Northern Ireland' and 'gay women's right to bear children'. It was not, you understand, that Graham doubted the candidate's sincerity, or questioned her democratic right to make these claims. It was merely that, from a purely pragmatic standpoint, the rhetoric, given general prejudices, reduced her electoral danger. Many of Graham's colleagues, far less agonizingly, referred to their opponent as 'the Marxist dyke'.

This time, however, the Nice People's personnel officer candidate, reselected by the Alliance despite a strong push by the BBC Education Producer, faced a Socialist who was a university lecturer, wearing expensive suits and answering all questions on policy with the words: 'Let me tell you what I don't stand for . . .' Even the incumbent Conservative was quietly telling voters and the press that, yes, perhaps Britain's first female Prime Minister had got a little carried away with herself in the previous term but that this criticism had been taken on board and that a listening government was now on the agenda.

'He's going to be much harder to beat this time,' said Hamster one evening as they trudged past two- or even three-car driveways in the smarter part of the borough.

'We, er, didn't beat him last time,' Graham pointed out.

'Ah, yes,' Hamster conceded. 'I suppose I mean he'll be easier to lose to.'

It was a rather tense and bickering election, both within

the parties and between them. The phrase 'hidden agenda', indicating policies which dare not speak their name in manifestos, was regularly used by the government against the opposition and by the opposition about the government. If Graham's party was spared this charge, it was only because it was regarded as not having a first agenda to hide a second one behind. Thus the general impression was given of a contest between two parties whose policies were other than they said they were and a third which had no policies at all.

The latter perception seemed to have spread to the doorsteps. More than one householder asked Graham and Hamster, 'What do you actually *believe*?' causing Graham to think of an aggressive Catholic girl at college, who would address this enquiry to Anglican students in support of her contention that the Established Church was a body without dogma. Now it seemed that Graham and his fellow party members were regarded as the dithering vicars of politics.

It was not that people canvassed were aggressive, but rather that they were either confused or treated Graham and Hamster with the elevated attentiveness and encouraging smiles which Graham recognized from his own uneasy treatment of those handicapped young adults who, in a new community initiative, sold hand-made dishcloths house to house.

After several years, and frequent cantilevered sub-committees, a joint colour had been agreed between the two halves of the Alliance – a kind of gold hue – but the variations in names had taken their effect. Canvassing in 1987 was, Graham found, like attempting to make a phone call to a girl who had opted to be called June on some days, Jane on others and Jan on feast days.

'Who are you from, then?'

'The, er, Alliance . . .'

'Oh, yes . . .'

'Do you mind if I ask who you voted for last time?'

'Do I mind? No, I don't mind. The . . . um . . . the, er, new lot, Social . . . Dr Owen.'

'I see . . .'

'What's happened to them, then?'

'Well, er, they, we, are part of the Alliance . . .'

'No, really? Well, I'll tell you this, I'll not be voting for them Liberals, not since that queer. . . .'

And so on. With a new party of barely recognized title now submerged under another one, and with joint leaders both called David, it was hard for Graham to raise local interest in the cause, or even to establish what the cause might be. Much would subsequently be written about tensions within the Alliance during the election. At the time, however, there was a public air of unity and bullishness, although there was a tacit understanding not to discuss nuclear weapons, which one David believed in while the other didn't. Graham's David spoke of a 'thoughtful election', in which 'seven million don't knows' would decide the outcome. Like a victim of a rare illness, Graham was glad to discover that the sufferers from his condition numbered seven million, but he was sceptical, from his own experience, about when they might be converted to certainty.

Until the last days of campaigning, the Alliance leaders kept insisting that 'the surge will come'. This was an expression which Graham, despite his best efforts to suppress the image, always associated with his own medical peculiarity.

As it turned out, the surge came neither for himself nor for his party. On June 11th, 1987, Margaret Thatcher was returned for a third term as Prime Minister. This was despite or because of an eve-of-poll reference to those 'who drool and drivel that they care'. It would also later be revealed that there had been furious dispute between Mrs Thatcher and her advisers about the management of the campaign. In a move which was perhaps symbolic of shifting political priorities, the Prime Minister had changed not her policies but her advertising agency. Retaining the same agency throughout, the Alliance polled 22 per cent of the votes, slightly lower than last time, for, again, 4 per cent of the seats in Parliament.

On the Sunday after polling day, the Liberal Party's David

called for a new, merged party, replacing the separate halves of the Alliance. It was pointless, said that David, for the two parties 'to be locked for ever in a wary and weary partnership of which the only guiding constitutional principle was mutual suspicion'.

Graham's David rejected this view, holding out for separate identities, and resigned when moves towards merger began. He was replaced by a man called Bob. This left the Sterlings and their friends with a difficult decision. Ben and Paula Waddle, for example, would effectively be rejoining a party they had painfully left a few years earlier. Graham, for his part, found it hard to reconcile the unpleasantness and talk of electoral pragmatism with the dream in which he had believed when he had first telephoned the credit card hotline in 1981. His temper was not helped by the election to a South-East constituency, with a Conservative landslide, of the journalist Timothy Duvet-Hogg.

His own disappointment mingling with envy of another, Graham lost himself in his job.

In the edition of September 6th, 1987, Graham published what he considered to be his best – or, anyway, not as bad as his usual standard – article for *Dentists and Dentistry*. Graham had persuaded McKenzie – or, in truth, tentatively suggested and met no resistance – that the magazine should return to its original title as part of the latest redesign and relaunch. A team of design consultants ('We tried them once. They're second rate,' said Eliza) suggested that the publication be printed on glossy paper and use larger photographs. The company also constructed a new bright blue masthead in which all of the title *Dentists and Dentistry* was in spidery lower-case writing except for the two bloated capital Ds, which had been filled in with even white teeth to suggest blue-lipped mouths turned vertically. ('People will think you're a paper for clowns or comedians,' Eliza commented.)

'Does this, er, mean we can go a little, er, upmarket again?'

asked Graham, when the proprietor approved the name re-instatement and grinning masthead.

'Upmarket! Downmarket!' shouted Mckenzie, 'I don't understand what those words mean. They're just North London liberal waffle, aren't they? I just want magazines people read. Give your readers what they want, Graham. That's the only motto, OK?'

This mandate was a complicated one. In his darker moments, Graham suspected that what his readers probably most wanted was for the magazine to be even more boring than it already was, drawing ever more arid distinctions between methods of extraction and preservation. Such an editorial policy was, however, unlikely to appeal to McKenzie, who almost certainly believed that the success of *Whopper!* was a commercial model for all editors. *Whopper!* had established a formula of floating an outrageous possibility on its front page, which, for legal protection, the accompanying story then repudiated. Weekly sales had passed four million since publicity attending the magazine's Is Prince Edward Gorby's Lovechild? exclusive.

However, the latest reader research for *Oral*, conducted in advance of the relaunch, had revealed that the subscribing dentists bought more hardback fiction and attended the theatre far more often than the national average. This information – which could be waved at the proprietor if necessary – gave Graham the courage to write the article for which he had been collecting information for many years: a two thousand word essay on characters in world literature who were dentists. The piece was run across the centre pages, illustrated by a faded George Bernard Shaw and a clearer Graham Greene. Anne Colledge invented the headline: Words of Mouth.

The article began:

It was once said that the great breakthrough of modern literature was that fictional characters started going to the lavatory! But it is hard not to notice that they also started going to the dentist!

For example, the opening stage direction of George Bernard Shaw's play *You Never Can Tell* (1897) reads: 'In a dentist's operating room on a fine August morning in 1896.' The playwright informs us of the character in question that: 'The professional manner of the newly set up dentist in search of patients is underlaid by a thoughtless pleasantry which betrays the young gentleman.' We may detect a certain disapproval of the tooth-puller here. A revenge for pain suffered by GBS in the dentist's chair?

Modern dramatists have, on the whole, been less interested in dentistry. Perhaps that is partly because, after John Osborne's famous *Look Back In Anger* in 1956, stage creations were less likely to have such a (generally!) middle-class occupation! However, Tom Stoppard did write a television play called *Teeth* (1966), in which a dentist takes revenge on his wife's lover, who is also (conveniently!, his patient, by extracting his (healthy) middle tooth. (The play was, of course, a black comedy: we all know that no member of the BDA would be so unethical!) Also on television, there was Carla Lane's situation comedy *Butterflies* (1979–83), in which a melancholy dentist had an unfaithful wife, played by Wendy Craig.

Graham had originally typed the sentence to hinge on the phrase 'his wife's infidelity', but he was tense at the time about a tall, superficially witty arts journalist, already published in the national press, who had been a member of Eliza's canvassing team in the 1987 General Election and had served with her on the publicity committee. Accordingly, he had inked liquid paper (he always seemed to need an entire bottle of the word-remover for each article) over the phrase 'his wife's infidelity', which sounded active and threatening, and substituted 'an unfaithful wife', which, with its connotations of passivity and historical fiction, was less personally disturbing.

His article continued:

That occasional playwright, Graham Greene, did, however,

make a dentist the central figure of his drama *The Complaisant Lover* (1959), although, oddly enough, it is not, as you might think, the character called Clive Root (an antiquarian bookseller, actually) but one called Victor Rhodes. This dentist, played by Ralph Richardson in the first stage production, is cuckolded by Root. In a painful scene, Victor discusses what he imagines to be the social inferiority (this was the snobbish 1950s, remember!) of his profession:

VICTOR: You weren't ashamed of marrying a dentist sixteen years ago.

MARY: I'm not ashamed, Victor. Not of you.

VICTOR: But people are. I don't know why. My patients don't ask us to dinner. Yet they ask their doctor. Though he deals in more ignoble parts of the body than I do.

MARY: I told you I'm not ashamed.

VICTOR: I wonder how many doctors could say they were as trained as I am. I have to know surgery, radiology, prosthesis . . .

At least one writer, then, has clearly done his research into the range of expertise which a modern tooth carer needs!

Graham had found the extract from the play thought-provoking. It was certainly true that society, even now, differentiated between doctors and dentists. Perhaps people had traditionally not asked their dentist to dine because of a fear that they would police people's eating (what dessert could you possibly serve?), but, then, the medical profession was increasingly moralistic as well. And surely it was also the case that Dr Owen, leader of the Nice People's Party, would have been taken less seriously – at the beginning that was; Graham accepted that there were a number of jokes about him now – if he had been a dentist rather than a physician. All of this, however, was merely a displacement of Graham's real fear: if, by some unexplained social consensus, dentists were judged to be funny, then what of dental journalists?

Words of Mouth went on:

Interestingly, Greene is also the novelist with, if we can use this term, the toothiest *œuvre*. *The Power and The Glory* (1948) uses the character of a dentist in Mexico as a symbol of spiritual emptiness (sorry, BDA members!). However, the later, blackly comic novella *Dr Fischer of Geneva* (1980) plays with the contrasts between a millionaire toothpaste tycoon and his son-in-law, an executive in a chocolate factory. One literary critic suggested that the dental decay caused by the confectionery represented evil and the toothpaste the possibility of salvation (our readers may like to wonder which brands!).

For many writers, however, dentistry seems to be associated with gloom. That great contemplator of death and decay, the poet Philip Larkin, produced no verse on the subject, but one of his two novels, *A Girl In Winter* (1947), includes a vivid scene of a tooth extraction. Professionally involved readers can only be sorry that Larkin produced no dental poetry!

It is often commented by members of the dental profession in this country that the Americans take their teeth more seriously than the British. It is interesting to note that this dichotomy seems to be represented in American literature too. John Updike, arguably the country's greatest living novelist, has written a short story 'Dentistry and Doubt', in which an American cleric, receiving emergency dental work in Oxford, reflects on the divine purpose of pain, while having a cavity drilled. Updike's novel *Couples* (1968) features a Massachussetts orthodontist who is also an abortionist. (The book, remember, is set in America!) With Updike, there may well be an element of revenge or catharsis in these scenes: he has written entertainingly, though painfully, in articles about the battle (literally losing!) he has fought with his own teeth.

Updike's great contemporary, Philip Roth, gave his *alter ego*, the Jewish-American novelist, Nathan Zuckerman, a dentist-brother called Henry, in his most recent book *The Counterlife*, published last year. Henry is having an affair with his dental nurse, Wendy. It is tempting to comment that Roth has usually been more interested in other functions of the mouth!

The last sentence gave him an erection. The improbable connection between sex and dentistry had recently been much on his mind. On a local radio advice show late at night, he had heard a pundit briskly outlining to a worried caller that what was described as 'woman on woman oral stimulation' (lesbian cunnilingus, he assumed) could be made safer in the time of Aids by 'the insertion of a dental dam in the vagina'. Graham had been tormented for days by this revelation of the procedures of pleasure in the modern world. Once you went as far as the use of dental dams, hadn't sex become like a holiday for which so many inoculations were required that it was hardly worth going?

He concluded his article with a brief résumé of celluloid dentists – particular reference was made to the scene in *Marathon Man*, in which Laurence Olivier uses drills and picks as instruments of Nazi torture. The final paragraph concentrated on texts with a high incidence of oral imagery, rather than characters who were specifically dentists. He noted the extended sore-tooth metaphors in the novels of Martin Amis, including *Money* (1984), in which the narrator's inflamed and cratered mouth was compared to a map of collapsing New York.

'Jolly nice piece,' said Anne Colledge, when she first read it. Graham, with a well-camouflaged minor confidence that this was a classy article, awaited the reaction.

Coming from Garry McKenzie, 'Get your arse down here pronto!' was not, of necessity, an unfriendly expression, but his voice on the telephone on that Monday morning lacked its usual harsh charm and Graham carefully arranged his face to show nothing of his fear as he passed Bernadette, the secretary, on his way to the third floor. He knew that the editor's summons to the proprietor would be the juicy lunchtime rumour.

McKenzie was waving a copy of *Dentists and Dentistry*. Graham realized from the large front-page picture of the Conservative government's new Health Secretary – a bland, blonde self-made millionaire who was said to have worked in America – that it was the most recent edition. The proprietor confirmed this by flapping open the magazine at the Words Of Mouth spread and jabbing at it with a sizeable fist.

'Trying to win the fucking Nobel Prize?' McKenzie asked. He pronounced it nobble. Graham found himself thinking of how John Durry said Cha-nobble, against the Cher-na-bil of others, for the Russian nuclear plant which had recently exploded, becoming a popular topic of London dinner party conversation, generally centring around the question: could it happen here?

'I mean, Graham. Listen to this . . .'

McKenzie was using a pair of gold half-moon spectacles like a field-marshal's baton. Now he tried to hook them on to his head with one hand in a self-conscious gesture of irritated busyness. But one of the arms of the glasses slipped and stabbed his cheek, forcing him to fumble with the other hand. The intended effect was further diminished by his needing to scan the pages awkwardly for at least a minute before finding the phrase he was seeking.

'Ah yes. this is the really rich bit,' McKenzie sighed. 'I mean, really, Graham. "It is interesting to note that the most fashionable school of modernist literature, Latin American magic realism, has so far shown little interest in the fictional potential of dentistry." I mean OK, Graham, yes, Rupert Murdoch owns the *Times Literary Supplement*, but, personally, I have no ambitions in that area. All right?'

He squashed the words as if he were boxing them. Latamerican. Modnist. Dentsry. And he said supp-ul-ment. Graham hated himself – no, hated was too strong a word, disliked perhaps – for noticing. One of the lessons of his upbringing which he most wanted to forget was a preference for how people spoke over what people said. He was glad that McKenzie seemed to require no answers. The admonitory monologue continued: 'I mean, Graham, I'm not complaining about the idea, don't get me wrong. It's the tone I didn't like. Elitism.' El-ee-isim. 'The point is, why those books particularly? Why not this book, for instance?'

The proprietor grabbed, more smoothly than for his previous props, a fat, battered paperback, which he skimmed towards Graham, who trapped and gathered it on the third bounce. He slightly recognized the cover from station bookstalls. It showed a tanned, black-haired man in a dental smock bending over a busty blonde, recumbent in a dentist's chair. Her glossy lips were wide apart but, although there were glinting mirror-sticks and silver picks in the man's hand, it was clear that his thick extended tongue would explore her mouth first. Wide gold lettering read: *The Dentist*. It was the latest book by one of the world's best-selling authoresses; the kind who was mentioned only sneeringly in the journals Graham read. Turning over the copy, he saw a large colour picture of the writer in a gold lurex jacket and earrings like Oscar statuettes, beneath the red-letter legend: 'The dentist . . . he filled all their cavities to satisfaction!' The word *all* was underlined twice.

'Well?' McKenzie pressed.

'I, er, I didn't know about it . . .'

'Ah. But, if you had, you would have mentioned it . . .'

'I . . . I, er . . .'

'Come on, Graham, you can tell me. You wouldn't have, would you?'

He recalled, as he often did when tempted by decisiveness, an anecdote which Graham's father had first told him when he could have been no more than four or five. 'Father, I cannot tell a lie. It was I,' confessed the young George Washington beside the stump of the felled family cherry tree. Although Graham now realized that the story had been parental propaganda for candour, and he suspected that most of the American presidents of his own lifetime would have replied 'Father, I cannot answer until my attorney gets here,' he was still visited by the story when an untruth loomed. To McKenzie's question about *The Dentist*, he chose to plead the fifth amendment.

'The point I'm making, Graham,' the proprietor went on, 'is that a guy in your position should have known about a book like that. I knew about it. In fact, I'd been reading it with a mind to buying the serial rights. In the end, I decided not to. The publishers got greedy. We couldn't find a price. But I knew about it. Don't get me wrong, Graham. All I'm talking about is balance. I don't want a magazine for dentists who speak Latin – I didn't know until I read your piece that people still wrote books in that – but no more do I want a paper only for the kind of dentists I got as a kid, who kicked your teeth in before they fixed them. I exaggerate to make a point. I want a magazine that every fucking dentist in the country feels they have to read. Or, anyway, buy. I want to get it so they'll be laughed off the podium at meetings of the, what is it?, British Dental Association if they haven't got the latest issue. All right?'

McKenzie was now cupping a hand around his left breast, which had a swell which would have pleased a teenage girl, and Graham wondered if he had some kind of cardiac alarm bells there. The proprietor paused and leaned forward, staring screw-eyed at Graham's face like a myopic trying to read a bus timetable.

'You're a hard man to argue with, Graham,' McKenzie growled. 'You just sit there, taking it, not reacting, choosing your words very carefully when you do speak. It's a clever trick. Letting – do you like cricket? – letting the ball come on to the bat.' Graham had nodded to concede an interest in the game. 'But I hope you've taken on board what I said. The point is, Graham, I'm not angry. I'm just disappointed. Now, get your arse back down to editorial and let's get on with being undisputed market-leader by the spring. All right?'

Graham told Bernadette that the meeting had been about some boring budget figures, but he sensed the rest of the staff watching him like relatives visiting a hospital, who have agreed to keep from the patient what the doctor said.

It was partly for this reason that few in the office were prepared to bet on Graham surviving what would become known in the folklore of *Dentists and Dentistry* as the Censorship Crisis.

It is a familiar trick of history that large conflagrations can start from distractingly minor sparks. The Falklands Crisis of 1982 had begun, somewhat comically, with scrap metal merchants landing on a rocky outcrop. The shade of Archduke Frans Ferdinand II must be flattered by the sheer scale of retribution occasioned by his shooting in 1914. In the same way, Graham's many antennae for potential embarrassment, failure, or shame registered no danger when he wrote a front-page story in early November 1987 about the government's plans to reform the National Health Service.

Under the new proposals, free dental check-ups would be abolished and patients would pay a larger percentage of any treatment. It would also become easier to make official complaints about a dentist. The white paper – on advance leaks of which Graham's story was based – regularly referred to patients as 'consumers' and used the expression 'patient throughput', presumably as an equivalent to 'productivity' in industry. ('Soon,' said John Durry, 'a dead body will be called a 'ground replenishment operative.' Graham shivered, for he disliked any reference to death.) Reforms for other sections of the National Health Service included the cancellation of free eye tests and a suggestion that hospitals should raise money through shops, cafés, and clubs. ('It'll be sponsored colostomy bags next,' joked Ben Waddle. Graham broadly approved of the sentiment, while feeling that the image might be hurtful to anyone who had undergone that particular surgical procedure.) These adjustments would save the government an amount of money which Durry said was equivalent to roughly six fighter aircraft or forty nuclear missiles.

Graham's article was short and factual, rounded off with one comment from a dental pressure group which supported reform but felt those reforms to be the wrong ones and another which, in the end, while having some quibbles with the detail, felt them to be a step in the right direction.

The day after publication, Graham arrived slightly late at the office after undergoing another series of tests on his semen at an expensive fertility specialist. The money apparently resulted in plusher premises and intense attention from nurses who were more like stewardesses.

'Do you have moral, religious, cultural, or medical objections to masturbation?' Graham was asked. He paused. There had been a similar entry on the questionnaire about fifteen years ago but it had not reappeared. He was able to reply: 'Er, no.'

Anyway, the alternative was worse. He had read in a pamphlet at the hospital that, for those with religious objections to self-manipulation, a special condom, without the usual spermicide, could be worn during the couple's regular love-making. The sheath then needed to be sealed and stored at room temperature (the cleavage of the female partner was recommended) during a dash to the laboratory. Graham thought of women in taxis, or even on buses, a twist of squidgy cooling rubber nuzzling their breasts in a tactless parody of suckling.

Ushered into the Harley Street beating-off suite, he noted with interest that the apparatus of encouragement in the private sector was more sophisticated. Instead of the torn and splattered magazines, he was allowed a radio, a television set with a remote control device, and a stack of audio and video cassettes. Apart from the inevitable *Last Tango In Paris* and the various *Spanking Sally* titles, the visual possibilities included the highlights of great soccer, cricket, and tennis matches. Arousal was obviously a subjective business. Graham flicked through the music library, looking for a requiem mass, his favourite relaxation. He finally chose Verdi over Fauré, distantly remembering that the former had more fast bits. Later, he freezeframed a dormitory scene from *Emanuelle Goes To College*, but his vigil was unproductive until he again thought of the moment in Jenny Cann's kitchen.

*

'Mr McKenzie called for you,' said Bernadette as he walked into his office. She used the voice of landladies in black-and-white movies, telling the lodger a policeman had visited.

Graham settled behind his desk, adjusting his shirt, which had snagged on a residue of stickiness which he had failed to remove with the fluffy monogrammed towel provided at the private clinic. He dialled the proprietor's extension.

'McKenzie.'

'Proprietor, it's, er, G-G-Graham. You, er ...'

'Graham, you old fucker, how are you?' He relaxed, realizing from this greeting that McKenzie was in a benevolent mood. 'Graham, you've probably got your brown trousers on, wondering what you've done ...'

'I, er ...'

'But it's not what you've done, it's what you're going to do.' Goantadoo. 'Maggie's glorious revolution of the dental industry. All right? Nice piece, this week. No complaints. Now, you know I have firm pledges on editorial independence ...'

'Yes. I ...'

'And those are – is this the word? – sacrosanct. You have got to believe them. Why have you got to believe them? Because the proprietor told you to. Joking, Graham. Joking. What I'm saying, if I can plant a root, is, how about a signed editorial – written by the editor – on whether *Dentists and Dentistry* thinks these reforms are a good thing or a bad thing? As the, no pun intended, mouthpiece of the profession, I think we owe it to our readers. No?'

'The, er, problem with committing ourselves one way or the other is that not everyone will, necessarily, agree ...'

Graham hoped that the proprietor would take this as a fear that the readers would be alienated by partiality on such a sensitive issue. In fact, he was voicing a wholly personal concern that McKenzie might not share whatever opinion his editor was eventually forced to opt for.

But McKenzie replied: 'Debate, Graham. Debate. Let's start a disagreement. In my view, that's what the media is for. As a

reader, I'd fancy having eight hundred words on what the editor
of the magazine thinks of these changes . . .'

Graham sensed his own next remark arriving, like a bomb
whose buzz betrays it in the air. He might have taken some
evasive action but a familiar paralysis afflicted him. 'Er, what,'
he asked, 'what do *you* think of the reforms?'

As soon as he had spoken, Graham heard a voice inside his
head: you are slime, it said, you are nothing, you are dung.
Telephonically distorted, McKenzie's laugh sounded half-way
between barking and choking. 'Graham! Graham!' he said. 'I
ought to report you under the articles of association. It's got
nothing to do with me. Just write whatever you think. Now,
fuck off, I'm busy defrauding the Inland Revenue. Joking. Only
joking. All right?'

The deadline for the editorial column to be given to Anne
Colledge for sub-editing was Wednesday lunchtime. That week,
Graham was in the office in time to hear the 8 a.m. news. He
had been praying – well, as an agnostic, he meant hoping, of
course – all night for a particularly gruesome event somewhere
in the world. And, more to the point, a relevantly terrible one,
like a terrorist massacre at the World Prosthetics Conference
in Mauritius; something awful enough to call for an editorial.
But, as the bulletin went on, it was clear that the world had
been cruel only in useless ways. There were continuing investi-
gations and condemnations over an IRA bomb at a Remembrance Day parade in Enniskillen, Northern Ireland. The news
ended with a report that a painting by Van Gogh had been sold
for $63 million. Graham distantly remembered reading that
Van Gogh had suffered serious trouble with his teeth but the
connection was probably too tenuous to merit a leader.

Graham was forced to accept that there was no option. He
silenced the radio, hacked out a clear space on his desk and
set down two sheets of white A4 paper. Although he typed news
stories, he always wrote opinions in longhand. It was a symbol
of solemnity, like wearing a hat in church. He cocked his pen
above the top of the first page, then paused and stared at the

two-foot long inflatable tube of fluoride toothpaste – a publicity gimmick picked up at an advertising presentation – which hung on the far wall of his office.

Eventually, Graham wrote: A) McKenzie genuinely wants me to express my own opinions and doesn't care what they are. Or, if he does care, will not interfere. B) McKenzie does care, will interfere, and wants an editorial supporting the government or, as he would put it, Margaret. C) Whatever his general opinions, McKenzie thinks that, on this occasion, the government has gone too far.

The sentences came to him with unusual fluency. This was pleasing. He might not be becoming more decisive but he was obviously developing a facility for summarizing the possibilities. Perhaps it was the influence of the questionnaire. On this occasion, at least, it was also surprisingly easy to choose between them. All sensible money was on B. He forced the sheet of paper into a ball and lobbed it at the bin. The projectile missed, ricocheting off the facsimile machine, on which foreign and freelance copy arrived.

At his desk, Graham set a new sheet of white paper on top of the second and wrote: 'There is no easy answer to the question of dental charges.' He stopped and wished he was a smoker, to fill the awkward gaps between inspirations. Burrowing in the bottom drawer, he found some of the packets of sweets which Eliza refused to let him eat at home. At 9.30 a.m. he swallowed a chocolate toffee with uncomfortable rapidity when Anne Colledge put her head round the door to ask how the leader was going.

'Oh, er, you know, slowly . . .'

'I hope we're going to give it to the bastards . . .'

'What do you mean?'

'Well, really. I mean, even my parents, who, in broad terms, tend to think that Pol Pot got an unfair press and that British elections ought to be suspended until Mrs Thatcher decides she might like to retire . . . even they draw the line at a pound for a tooth and a fiver for an eye . . .'

'You think most people are against. . . .'

'It wouldn't even count as controversial.'

Graham had become increasingly friendly with Anne – and not just because she was also a member of the Nice People's Party – and was persuaded by her argument for at least a quarter of an hour. This impetus permitted him to add a second sentence to his editorial. 'However, the National Health Service, of all British institutions . . .' At 10.15 a.m., however, Graham decided, after reflection, to call a short editorial meeting at which he suggested that, given the importance of the issues and the complexity of the options, he felt they should collectively decide the magazine's line.

Eric Foster-Thomas said, with rare animation, that, although he was not political, he thought the charges were a 'scandal, a damn scandal'. Graham suspected that, with Eric's complicated table of alimony and maintenance payments, a reduction in state benefits was potentially ruinous. Eric's private life was rumoured to have become even more complex. Bernadette told Graham that Anne had said that, for the last fortnight, all Eric's calls had been diverted to her and that she was instructed to say that Eric was off sick, although nobody was sure whether he was evading bailiffs or boyfriends. Graham thought: people's lives.

The meeting was also attended by Derek Dobbs, a loud-voiced but affable Scot in his late thirties who had been poached from the rival *Dental Weekly* to fill Graham's former post of Chief Reporter and *de facto* Features Editor. Dobbs voted for the editorial to attack the charges (Graham blinked) and call for their repeal (Graham blushed). Also in favour of a critical position was Abigail Adams, the junior reporter, whom, as a deliberate antidote to her predecessor Timmy Duvet-Hogg, Graham had recruited directly from a local state school.

Anne Colledge said: 'You know what I think already. So, four-nil. You wanted our opinion and now you've got it.'

For the approach of winter, Anne was out of dresses and into jeans and baggy sweaters, a combination which, emphasizing her lower curves and tantalizingly disguising her higher ones, did not help Graham's mood. The others did not bother him. It was Anne he knew he could not overrule. As the staff left the office, she turned back, winked and said, 'Deadline's one. Good luck. Kick their teeth in. As it were.'

Graham screwed up the top sheet, with its two equivocating phrases and wrote at the top of pure foolscap: Why The Government Are Wrong. He stopped, hunted for a ruler and underlined the words. He stared at the paper, then swore, fumbled for a bottle of liquid paper and replaced the word 'are' with 'is'.

At 11.30 a.m. Graham telephoned John Durry.

'Yeah?'

'John, er . . .'

'Graham. Strange time. Shouldn't you be writing *incisive* journalism . . .'

Graham stammered an explanation. Durry said that he was busy on a chapter of his next book – provisionally entitled *Love You To Death*, it was a study of Western arms sales to various dictators – but that he would see what he could do. 'You know how pregnant women say they're eating for two?' murmured Durry. 'With you, Graham, I always think I'm having opinions for two.'

At 12.30 p.m., the red light on the facsimile machine winked knowingly at Graham. Heart alarmingly fast, he read the words upside down as they emerged. The opening paragraph was: 'In Victorian times, before the wide availability of dentures, the poor would sell their teeth to the rich for attempted implantation in the jowly jaws of privilege. Rarely has there been a more eloquent symbol of social inequality. Who, though, would have thought that, in the Britain of the 1980s, a price would again be put on the teeth of the poor in order to benefit the rich?'

At first, Graham thought: this deception is ridiculous, like a political equivalent of the balcony scene in *Cyrano de Bergerac*. But he also knew that he was saved. Such was his elation that he almost rushed and handed the waxy, still faintly warm pages straight to Anne Colledge, like a Valentine. Then he realized that the sheets were quite evidently a fax message and, furthermore, had the name of the sender at the top. He sat and retyped the editorial, deleting, largely on the grounds of length, a paragraph of comparison between the present British government and dental experimentation by the Nazis, and twice changing 'proletariat' to 'poor' and, elsewhere, 'smug beneficiaries of capitalism's largess' to 'rich'.

At 1.10 p.m., Anne Colledge said: 'Don't want to rush you, but . . .' Graham typed the final phrase – '. . . the latest vengeful lunge of a toothless political tiger' – and handed over the pages. Fifteen minutes later, Anne rang on his internal extension to say: 'It's brilliant. Best you've ever done, if I may say so.'

At 4.15 p.m., just after Graham had authorized a payment to John Durry for 'background information towards article', the door of his office opened without warning and revealed an insincerely beaming Garry McKenzie. Standing, his large cigar raised, the proprietor looked more than ever like a conductor in search of an orchestra.

'Graham!' he bellowed. 'All right?'

'Er, yes . . .'

'I decided I couldn't bear the suspense. Why wait till Friday morning to see what my editor thinks of these revolutionary new policies, I said to myself, when one of the few remaining privileges of a proprietor, in this age of necessarily rigorous guarantees of editorial freedom, is to find out a little bit early?'

'I'm er, not sure where the proofs are. The, er, paper's practically gone . . .'

'Got one!' McKenzie moved a hand which had been hidden by the door-frame to reveal a photocopy of the editorial page. Graham's eye took in the headline: Tooth – The First Casualty Of Class War.

'I picked one up from that cute little sub with the dark hair. Stroppy little cunt, actually. Said something about unions but luckily my deaf aid's on the blink. I told her I had your permission. For which I now humbly apply . . .'

'Oh, er, yes.'

McKenzie said that he was taking the piece down to his office to read with a nice cup of char. Waiting for the phone to ring, Graham felt the sting of tears in his eyes. He thought of telephoning Ben, or Durry, or Eliza, but he had so perfected the art of keeping up a pretence of equilibrium, no matter how deep his unease, that he could no longer admit despair to another. These were England's rules, to which he had added a few more of his own. He often thought that, even if he were dying, he would reply to the thoughtless pleasantry 'How are you?' with the reflex answer 'Fine.'

At 4.30 p.m., McKenzie rang and said: 'Graham, get your fat arse down here.' It was the first time he had ever said 'fat' and Graham feared that it meant an escalation of abuse but, in person, the proprietor was frostily serene, sure of his superiority over his opponent.

'We can't print this, Graham,' he began. 'It's, it's ... it's shrill. And don't let's have any loose talk about censorship. I'd say exactly the same if it supported the government in those kind of terms. In a magazine of this quality, we want reasoned argument. Frankly, Graham, when I give my editors a free hand, I give them a free hand to be responsible ...'

In the lift, on the way to McKenzie's room, Graham had worked out his answer. It was one he regarded as unarguable.

'I'm sorry you think that,' he said. 'I really am. But we have to be off stone in an hour and there's no time to do anything else ...'

'I'd anticipated that one,' the proprietor replied. 'Why not, given the significance of the issues, have an outside leader this week? By a big name. You could get this set.'

He shunted a wedge of expensive typing paper across the desk and Graham thought: Oh, God, no, it's going to be a piece by him. However, it proved to be an article by a government junior health minister which, in these circumstances, counted as a relief. The article began: 'We all want to be leaner and fitter. A leaner, fitter National Health Service can help us to be just that.'

McKenzie leaned forward. 'Graham, in fifteen minutes, I will ring your office and you will tell me what you've decided. And, just in case that little cunt in editorial starts menstruating about guarantees, you remember that the agreement says that I will not interfere *unreasonably* in editorial matters. It would only apply if I were ever not a reasonable man. Which I am. And I would bet that the independent directors will agree. All right?'

Graham tried to avoid Bernadette's eye, but she said 'Everything OK?' and he was forced to reply 'Fine.' Back in his office, Graham stared at the inflatable tube of toothpaste and wondered how he would tell Eliza what had happened. He knew that both she and anyone they met at dinner parties would tacitly assume that he had been sacked for incompetence. They would believe that his claim of a principled stand was just a self-delusionary excuse. Only Durry might accept the story, because it confirmed his beliefs about capitalism. Graham was glad that, by never crying since early childhood, he seemed to have banished the possibility: dried up the ducts.

At 4.40 p.m., he worked out what he would do. Telling his staff that he had decided, on reflection, that the first piece was too strident, he would, adrenalin lending fluency, produce a hasty piece of consensus pontificating – room for more efficiency in dentistry, but, on the other hand, not too many working-class children with gum disease, please – and offer it to McKenzie as a compromise. He would not, however, print the junior minister's apologia. He was craven, but not limitlessly so.

At 4.41 p.m., there was a knock on the door and Anne Colledge came in.

'We've heard from Bernadette what happened,' she said.

'From Bernadette . . . ?'

'Yes. I've rung the printers and they're going to pull the plug unless your editorial is run. All of us, and advertising as well, are, well, withdrawing labour sounds ridiculous, but we're stopping work until this is sorted out.'

'Sit down,' said Graham, and, to his surprise, his voice sounded satisfyingly cool and mature. As a boy, he had read stories of escaping prisoners of war suddenly discovering themselves able to perform feats – scaling walls, swimming rapids – which they would never have contemplated in safety. Perhaps he was now experiencing the liberal ditherer's equivalent.

'Anne,' he said. 'It's not that I don't appreciate it. It's just that, well, it isn't like that any more. He's probably already got Napier standing by as caretaker editor and all of you can be replaced by the end of the week by bright, young things – not that I'm, er, saying you're, er, well you know what I mean. As for the printers, he'll have some kind of arrangement in Sweden, Germany, Amsterdam, somewhere like that. It's not worth fighting. They can do what they like, these people. Because enough people want them to do it.'

'You can't just give in,' said Anne.

But a voice inside Graham's head said, with defiant insouciance: Oh yes, I can. Publicly, however, he told her: 'I'll think about what you said.'

At 4.44 p.m., Graham rang Eliza at Dazzlem. To his relief – and, he feared to admit, surprise – her tone was first encouraging and then attentive. He briefly told her everything except that the contentious editorial had been ghost-written by Durry.

'So what have you told him?' asked Eliza.

'I, er, haven't decided. I thought I'd offer him a compromise . . .'

'No. Look, I'll call you back. I find it helps to write things down when solving problems.' Her voice took on a familiar strictness. 'Listen Graham. Don't crumble until I call you back. How long do I have. . . ?'

'Oh, I don't know. Minutes . . .'

The phone went dead. Graham's mind was suddenly filled with images from thriller films in which experts sweated to defuse a timer device. But, in films, particularly if a star was

221

involved, you always knew, even as your pulse responded to the tension, they would succeed. At 4.49 p.m., the telephone rang. He tried to guess from the bell whether it was an internal or an external call but his clenched mind refused to decide. He picked it up.

'Darling?'

'Oh, God, I thought it was going to be him.'

'Look, I think I've got it. It's pretty obvious, actually. I don't know because you haven't told me but I would suspect you've drawn the battlelines on principle, integrity, editorial guarantees, that kind of thing . . .'

'Yes . . .'

'With a man like him, you're pissing in a hurricane. He thinks principles are women who run ballet schools. You've got to pitch it at a level he understands. Look, anyone with any sense can see that most of your readers are going to be against these reforms, particularly those with a lot of NHS patients: partly on the grounds of, well, compassion, partly because of loss of their own income if the poorer stop coming. Leader columns contain the opinions that a majority of their readers most want to hear. Isn't that how newspapers work? Anything else is commercial madness. Tell him supporting the reforms would be like *Whopper!* printing a true story. Well, don't tell him that, but you know what I mean. Tell him your editorial will make dentists feel good about their magazine. Actually, the bits you read me sounded terrific. I didn't know you had it in you . . .'

'Thanks . . .'

'I was only teasing.'

'No, I mean, thank you. For finding the answer.'

'Well, it was hardly quantum physics, my love. You just don't have a business brain. Do you want me to run through it all again?'

'No, I think I can . . .'

As soon as he put the phone down, it rang again. He braced himself. It was, however, Bernadette.

'Mr McKenzie was trying to get hold of you, Mr Sterling.'

'Yes. Ring through and say I'm coming down to see him.'

At 4.50 p.m., opening his door, he found both the editorial and advertising departments loitering around it, so that he felt like a controversial public figure ducking through the throng to reach their car. Extending the analogy, Anne Colledge now shouted, like a television reporter, 'What are you going to say to him?'

He shrugged. They must have thought it was a gesture of helplessness – he thought he noticed Anne raising her eyebrows as she turned away – and he could understand why they had made that assumption. But knowing they were wrong was a rare and appealing feeling.

'All right,' said McKenzie.

Graham presented Eliza's argument with reassuringly little hesitation from himself or interruption from McKenzie. He said only one thing of which he would later feel ashamed. It was the qualification 'whatever you and I think of the changes', which indicated, falsely, that he was on the same side as McKenzie but succumbing to commercial logic, where the truth was that he was on the opposite side from McKenzie but succumbing to employment logic. Graham ended with an image of his own: 'If you ran a football magazine, you wouldn't tell them cricket was the better game.'

McKenzie looked solemn, like a politician at a party conference who thought the camera was on them.

'You're a cool fucker, Graham,' he said. 'You really are a cool bloody fucker. I thought I'd put you through the blender good and proper. Do you know, I'd actually already rung Ernest Napier with a view to an emergency secondment back here? But, all the time, you were sitting it out, quietly, like you do, waiting to come back in here, right up at the deadline, like the fucking Cuban Missile Crisis, and tell me what a dickhead I've been...'

'No, I...'

'You're right, Graham. The editorial runs as written. Will you ring the printers and tell them or will I? Joking, only joking.

223

The rules mean I can't speak to printers.' He paused and, leaning back, massaged his left breast in wide circles. 'I made the worst mistake a man can make. You know what that is, Graham?'

'No, I, er . . .'

'I allowed what I might personally believe to get in the way of making money.'

So novel – and, admittedly, complicated – were the emotions that he was experiencing that Graham made the walk back to the editorial floor as slow as he could. As he turned the corner, he froze his face, to hold off the revelation as late as possible. He stopped in front of the huddle by his door and waited for silence.

'All I, er, want to say,' he announced, 'is that the editorial will now appear as it was written.'

In the whooping that followed, Anne Colledge hugged Graham, until an all too apparent erection made him redden and her look pensive.

As a result of these events, Graham was now perceived, a little guiltily, as a strong man, but he was also more professionally secure, which was useful. And, shortly after the Censorship Crisis, he was offered an opportunity to become rich. He missed it, not from scruple but from, well, something closer to stupidity. In retrospect, this was another of his Temptations, which he failed to detect at the time.

Returning one afternoon from lunch with his advertising manager, Graham found a message to call Alastair at Hanratty's. His friend still used that name for the company, although, when Graham called back, the bored voice on the switchboard said the correct 'Potomac Johnson Hodge'. Via a suspicious secretary, who, when he gave his name, said icily that she would check, Graham was put through to Alastair.

'Dear boy!' said Alastair. 'Sweet of you to call back. Look, how about a drink this week? There's something I want to run past you . . .'

They agreed to meet after work in a wine bar near Alastair's office, frequented by financiers and journalists on what Graham thought of as proper newspapers. Alastair collected a bottle of iced champagne, handing a card to the barman to add the cost to his company's account, and joined Graham at one of the tables made from beer kegs. The room had the damp-brick feel of having been a cellar. There was sawdust on the floor. For some reason, it was this primitive chic which appealed to those who shunted money to and fro from London.

'It's very passable, this place,' shouted Alastair. 'Sorry about the din. I'm afraid the oiks have discovered it.'

The oiks, Graham knew from previous conversations, were a new generation of commodity dealers, who had not been to public school or, Alastair had added in scandalized tones, 'to any school at all. Well, not after fourteen or sixteen or whatever.'

Alastair now treated Graham to another disquisition on the oiks. 'I mean, Gray, really, these are people who pronounce Porsche as if they're talking about Shylock's defence counsel. A sufficient disqualification from owning one, I would have thought. However, if you're lucky later, you might catch this pretty little trick they do with Moët. Stack up the bottles like a Carmen Miranda hat and then pop the top one. It looks like, like . . .'

Graham could all too easily have provided a visual comparison, but Alastair had been reminded of another oik anecdote. 'They did it in here the other day. One of them from Hanratty – we're on kind of lift, escalator, and urinal terms, you know – said "Cor, Al, ain't that something? Looks like Trevor's Fountain." I said, like what? He said, "You know, Trevor's Fountain in Rome. Ain't you seen it?" I mean, please.'

Graham broke the first silence by asking after Hamster. 'Stocks in Hamster are high,' her husband smiled. 'You must have seen a lot of each other during the election.'

'Yes . . .'

'Pity it wasn't in happier circumstances, what?'

There was another pause, during which Graham thought:

Oh my God, he's going to accuse me of having an affair with Hamster. But what Alastair said was: 'Look, what I wanted to suggest . . . we should be drinking beer, really. What label do you drink?'

'Oh, er, lager, mainly. I like that one they advertise with. . . .'

'You've never had Clifford's Particular . . .'

'No. I, er . . .'

'Pity. You know my uncle's . . .'

'Yes . . .'

As had been let slip more than once at dinner parties, Alastair's mother's brother-in-law was the chairman of a profitable family brewing firm, which specialized in authentically powerful bitters. The Macleods would often stay at the castles, villas, and paradors belonging to that branch of the family when the castles, villas, and paradors belonging to their own side of the line were fully occupied.

'Very very good time to be drinking unc's little number, at this moment in time,' said Alastair, lowering his voice and leaning inwards, so that Graham noticed a new intensity in his eyes.

'Is it?' said Graham.

'Yes, indeed. Even if you don't drink it, it's a good time for laying down stocks, if you see what I mean. Unc's little brew, I think I can assure you, will mature very well, and quicker than you'd think . . .'

'As I said, I don't really drink bitter . . .'

Alastair looked agitated. 'Even so, Gray, there are definite advantages to having some stored away for a rainy day.' He winked. 'Look, if you decide you want to lay some down, ring this number – it's a chap I know from school, safe as houses – and say that Ally asked you to find out how Cliff was. Ally asked you to find out how Cliff was. He'll take it from there. Only thing is, I'd do it soonest.'

Alastair changed the conversation to cricket and then a complaint about how the Chucks and Hanks at Hanratty's all went on about American football, which was even more damn barbaric than British football, and which, now he came to think about it, the oiks had taken a fancy to as well.

Afterwards, Graham was perplexed by the conversation. He tried to remember if Alastair had ever asked for beer at their house and they had been unable to provide it. Or had Ben – who, in the way of jazz buffs, was just a little bit of a beer bore as well – dropped a hint to Alastair, who was passing it on? Social codes were so complicated in England. For example, if anyone ever told you, in your teens, a convoluted story about their struggle tactfully to tell a friend that he or she had body odour, they were almost certainly telling you that it was you who smelled. In other countries, they would probably just have held their nose and retched.

The following week, Eliza came home one night and said: 'I need a drink. Is there any of that Burgundy from last night? Hamster was unbearably bouncy today. That brewery on Ally's side's been taken over. Happy Birthday to the shareholders, including Mr & Mrs A. Macleod, who have been spending their pocket money on them for at least the last year. At times like this, it becomes easy to believe in the redistribution of wealth. The *limited* redistribution.'

Two weeks after that, Eliza rang Graham at the office and said: 'Darling, just to warn you, I think we might be required for some social first aid tonight. Ally's been interviewed by the DTI. That's the Department of Trade and Industry, Graham. They're after him for insider dealing . . .'

'God. How's she taking it . . . ?'

'Theatrically. She keeps saying, over and over again, this isn't crime, crime is beating up old grannies and holding up building societies. She says it's not as if there were any victims. Ally was just helping people, not hurting them, she says . . .'

'Will he go to jail . . . ?'

'Don't jump the . . . They haven't even charged him yet. It's a matter of what they can prove, I suppose. Apparently, he was tipping off his friends about the beer deal. I thought, it's a pity he didn't include us among his friends . . .'

'Yes.'

And so it was that Graham remained both poor and pure, though both measures were, of course, relative.

The hotel bed was large – it was the kind of plasticated, sub-American place that hoped to attract businessmen's conventions – but, on that Friday night at the end of January 1988, Graham and Eliza both slept clinging to the outer edges, like fallen mountaineers in a thriller film. They had dined the night before in different groups at separate restaurants and, when Graham returned before midnight, fighting to contain belches, although, as always, he had ordered the mildest curry on the menu, and drunk only one and a half pints of low-alcohol lager, Eliza was already asleep. When his hand eventually bumped the light switch in the darkened room, it rustled a piece of paper. Detaching it, and retreating to the corridor, he read: 'I'm in bed. Do NOT put on main light. Undress in bathroom. Do NOT wake me up.'

In the morning, when the alarm clock roused them, they washed and dressed without speaking, their communication restricted to an admonitory scowl from Eliza when Graham made as if to overtake her as she headed for first use of the bathroom. In fact, it was merely that, without his glasses, he had not seen her. He felt new resentment on top of all the wrongs already catalogued, and assumed that the same would be true for Eliza, so that the balance of anger remained constant. They descended silently in a crowded elevator – acknowledging acquaintances squashed on either side, without looking at each other – to the garishly marbled first floor where they queued at the entrance to the breakfast room, the doors of which had gold, or more likely gold-coloured, handles, big as steering wheels and embossed with the crest of the hotel chain. In the queue, an orderly line of the kind which only Noah and the English had ever successfully enforced, Graham parried banalities with the husband of the couple behind, and Eliza with a young woman in front, who was one of the few guests travelling alone. The Sterlings were first in the queue.

'Smoking or non-smoking?' asked the waitress, a plump teen-ager, with a Northern accent modulated towards an attempt at hotel-posh.

'Non-smoking,' said Eliza.

'Er, non-smoking,' said Graham.

'Merger or anti-merger?' asked the waitress.

'Merger,' said Eliza.

'Er, anti-merger,' said Graham.

'Madam,' said the waitress (it came out may-dem), and led Eliza to a non-smoking, pro-merger table. Graham recognized the bossy BBC Education Producer from their own branch among those she joined. He was taken to a non-smoking, anti-merger table, where he knew no one. 'Good man. Good man,' said a red-faced bearded weekend-sailor type, as Graham sat down. 'One of the quisling tables tried to borrow our marma-lade. It's in short supply in here,' he added. 'But we told them to bugger off.'

The Nice People's Party had summoned members of its ruling body – the Council For Social Democracy – to Sheffield for an emergency conference on the future of the organization. Eliza was a Council member, with Graham attending as a non-voting observer. Sheffield, although its former status could be gauged from the fact that it was one of the relatively few two-football-team towns in Britain, had suffered badly in the industrial recession of the early 1980s and was now a grey, damp city, where, even on dry days, it seemed to have rained and the shopping centre, with most windows boasting Final Reductions, rang to a cacophony of smokers' coughs. The new party had adopted a deliberate policy of holding court in places other than the hoary seaside resorts – Blackpool, Brighton, Bournemouth – favoured by the established conference-plan-ners. Coming to Sheffield (as, in pre-crisis days, the Nice People had visited Buxton) was symbolic of one-nation politics, of faith in the North of Britain. Perhaps more realistically, the hotel had taken on extra car-park staff for the weekend, to protect the hub-caps and stereo radios in the Volvos and Audis which most of those attending drove.

Non-delegate guests in the breakfast room on that Saturday morning would probably have assumed, from eavesdropped conversations, that the conference group was a medical seminar or a meeting for people with the same disease – haemophiliacs, perhaps, injected with imported Aids-infected blood by the NHS – because one table would be saying 'the doctor' with impressive venom and the other with sentimental contentment. For example, a middle-aged lady was to be heard saying: 'I think we owe it all to the doctor and I'm sticking with him!' In fact, these were references to Dr David Owen, whose refusal to form a new party with the Liberals had resulted in the need for four different sections – pro-merger smokers, anti-merger non-smokers, pro-merger non-smokers, anti-merger smokers – in the hotel breakfast room. Often, as was the case with the Sterlings, married couples encompassed one of each persuasion.

Many of that morning's newspapers were recalling with ironic relish the Duke of Burgundy's comments in the 1979 lecture which had begun the march of the moderates. The Duke had said: 'This is not to argue against some dispute and tension within parties being inevitable and even desirable. Such reasonable and creative tension is, however, a far cry from a position in which internecine warfare is the constant and major purpose of a party's life.' A clever sub-editor, recalling the lecture's invocation of Yeats against the Socialists, had appended the headline The Centre Cannot Hold to a columnist's reflections on the comedy of the vaunted antidote to political hostility ending in this way. Another writer, recalling the election slogan 'Breaking The Mould', concluded his piece: 'The mould broke them.'

Journalists trawling for more such collisions between intention and outcome were amply rewarded by events at the conference on that Saturday. The venue was the Octagon, the arts centre of the university; a grey concrete memento of the 1970s

230

nuclear-bunker school of urban architecture. Eliza, sitting on the left side of the auditorium near the front, cheered and applauded when a Welsh delegate, supporting merger, said, in reference to the controversial doctor: 'You cannot base a party on hero worship . . . you cannot base it on the concept of a Man of Destiny.' Graham, sitting near the back on the right, tried not to betray his allegiance when those sitting near him laughed and cheered at references to a 'fan club' or 'rump' supporting the doctor.

He was, however, undemonstratively pleased when other delegates screamed 'Liar!' and 'You tricked us all!', during an address, also urging merger, by the Duke of Burgundy. The only matter on which the two factions were united was on bitter criticism of the media for their reporting of events. Very few delegates spoke against a merger, which worried Graham, but the doctor's aides insisted that many of his supporters had refused to attend the conference because of prior disillusionment.

The former leader was due to address a meeting on the Saturday evening and it was then that those journalists whose selected story for the weekend was Nice People's Party Turns Nasty hit what Alastair Macleod had started to call, to Graham's discomfiture, pay dirt. The pro-merger section of the party, led by the Duke of Burgundy and the man called Bob, objected that the doctor's speech was a fringe meeting and should therefore not be held in the main auditorium. The former leader's team riposted that this was the only hall in the complex large enough to accommodate all his supporters. After a day of conflict, gossip, smear and counter-smear, it was agreed that green drapes would be hung over the main conference podium, in party colours, before the meeting started.

Of his friends who were also Nice People, Paula Waddle (anti-merger) had felt unable to leave the children for a weekend, and Alastair had refused to let Hamster (pro-merger) go away. Alastair was still twitchy after his sizeable fine and formal warning for insider dealing, althougl. he had kept his job. It seemed to be quite difficult to become an unfrocked financier. Alastair had also survived Black Monday, when, in November 1987, the financial markets had staged an unpopular one-day revival of 1929.

So, on that Saturday in Sheffield, Graham had lunched alone, spotting Eliza on the other side of the canteen, with two couples and, he noticed, the partner-radar working even in these circumstances, one spare man. The only other delegate Graham knew was Anne Colledge (anti-merger), whom, despite extensive casual scanning, he had failed to spot. It was not until just before Dr Owen rose to speak that he saw her, in a bright red rugby shirt, reading a newspaper in the second row. Alone. Graham, sitting near the back, calculated the angles and distances involved in intercepting her at the door when the meeting ended. He was pleased, in this regard at least, that the audience was not as large as had been predicted.

Political speeches, as the Duke of Burgundy's 1979 remarks to Graham, Eliza, and others had demonstrated, can work like amphetamines, but they can also be like LSD and the doctor's intention that night was that his audience should begin to see things which were not there. 'We are all embarked on a Great Adventure,' he said. 'It will take Courage. Commitment. Nerve.' The more facetious political commentators observed that the best-known meaning of the expression 'Great Adventure' was death, in J. M. Barrie's *Peter Pan*. 'A Freudian slip,' crowed the pro-merger delegates. Others joked that, *in extremis*, the orator had abandoned his lifelong commitment to alliteration. 'In his great days,' noted one columnist, 'he would have invoked courage, commitment, coolness. The uncharacteristic injunction to courage, commitment, nerve, suggested that his own supply of the final quality was going.'

As the meeting dispersed, Anne turned round before Graham reached her and said, with what looked like genuine pleasure, 'Hello, sir. I was looking out for you.' (As they had become friendly, she had started to call him 'sir', in a way which he found endearing after convincing himself that it was not an expression of incredulity at his having become editor.) There was a brief flurry of ducking and bending before they decided not to greet each other with a kiss, she uncertain because he was her superior and he uncertain because he was Graham.

'What are you doing tonight?' she asked, and then giggled. 'I'm sorry, it sounds like a fourth form chat-up line. What I mean is, are you off to any fringe meetings on European Federalism or The Case For Proportional Representation or are you free to go and get something to eat? Assuming, that is, that a humble galley-slave can ask her captain such a thing.'

What he liked about Anne – one of the things he liked about Anne – was that her questions to him somehow incorporated and dealt with all the possible alternatives and objections, so that the reply was more a matter of choosing an answer than thinking of one. At work, when she brought a page proof into his office, she would say: 'See what you think of this page one lay-out. Some of the readers might find the headline a bit racy. But the president of the European Periodental Conference isn't Martin Luther King and may need some help from us to get his message over. On the other hand, you might want to think about leading with the gum disease breakthrough at Leeds University, although the picture will need careful cropping if our readers want to keep their breakfast down. And, for that matter, we led on gum disease three weeks ago . . .'

Faced with her range of possibilities with regard to an evening in Sheffield, he told her that he, er, had nothing planned (did she know Eliza was at the conference?) and that, er, supper sounded, er, great. They found an almost empty Greek restaurant in a street whose dereliction looked fairly recent. Sudden self-consciousness about his bulk made Graham ignore the complimentary pitta bread, but then nervousness made him chain-eat it. And, anyway, Anne wasn't fat, but nor was she skeletal-evangelical, like Eliza and Paula and others with whom he tended to share meals. They clinked glasses of a rough red wine with a Greek dancer on the label. It was Anne who cut into the first pause.

'What did you think about today?'

'I don't know. What did you think?'

'Well, it's all over, isn't it, frankly? I mean, we'll lose the vote tomorrow and then it's downhill until the money runs out. I'm not holding out because I still believe. I'm holding out because if I'd wanted to join the Liberal Party, I'd have done so seven years ago. Giving in now would mean it had all just been a bloody complicated way of belonging to a party which existed, anyway. I mean, it must have been about more than that, mustn't it?'

'Yes. Yes, I think so.'

He filled up her glass.

'Thank you, sir. Not too much, I'm walking. Eliza's on the other side, isn't she?'

'Yes. Yes, she is.'

'Has that been very difficult?'

'I . . . well, to be honest, things hadn't been . . .'

'Look, I should never have mentioned it and you shouldn't tell me. I don't have many rules but one of them is that husbands don't slag off their wives to other women . . .'

At once, counsel for the libido was on his feet, arguing that the use of the phrases 'don't have many rules but' and 'other women' strongly indicated that she was happy to sleep with married men, as long as their wives weren't defamed as part of the foreplay. Counsel for the conscience quoted at length the precedent of Sterling v. Cann (1983), with regard to the uncertain relationship between words and deeds, and was strongly supported in this submission by counsel for commonsense. Counsel for the libido conceded, saying that there would be no further questions for the moment.

Their first courses, of a pink mush and a green mush respectively, arrived. Over these, Anne said: 'Sometimes, I see Thatcher going on for ever. Particularly if Denis dies. We'll have the Widow Thatcher, like the Widow Gandhi. I mean, what's that thing the right-wing papers all point out? That she's still younger than Ronald Reagan was when he first entered politics?

Something like that.' Over their greasy, grilled meat, with congealed yellow rice, they concurred that the world seemed a much safer place with Gorbachov running Russia. 'I mean,' said Anne, 'the truth is that politics in this country is going to matter less and less. Do you know, there were people in my branch who talked about us as revolutionaries, the English middle-class answer to Marxism? Well, really.' Graham admitted that he quite admired Lech Walesa, and Anne said: 'I know what you mean, but he's finished, isn't he? But that's partly my point. Solidarity in Poland – now that really was people who hadn't been involved in politics before standing up to be counted. They were risking their lives. Our thing was just people who had got a little bit sick of democratically elected politicians yelling at each other all the time.'

It was well past eleven when the waiter brought the bill, with two small glasses, on the house, of a liqueur which tasted like melted marzipan. When they were outside on the pavement, theatrically shivering against the cold, and muttering about looking for taxis, perhaps stressing the plural rather self-consciously, Anne said, glancing away, as if scanning the road for cabs: 'Look, Graham, I've never been good at these conversations, and report me to the Press Council if I've got it all completely wrong, but . . . are you pro-merger or anti-merger . . . ?'

Graham was confused. He assumed that she was attempting to persuade him to change his mind and join the new party. He did not have so many certainties that he could afford to surrender them casually, and he was constructing an answer about reflection on the options overnight, when she suddenly buried her head against his waxed jacket and said: 'Because I'm afraid I'm feeling pretty strongly pro-merger . . . I'm speaking metaphorically.'

'Oh.'

Graham had caught up with developments. Counsel for the libido announced that the prosecution felt entirely vindicated and wished the precedent of Sterling v Cann (1983) to be wiped from the record and the case thrown out. Shouting objection, however, counsel for the conscience asked permission to put a written document into court:

22: In your opinion, is the concept of sexual fidelity between two established partners:

☐ **A:** A killjoy device of sex-fearing Christianity [*Judaism/Islam may be inserted. Mormons may ignore this option*], irrelevant in a secular age.

· ☐ **B:** Commonsense, given the endemic spread of Aids [*Acquired Immune Deficiency Syndrome*].

☐ **C:** A denial of man's [*or men's*] genetic instinct to impregnate as generally as possible.

☐ **D:** The only way to avoid an eternity of hellfire.

[*NB: those selecting B or D, move on to final question: What's It All About? Otherwise, proceed to supplementary question 22a.*]

Graham recognized the question, and most of the options, but the rubric of the questionnaire made clear: 'Certain questions may recur in a slightly different form.' His initial reaction was to answer 'It's practically over with Eliza' and/or 'I'll use a condom,' but the rubric also insisted: 'Each question must be answered with one of the [generally comprehensive] options offered. Nothing may be written on the paper.'

'Look, are you . . . ?' he began.

'Graham,' she said, an edge to her tenderness now, 'I'm not going to make this decision for you. This one has to be you . . .'

7

The Last Supper Party

As if by common consent, they saved the fall of the Berlin Wall until the tortelloni.

'My grandfather fought the Germans, my father fought the Germans, and I'd have thought, now, after this, you'd have to have a Deutschmark on Christopher being forced to turn out for a rematch,' said Alastair Macleod.

'Only if he genetically inherits his father's belief in racial stereotypes,' muttered John Durry.

'Cheap shot, old man,' said Alastair Macleod, laughing, so that a small dribble of Chianti had to be retrieved by his tongue.

'The point is,' interrupted Ben Waddle, 'isn't the point, Ally, that we in the West – well, our politicians particularly – have spent twenty years standing in front of that wall, saying, which man who believes in democracy can look upon this wall and not weep, and ich bein ein bloody Berliner and so on? And now, now they've taken it down, we say, steady on, I hear the tramp of jackboots. I mean, are we now saying the wall was a good idea, a guarantee of European security . . . ?'

'Personally,' said Alastair. 'Personally, I could never get very worked up about the wall being there or, indeed, whether that negro terrorist Nelson Mandela was in jail or . . .'

'Oh, now come *on*,' said a combination of Durry, Hamster, the Waddles, and the Sterlings.

'Oh, dear, it's so easy,' sighed Alastair. 'I only said it to annoy because I, et cetera. It's not even satisfying any more. Pavlov's moderates!'

'Well, he is a negro terrorist. It's a simple factual description,' insisted Timmy Duvet-Hogg, MP, who was one of only two people at the table who had not reacted to Alastair's remark. The second was Rosinia Duvet-Hogg.

'The other thing is,' said Paula Waddle, her instinct for conversational diversion intact, 'going back to the wall, and Germany and all that, is, if, as Alastair seems to want, we mistrust our old enemies for ever, then we're just apes with clothes on, aren't we? The whole point of history is that countries are endlessly repainted in new colours, like charter aircraft. My granny never quite got out of liking Stalin, because of what she calls her war, so the Cold War sort of passed her by, but now, without really knowing it, she's back in fashion again . . .'

'Yes. Isn't Gorby great?' said Hamster. 'Don't you wish he'd just run for leader of the whole world . . . ?'

'What I do know and I think Gorbachov knows this too,' Alastair Macleod contributed, 'is that Communism has failed. If the events of the last year have taught us anything, it's that Marxism is dead, kaput, no more, pushing up the daisies, rung down the curtain and joined the choir invisible. Darling, I think we're running out of Parmesan . . .'

'Maria!' shouted Hamster. 'Capisco!'

'Does capisco mean quickly?' wondered Rosinia Duvet-Hogg.

'Doesn't it?' Hamster said.

'It might be argued that Communism hasn't failed,' suggested John Durry, 'because Communism hasn't been tried. What the people were offered in Eastern Europe wasn't Communism . . .'

'Steady on, dear boy!' said Alastair Macleod.

'Bloody bonkers, if you ask me!' snorted Timmy Duvet-Hogg.

'Oh, God, I thought I heard one of the monsters calling,' said Paula Waddle. 'Emily had a tummy upset earlier. I'd better . . .'

'Can you look in on poppet?' asked Hamster Macleod. 'She's due a feed ...'

'I hope it isn't Jess. She had sunburn,' worried Rosinia Duvet-Hogg. 'Could you just stick your head round the door ...?'

'Yes, yes, yes. Mother Courage and all her children,' complained Paula Waddle, with a quick charade of a crone's stoop and shawl.

'Oh dear, don't say any more. You'll put Graham off children again,' said Anne Sterling, touching by reflex her smock, where it now brushed the table, like a businessman's gut at lunch.

This was late July, 1990, at one of the many Tuscan farmhouses to which the Macleods had access. They were spending six weeks in Italy, inviting friends to visit for days or weeks or fortnights. There was a chlorinated pool, and olive groves for strolling, and a local couple – 'Communists, of course, like all the peasants here, but work like blacks,' said Alastair – to help prepare and clear away the alcoholic, disputatious meals.

The theory had been that July and August would be scorching, but an unpredicted dullness had struck the region that summer, with the result that one day out of two brought cloud in the English manner, faintly backlit by a struggling sun, like tiny bulbs through tissue paper in a toy theatre. This worried the visitors at a level beyond mere irritation about its disruption of their holiday. Hamster often spoke of a television documentary about the Greenhouse Effect and the changes in the weather caused by man's scourging of the earth.

'You realize what all this means,' said Hamster. 'One day, our grandchildren might come skiing in Tuscany.'

'Mmm, I fear the environmental consequences may be more far-reaching than that,' suggested Ben Waddle gently.

'Will there be any grandchildren?' worried Paula Waddle.

No rent was asked by the Macleods, which meant that, with cheap flights, the Waddles could afford a vacation beyond the scope of most two-schoolteacher couples with three children.

Occasionally, awakened by mosquitoes, the lovemaking of other couples (Hamster seemed especially demonstrative) or Chianti bladder in the middle of the night, Ben would fret to Paula about 'private sector handouts'. It was true that Alastair's largess contained an element of arrogant display, of status games, but sun and wine were Paula and Ben's respective Mephistopholeses, and their guilt was soon suppressed.

On the night of the row about the Berlin Wall, the Waddles were enjoying their second week in Italy. With tact planned like a battle, Hamster operating as Etiquette-General, it had been arranged that the Waddles, who had been close to both Graham and Eliza, would be invited for a strategic fortnight. The first week coincided with the second week of Eliza's trip, with her new boyfriend, and the second week crossed over with the first seven of the fourteen days spent by Graham and his new wife, Anne. The other guests in this section of the entertainment schedule were Timmy and Rosinia Duvet-Hogg, who had become firm friends of the Macleods after meeting them at Graham and Eliza's. Alastair was excited by knowing a Conservative MP, even a backbencher.

Less predictable was the invitation to Durry. However, dinner party politicians divide into those who like to lecture and those who genuinely enjoy debate, and Alastair was strongly of the second group. He tolerated Durry like a king employs a jester, although, with what may have been a calculated slight, he invited his clown for one week only and Hamster explained that, while he was welcome to bring a friend, conditions might be a little cramped. Why, then, did Durry accept, even obeying the hint to visit alone? Ben put this question to him in the swimming pool on a rare gas-mark seven afternoon. 'Know thine enemy,' replied Durry, ducking his head under water to cool down. 'Most people in my position aren't allowed such a perfect opportunity to examine the texture of what they despise.' Ben was half-sighted from the treated water but he suspected that, for the first time ever, he had seen Durry wink.

Graham, at least, was glad of Durry's presence. He appreciated the sensitivity of Hamster's arrangements but there was still a tension which intensified his guilt. He was often conscious of the others biting back, or hastily rewriting, any shared memory they voiced which involved Eliza. He also found himself frequently required to explain whisperingly to Anne the kind of coded jokes which old friends share.

And, on one of the gloomier afternoons, when Graham retreated inside to collect a pullover and a paperback, Hamster, supervising the chopping and boiling by the communist peasants in the kitchen, bustled him into the corner, next to the huge and sooted cooking range.

'Gray, you needn't be afraid, *entre nous*, to ask about Lizzy, you know . . .'

'No. I'm, er . . . Whatever makes you . . .'

'She was here last week with her new man. He's fine – a cousin of Ally's, it turns out, but then most people in the City are – but I don't think it's some, you know, grand passion, like you and Annie. No, don't look like that. I'm not being funny. The point is, Eliza and Derek, well, she has him because it's easier for people like us to have someone than not to have someone – it's sort of expected and hostesses hate singles. But she's confused, Gray. Hurt. She says she doesn't know what happened. She just somehow lost you. Frankly, it surprised us all. I mean it never occurred to us that you of all people – not that I'm suggesting anything about you – would run off for a bit of bonking on the side. And, as Ally says, Eliza's sexier and prettier than Annie by a long chalk. Oh, cripes, I don't mean to be bitchy. Ben – don't tell him I told you – has this theory that you were so terrified Lizzy would hurt you that you got in and hurt her first. Your friend Durry – we were discussing you and Lizzy at supper when she and Derek went to Siena for the night – said your relationship with Lizzy was – you know how he talks – a, what was it?, an example of the ordered being drawn to the chaotic. What was the other bit? Oh, yes. An unarguable force meets an unarguing object. "Reader, she carried him," he said. Ben and Paula laughed. It's from a book,

isn't it? Durry also said – I suppose I shouldn't be saying this
– that Annie looks like your mother, at least as he remembers
her from your wedding. Your first wedding. All I'm saying is,
Gray, is that I don't know what you might have thought about
Lizzy in the end. But she talked about you all the time. Little
stories in the office about how, oh I don't know, you'd locked
yourself out of the house, got on the wrong bus, booked at the
wrong restaurant, mixed up the sugar and the salt in a recipe.
But not, you know, nastily. She was barmy about you. Actually,
sometimes I think she was just barmy. Only joking. But you're
not the easiest person in the world to live with, I shouldn't
think. And – I can say this to you because I'm your friend –
you might not always, all the time, be quite as nice and decent
as you think you are . . .'

Graham shuddered. It was the first time that his private
estimation of himself had ever been publicly challenged. Hamster's monologue had also forced him to think about his treatment of Eliza and the fact that, when you were not present,
your friends might talk about you. These were two areas which
he was reluctant to explore.

'Oh, dear,' pouted Hamster. 'I've said too much . . .'

'No. No, er, really . . .'

'I sometimes think if maybe you and Lizzy had had
kiddies . . . I don't mean to pry, but you'd been trying, hadn't
you? . . . Funny that Anne . . . Oh, don't blush . . .'

Graham had married Anne in March of that year. His relationship with Eliza, already strained, had been irretrievable since
the Saturday night in Sheffield, when he had not returned to
their hotel until breakfast. It had been his first night with Anne.
They had taken a taxi to her rented college room where, on a
narrow mattress, concave from age and the sexual athleticism
of emancipated '80s students, he had broken his marriage vows
for the first time. The educational location lent the encounter
a Lolitan element, which raised the erotic stakes for Graham,
although he and Anne were the same generation. Afterwards,

as they lay huddled under a cheap brown blanket, Anne said: 'Are you sure you're? . . . you didn't come . . .'

'No. No, I don't. . . .'

'What? Never?'

'No. Not really.'

'You're joking . . . no, don't, I don't mean . . . It's the opposite problem you meet more often. Nice for your . . . nice for the girl. You must be quite in demand . . .'

'No. No, not at all . . . You're the . . . I've never . . .'

'Do you mind not . . . not . . . finishing off?'

'I don't know . . . Sometimes, I think I'm a kind of throwback to women who . . . I'm sorry, that's terribly, er, sexist . . .'

'No. I know what you mean. Well, sir, let's see if we can't sort you out . . .'

She had straddled him and pulled and squeezed and rocked, not unpleasantly, until she asked if it was all right to stop, but his problem remained his problem, which relieved him, for it would have been depressing if the solution had been as mundane as a change of wives. For some reason, perhaps the conformity of his thought processes, he already considered Anne as his potential second wife instead of his first mistress.

On their return to London, Graham and Eliza's marriage was concluded, as it had been conducted, with minimal emotion or even discussion. In fact, the mechanics of the separation were a parody of their relationship. Graham, after Sheffield, vaguely supposed their marriage might be over and that it seemed to be assumed he had a future with Anne, who, on their student bed, had said: 'Actually, sir, I don't mind admitting, I've wanted this for quite a long time . . .' And yet Graham had no idea how the change from one state to the other might be effected.

It was Eliza who took control. 'OK,' she said, back in their flat on the Sunday evening, 'I think there's someone else and I think it's probably that little girl from your office. I've never seen the point of melodrama. So I wouldn't waste my breath fighting for your affections. Actually, take that how you may, but it wasn't meant nastily, particularly. I wouldn't fight for anyone's. There aren't going to be any big speeches. I don't really go for those. It's just a matter of sorting things out. One, accommodation. A: I move out, while we sell. B: You move out, while we sell. Of course, our cut of the money will be in line with our shares of the mortgage . . .'

He almost, from reflex, said that, on balance, he would go for A, but he replied: 'It's all right. It ought to be me that moves out . . .'

'Fine,' said Eliza.

The nastiest part of himself wanted to see her cry, but a more palatable region of his feelings admired her civilized handling of this impasse. He felt again the sense of being a spectator even at his own most important events. He had wandered into a marriage and now he was wandering out of it. As he left the flat, he suddenly thought: we have actually never had an argument. And yet, except for a particular circumstance, this cool, rootless union – the English middle-class equivalent, perhaps, of a marriage of convenience – might have resulted in other lives.

He suddenly understood the aptness of the legal phrase 'marriage dissolved'. Their liaison had melted quickly away, like one of those hangover or flu powders: dust you poured into water and stirred. The other available phrases – to do with marriages breaking up, splitting, falling apart – were inappropriate. Graham and Eliza's marriage had, indeed, dissolved. His brain characteristically choosing to analyse language rather than face pain, he reflected that a dissolution was what you got when marital problems became insoluble. How typical of English. It was scarcely surprising that the race was so poor at intimate communication, given the language it had been allotted for these procedures.

Graham stayed first at Durry's council flat. 'Seeking political asylum, are you?' Durry had smirked, opening the door on the first night. The only available space was the living-room floor, but this necessity held a suggestion of penance which suited

Graham's mood. His amount of sleep was decided by whatever hour the political discussions between Durry and his flatmates, all connected with the magazines or pressure groups of the Left, were abandoned. One of the men, a Geordie who wore a fez indoors, had declared himself an Albanian Maoist, a sect so undocumented that the others treated him with an edgy respect, permanently uncertain what line he might take on any subject. Graham rarely contributed to these sessions and refused the generously proffered substances, which he suspected might be drugs. Otherwise, he was generally left alone. 'Where would you place yourself politically?' asked one flatmate. 'Well, I, er . . .' began Graham. 'He's a lapsed Social Democrat,' explained Durry. 'Weee-errdd,' said a blonde girl who occasionally slept in Durry's room.

There was little talk about the end of Graham's marriage. (Eliza's solicitor was already efficiently filing for divorce.) But, late one evening, woozy from wine, Graham said self-pityingly: 'Perhaps, if we'd never heard that speech . . .' And Durry cut in: 'Oh, spare us. I was waiting for that one. You blame it on politics because it glamorizes everything, makes it seem worthwhile . . . why can't it be over leaving the bog seat up, or wanting to fuck other people, like everyone else?'

Gradually, Graham spent fewer nights at his first refuge and more at Anne's bright, cramped, and highly mortgaged house in North London. Eventually, her flat-mate was given notice and Graham moved in. He worried about money, although he suspected, when the deal was completed, that Eliza had, despite her warning, divided the proceeds unevenly in his favour. And McKenzie, increasingly convinced since the Great Censorship Crisis that he and his editor were soul-mates, had recently appointed Graham, with appropriate recompense, Group Editorial Director (Medical Titles), which gave him sway over gynaecological, aural, nursing, and rectal publications as well as his own (to his bemusement, there was even a news-sheet called *Diarrhoea Weekly*). Anne, as soon as their relationship was formalized, applied for other jobs – 'I know you'd agonize about other people knowing your were screwing one of your staff' – and became production editor of a computer monthly not in the McKenzie stable.

Sometimes, for entire evenings, Graham's swell of happiness would overcome his drag of guilt and failure. The questionnaire no longer troubled him, not, he suspected, because he had satisfactorily answered it, but because he no longer qualified to belong to the sample. The invigilator had stepped in. And, anyway, Graham did not agonize over decisions any more but simply followed his first instinct, or the lead of others, trying to blind himself to complexity or options in case the file on his recent behaviour was reopened for him. It was Anne who said, in bed, 'I'd quite like to get married, if that's all right with you, sir,' and Graham who agreed, merely turning up at the register office as instructed.

In the months before the wedding, Anne's sexual therapy had continued. After each coupling, she would look disappointed, not, or at least he hoped not, because of any lack of pleasure for herself, but because of solicitude towards his own dry dividend.

'Look,' she said, after another anticlimactic encounter, 'armchair psychiatry and all of that, and Freud was a mispelling for fraud, but ... did you ever know anyone who had an abortion ... ?'

'Yes. Yes. I ...'

'Ah! We're getting somewhere ...'

'No. No, I mean it wasn't ...'

'Don't worry, love.' She cuddled closer. 'We ought to be able to talk about these things ...'

'No. I mean, it wasn't my baby she got rid of. It was Durry's ... or rather she didn't. He wanted her to. She called it Jack. So, actually, I'm sorry, no, I don't know anyone who's had an abortion ...'

'Oh. You see, I had this theory that the reason that you don't, you know, come, is that, deep down, you were terrified of getting someone pregnant. I thought, maybe, once you had ...'

'No. Er . . .'

'And you're not terrified of getting someone pregnant . . . ?'

He pushed himself away from her.

'You're not, are you, Anne?'

'No. How? I mean, in theory. Look, I'm thirty, you're thirty-five. If we wait any longer, we'll be able to put two walking frames together for a play-pen . . .'

'I'd never really decided whether I wanted to have children or not . . .'

'But you wouldn't mind, if we can overcome . . . if we can sort something out . . .'

'I don't think so.'

But he constantly replayed this conversation in the following days. He had suspected as soon as she said it that she was right. It seemed more and more plausible that, although he was an evolutionary mutant, the reason was not, as he had once arrogantly imagined, that his mental sensitivity had adjusted his body to provide fun only for his partners, but because he was subconsciously terrified of reproduction. He was particularly frightened of a son, who might, at worst, replicate his own limitations and failures, and, at best, be so much stronger, because of the dilution of the pooled genes, that he mocked his father for his weakness. Here, starkly, he had the answer. His sense of worthlessness had rendered him a self-contracepting human being.

Admitting the difficulty did not, immediately, fix it. But, although he never admitted to Anne the merit of her theory, she, perhaps suspecting success, would talk about his suitability for fatherhood, praise his articles, and laugh at his remarks. He was encouraged to complete sentences and express thoughts and ideas, like a student learning a new language. Graham slowly appreciated that she had begun a complete re-education, in which all of those tasks which he seemed to have avoided in his first marriage – like shopping, cleaning, washing, driving – were introduced to him in stages. Anne, for her part, believed that she was engaged in the long, slow process of making his behaviour compatible with his beliefs.

But what beliefs? It was a myth, a cruel American rumour, that self-discovery was automatically beneficial. Suppose, like Graham Sterling, you were horrified by what you found? His self-image had always been of himself as a liberal, unsullied by prejudice. And yet he had ended up despising and fearing his wife like the husbands in the kind of situation comedies he never watched; the kind he never watched because he thought that they were for the brainless proletariat, a sentiment which was a compounding extra sin of illiberalism. He had been, now he looked back, convinced that any man who made a gesture of kindness towards him was a homosexual, intent on sodomy. He involuntarily flinched when he passed a person of another colour in the street or, when he met a member of a different race socially, extended a fake, exaggerated kindness. From an ambitious blueprint, in adolescence, of universal tolerance, he was, now, not entirely able to convince himself that he had not become a chauvinist, misogynist, homophobe, racialist, and all those other villains of his morning newspaper.

He had obsessively suspected Eliza of infidelity, a contention for which no evidence existed. Indeed, it had been he who had his penis bitten on the kitchen floor by the estranged common-law wife of his best friend and who had allowed himself – no, that was unfair, he was relying again on the escape clause of passivity – who had adulterously fucked one of his colleagues in the draughty hall of residence in Sheffield. Did he hate all women or merely his unfortunate first wife? Ah, well, she would find out.

These realizations, allied to Anne's regimen, seemed to have a cathartic effect. One night, during their love-making, both Anne and Graham, almost simultaneously, grunted something like 'Yeah!', a version of a sportsman's roar of triumph. The impetus was novelty rather than, entirely, ecstasy. 'Good boy!' said Graham's wife/diagnostician. 'Er, thank you,' he gasped. Next morning, when Anne was in the bathroom, he surreptitiously inspected the proof of the dried-up pool on the undersheet.

And now, in Tuscany, in late July 1990, Anne was four months pregnant. Graham was adjusting to the knowledge. While she slept naked behind woodwormed shutters in the afternoon, he would stare at her fleshed-out belly and try to envisage the previously inconceivable being. His son – for he had a conviction that it would be a boy – would be bigger and slimmer than himself, with more luxuriant and durable hair. He would be picked first, instead of last, when football teams were being selected for PE. Confident but courteous in conversation, he would habitually pull out the clinching statistic which trounced the bore over the port. More in demand from women and, at the supplier's end, with more testosterone on tap, he would commit adultery without being discovered and without anyone else ever being upset. And of one thing above all Graham was convinced: he would not be a decent English liberal.

He would also, Graham hoped, not be a sufferer from Donne's Syndrome, as his expectant father still was. In the previous two years, Britain had become disturbingly prone to transport disasters: a ferry sank, a jumbo jet exploded, two trains crashed, a railway station blazed. Graham noticed a new social phenomenon by which people would claim to have avoided, by the merest quirk of circumstance, having been a passenger on the wrecked vessel. 'If I hadn't missed the train . . .' they would say. Or: 'If I hadn't had a conference at our other office . . .'

And yet, in most cases, Graham knew that the speakers never used the doomed routes. Why, then, was there this general need to feel spared, anointed, special? Was it an expression of what seemed to be the increasing improbability, in the twentieth century, of getting through the day without becoming a victim of illness, malevolence, or chance? There seemed to be more and more ways of dying. Was to be spared now regarded as a kind of secular blessing: there, but for the grace of Non-God?

However, even Graham found that he did not bear every reported death as grievously as he once had. These days, he could pass over a newspaper report of an estimated fifty thousand killed by death squads in Sri Lanka, or fifteen hundred drowned when a ferry in the Philippines capsized, without serious alarm. In a way, the best cure for Donne's Syndrome was news. As global populations expanded, so did information about their fates. However well meaning you were, it was not really possible to think: send not to know for whom the news flashes, it flashes for thee. Callousness was becoming natural to human beings. It was another Darwinist adjustment; upwards or downwards, depending on your prejudices.

Inevitably, they reached Death one night in Tuscany over the tagliatelli carbonara. Graham confessed the calculation he had made after Appleton's funeral.

'Statistically,' he explained, 'the chances of two people who know each other – who travel regularly on the same train – both dying young must be quite slight . . .'

'Mmmm,' said Durry. 'Unless the train crashes . . .'

'Oh, God,' Graham acknowledged. 'Yes, I hadn't thought of that . . .'

'I always remember breaking it to Russell about the Big D,' said Paula Waddle. 'His reaction was a lesson to us all, really. At his little school, Roger, the class guinea-pig, had fallen off his perch, or the guinea-pig equivalent. Mrs Walsh broke it quietly to the mums at night. Ben and I sat Russ down, our pockets full of chocolate bars, just in case. "Roger is dead," said Ben, solemnly, like, you know, them announcing George V had popped it on the radio. He was just about to do the spiel on guinea-pig-heaven, life cycles, and the replenishment of the earth when Russ piped up: "Oh good, we might get a black one next." Roger was tawny . . .'

'Bravo! What an epitaph! Roger was tawny,' Alastair declaimed, the grape already muddling his enunciation.

'Of course, it's tempting to believe,' said Ben Waddle, 'that there are more and more different ways of dying or being killed but, one, we simply know more about what's going on elsewhere and, two, I can never remember the figure, but millions and millions of men have died in wars this century, whole generations wiped out. We were spared that. We were even spared National Service . . .'

'Ben's right,' said Anne. 'Whatever Ally says about Germany, we live in a safer world than any of the last few lots. When I was a teenager, riding my horse, I used to imagine the English landscape radioactive. It was commonplace to think you wouldn't grow up . . . but, now, I mean, our children . . .'

She touched her stomach. The other mothers smiled indulgently.

'And never let us forget that it was nuclear weapons that won this peace,' said Timmy Duvet-Hogg, MP.

Durry jumped in, but Paula Waddle cut him off. 'Now, Timmy. You know the house rules. No first-use of nuclear weapons argument by anyone. It's kept the peace – or a kind of peace – for ten days now, and we're not throwing it away . . .'

'Oooh, when you're angry you remind me of Margaret,' Duvet-Hogg shivered theatrically.

'Bugger off,' said Paula.

'Margaret Thatcher,' said John Durry. 'Now there's a regrettable constant in an otherwise bizarrely changing world . . .'

'Ten more years! Ten more years!' half-sang Duvet-Hogg, with Rosinia as soprano backing. Alastair banged a pair of silver nutcrackers on the table in support.

'I fear you may be right,' grunted Durry. 'Unless someone shoots her . . .'

'The point is,' said Ben, 'getting back to what Anne said about peace is that, well, really, who would have thought, ten or twenty years ago, that, in 1990, we'd be talking about what things to spend all the money on that we don't need to spend on weapons any more . . .'

'Don't talk to me about the Peace Dividend,' said Alastair Macleod. 'It's madness. The Bear hasn't changed his spots, you mark my words . . .'

But, despite Alastair's attempt to keep the Cold War going, there was a general mood of optimism around the swimming pool during the day and the dining-table at nights. For Ben and Paula, Graham and Anne, it suddenly seemed easier to be liberals. Even Durry, who believed in neither the possession of military weapons (including non-nuclear ones) nor that the Soviet Union had ever invaded a country which had not invited it to, was less vulnerable on these points than he had been previously.

The treacherous subject of sex was also navigated safely, despite the presence of Graham and the fact that Duvet-Hogg was generally said to be sleeping with both his constituency and his House of Commons secretaries. It was, perhaps revealingly, Ben and Paula who spoke with most gusto and least embarrassment on the topic.

'Have you noticed when men talk about sex now...' said Ben, 'among men I know, that is, who talk about sex...'

'Not yourself, obviously...' Paula teased him.

'The odd thing is that the boast is not how many women they've had – as it would have been a few years ago – but how many orgasms they'd given this girl of theirs. So even male sensitivity becomes macho, a contest...'

'A pity all men don't compete, then,' muttered Hamster.

There was one subject which, despite intensive efforts at deflection, made an appearance during most meals. It was the poll tax (officially called the community charge): Margaret Thatcher's attempt to ensure that the cost of the services provided by the local council, from education to refuse collection, was divided equally between residents. In fact, as any Socialist could have told her, such equality was an elusive goal. Through quirks of local payment-calculation, the loaded Macleods would pay less for their British residences combined than Graham's incomeless widowed mother had been quoted for her solitary home. Graham, who now lived in a show-off Tory borough which had sold off its schools and privatized its services, was paying so little that guilt led him to consider moving to an area where he might pay more. That the new tax was a miscalculation was one of the few subjects on which all the guests easily agreed, though from perspectives as different as private greed and public spirit.

Even so, there were only two real conversational danger topics among the group. One was Salman Rushdie, the Indian-born British novelist who was in hiding, under armed guard, after a death threat from the spiritual leader of Iran for alleged blasphemy against Islam in a novel called *The Satanic Verses*.

'Are you aware of the stuff he wrote and said about Margaret and the British police?' Timmy Duvet-Hogg, MP, asked more than once. 'He can pay for his own damn protection, if you ask me . . .'

'Ah, now,' replied Ben Waddle. 'I thought we were supposed to be proud of living in a democracy. Anyway, it's entirely pernicious to go on about the cost of protecting him. We're all paying, already, God knows how much to provide round-the-clock Rottweilers for minor members of the Royal Family and forgotten politicians. Why don't *they* pay for their own security . . . ?'

'Well, I tried reading that book,' Hamster volunteered, 'and I couldn't get past page thirteen . . .'

'Yes, well, you have to be a little careful, Hamster, on that one,' said Ben. 'I mean, the death threat wasn't actually literary criticism, you know. "A grave disappointment after his earlier work" – *Tehran Times*. I assume that none of us here actually believes that writers whose books we don't like therefore automatically deserve to die . . .'

'That's a pretty debating point,' interrupted John Durry. 'But the question isn't whether this might have been a blasphemous book, but whether it is a racist one. I think it's a pity that Rushdie, a non-white himself, of course, should have provided such a convenient focus for hostility to British Moslems . . .'

'Hostility to them,' spluttered Ben. 'What about their fucking hostility towards him . . . ?'

'Boys, boys,' Hamster crooned.

'What do you think, Graham?' asked Durry, shrewdly diverting the fire.

'I, er, I suppose I believe in freedom of speech, don't I?' replied Graham.

'Well, Moslems are exercising it, no?' Durry asked.

'John, leave Graham alone,' Paula said. 'Graham's right. It's perfectly possible, in this, to believe in freedom of speech, subject to the laws of libel and, in this case, murder ...'

'What about the laws of blasphemy?' asked Durry.

'Ah, yes, well, that's tricky,' Paula conceded. 'I won't deny that there's a problem with the laws of blasphemy. Probably, yes, in the end they should apply to all our Gods or none, but certainly not just ours ... not that I personally, actually, you know, believe, but ...'

'What I really want to know,' Hamster wondered, 'is how did he get those funny eyelids ...'

'There's a joke at the House,' said Timmy Duvet-Hogg. 'Question: What's the cruellest thing you can do to your enemy? Answer: shout out "God, Salman, you've changed!" on Bradford station ...'

Alastair Macleod hit the table with a spoon to demonstrate his approval of this humour.

'In the end,' said Ben Waddle, 'and I'm sorry our resident MP doesn't begin to see this, what it comes down to is that a British citizen is unable to walk the streets of his own country ...'

'A sort of British citizen,' said Alastair.

'A British citizen. ...' insisted Ben.

'Cheese or ice-cream, anyone?' Paula intervened.

The other reliable flashpoint was any reference to their own political pasts. The Nice People's Party had officially been disbanded three months earlier, nine years after its foundation.

'In these last ten years,' said Ben Waddle one evening, 'Thatcher has got away with the crime of the century. Domination without opposition. And we were accomplices in that crime ...

us, shunting between hopeless parties, John rendering another unelectable . . .'

'That's classic short-termism, Ben,' complained Durry. 'Historically, it will be seen. . .'

'Yes, it's true, we were not helped by the voting system,' continued Ben. 'But might we not also have been short of a motivating idea beyond a vague belief in things being a bit fairer and nicer? We were so frightened of prejudice or dogma that all our thinking steered a rough course between extremes. I wonder if it's possible that all opinions, ideas – decent ones – depend on prejudices. Where what we had was the steady drip-drip-drip of liberal humanism . . .'

'I'm not sure that's entirely fair,' said Graham. Everybody laughed. When Graham saw the joke, he looked down and examined his napkin. He was glad of Anne's squeeze of his hand.

Duvet-Hogg asked, from what were probably show-off motives, whether any of them had ever dreamed of being politicians. Ben and Alastair owned up, while Graham and, unusually, Durry tried to look as if the question had not been meant for them.

'I think,' said Ben, 'and I'm not intending to be rude to Timmy, that it's something you grow out of. Look, if you think about it, it's very hard for any politician to make a lasting impact . . .'

'Well, it's hard for anyone to make a *lasting* impact,' said Anne. Graham thought of Appleton.

'Yes. Yes, all right,' Ben agreed. 'But politicians think they're going to. The whole idea of politics is that they will. And, in fact, could anyone here name me one single achievement of, oh, Macmillan or Alec Douglas-Home . . .'

'Oooh, you wouldn't say that if you were a pheasant or a grouse,' Durry smirked.

'Or really any British politician apart from Churchill?' Ben went on. 'In fact, I would suggest that the only way to change a country absolutely is to lose or win a war. And a war of national self-defence, not like the Falklands . . .'

'Rot!' insisted Alastair Macleod. 'You just never understood what the Falklands was all about. It had, sod all, frankly, to do with what colour passports sheepshaggers got. It was about Margaret teaching the world that it couldn't kick sand in our faces . . .'

'Putting the Great back into –' began Timmy Duvet-Hogg.

'Oh, please, not that bloody cliché,' Durry interrupted him.

'I suppose John F. Kennedy is generally remembered,' Ben developed his theme. 'But not for anything he did, more for what he might have done if he hadn't been shot. So, in a sense, he owes his reputation to Lee Harvey Oswald. Assassination or battle? Dead young and remembered, alive old and forgotten or alive and remembered with the blood of your countrymen on your hands? Wow. Talk about multiple choice . . .'

Graham wondered, from these words, whether Ben was also subject to the questionnaire. 'Maybe that's what they mean about politics consisting of hard choices,' his friend continued. 'The point I'm making is that almost no peace-time politicians actually make any difference. You get some basic choices – will I have inflation or unemployment? Remember those fifth-form graphs – but, otherwise, economies throw up waves, which you might be lucky enough to ride. You're not God. You're a surfer . . .'

'Mmmm, but isn't it the fault of politicians for thinking in terms of immortality?' said Anne Sterling. 'What's wrong with just minding the shop for a few years and passing it on in decent shape, like the MD of a famous company? Try to avoid bankruptcy and take-overs but don't expect to remake the place in your own image . . .'

'Anyway,' challenged Timmy Duvet-Hogg. 'Who says all politicians want immortality? I don't want to be remembered. I want to be known. And sucked up to . . .'

'And sucked off,' giggled Rosinia.

This line of enquiry broke down. The conversation changed

to their political allegiances now. Graham was seriously considering joining the Green Party – Anne was already signed up – but he did not risk admitting this.

Ben said: 'I sort of feel that those of us who joined the Nice People's Party, who really, let's remember this, believed in it, should be excused from politics for the next ten years, like jurors in a particularly gruesome trial. I think I may have come to the conclusion, which is exactly what I've never wanted to believe, that politics is just self-interest. It may occasionally be necessary for a politician, in pursuit of his ambition, to do something altruistic, but that's about as far as it goes. We are opposed to nuclear weapons not because we think they are absolutely morally wrong but because we have read articles on fall-out and do not want to die. We give money to medical charities as a kind of shifty superstition against being stricken ourselves. We secretly appreciate Thatcherism, because, in opposition, we can moan about public spending priorities while benefiting from tax cuts . . .'

'Great speech,' said Duvet-Hogg. 'You should have been a politician!'

Graham agreed with a lot of what Ben had said, although he would not have gone quite so far. Even after all Anne's therapy, he still found difficulty in either holding opinions or in expressing them. It frightened him that already, five months into his second marriage, he was subject to spells of insecurity about Anne's love. Why was he incapable of believing in anyone or anything? He feared that he was, in some absolute sense that went beyond politics, a Don't Know; in some absolute sense that went beyond religion, an unbeliever.

And yet, perhaps, in the world which was emerging, this would matter less. As the countries of Eastern Europe proclaimed democracy, maybe it really would be a future in which only those who adhered to one creed – the ideology of decency – would prosper. The march of the Nice People might have been halted in Britain but there was reason to believe that it was proceeding everywhere else. Nelson Mandela, whose poster had been on the college walls of the liberals at the dinner party, had walked free from his twenty-seven-year cell. Now there was talk of the dismantling of apartheid in South Africa. Graham's secret *alter ego*, the shabby electrician Lech Walesa, had even become President of Poland. Graham hoped that, in this new world, just as there would be less need for nuclear weapons, so there would be less need for opinions, for the taking of sides.

And, anyway, he would bullishly tell himself, what was so bad about being a Don't Know? You only had to look at the trouble caused by the Knows. Margaret Thatcher had been a Know. Ronald Reagan had been a Know. The Ayatollah Khomeinie had been a Know. It was not an impressive record.

On the Thursday of his first week in Tuscany, Graham joined Ben in the kitchen of the farmhouse to search for the BBC World Service on the radio. They were trying to find the cricket scores. They heard the World News first. The newsreader announced the headline in a voice of special heaviness.

'Oh,' said Graham.

'Yes. I know,' said Ben.

It was another day when clouds had mounted a flying picket of the sun and shirts and even jerseys were worn around the pool.

'Any news?' asked Paula. 'Non-cricket news?'

'Yes,' said Graham. 'Kuwait's been invaded by . . .' He looked round for help from Ben.

'Iran. I mean, Iraq. Er, yes, Iraq, it would be, wouldn't it . . . ?' clarified Ben.

'Is that . . . Russell, stay away from that bush, it's full of nasty sting-stings . . . is that the Ayatollahs?'

'That's Iran,' said Durry. 'Easily confused. What's a consonant between friends? Quite a lot, actually. Iraq-q-q was a friend and customer of the West during its war against Iran-n-n . . .'

Durry had in his luggage the completed manuscript of *Love You To Death*. Graham tried not to think that the new world

258

situation would help sales of Durry's book. Failing not to think about it, his next attempt was to keep envy from his reflections.

'Well,' said Hamster, after a while, 'it's unlikely to affect us . . .'

'There's always trouble for someone,' said Ben Waddle, in a cod Northern accent.

Russell Waddle ran over and playfully punched his father's surging girth.

And, as John Durry spoke of hypocritical Western arms dealers, Graham felt helpless again. As a boy, he had dreamed, as most children in democracies surely do, of becoming Prime Minister. Occasionally, watching the television news, he would try to imagine himself as part of that world of handshakes, statements, speeches, wars, and peace conferences. But it would never be. There were two groups of people in the world – the powerful and the overpowered – and he belonged to the second category.

Bloody Margaret

'She is without doubt the most significant female historical figure since Bloody Mary.'

LORD HAILSHAM OF SAINT MARYLEBONE, 1989

'Many of the big animals of Africa – eland and buffalo, warthog and rhino – are attended by oxpeckers, birds that belong to the starling family... They scuttle over its body, picking off fleas and ticks and maggots... But the birds are not an unqualified benefit. Blood is a major part of their diet... And they are not always content to take it second-hand.'

DAVID ATTENBOROUGH – *The Trials of Life*

Bloody Margaret

1

Blackpool (1987)

'BOADICEA to Imperial.' My radio crackles with these words. 'Roger,' I acknowledge, the boy in me still rising to the line. I admit that the cult of the portable telephone – businessmen dialling from trains and even the street – has slightly reduced the uniqueness you got used to as a policeman: of speaking into your sleeve. From a bird-shitted window in this office in the Blackpool Winter Gardens, glumly stuck with posters puffing long-dead double-acts, I look down at the crowd.

Most of them, it seems, are pensioners, scarved and overcoated against a sea-fret cruel even for bloody October in bleedin' Blackpool. I think, as you always do: Will it be today? Is her Hinckley, her Lee Harvey Oswald, or that one with the foreign name that shot the other Kennedy, down there in the shadow of the rock shop? Blackpool rock. Some shithead sick of his own uselessness sticking her pictures in a scrapbook in a bedsit stinking of armpit and fart. 'Boadicea at Imperial,' my radio croaks. I am her bodyguard.

In a traffic jam, the black episcopal Rover, as big and shiny as a South African bishop, is stalled for several minutes. Some old biddy, out shopping, gapes in, her teeth – my dear, her teeth! – as rough and discoloured as, ironically, brown sugar. Do they have brown sugar in these parts? She smiles and does a nod, more reverential than friendly, of the kind that women of her class still give to clergymen. I beam back. My hand begins to twitch towards a full-scale blessing but I decide it might be ostentatious and halt it by my solid silver pectoral cross.

It seems safer. I have not often before been to the Northern parts of England. I wonder, not for the first time since this all began, whether the old dear would still smile if she knew where I was going. What do the people think of my mistress? Is she just some fiscal fruit machine showing three lemons, a crazed television game show host doling out consumer durables? For the moment. For the moment. Do they – to use the word prevalent in those works of populist theology which aim, the heavens help us, to sell copies – love her? I am her priest.

Mornin', mornin', mornin'. 'Ow's the cold, John? Oh, dear. You want a nip of something for that. What's that, John? Is it official government advice? Let's say sources close to the Prime Minister. OK, settle down now. Sorry it's a bit cramped 'ere. Not our customary, um, palatial arrangements, I know. Now, prison riots. The government stresses that it has spent more on the prison system than any previous administration. If prisoners behave like animals, they will be treated like animals.

Reminds me. I said to an old bloke in the Pig and Whistle at the weekend: 'What do you think of these prisoners rioting?' He says: 'It's scandalous. They want locking up.' Well, you might say at the moment, they're proving that they do. However, in 'er speech to conference this afternoon, the Prime Minister will . . . Surrounded by journalists, famished for scraps, speaking off the record at a meeting which officially has never taken place, I am her Chief Press Secretary.

One potato, two potato, three potato, four, Snobby Roberts is a whore . . . We'd have said foo-er, and who-er then, of course. Some of us still do. Though most of our accents have come a long way since Kesteven and Grantham Girls' School. Hers further than most. Who–er was just lasses' spite. Lads were in short supply where we lived and Margaret wasn't even in the market. I sometimes think that may explain her liking for slightly fast men, the blazer and Brylcreem types: the one that got his secretary in the pudding club, the one that paid the tart to scarper. Somewhere in her mind she's running to the bikesheds with them after class.

I have my television switched on to catch her speech this afternoon. We, I suppose, watch her with a special fascination. Maybe the old chums – though chummy she never was – of the great and good always say this but, if we could have voted for one lass from our year to run the country, she wouldn't have made the Top Ten. We'd have been too frightened – frit! (remember when she suddenly said that in the House of Commons?) – of a Snobby Britain in her own image.

For this afternoon's engagement, we have selected, after a brief flirtation with a two-piece in cruise-missile grey, the usual Tory-blue suit, set off by her husband's pearls. One of her favourite combinations, particularly when the Nuremberg revival comes to Blackpool or Brighton. We've ditched the shoulder padding, an experiment during the last general election to make her head look smaller. One of her difficulties, from a dressing point of view, is that her bonce is unnaturally large. I said to her once: 'Don't fret, petal, it's all them brains inside it!' I'd like to tell you that she laughed.

Equally, from the fashion purist's point of view, the bullet-proof vest is a bit of a minus but Special Branch won't budge. So we sort of work round it, those layers of flounce on the blouse. Otherwise she'd look stacked like Jayne Mansfield. At least she gets away with it better than old President Reagan. You'd have thought he had a door down his shirtfront or a ledge for putting drinks on. Her knickers will be – this is not a leak, she has said it on national television – from Marks & Spencer. A bit cheap, completely non-erotic, but won't let you down in a crisis. Bit like her, really. Stop it, I'm being a bitch. I am her Image Man.

*

Hair and skin grow back softer, like a baby's. But babies are lucky; they don't know how they should look. I remember, in the day rooms, patients from the cancer wards fluffing up their down – like bum-fluff it was at first – above their collars. Checking it was still there, like buggers going bald. Of course, even with your bandages, like Claude bloody Rains, and the sodding throbbing all the time, and the parts where nothing hurt or felt at all, you knew they envied you. We just had a long time getting better, mostly better; they couldn't talk about time. I still find mirrors difficult, though not as hard as strangers in the street.

The thing about mirrors is – people say getting old is seeing the face of your Mam and Dad, like when you're washing or shaving. Our way is queerer, watching your young face come back. Well, most of it. Well, some of it. I have about one and a half ears now, which they say will be my lot. I'm not complaining. I can turn it to advantage, like Nelson's eye, listening to what they say about our war with my half ear. Perhaps I will direct it towards her speech this afternoon. I'm not specially bitter about her. I count myself lucky. An estimated seven further operations will put back some more of my face, though not so that a girl would want the light on. I can get up stairs, slowly, and past stares, daring them to look away.

Some of the other poor sods have got the worst of it, not knowing when you might shit your knickers, that kind of thing. Oh, yes, some of the other buggers – I'll get in before you do – are dead. Getting over that was the first hard part. The being lucky. You begin to understand that thing you read about, that thing that never makes sense, of Jews who got out of the death camps alive, committing suicide, years later. I understood that, in there. The day I started pulling through was when I realized the irony of it. The ones with cancer sitting there, groaning, somewhere inside, 'Why me?', and us, the lucky buggers, moaning 'Why not me?' The question now is: why any of us?

Oh, before you pounce, before the Paper That Supports Our Boys jumps on us, I know it was part of our deal. I'm not moaning. But I do think that those of us who got out can say, for the sakes of those that didn't, that there hasn't been very much of Remembering Them in the morning and at the going down of the sun or any other time, really. I was her soldier.

I am rubbing the head of the Conservative Party Chairman. Now I am rubbing across his stomach and, briskly, between his legs, against the hard bulge there. I give him a last brush with my duster and return him to the shelf. I am her cleaner, with special responsibility for her treasured collection of porcelain.

Inside the Empress Ballroom, where she will perform in ninety minutes, the faithful, loath to lose their places for the Apotheosis, have brought sandwiches today and stayed in their places through lunch. The Empress Ballroom. Almost her ideal setting, although she once launched one of her Inner-City Initiatives (whatever happened to them?) in the Winston Churchill Suite of the Queen Elizabeth II Conference Centre, the most name-dropping location in British politics.

I have spoken to my news desk, who want seven hundred words of colour by 7 p.m. There is plenty of colour. Young men in bulging waistcoats, tiny Union Jack paper hats perched on their fat heads like cherries on a cake, a strand of elastic slicing their second chins, are standing on their chairs. They are rhythmically throwing out and pulling back their arms at a slant above shoulder level, in a gesture like ... I am a wet liberal, who is paralysed by what she has made of this country, so let me say: in a gesture like that of someone reaching for a book from a topmost shelf. A German book, say, published in the 1930s.

'Maggie! Maggie! Maggie! Oi! Oi! Oi!' they are chanting. On the platform, someone is testing the inevitable autocue. A state-of-the-art affair involving slanting perspex reflectors like oblong ping-pong bats, it is a trick picked up from her long-time international political contemporary in the White House. Skilled apotheosis-organizers – Jesus Christ would be alive today if these guys had run a Jerusalem branch back then – her team have left little to the market of chance and ambush in which politicians operate but have banked without the organist. Evidently a closet lefty, he eases his keys into Kander and Ebb's 'Come to the Cabaret', a tactless selection from the juke-box of right-wing tunes. Busy with some truculent bunting on the platform, her image men, ignorant of popular culture – art, even of this coin, is for wimps, pooves, stay-a-beds – let it go. I am a – definitely not *her* – journalist.

Oh, God, the stench, from their breath and beneath! Picnic claret, in dinky plastic bottles, and expensive perfume, never quite masking the olfactory evidence of quite disastrous under-arms. If you were to ask me what is the single greatest price to be paid for political power, I would say to you, with regard to my own party at least, it is this: the Tory Women. The party conference is a penance, even if, like I, one tips the schedule towards partying over conferring.

Tanned from my month in a still unspoiled part of Tuscany, I plunge among them on their stalls – packed, teeming, and pungent as a street bazaar in the Third World on a television documentary – outside the Empress Ballroom. It is dark and lonely work but the ambitious have to do it. My party asks it. Party! Of all the ridiculous coincidences in English, a language which is rich in them, there can be none odder than the use of the single word 'party' to describe a private grouping of people most of whom like each other and a public grouping of people most of whom don't. I am asked to guess the weight of the cake; a flat and compact curranty number about an inch thick. Trained in opinion polls and the deployment of government statistics, I very nearly say two tons but catch my tongue in time.

The stunt is, I suppose, for charity, although it is hard to guess which one. It is not, in fact, impossible that it is part of a new government policy for the funding of the National Health Service by jumble sales. 'Let them weigh cake!' Perhaps I was omitted from that particular cabinet sub-committee at which she, *primus inter pares*, decided this. The ladies chuckle unbecomingly as they enter my guess in their book. Their twinkles tell me that it is a quite improbable estimate but a man who does not know such things is, by their parameters, a real man. The wife he cheats on with his secretary fails to trouble his great and nation-serving brain with cake information, cookery chat, and that is good. The ladies are, this afternoon, even more tumescent than usual, as they always are before She addresses them. For She comes, they believe, from their own bosom. (A formidable organ. Did child ever suckle there or man foreplay?) But in this belief, they are, as I hope to explain, mistaken.

I almost never watch television – we only have it for the lads; Sheila and I are wireless people – but we enjoy those wildlife programmes by that chap with the quiet voice and sweaty shirt. In one of them, he covered the human-Hoover service provided to the bigger buggers of nature by something called oxpeckers. The deal is that the tweeters clean away the rubbish but they want blood in return (not unlike the dustbin men in Labour boroughs, eh?)

I stored the image away. For we, all of us who attend our leader in our different humble ways, are her rhinoceros birds. That analogy, I'm afraid, makes Margaret a rhinoceros, but there we are. It also, if you think about it, makes us bloodsuckers. For my part, I was for quite some years – to the surprise of political journalists who habitually predicted my imminent reshuffling – her loyal (well, -ish) minister. I am now without portfolio, though not, but whisper it, without ambition.

I find it hard to offer you a comparison for the quickening within me as I anticipate Margaret's speech this afternoon. The nearest analogy would be the periods when I was first courting my two wives. A not-long-until-I-see-her-now sensation. A difficulty in concentrating on any other matter, a mind which keeps returning to her face. Of course, in the case of one's spouses, there was also an element of not-long-until-I-have-her. Can I just make clear that, whatever some facetious liberal journalists suggest, sexual attraction is only a very small part of the emotions felt towards Margaret by myself and other members of the Hard And Straight Group (a reference, incidentally, to the way in which we feel government policy should proceed) among Conservative MPs? I am her loyal, ultra-loyal, back-bencher.

'Boadicea from Imperial, ten minutes.' Again, I give Roger a name-check. Who was Roger, I often wonder? Some kid assistant of Alexander Graham Bell's? Is that it? So, if he'd had a girl working for him, there'd be grown policemen standing around saying 'Suzy' every time they got a message. In posh circles, Roger means a fuck, doesn't it? Although, in fact, I worked with a Roger, in Fraud Squad, who's common as a cold, but who the same applies to. From my perch, I look for Boadicea's black 3.5 litre chariot. When I say I am her body-guard, I mean, of course, that I am one of many. The cost of policing this conference is £1.5 million, half of it from the rates of those who hate her. The thin blue line is deep and wide. More coppers than a charity collection. A canny crook could clean out Lancashire today.

A black Jaguar brakes, bears left, takes the corner by a poster announcing next week's attraction, a brace of Northern comics called Hammer and Bolt. As the car passes, the crowd crushed behind the barriers has no way of knowing that they are venerating a Special Branch officer in a yellow wig; the man we call – not, I reckon, without some justice – the Dummy. That is an operational term. As the Jaguar accelerates down a side-street, some young buggers start a chant. A number have that queer hair-do: stiff, painted pricks in the middle of bald bonces. Mohican, is it? Others wear canvas jackets thick with badges. Left-wing shit-stirrers, I shouldn't wonder. 'Cunt!' they are screaming. 'Cunt! Cunt! Cunt!'

This is technically an offence against public order and a party official approached us at a previous conference with a view to

274

arrests. The guvnor, after due consideration, took the view that it was best regarded as free speech. The word was, he said, anyway, an acknowledgement of her single unique attribute among British Prime Ministers. Don't get me wrong. The guvnor's not a Liberal or anything. This was an individual operational decision. 'Cunt! Cunt! Cunt!' they screech. The old dears, almost certainly too deaf to think this other than three cheers, are shouting only 'Maggie! Maggie! Maggie!' I lift the radio to my lips again. 'Dummy to Winter.'

A cry is carried on the wind as my Rover follows the signs towards the Winter Gardens, past the Imperial Hotel. Although fate once nearly delivered me to a theological college higher up than Suffolk, I have always previously succeeded in performing God's works in the South of England. So this, then, is Blackpool. How apt. One understands that, in the United States of America, a town called Condom or Enema may turn out to be perfectly amenable, but English cartography seems to be less metaphorical. I do not think that Blackpool is a metaphor but rather a literal description. Black pool. In ancient times, there was a large stretch of dark water here and now there is this leisure resort. The Winter Gardens beckon and the cry becomes decipherable. It is, I realize with dread, a voluble reference to the feminine pudenda. *Dominus vobiscum, dominus vobiscum,* I murmur to myself as a purgative.

It seems increasingly probable that I will have to marry the burly policeman who, each morning and lunchtime this week, has subjected me to the very public heavy petting which is disguised as security at Conservative Party conferences. Looking for suspicious bulges in your trousers, the police are not always as gentle as they might be with the unsuspicious ones. Several journalists more celebrated than myself, furious at apparently not being believed to be the person whom the officer must surely know they were, have already devoted whole columns to the repressive protection on display here. Well, no policeman does or should know me from a nutter with gelignite packed up his bum but I do wonder if we're not in to designer paranoia here.

I mean, to some extent, it's a risk she takes if she wants to be a *grande fromage*, as they say. The screen around her is getting to be like a permanent sick note for Games. I've been nosing around on the security here. I've discovered a funny thing and a serious thing. The light fact is that her Special Branch codename at this conference is Boadicea. They're neat, these radio identifications. President Ronald Reagan's, for a while, was Rawhide. And the entourage of the Rev. Jesse Jackson, during the present American presidential race, is known to have objected to his alloted tag of Pontiac, a make of car popularly acrosticked by Americans into Poor Old Nigger Thinks It's A Cadillac. Short-wave racism, perhaps; a warning to the black man not to aspire to the presidential limousine? However, there is little chance of her supporters objecting to Boadicea.

Now the heavy thing that I have discovered this morning is that the overall cost of the security for this five-day conference is £2.25 million: police overtime, food and grooming for a whole bloody Cruft's of sniffer dogs; a Navy frigate grimly tramping the coast of Blackpool in case the Boyos have started up an aquatic wing. She is the best-protected politician in history. She is also, of course, the one that has most need of it. Oh, few people would grudge her some of that two and a quarter million. Most even theoretical democrats would expect the Prime Minister to be as bomb-proof as possible. Imagine if she had been cleaning her teeth that night in Brighton in 1984 when her fourth-floor bathroom hit the basement. And it would be harsh to say that the Irish threat was one she had brought on herself. Superannuated Socialist politicians now quite forgotten are still, at the taxpayers' expense, not allowed to go to the lavatory away from home without a sniffer dog going first.

Forget the Boyos for the moment. There's something else you see in this job: the hatred she inspires not from the Irish but from the English, a feeling deeper than any previous Prime Minister has ever known. It is convenient to suggest that the reason for her not doing walkabouts is the terrorist threat but it is equally the danger from the electorate – fists, eggs, paint, and spittle, and the kinds of weapons which run on a timeless time-fuse. She went walkabout in Australia once – walkabout in that country usually means alone, in the desert, at the mercy of dingos, but no such luck – and was nearly lynched. 'A lot of Provos and Homos,' her Chief Press Secretary is reported to have said, unattributably of course, his bluff Northern accent making both social groupings sound like Greek *hors-d'oeuvres*.

That would be the conventional view in government and authority: Lefties, benders, shit-stirrers. But suppose it isn't just an easily dismissable minority but a deep seething, silting up slowly like coral: a terminated work-force here, an unjust Budget there, a piece of primitively queer-bashing legislation here, some over-keen policemen somewhere else. During the Election this year, one of her ministers, out campaigning, limped, still wincing visibly from a Brighton-shattered hip, in to a crowd of jobless youth. 'Brighton! Brighton! Brighton! Brighton!' they taunted him. Where does such raw hatred come from? Where does it go?

Inside the conference hall, the subversive organist has switched to 'The Lady is a Tramp', which is a little, though not a lot, better.

In the press centre, on the tapes, 'senior government sources' are rubbishing those here and elsewhere in the world who have views different from hers. Where can it have originated, this anonymous mocking?

She is certainly not one for chattering as she sits in the electric bath. I minister now to most of the great ladies of our age – and, by a postal scheme, to female leaders on the sub-continent also – and some of them, they gossip like nobodies. Not her. Once a month she comes here. She wears a swimsuit, to be private. 'Madame Arcati,' she said to me once. 'Only my hus-

band and my bathroom wall see me without my clothes on.'
Such a lovely sense of humour she has. The system I employ
is called Ayurveda. It is of Hindu origin. Flower oils mainly,
you see, for the skin and the hair and the eyes. I have added
to this the bath.

A lot of your papers say I am electrocuting your Prime Minister – I think some of them would think this was a good idea –
but this is nonsense. My ladies are not in any danger. They sit
and a small charge of electric is passed through the water. The
result is a release of energy. And also an eternal youthfulness.
Often in the street it is being said to me that my daughter is
my mother. I tell this to my famous lady and she laughs. Such
a lovely sense of humour she has. She herself is a mother. I
think this is so important to what she has done. Call me
Madame. I am her Ayurveda teacher.

'Boadicea to Winter. One minute Winter.' The work-shy down
below, perhaps sensing her arrival in the sudden busyness of
the police lining the street, take up their song again: 'Cunt!
Cunt! Cunt!' Foulmouthed fuckpigs. Also, it has to be accepted
that, because of our radios, policemen watching the crowd
crackle just before anything happens, like that satisfying sound
you get when running the metal-detector over someone for
guns or explosives, although usually, of course, you have a pretty
good idea as soon as you hear their Paddy accent.

On that point, incidentally, there has been a lot of gossip in
the press about, I may have got the numbers wrong, the Guildford Four, the Birmingham Six, the Magnificent Seven and
very probably, I wouldn't wonder, the Famous Five. There is
talk of forensic errors, of members of Her Majesty's Constabu-
lary falsifying confessions. OK, let me just make two points
about this. One, for security reasons, the public do not have,
and cannot possibly be allowed, the full range of information
on any given issue. If those Micks didn't do what we said they
did at the time, they almost certainly did something else. Forgive
me, ladies, but if it wasn't that shit on their boxers, it was some

other shit. Two, both forensic scientists and interviewing police officers are, given the cesspit of a world in which we live, overworked. Sometimes, OK, they're going to cross the wrong i or dot the wrong t. Written evidence is not intended to be pored over like some little poem at school.

The kind of stuff the newspapers are printing about mistaken imprisonment reduces respect for the police force and, if that happens, we are all losers. Better one innocent man hung, than ninety-nine others mistrusting the system. Of course, I'm just a dumb plod but I think you'll find that a lot of distinguished judges agree with me.

I have now moved to a window at the rear of the room. Well, you didn't think we were going to let her drive through those fuckpigs down there, did you? Ah, now I've eyeballed the car. We have our own way of talking in the force. We always say 'eyeballed' instead of 'saw'.

I suppose, if you want to make an issue out of it, our way's actually more bother – the word *is* longer – but there you are. Her car – a black Daimler – is accompanied by police outriders. It is an impressive sight. The drivers have a system of blowing whistles to communicate with each other as they change formation. I have never worked on Traffic – and, please God and Freemasonry, never will – but it is certainly something to witness. To eyeball. I have never seen a ballet but I think a ballet must look like that.

Conspicuous as the only clergyman in the building, I take my seat in the hall. Several of the purple-permed ladies give me the kind of smile that you usually have to be a baby or disabled to secure. I suppose that my presence lends them a certain reassurance. A kind of moral equivalent of: Le patron mange ici. I wonder why it seems to matter so much to them – to her particularly, I feel – to be told that God is a member of the party. Is it just an English social reflex? Or does she actually believe that she is guided by God, that she rules, if not precisely by divine right, then by divine preference? Contrary to what you might think, I would consider that bad for business. The most dangerous leaders are those, of any faith, who think they have an extra hot-line on their desks, not available to their rivals or predecessors. It doesn't really matter if the voice they think they hear belongs to that whom or that which we choose, in our Church, to call God. Hearing voices is a bad idea for politicians, full stop.

Oh, God, no, as I move towards my seat, I am spied by my constituency secretary, doubtless intent on bearding me, as she would certainly put it, about my views on hanging. We differ on this issue. I am against it in all cases; many of my constituents are against it only in the cases of crimes committed by unbaptized babies. My constituency secretary is particularly zealous, having, at a meeting this week, promoted the idea of a 'retrospective death penalty', applied to most of those already in jail, who, in her words, 'slipped through the net' between the abolition of the death penalty and what she hopes will be its restoration. Oh, the sour penances of power. Surreptitiously, I consult my watch. Two minutes to the Triumphal Entry of The Leader. I will never have been so glad to see her.

Six of us in the Hard And Straight Group are sitting in a row, where she can see us, for encouragement, when she looks down. By a combination of being early in the queue and strategic smarming to the organizing committee, we have ensured far better seats for ourselves than any of the Wets. Even historical legends need reassurance sometimes. We have sent a bouquet of red carnations to the stage door from the Hard And Straight members. And, if she should pass by us afterwards as she leaves, one of us might say: 'You look particularly sparkling today, Prime Minister.' Already I have an erection.

Munching a second biscuit – comfort eating, I know – I turn the set to one of the two sides showing Snobby's speech. The man from the television is saying that in this afternoon's speech she will set out her policies for the next four or five years. It comes home to you when it's put like that. I often think that other folks whose classmates go on to be famous – film stars and announcers and so on – probably feel a bit of envy, a bit of you'd-not-have-thought-it-of-them but we feel something different. A sort of dread.

I am not going to sit at the press benches, which are set to one side of the sky blue podium with its slogan: THE NEXT STEP FORWARD. I wonder if, in a liberal newspaper, I could get away with a joke about it being a goosestep. I sit instead between two anticipatory shire matrons in the middle of the auditorium. Such infiltration can be risky. During the education debate this week, a colleague and I were the only two people in the body of the hall not to join in the ovation for the minister. 'Ah,' said one of the applauders, 'you must be teachers.' It seemed self-evident to them that the more their education policy displeased the teachers, the better it must be. Ah, here she comes . . .

Oh, Lord, look at those constituency bosoms pumped out with pride. To what extent do they begin to suspect the heterodoxy of me, their elected representative. I no more represent them than a broken mirror represents a face. Yes, not a bad conceit. I may use it in a freelance article, applying it to the Leader of the Opposition.

Oh, God, in your wisdom, give her humility to rule with reference to the needs of others . . .

Maggie! Maggie! Maggie! Oi! Oi! Oi!

Beautiful in blue, not looking in any way at all the sixty-two she will be next week, a walking advertisement she is giving me for the Ayurveda method. Soon – such is the demand from clients – I will need to buy another bath!

*

281

Bonkers, she looks, if you ask me. Smooth for sixty-two, admittedly, and improbably alert for the three hours' sleep she claims to take, but a quality of derangement emanates from her. Although it may be hard to find a way of saying so in my seven hundred words of colour. Bonkers and derangement are clinically inaccurate, liberally indefensible words, I know, but I really think she may be, as an American journalist put it to me when we were covering her visit to Reagan earlier this year, a few tacos short of a combination platter.

In my opinion, prolonged exposure to power always takes the same toll. And this applies whether you are elected three times in a row, as she has just been, or whether you seize power in a military coup and successfully prevent subsequent disgruntled generals from taking it away from you. Given the modern security cocoon – and, in her case, a refusal to read newspapers other than through the sanitized cuttings service provided by her chief press secretary – there is no reason to believe that she retains much access to reality. And her cyclical winnowings-out of dissent in the cabinet, when allied to the argumental cowardice of ambitious ministers, guarantee that she rarely hears disagreement. Democracies should never forget that their leaders may, between or despite check-ups from the electorate, become quite as removed from their roots as long-term dictators who take to drinking their own urine and shooting anyone who disagrees with them. The consequences are less grave, but the condition is the same.

How sensible America's two-term rule now looks. If you doubt it, ask yourself who were the two American Presidents to wonder aloud to their aides if the regulation might be changed to permit the public four more years of them. Richard Milhous Nixon and Ronald Wilson Reagan: a crook and a crock. As for our Margaret Hilda, that incident the night before the election this June, when she suddenly started snarling about people who 'drool and drivel that they care' looked suspiciously like the scene in all werewolf movies when the effects of the full moon begin to show. Is it in *Hamlet*, that line about how madness in great ones should not unwatched go? Anyway, I am a journalist, not a psychiatrist, and this discussion must wait, for, the euphoria turned down to simmer for the moment, she is beginning to speak ...

'A lot has happened since we last met,' she says. We all laugh, particularly long and loud in the Hard And Straight Group section of the audience. We know what she is getting at. Some applaud this single line but my colleagues and I are nervous of peaking too early in her performance. 'There was, for instance, our election victory in June,' she continues, prompting another chuckle from us all. How lightly she presents her role in history! 'They tell me that makes it three wins in a row. Just like Lord Liverpool. And he was Prime Minister for fifteen years. It's rather encouraging.' We roar with laughter. It is clear that she is in terrific form.

Pass the sickbag quickly. It is now that I begin to regret my decision to secrete myself among the true believers. Over on the press tables, the hard news boys are banging at their portable word processors like pub pianists. I suppose they've already got their line, the people from the the 90 per cent of papers which adore her: Maggie Hints At Eight More Years. Thank God I write facetious journalism for a newspaper which is at least equivocal about her. The odd thing about all this obsession with an assault on Lord Liverpool's record is that at least part of the point of continuing that long – 'I will go on and on and on,' she has recently said – must be the assumption that longevity confers immortality.

And yet even the pickled pedants among political correspondents – the ones who can not only pronounce Bagehot but quote him – can tell you almost nothing about Lord Liverpool. I am not sure that, even if she beats his record, the Blessed Margaret should be sure of being remembered for anything more than endurance. Certainly, she will not be immortal for her oratory. She's just done a bit about how it was said in the early '70s that you couldn't behave like a Conservative and be elected. 'Don't you harbour just the faintest suspicion that somewhere along the line something went wrong with that theory?' she asks, lowering her husky lisp, inclining her head and fluttering her eyelids, as if trying to teach a group of two-year olds what irony is. I scribble in my notebook a proto-joke about how she might be called the Iron Lady but she'll never be called the ironic one.

Watching her again, the voice and manner remind you that she is the most extensively remodelled politician in recent history. The Reagan who negotiated with Gorbachov in the '80s was recognizable as the Reagan who went to bed with Bonzo in the '50s movies, allowing for the accretions of a few decades. She, however, has changed in a way beyond the dictates of ageing and the protocols of hemline and fabric. Cosmetic dentistry was coupled with voice coaching. There exists a film clip of one of her pack of flatterers, Higgins to her Eliza, coaching her to go lower and huskier on a reply about her government's compassion. She was given the PR equivalent of plastic surgery.

Oh, here we go, Snobby has just got on to Education, a subject on which she had strong views even at school. Actually, she had strong views on most things. She was a bastion of the Debating Society. Was she good? She was keen. It wasn't that she kept you listening, certainly not that she kept you amused – there were never any jokes that I remember – but more that she kept going. She's a touch lighter now. I suppose she has people to write these things for her, has she? 'Children who need to be able to count and multiply are learning anti-racist mathematics, whatever that is,' she is saying. 'Children who need to be able to express themselves in clear English are being taught political slogans.'

Look at them in the crowd honking like sealions. But is it true what she says? Oh, there probably are bad teachers, but every profession has its wretches, including politics, and they show damn all sign of reforming that. I would have thought that there are still a lot of teachers around as good as ours were and, anyway, if you're teaching the kind of class they have nowadays – I saw a thing on the television – half-white, half-black in some London slum, you want a bit more from the government than jokes about anti-racist mathematics, whatever they are.

Snobby was a scholarship girl – my old dad, like most people's, paid part-fees – so you would think she might retain some affection for our schooling system, a sense of her own luck. But, no, everything she does looks like a kind of revenge. But for what? She could not, surely, have accomplished more.

'It's not just that violent crime is worse than other crime,' she is saying. 'It's much worse.' This epigram wins another spatter of applause. I wish journalists could write so flatly and receive such a rapturous response. Although many articles are published – I have written some of them myself – about the growing influence of speechwriters in Western politics, the truth is that this Prime Minister is no puppet of a word processor. Ronald Reagan – who, as an actor, was perhaps more sanguine about sending out for takeaway phrases – was genuinely a written politician, a conduit for the corny pith of others. Remember, when the spaceship Challenger blew a gasket or whatever, how the astronauts, far from being victims of a Nasa cock-up, had, apparently, 'slipped the surly bonds of earth and touched the face of God'. Or, in fact, Gard.

It is impossible to imagine our own dear leader saying that. Partly, it's a cultural distinction. The level of rhetoric required to engage an American is already nausea level for Europeans. But, even with that allowance, there's a difference in expertise. American speeches are corn but the harvest is toiled for. Set-piece English addresses, like the one we're hearing now, are inelegant tapestries of official statistics, party braggadocio, lumpen puns and leaden ironies. The leader of a country of middling importance, who claims for herself and her nation a grander status, speaks with no more zest than an averagely competent headmistress at prizegiving. 'Civilized society doesn't just happen,' she is saying. 'It has to be sustained by standards widely accepted and upheld.'

Her delivery, though, is at least efficient, aided by one of those invisible moron-boards, also pioneered for her special relation President Reagan, which permit the modern politician the secondary oratorical illusion that they are inventing – or, at the very least have memorized – the words which have been written for them. It is an elegant illusion. I was once seated behind a speaker who was using one of these secret screens. The words surged past at eye-level, apparently unsupported, like sky-writing, or like a production of *Macbeth* I saw recently, in which the fantastical dagger was done by laser. It seemed to me a useful image for political oratory: sentences in the emptiness.

'We must draw on the moral energy of society,' she is saying. 'And we must draw on the values of family life.' Aha, they are playing my song. My hymn, should I say? Although I must admit that if, as her unofficial theological adviser, I have tried to make one point, while of course expressing it obliquely in her presence, it is that this constant ringing mantra of the Family may be taken amiss, or with amusement, given that such a very significant proportion of her ministers have married their secretaries after divorcing their wives. Indeed, she herself is her husband's second wife.

I find this one of the oddest aspects of her character. Although a public scold – 'those habits of mutual love, tolerance and service on which every healthy nation depends', she now hurls her words into the grim black pool – she is the very opposite of a private moralist. To my personal knowledge, her entourage has included two adulterers-with-progeny, a drug addict, and a homosexual. And yet she fingerwags me over the Synod's equivocations, as she sees it, on gay clergy, and introduced legislation which stopped only just short of sewing up the bottoms of homosexuals. Britain's first woman Prime

Minister, she was opposed to female clergy. Hypocrisy? I would prefer to call it moral complexity.

'Mr President,' she is saying, 'it is a great trust which has been placed in our care. May we never fail that trust.' And may we never fail hers! On the first syllable of the last word, the Hard And Straight Group are on our feet, which we are stamping, our hands meeting at first with no more urgency than those of a woman winding wool. It is vital to pace our ovation. Anything less than ten minutes and mischievous journalists will be hinting that she might be out of office before the millennium.

You will, I know, accuse a sacked minister of bitterness in his reactions to this speech. I am perfectly happy not entirely to deny that personal emotions enter into my assessment of the Prime Minister. For English males of my generation, embodiments of female power were rare outside of the school sanatorium and Margaret has necessitated a substantial mental readjustment. I suspect that many of my colleagues could never quite rid themselves in her presence of the fear that she was about to insert a thermometer in their bottoms. But she also – I realize that this sounds, dread word, wet – took advantage of our upbringing.

Educated to be polite to women – taught also, of course, it is true, that women would never be in charge of us – we found ourselves being shouted down and bawled out by one of this supposedly deferential gender. Margaret was like a nanny with bad manners and with no sense at all of the loftier social status of her charges. But I do also have political differences with her. English males of my background and political persuasion were educated never to do anything which would render one unable to look one's servants squarely in the eye. This was one nation, whether or not we owned a somewhat higher proportion of its assets. The current government has played what I believe our friends across the pond call a Percentage Game. Don't whinge about unemployment, think rather of those millions of voters who do have jobs and whose taxation burden we may reduce to help them celebrate their fortune. Do not talk about the homeless, speak rather of those who have bought their own homes. Divide and rule.

Of course, I'm accused of being an 'old fashioned paternalist', isn't that the phrase? Well, so be it. I still, however, hold that doctrine preferable to her new-fashioned maternalism. Ah, at last, the embers of applause. I check my watch. Ten minutes. A small orgasm by the standards traditionally applying at this address.

Two hours until I file. In the crush around her as she left the podium, I was thrown next to our political editor, a brilliant, obsessive ferret of a man. He's inflamed at the moment with this idea of Year Zero. She and all her ministers have talked all week about correcting what went wrong before 1979, the date of her own elevation. And yet exactly half of the thirty-four post-war, pre-her years were filled by governments of her own colour, now disowned. He believes she is Messianic, he believes she is mad. I ask him if he can stand it up and he responds with a cackling joke about impotency. He is like that. Journalists are like that.

It is perhaps a good thing that his machine-gun delivery of these thoughts cannot be heard above the singing of 'Land of Hope and Glory', the stamp of boots and the flap of paper and fabric Union Jacks. She shakes, or squeezes, random hands, many of which, after she has released them – I am not making this up – rise to rub brimming eyes. Next to them, friends or spouses tremulously Polaroid the moment, for future generations to relish. Although you are observing it, this remains a phenomenon as mysterious as the sex lives of others. For my part, if I have grandchildren, I will show them her picture and say: stay well away from strangers, particularly any who look anything like this.

As she reaches the door of the hall and I am strong-armed away by a bodyguard I hear a grey-haired lady festooned in blue telling a radio reporter: 'I think she should go on for ever, as long as she wants to go on. I think – a lot of us think – we should make her life president of Great Britain.' Oh, shit is it in this dawn to be alive.

'Boadicea from Winter.' The buggers down below are still chanting 'Cunt!' Haven't they got any jobs to go to? And, ho, ho, won't they be angry when they realize that the glimpse of black limousine by the sea front ninety seconds from now is as close as they're going to get to inflicting their filth on her. From my high window, I sneak a picture of her for my private album. For a few moments, I listen to other voices receding on my radio. 'Boadicea home. Boadicea home.'

2

Toronto (1988)

IF I REMEMBER anything of this, it will be the Buddhist monks. In fact, like most of the world's journalists gathered here for this Global Economic Summit – and most of those in the world do seem to be here – I had low hopes for Canada as a whole. That isn't to say I didn't want to come. Oh, journalists will go anywhere abroad. It's arguable that this childish side of the personality – wanting to poke and point and ask 'But, why?' – is vital to the craft. When I fly, I have a thing about being allowed in the cockpit, particularly of 747s, for take-off or landing. Once, when I asked the stewardess of an American airline whether this might be possible, she looked doubtful but said she'd check and get right back to me. When she returned, smiling, she said that was fine. The captain had informed her that the company offered this facility to small boys and journalists.

The pairing seemed a fair one. Certainly, there's always a school-trip mood among the press on these international junkets. Distinguished columnists and reporters – the prefects of our profession – get very drunk and visit brothels. Although, on this occasion, Canada seems to have been something of a challenge for the sybarites. That's the night-time problem here. The daytime problem is that there isn't actually much of a yarn. It's Reagan's last summit – which offers some potential for cowboy and sunset metaphors – but advance briefings indicated that the British Prime Minister has decided not to put her bovver boots into Germany and France on this occasion, which is a novelty (she tends to regard Europe as a Socialist plot), but leaves us short of splashes.

No, the only surprise has been the Buddhist monks. There are a dozen of them, flown in from Tokyo, in saffron robes, beating drums day and night beside the security fence surrounding the summit venue. They say they are drumming for world peace. It's a nice idea but they seem not to have realized that the President of the United States wears a deaf aid, while our Prime Minister might as well be so equipped, given her record for listening to people. They are drumming against thunder.

Those drums, those damned drums. I hardly had a wink of sleep last night, which was a bore as I'd been up late ironing her glad rags for today. For the official group photograph, we selected a rather jazzy little jacket: white, overprinted with red roses and green foliage. She'll wear it over dark, calf-length skirt and coal-coloured blouse, with high-heeled patent leather shoes of the same shade, and crocodile-skin handbag. The high heels are the teeniest little bit political, I admit, because France is a small man, as is the European Community, and Japan, who's not been on the Christmas card list until now, so he's a bit of an unknown quantity, is, it goes without saying, diminutive. America's high in the saddle and Germany's as high as he is wide, which is saying something. And Canada's not tiny either. The idea is, the heels will have her towering humiliatingly above the tinies and within spitting distance of the biggies, which is the best to be hoped for with a domineering woman of moderate height. As I always say to my friends, it's all political. They also serve who only stand and iron. Take the summer-garden jacket for today. At these diplomatic gangbangs, we use fashion to make capital from the fact that she, alone of *les grandes fromages du monde*, isn't a chap in a lounge suit. She'll look like oil against charcoal in the photographs.

As we wait in the press centre for the end of the latest session,

I flick through the local papers. She's in the middle of every team photo. Although some feminist journalists dispute that she is a woman at all, I don't think you can underestimate the importance of the novelty of gender to the perception of her around the world. In the picture library at my office, the fattest file of all those on the long shelf she now merits is marked 'With Others (Famous)'. Her supporters would attribute her global visibility and reputation solely to her policies and stature, but I think you can't ignore the simple fact of her disruption of the visual status quo. Blow-wave, handbag and pissing sitting down were bound to give her prominence in the man's cabal of politics.

As a lone skirt among suits, it also tends to seem sensible that she should stand in the middle of the group. And she, it must be noted, helped to encourage this logic. There exists a splendid film clip of Britain's first woman Prime Minister, at one of her earliest summits, grimly elbowing her way through the chaps, with crisp excuse-mes, from top row right to front row centre. She was helped in doing so by masculine deference or confusion. As enacted by men, politics has always been, one way or another, a cock-measuring contest, whether the boys whip them out in the cabinet room or on the international stage.

Minister A is not going to give in to Minister B or, at a global level, Chancellor A to Prime Minister B or President C because, at a not particularly subconscious level, A believes himself to have a bigger one than B. Now, Margaret comes along and has nothing to put on the table in the donger competition. To continue this indelicate but, I think, helpful analogy, it is a fact of male psychology that the chap found lacking, size-wise, in the locker room or showers is only half as humiliated as the chap found wanting in the bedroom. So, with Margaret on the scene, the boys begin to be nervous of even taking them out. It helps that she has a manner which suggests she knows they're going to be tiny anyway. So, in the Cabinet Room, helped by the English public schoolboy's (80 per cent of her ministers in 1988) terror of the feminine, she is able to win 1–20.

Her femininity – or, if you prefer, female gender – has also helped her to develop the myth of her own, and her country's, international importance. The clear subtext of her photocalls with Gorbachov or Reagan is romance, particularly to readers of the popular press, for whom the phrase 'Special Relationship' has what are essentially Valentine card connections. Playing up to this, she would gaze deep into the American President's eyes, as he delivered a speech, with what was the body language of the adoring political wife. It is true that, through a combination of old-fashioned gallantry, ideological coincidence, and perhaps even subliminal sexual attraction, the men, particularly those from America and Russia, gave as soppy as they got, but the effect was to disguise the true nature of the relationships between the nations. Reagan treated her like a fellow landlord when she was effectively his lodger.

Consider her statement about Gorbachov, when he was first, I nearly said elected, when he was first promoted: 'Here is a man I can do business with.' Oh, yes? What business exactly? The claim was logically ridiculous, as the serious job to be done was the arms negotiations between Russia and America, in which she had no role. Our nuclear weapons would always point in the same direction as America's, whatever business she thought she could do with the Kremlin. And yet that is not the story the newspapers and news bulletins tell. The effects of arrogance, novelty, and chemistry allow her the illusion of equal status with the superpowers. As a politician, she is a considerable magician. And, of course, the British press, or most of them, are happy to pretend they haven't seen the rabbit being hidden in the hat.

Morning, morning. I trust you're not too etiolated – look it up in a dictionary later, Simon – by Canadian nightlife. In which connection, welcome to some of our friends from the foreign press. Perhaps I'd better stress, usual British lobby rules. These remarks attributable to 'British sources' or 'Senior British officials'. Clear? Right, the leaders are sending a joint appeal to the South African government for clemency in the matter of the Sharpeville Six, who, those of you who read newspapers as well as write them will be aware, are sentenced to hang. Although it is a joint appeal, it's fairly widely accepted that the British Prime Minister's is the name on the paper with the proper clout.

While she, of course, wholly disapproves of apartheid, she has been careful to keep a line open to the South African President. You might want to reflect that a situation like this – in which a letter or even, at a later stage, a phone call, might have some effect – shows the danger of isolating South Africa completely, through sanctions and so on, a course of action against which the British Prime Minister 'as consistently warned.

Meanwhile, discussion continues on rescheduling of Third World debt and, inevitably, farm subsidies. It's no secret that talks on this subject have gone on rather longer than expected. The reason, I regret to say, is that our American brethren are being pig-headed over this cock-eyed plan of theirs to wipe out subsidies completely by the end of the century. Britain has emphasized that the ambition is admirable but the timetable impractical. Indeed, Britain 'as become a smidgin irritated with America's refusal to see sense on this point. It 'asn't affected their very close friendship, but the Prime Minister, frankly, believes her senior international colleague is, how shall we put this, shooting from the hip on this occasion. Yes, John? No, no, they 'aven't 'ad a row. Absolutely not. They may be Western leaders but don't get carried away by John Wayne metaphors. We're not talking showdown at Dead Man's Gulch. We're talking a friendly word from the sheriff.

In which connection, and I'll be expanding on this point in a briefing after the final communiqué tomorrow afternoon, I think it's generally accepted here that, this being the, if I may, last reel for President Reagan, the *de facto* leadership of the free world passes to the British Prime Minister on account of 'er unrivalled length of time in office and worldwide reputation.

Finally, official dinner this evening. I'll have the menus for you later, if you want them. The idea is that the cuisine will incorporate an element from all the participating nations. So, the Am_ricans will be eating humble pie. Forgive my little joke.

Yes, Simon? The British dish. I don't have that information at the moment, but I've made a formidable case for Yorkshire pudding. Yes, small Japanese gentleman standing at the back? No, no, you don't 'ave to attribute the menu to British sources. You can say what you bloody well like about the menu. Right, any other questions?

At the moment, there is little actual writing going on in the press centre. What seems to be hundreds of Americans are slumped glumly before portable word processors and mobile telephones amid pungent and greasy hamburger and pizza debris. The Americans are not happy to be in Canada, which they seem to regard as a kind of sewage inlet for their own part of the continent. On the first day, they grouched around the hotel muttering things like: 'Hell, until now, I thought Toronto was the Lone Ranger's friend.'

Although some of us culture-hungry Europeans have ventured out, clutching our folder with its suggested visits ('This futuristic ninety-six-acre recreation complex on Lake Ontario is a real must-see') and useful list of Some Important Toronto Dates ('1842 – streets are gas lit'), the Americans never leave the press centre. But they do not intend a specific rebuke to Canadian scenery and sight-seeing. At summits in Paris and Tokyo, it was the same. Studiously incurious about the Louvre or even the Hiroshima crater, they stared at the TV screens, phoning out to the local McDonald's twice a day for meals.

Apart from a natural lack of interest in any country not their own, this is because all American reporters are obsessed with the possibility of missing their President being shot or, in the case of Reagan, dying quietly of old age. An anecdote is shiveringly told about a reporter who dutifully followed Governor Wallace of Alabama for two years but, taking an afternoon off to go shopping, missed the politician getting drilled. Whatever people think about journalism being a permanent holiday, reporting politics is a way of travelling and not seeing the world. By contrast, the British Prime Minister is demonstrating that being a politician is a way of travelling and not hearing the world.

Myself, in between listening to the drums, I've been reading the agency tapes in the press centre, along with some faxes of yesterday's British front pages sent over by my office. The line seems to be that Reagan has handed on the lump of kryptonite to the British representative. For Superman, read Superwoman. My sniffy liberal newspaper refuses to attend these briefings – regarding them as a sort of official equivalent of anonymous poison-pen letters – and I can see the point. The present Chief Press Secretary has clearly operated at times as a secret assassin of politicians whom the Prime Minister was publicly defending. But to fume about those holding the spoon is to avoid the trickier point of why this nation's journalists are so willing to be spoonfed.

I suppose that there is laziness: a dazed, hungover gratitude to this man handing out what are, after all, juicy titbits and lively angles. There's a particular problem with politics, which is that so much of what goes on is dull or complex or actually incomprehensible. The columnists and the serious news boys all spout forth about the Uruguay Round of the GATT Talks, but I doubt that anyone, if asked for a concise summary at gunpoint, could give one. So take-away angles from government sources have the benefit of clarity. And editors like them because, at this period in history, their content coincides with the right-wing politics of those rich men who own newspapers. And, indeed, with their patriotism, which, curiously, extends even to those proprietors born in other countries, presumably on the basis that such inaccurate triumphalism sells.

Ah, a flurry of activity. Americans shouting things like 'Bob, do we have a live feed?' I think the leaders of the free world are ready to pronounce.

*

OK, usual terms, British sources. You'll have read – those of you as can read – the communiqué. The important point, as you'll gather, is that the kind of strong, sensible economic policies followed in Britain and America have promoted an unprecedented period of world prosperity. However, with this prosperity comes a responsibility towards the less fortunate, less, er, organized nations of the world. So the debt burdens of these countries will be lessened, although the precise details will be worked out later by what is known as the Paris Club – sounds a sight saucier than it is, I can tell you – of international finance ministers. It might interest you to know that the plan adopted on this matter was effectively the British blueprint.

Otherwise, the main business was saying farewell to the American President, although special friends, like the British Prime Minister, will be seeing him in Washington before he leaves office. I think it wouldn't be misreading the tea-leaves to say that, as the great ex-actor leaves the stage, he's secure in the knowledge that he has a brilliant understudy. She's word-perfect and ready to take over the role. Any other questions?

My dears, the outfit worked like a dream. The men's conformity was all we had hoped for. Canada, Germany, and Japan all wore black suits. Even their neckties spurned surprise. Italy and the European Community chose grey two-pieces, and France a sort of grey-beige which had a worrying whiff of off-the-peg to me. America plumped for a navy blazer and charcoal slacks, giving him the look, it was hard not to feel, of an elderly Yank on vacation, which, on reflection, I suppose he was. And, at ground-level, we had seven pairs of black lace-ups, which was at least an improvement as, in the past, France has had a penchant for slip-ons, which I think a mistake. Anyway, the net effect was that, sartorially, there was no contest. She stood out like a gâteau in a bread shop.

We in the lofty press are taking the line of a 'turgid and wordy' communiqué, calculated to allow all the participants to claim they got exactly what they wanted. A summit of show above substance. Which is probably a working definition of all these meetings. According to a colleague, one of the leaders said, off the record, 'Why do we come? Because it says in our diaries that we ought to come.' Such honesty from a politician would, I suppose, have to be unattributable, but this kind of cynicism is surely the correct approach.

Consider the fact that these economic summits are billed as bringing together the G7 countries, the world's main creditor nations, although, in fact, America is a substantial debtor. Even more bizarrely, her debt is largely to Japan, a junior member of G7. This anomaly results from what might be called the decent-chap theory of politics. One example is that nuclear weapons are such terrible things that only decent, sensible, usually Western countries may be permitted to possess them. In the same way, a huge debt held by a decent, sensible, Western country is regarded as a kind of legitimate tick – a Japanese Express account, if you like – while a sizeable deficit sustained by a Third World country is bankruptcy. Under this arrangement, the President of the United States of America, whose economy is measured in red-coloured zeros recurring, gets to call other nations economic basket-cases.

But these summits are not about logic. Their importance is symbolic. The Canadian opposition parties have complained that this event amounts to a $20 million dollar photo-opportunity for the Canadian Prime Minister and there must be a certain justice in that view. His image as a global hob-nobber is supposed to raise his profile at home. Britain's Prime Minister, too, has developed a tendency to absent herself abroad during election campaigns, to stress that her constituency is international. Small or unimportant countries or their leaders have learned, in a television age, to work the world circuit like autograph hunters. Triumphantly, they flash their albums at the domestic electorate: 'That's me with America. And here's me with Germany.'

A foreign correspondent once told me of the leader of a

medium-nowhere nation, who, on a state trip to Paris, entered town ahead of a line of twenty rented thin black limousines, many of them empty. It is a safe bet that the cost of the petrol and the hire was more than recompensed in false prestige. At any of these summits – or the funerals of statesmen – I like to hang around the airport when the leaders are arriving. It's hard not to conclude that transport decisions have more to do with politics than aeronautics. France likes to use a Concorde, even when distances mean frequent refuelling, presumably because, parked on the tarmac, the plane looks so grand and fuck-you. I have watched the leaders of poor countries arrive, with tiny entourages, in greedy, empty jumbo jets.

I toy with writing a plane spotter's guide to world power. There are so many airport nuances, like whether you get a manually unfurled red carpet or the state-of-the-art sort where the roll shoots out from the aircraft steps, like a tongue, when a button is pressed. So much of modern politics is in these details. In this way, a summit which accomplishes nothing can be entirely satisfactory to those who take part.

3

St James's Park (1988)

IT IS OVERCOAT WEATHER, although it is spring. It is also before breakfast, as several other journalists and I loiter in St James's Park, swapping gossip about ministers' mistresses and editors' eccentricities. We are gathered here today, plucked untimely from our hangovers, unfinished novels, and early morning projects for other employers, by the promise of a photo-opportunity involving the Prime Minister.

The point is that, whatever the fashion mafia might think, it's important to take on board that our bywords while sorting through the wardrobe before today's event were warmth and mobility. For a summit team-shot or a treaty signing, your options are wider. This morning, we've gone for a low, wide heel, because the scenario is movement-led, and a vented check tweed top-coat, which permits her speed across the ground while keeping out the chill.

I asked one of the sniffer-dog boys from Special if he'd be an absolute love while staking out the site and stick a heel in the grass to test the going. He reckoned it was firm to soft, so I'm holding to my first hunch on footwear, while keeping an alternative heel to hand in case of drizzle. Decisions! Decisions!

We fumble for our notebooks as she comes. The chuckling begins. It is apparent early on that this is one of those satisfying set-ups in which the line between publicity and stupidity has become blurred. As she steps from her limousine, she passes her handbag to an aide and cradles in its place a large black plastic bag and a long white stick with a hinged flap at its base. On grass of tennis-court perfection, ringed by vivid, overlapping daffodils, neat stacks of rubbish wait at one-yard intervals.

It is strangely decorous detritus. The park is, for example, devoid, for once, of dog-shit. And the jumbles of cigarette packets, chocolate wrappers and plastic bottles look almost clean and washed. Their arrangement, as staggered as jumps on a race track, is equally paradoxical. It is as if they were scattered by – an unlikely personality disorder, surely – an organized and anally-retentive litter lout.

With her funny, crouching Groucho run, she stalks a swirling cardboard packet, attempting to snare it in the maw of her stick, like one of those mechanical grabber games in arcades. An aide chases after her and steers her back to the pre-arranged steeplechase of garbage. Suddenly, you realize that – what is going on here? – she seems to have chosen the wrong rubbish. Those of us whose newspapers permit jokes against her sacred person begin to sense that this is Christmas.

OK, OK, is everybody 'ere? Sorry to get you out of other people's beds at this hour. The purpose of this morning's exercise is that the Prime Minister is setting an example of civic responsibility. It has frequently occurred to her, while driving through the capital with the ever-increasing number of international heads of state who wish to consult or visit her, that she needs to avert their eyes from the streets with economic discourse. Britain, she feels, has become the Untidy Man of Europe. To encourage the example she is setting, a grant will be announced later today to the Keep Britain Tidy Group to examine the phenomenon of public rubbish. And we're not talking about speeches by the Leader of the Opposition. Forgive my little jest.

As she scuttles from pile to pile, spiking and filling her bag, her Environment Secretary trails in her wake. A somewhat grumpy man from an age of politics before the use of words like Presentation and Communication, he makes some desultory lunges at large and stationary shards of garbage. Good God, I don't believe this. From his mouth, there hangs a characteristic but, on this occasion surely tactless, dripping cigarette.

Now my fingers brush the trousers of the Foreign Secretary, seeking out the crevices, making sure that there are no stains there, for the Prime Minister is very keen on cleanliness. In my career as a cleaner, I have never before had an employer who took so much interest in my work. I rub a stubborn smear of dust on the elder statesman's thigh. Look at the way in which the potter has captured the exact shade of grey for the garment.

Note how the artist – whose masterpiece, *Triumph in the Falklands*, I am deliberately saving until last – has simulated deep suit-creases by sharp scoring with a knife. With a little bit of spit, I gleam his glasses and pop him back on the top shelf, second from the right in what she always calls the Porcelain Cabinet (the potter can provide replacements within two months of a reshuffle.) Once, I opened a sort of wardrobe in the corner and found a pile of pottery men, lying like skittles. They were people I had vaguely seen on television years ago, all cobwebbed and horrible now. The cupboard was stuffed with them.

She has just rushed over to us and gabbled on about her embarrassment at the state of the capital. 'You actually feel ashamed,' she says in her talking-to-morons voice. We dutifully took it down in shorthand but I fear the story isn't any more the yarn she wanted it to be. Some colleagues and I have been chatting to a park attendant. Presumably, we asked sarcastically, the litter had not been originally dropped in these neat hillocks of filth? Who had asked the staff to sweep the pieces into easy targets for her?

At this, the bloke looks a bit shifty, lowers his voice, and says it's more complicated than that. Apparently, they cleaned the park as normal last night, tipped out the bags and did some quality control: no shit, squashy condoms, broken glass, or rusty needles. Then, in a scene which presumably resembled an unknown Magritte called *The Park Keepers*, they roamed around the greensward, redistributing the litter. This customized debris, I now notice, includes a large number of banana skins. I feel a metaphor coming on.

The fact is, between you and me, and not a word to my constituents I even thought this, is that it's no longer a minority view that she's gone loopy. No one at home. The elevator doesn't go all the way to the top, as our special relations across the pond put it. Exhibit one is that she has begun to refer to herself by the first person plural. 'We think' and so on. I am not a psychiatrist, but I am a grammarian and I regard that as a danger sign.

Her fans insist that, when she does says 'we', she is speaking for the cabinet, to which this discarded minister can only reply that it would be most out of character for her suddenly to seek to spread the credit. Her detractors note, with elation, that this particular part of speech is associated with The Queen. It is a tempting hypothesis but I confess to remaining somewhat agnostic. Given that monarch and first minister are, for the first time in history, ladies of the same certain age, bound by the same rigid dress regulations at public occasions, Margaret is uniquely open to the accusation of regal delusion. In the past, a male prime minister who wore a morning suit was not accused of thinking he was king.

And yet. And yet. It is whispered that this prime minister has taken to dispatching her own telegrams to those of her subjects, I mean voters, who attain the age of a hundred. And it is also true that, after disasters, she has frequently given the impression of being involved in a hundred-yard dash against the Royal Family to reach the clinic first. My biggest lad tells me that he and his college friends carry cards in their wallets – you write off to some company, apparently – saying 'In the event of serious injury, not to be visited by the Prime Minister'. I hope that Margaret's historians, when the time comes, do not miss details like that.

However, on this matter of the relationship between our hereditary and our elected heads of state, it is also widely whispered that our leader and HMQ do not get on. They disagreed, it is suggested, over such subjects as the Miners' Strike of 1984 (Real Queen compassionate and agonizing, fake Queen resolute) and the imposition of sanctions against South Africa (Real Queen pro, fake Queen anti). On the basis of this, it is often somewhat improbably claimed by liberal journalists and left-wing politicians that the monarch and her eldest son are a variety of closet opposition to the government: billionaire radicals.

Steady on, say I. On South Africa, Her Majesty's apparent support for sanctions happens to coincide with the position of the African National Congress, but the motives are rather different. The Queen is desperate to hold together the Commonwealth, her increasingly lukewarm global supporters' club, many of whose branches have been disbanded. The remaining branches support sanctions, therefore so does she. And yet the monarch, cheered by the Left for this, is surely, in truth, driven by old-fashioned colonialist motives, somewhere to the right of even she who sent an Armada to the Falklands. The point is, never, in politics, take bedfellows – private or public – at face value. Ask what there is to be gained from the transaction.

And yet, on the subject of domestic issues, particularly strikes and unemployment, I do think the rumoured disagreement between, as it were, crown and town is interesting. There, I think the tension, if it exists, would be connected with what I have called elsewhere, in brave but lucrative articles for the liberal press, the government's Percentage Game. Monarchs seek to rule whole nations; politicians can rely on pockets of support, ignoring others. Queens and Kings do not have constituencies. This, I think, would have been a useful point for them to make. And yet, it must be faced: Margaret thinking she might be Queen would still be different from, say, my thinking that I might be Napoleon. The jury remains out on our Prime Minister's neurotic condition.

I will say only this. Leaders, the longer they are in office, are surrounded by ever larger entourages, advisers who fawn more and more. This cosseting has only one result. They are protected from everything except their own nature. And Margaret has no other interests, beyond a collection of rather tacky porcelain. Questioned on television about literary interests, she announced that she was 're-reading' a paperback thriller. It is not that I think she should be reading Trollope, although I might warm to her more if she did, but that there is something more than odd about a busy woman reading for a *second* time a book whose primary interest is suspense.

It is, therefore, with a mixture of interest and dread that I note reports that she is to be found this morning chasing sweetpapers across St James's Park with the intention of teaching the electorate a lesson about public hygiene. Frankly, you know, alarm bells ring, though not, I suspect, yet with my constituency or a sufficient quantity of my colleagues.

Inspired by her marvellous example this morning, we in the Hard And Straight Group have instituted Litterbug Boxes in our offices at the Commons. Anyone dropping ash, or failing to hit the bin while chucking scrunched-up rubbish backwards over their shoulder from their desks (we like to play a sort of garbage basketball to pass the time), is forced to put a forfeit in a tin. The amount is discretionary, but, psychologically, which of us wants to be seen by his peers to have so little money he needs to think about it? Accordingly, when you pick the Litterbug Box and shake it, there is no sound at all. All the forfeits so far have been paper money. At the end of each month, we will give the surplus, after the subtraction of certain administrative costs, to buy rifles for white South Africans or some such worthwhile cause. No, I'm joking. We'll find a charity for one-legged lesbians or something similar. Something more acceptable to liberals. That was another joke, incidentally.

Handing her symbolically filled bag to an assistant, her hinged scoop held momentarily aloft in front of her like Britannia's trident, she leaves in her limousine. The minister of state with responsibility for the preservation of the Earth flicks a little more ash on to it and departs in another car. The press is ecstatic, the only gloom among those reporters whose proprietors and mortgage repayments will not allow them to be rude. We all write articles and take part in late-night television discussions about image-management in modern politics, but it is rare to see such a fine example of image-mismanagement.

I find the idea that photo-opportunities are dangerous for democracy, reducing complex issues to a single picture, a peculiar one. In my experience, they are dangerous mainly for politicians. What's the political image you see most often in modern newspapers? A photograph of all the photographers photographing a politician. The minister, cuddling a fluffy lamb as part of an event cunningly constructed to encourage consumption of domestic mutton, is a small foreground detail in a composition which chortlingly draws attention to the manipulation he is crassly attempting. And we fear that this subverts democracy?

It may be worth pointing out that the present Prime Minister, victor in three successive elections, has been involved in hundreds of these set-ups – a photo-opportunist, you might call her – but that, increasingly, they have been subject to disruption like this morning's. In the North of England, for what her aides had calculated as a photocall in front of a new industrial development, she cheerfully accepted the invitation of photographers, who used an excuse about light, to stride away across some rubble-littered scrub, thus inadvertently colluding in the Our Lady of the Wasteland pictures which remain the most popular symbol of her attitude towards the top half of the country she led. A mistress of the manipulative image? I don't see that at all.

In fact, her most startling paradox as a politician has been that a tendency to do the exact opposite of what her colleagues or international counterparts wanted has co-existed with a willingness to obey to the letter the requests of her image consultants. For example, it was recently revealed – and has never been denied by any of the professional story-abortionists who surround her – that she submits to controlled electrocutions in a bathtub in Shepherd's Bush in the interests of a youthful demeanour.

This is pretty weird stuff. How far away is she now from the Emperor Haile Selassie, whose faeces, I read somewhere, were transported in vented jars around his kingdom with the intention of giving his subjects a medicinal whiff? That has always seemed a perfect image of the illogical extension of the cult of person-worship: the belief that even a leader's excreta must be significant. Perhaps, even now, our own leader's image advisers are bottling her special bathwater.

Breaking off from producing what a youth in her office called 'some general background guff on God and politics' for a speech she is to give shortly to clergymen – Scottish clergymen, may God go with her – I see her on the lunchtime news, being ridiculed for some rather puerile-looking stunt proselytizing tidiness. She was not, I felt, God forgive me, at her best in this performance. There was a manic quality in her aspect which used to be an exception but which I fear is becoming a rule.

The truth is that she has also recently begun to talk about God and Jesus as if they were members of her cabinet, which is a tricky one theologically, even for as skilful a trimmer as me. *Margaret and God: A Brief History.* She is a lapsed Methodist who seems, with no formal ceremony, at some point to have moved across to the Church of which the Queen is head. There was, inevitably, a certain perkiness in the Church of England when, on the steps of Number 10, after election, the Prime Minister pulled from her handbag the prayer traditionally attributed to St Francis but, in fact, the product of an anonymous divine.

But no matter. 'Where there is hatred, we will bring love,' she promised, and so on. Well, for priests, this was, I suppose, like a sports goods manufacturer having the England Captain wearing his brand of boots. Many of my colleagues were less keen when it became clear precisely which gloss was put on that beautiful prayer by her policies, but I have remained a supporter. I confess, however, to a period of doubt when she informed a television interviewer, when pressed on the needs of the weakest in the Community, that the Good Samaritan was only able to be Good because he had money. I had never read the parable that way. Frankly, you might as well say that the moral of the Wedding Feast at Cana story is the lack of an off-licence in the vicinity.

But, at about this time, because I was known, I suppose, to be on the right of the Church – there had been a Gadarene rush, particularly episcopal, towards the Nice People's Party (remember that?) – I was invited to contribute what was described as 'moral input' to her speeches. I remember, at the time of the Falklands Conflict, one of her closest advisers saying: 'Is there any sense, at all, Reverend, in which this business could be thought a Holy War?' I gently explained that the C. of E. has no theology of jihad, but rather the concept of just war, which the present Archbishop and Synod had further diluted to a sort of if-you-absolutely-must war. They did not like this, nor the altar-time given to the theme of the pity of war at what they had hoped would be a Thanksgiving service after the conflict.

Then, after the Falklands, there was a trend of bishops speaking up for the miners, the homeless and so on, some of them combining this secular fretting with a religious quizzicality about whether, for example, the Garden of Eden was an actual literal municipal park (cf. St James's) or a metaphor. You know the kind of thing. Articles on the Annunciation by obstetricians, arguing that the details of the Virgin Birth did not fit their experience in ante-natal clinics. She and those around her started off by complaining that religion had too much politics in it, gradually moving round to the graver accusation that the religion had too little religion in it. I remember one of her circle saying to me – he was the kind of evangelical who reads the lesson in a ham actor's yell – at a dinner: 'Suppose the Church slips too far – a lesbian becomes Archbishop of Canterbury, let's say – would you be interested in coming on board for a rival communion?' I equivocated.

But they would whisper, of some emergent clergyman, 'Reverend, is he one of us?' And they would talk of hitting back at the liberals with scripture of their own. If my relationship with the party has ever been strained, it has been because of the periodic insistence of her team that there 'must be something in the Bible' to justify whatever radical new policy they have just constructed. This puts me in a delicate position. Although the established Church succeeds in being a suitably elastic corset for an improbable number of doctrinal bulges, the Bible, in itself, is not an equivocal document. It has an awful tendency towards absolutes like 'Thou shalt not kill' and 'Do not covet thy neighbour's ox', which, if you're not very slippery in the exegesis, can make both domestic and foreign policy a no-go area for theology.

However, I now find myself providing some material for her address – her staff are referring to it as a sermon, whether with irony or not I am unsure – to the General Assembly of the Church of Scotland. I have in front of me her own rough notes, which demonstrate that she intends to be rather more specific about her religious beliefs than has been normal for prime ministers. And, indeed, rather more so than American presidents, who now need to be believers to be elected, but who are rarely theologically more complex than saying 'God Bless America' as often as possible. Margaret, however, intends to affirm that: 'Our Lord Jesus Christ, the Son of God, when faced with His terrible choice and lonely vigil, chose to lay down His life that our sins may be forgiven.' I suppose this is very Church of England of me, but I wonder, given that She presides over the most ethnically various British electorate in history, whether the speech might not verge on public tactlessness. Perhaps I am just being wet.

For my own part, and God have mercy on my soul, I have minted for her the line: 'It is not the creation of wealth which is wrong, but love of money for its own sake.' It is a phrase sufficiently vague to assuage both my conscience and theirs, in different ways. And in St Paul I have located two useful pieces from the epistles: 'If a man shall not work, he shall not eat' (Thessalonians) and a warning from Paul to Timothy about the evils of a man neglecting to provide for his own house. Thus does the reliable old grump conveniently denigrate the welfare state and support home ownership. It will do. I have been thinking about modern politicians and their scriptwriters. I suppose that if Pontius Pilate were around now, he would have to say: 'It *was* written.' I would not hazard such a joke with Her.

Over lunch today, a writer on another paper told me a nice yarn. A British television programme had been trying for months to get an interview with Reagan for a documentary about Margaret Hilda. The message comes back: He'll do it because of his very high regard for your Prime Minister but he's a busy busy man and that's a busy busy day and you got ten minutes, OK?

On the appointed day, crew and interviewer turn up. Lights and cameras are installed in an anteroom of the Oval Office. At the appointed hour, the doors crash back and an aide jumps in and shouts, in this mad pompous way they have, 'The President of the United States!' Reagan ambles in and sits down. The first question is ready when the American cameraman whips a piece of paper from his pocket – the G-men tensing at the sudden movement – and shows it to the President. It is a picture of Spot, a dog belonging to the cameraman's young daughter. She has noticed a close resemblance between Spot and Lucky, the presidential pooch, and wishes the matter to be brought to the attention of the Commander-in-Chief of the US

Forces. The President stares at the snapshot – the interviewer conscious of his minutes elapsing – and cracks his dotty, harmless grin. 'Hey, would you believe that? They could be twins!' Thankfully, the interview is accomplished and the President retreats to his office and affairs of state.

The crew has almost stowed its gear when, fifteen minutes later, the big doors split again and an aide shouts, again, 'The President of the United States!' Reagan ambles back. He approaches the cameraman and hands him a sheet of paper. On it, the President has drawn two black and white mutts, similar as twins, and labelled them Lucky and Spot. Even now, he is reluctant to go, hanging back for some more doggy chat, and, finally, his aides nudge him back to his desk.

We chuckle. But this man – who, also, apparently, employed an astrologer to chart his presidential schedule by the heavens – has run a country for eight years. And this woman – who believes in magic baths, a personal divine involvement in her destiny and calls herself 'we' – has run a country for nine years. A photographer once told me that Margaret and Ronnie had an arrangement, when appearing in public. If his deaf aid went, he would nudge her and she would step across, pontificating furiously on some ideological topic, to shield him from the snappers while he fixed it. This is the way the West was run during what it liked to present as a period of unprecedented moral vigour. The message is clear. Power is not a sun that can be stared at for too long.

Walking back from lunch, to begin my piece on the Prime Minister's clean-up campaign, I see that St James's Park is filling up with authentic litter: smeared, squelchy, sopping stuff, a metamorphosis or two ahead of this morning's designer debris. Oddly, though, no responsible citizens dart around with bags and little grabbers, in imitation of their leader.

4

London (1990)

ALWAYS BEFORE she looks serene but, this month, I can see that she is *distraite*. 'More power,' she says as she sits in the bath, 'more power.' I say to her I am on no account taking this silly risk. 'What if anything happens?' I say. 'No. No. May you reign for a thousand years!' She looks thoughtful.

My duster can barely keep up with the reshuffles. In the middle of last year, she sacked her Foreign Secretary and scarcely was the new one back from the potter's before her Chancellor of the Exchequer resigns – apparently she'd been supporting him in public and ignoring him in private, which wouldn't be the first time – and the Foreign Secretary – a quiet-looking boy with glasses, nice smile, called Major – becomes the Chancellor. That isn't a problem from a porcelain standpoint – he just moves along the shelf, closer to the Toby Jug version of herself – but it meant a rush job for the potter to do the new men in the cabinet.

Next thing I know, I've lost two from the back row, both of them I'd been dusting for donkey's years. They both told her they wanted to 'spend more time with my family', but I think there's a feeling that might be a polite way of saying it. My husband now, when he goes down to the pub in the evening, always says: 'I wish to spend less time with my family.' We laugh.

Anyway, then, wouldn't you know, we've only just got both

shelves full again, when her Environment Secretary compares
the new, united Germany to the Nazis, so he resigns – although,
apparently, she didn't want him to – and the whole lot moves
round again, which left me with gaps for at least a fortnight,
which means she can't show the collection to guests, in case
they comment. Well, we got through September and October
without her sacking anyone or anyone resigning, which was a
novelty, but now, as if we didn't have enough trouble, the
deputy Prime Minister has just resigned, saying she's gone
loony on Europe.

Well, I don't know a thing about politics but we saw her on
television the other night – spitting and swivelling her eyes
about the French and the Germans making us all eat snails for
breakfast, if they get their way – and my husband, who's never
been a malicious man, said, well, really, if she was a member
of your family, you'd walk slowly backwards out of the door
and make a phone call. It's true. I mean, it can't go on. At this
moment in time, I've got more gaps than dusting. The potter
says to me, when he brings in the last box of replacements, 'If
she keeps this up, I'm going to have to send them back without
a final glaze, some of them.' I said, some of them, it wouldn't
make much difference. He laughed.

'New par. Speculation has comma however comma intensified
at cap W Westminster that Sir Geoffrey's ee-oh-eff-eff apostrophe s departure comma and the remarks in his resignation
letter about her negative attitude to closer links with Europe
comma may prompt a challenge to her position by the former
Defence Secretary, comma Michael Heseltine comma who
resigned four years ago over the very same issue of Europe.
Stop. Thanks. Can you give me Home?'

Listen, gentlemen, I'll tell you this for free. Talk about 'is
resignation won't be steaming up the windows of the Plough
and Whistle. Nah. His differences with the Prime Minister are
over tone and style, not policies. Anyway, deputy Prime Minis-

ter. Deputy schmeputy. This resignation, it reminds me of when you read in the paper that someone – a film star, mebbe – has died and you think: 'I thought they were dead already.' You know what I mean?

The point, the absolute point, is that we in the Hard And Straight Group are not just fair-weather friends, boon buddies, like some of our Parliamentary colleagues. We accept that she is not at the peak of her personal popularity but mid-term downswings are a fact of political life. Throughout my career, I have held to two rough creeds – never trust a poll and never trust a Pole – and while recent events in Eastern Europe have undermined the latter principle, the first remains intact. We would also accept that there has been something of an economic downturn in recent months. Yes, we too have received letters from constituents whose businesses have collapsed or whose homes have been reclaimed by the building society. We prefer, however, to look at it this way: yes, it looks like a lot of homes, a lot of businesses, but *only because so many were created*! To the Jeremiah Jims, Moaning Minnies, and Tired Tims who mutter in their cups that it might be time for a change, we would say only this: hasn't she, by her devotion, by her actions, by her victories, her three victories, earned the benefit of the doubt?

I passed another of her sacked ministers in the corridor. Statistically, there's quite a high chance of bumping into one. He said – we have known each other since Oxford – 'Well, old boy, are you jubilant?' Mmm, I said, I was on stand by to be jubilant. 'Yes,' he chuckled, 'what's that phrase the Pentagon has? I'm in a high state of readiness.'

I know a political columnist on another newspaper, who reckons that, in the last eleven years, he has now written nine columns on the general theme of 'this time, she's finished'. However, even he now feels relatively optimistic about his latest such prophecy, published last month. He thinks that history will know sod all about the poll tax but that that tax will be her asp. They're fond of allusion, the older columnists. His only caveat is that it's no good hoping for anything from the resignation speech in parliament of Sir Geoffrey, a famously sedative temperament.

With hindsight, we political analysts convince ourselves that the portents of crisis were there all along. I would cite four. First, on the recent birth of her son's child, she used the first person plural in a sense – 'We have become a grandmother' – which was excusable by no known rule of grammar or political convention, intensifying speculation that she – or do I mean they? – is or are no longer operating on local time. Secondly, credence was lent to this belief by the fact that her opinions have become both more wilful and more dogmatically held. Take her speech at a banquet in Paris last year to mark the two hundredth anniversary of the French Revolution. She said: 'It took us a long time to get rid of the effects of the French Revolution two hundred years ago. We don't want another one.' Is it possible to imagine a more paranoid tactlessness, a worse example of international anti-diplomacy? Thirdly, after the 1988 American election, she specifically commended the graciousness of the defeated Democrat's speech. An unexpected sensitivity on her part, it now seems likely to have been the result of a spreading premonition that, one day, she herself might have to make a speech in defeat. Fourthly, there was the duck.

According (a necessary qualification) to reports in the tabloid newspapers, a damaged mallard was discovered, in the garden of 10 Downing Street, unable to fly further. The Prime Minister – Animal Lover Maggie, as the headlines had it – gave her 'personal instructions' (nice phrase that, often used of the lofty, but how would impersonal instructions sound?) that it was to be nursed back to health. The Lucky Duck is now, apparently, driven down to Chequers at weekends with the red boxes to encourage rural recuperation. A member of her Special Branch protection squad is supposedly instructed to supervise the duck's morning constitutional in St James's Park. Well Cor,

Love A Duck!, as one tabloid sub-editor has headlined the story.

The press's usual stupidities on her behalf? Perhaps it's more complex than that. What has been the phrase used by the press and her opponents about the Prime Minister in her current troubles? A 'lame duck' leader. Only last year, she was forced to insist to an interviewer: 'I have never been a lame duck in my life and I don't intend to start now. I will go on for as long as I am wanted.' And how did her image consultants and her newspaper cheerleaders seek to counter her negative image? By promoting the story of her kindness to, yes, a lame duck. The metaphorical structure is bizarre. It is partly explained by the curious priorities of the English, who are far less sanguine about the mistreatment of animals than cruelty to human beings. When an atrocity committed by the Irish Republican Army severely injured mounted policemen, it was medical bulletins on their steeds (Some Improvement, Say Vets) which took prominence in the popular press in subsequent days.

Similarly, an electorate which would happily accept the removal of sticks and pills from the elderly, the renting-out of English hamlets for the bombing of Libya by America, the calculation of unemployment figures by a method equivalent to counting on six fingers and calling it two hands, the triumphant return to the Government of the Family of a minister who abandoned his secretary pregnant with child, would be thrown into moral convulsions by any suspicion of indifference to animals. Therefore, it should not be thought surprising that the full machinery of government was employed to prevent a lame duck turning into a dead duck.

As a companion to *The Plane Spotter's Guide to World Power*, I have toyed with *The Use of the Animal in Political Image-Management*. There would be Checkers, the puppy which the young (then Vice-President) Richard Nixon was accused of taking as a campaign bribe. He was also accused of taking furs and money, but, in a live television defence, concentrated soppily on the dog – the kids had loved it, so he'd kept it – thus,

316

as subsequent events showed, selling the public a pup. The book would also consider Millie, the pooch owned by President George Bush, who, in one of the most remarkable examples of the phenomenon of the elected pet, recently published her memoirs, a runaway bestseller in America.

Mention would also be made of a Labrador retriever given to President Ceausescu of Romania by an English liberal politician and the Japanese poodle called Lulu, who slept on the bed of the Emperor Haile Selassie of Ethiopia and pissed on the shoes of his entourage and visiting ambassadors. The imperial staff was expanded to accommodate a urine-remover.

The volume would consider at some length the significance of pandas in Sino-West relations. Barely off the plane in Peking, the visiting politician is told: 'Here, have a panda. You got one last time? No worries. Have another. Your capitalist press will take pictures of it and forget to ask questions about human rights abuses.'

In the Thatcher chapter, there would be a baby lamb who nearly expired in her arms during a photo-opportunity at a farm, the lame duck, and Kitty (also known as Tabby), the Downing Street Cat. A couple of years ago, speaking by radio to Australian children, students of the School of the Air, the Prime Minister revealed that she had adopted a two-year-old maltreated cat which had appeared in the garden of Chequers. The cat, which apparently had a passion for cheese and onion crisps, was referred to by the Prime Minister as Tabby, thereby contradicting an off-the-record briefing by her Chief Press Secretary that the creature was called Kitty. You rather hope that the visits of the lame duck and the maltreated cat to Chequers are staggered as the consumption of the former by the latter would be an unfortunate manifestation of the free market.

Also in this chapter would be Wilberforce, the fat, happy Downing Street cat, who served three prime ministers, but recently suffered a cardiac arrest. It was reported by the popular press, presumably informed of the fact off the record, that Mrs Thatcher had shed a tear.

It is all very odd. If, in America, aspirant presidents have to mention God a lot, perhaps, in Britain, ambitious politicians should run for office prominently holding up a litter tray or absently carrying a dog lead. How long in the process of democratic evolution will it be before the electorate's biggest concern is choosing a politician who is kind to human beings?

Perhaps, when she read that prayer from St Francis of Assisi on the day of her election, all she meant was that, like him, she was going to be nice to animals. However, I think, if she goes, a case could be made for dating her demise from the duck.

'Donald to James's. Donald to James's.' I sense the amusement of my colleague at the other end of the radio link. When I joined Special Branch, I never seriously expected to be detailed to escort a crippled duck – codename, ho bloody ho, Donald – on its morning walk.

'Breaking the tradition of anodyne ay-en-oh-dee-why-en-ee and coded resignation statements to MPs plural comma Sir Geoffrey ee-oh-eff-eff astonished colleagues with a far hyphen reaching condemnation of the Prime Minister's apostrophe s attitude to Europe and style of government. Stop. He suggested that her dogmatic refusal to contemplate such possibilities plural as a common European currency threatened to reduce Britain's influence within Europe. Stop. New par. A well hyphen placed ministerial source indicated that the Prime Minister had been openly mocking and dismissive of her senior colleague in recent weeks. Stop. The speech will further intensify speculation about a challenge to the Prime Minister's position. Stop. One well hyphen respected backbencher said afterwards colon quote She is a lame duck now comma holed below the waterline endquote stop. Cheers. Can you give me Home?'

*

A lame duck? Nah. Wounded tigress, more like. She reads Kipling, you know. Favourite author. That line about the female of the species. Think on that a while, gentlemen, before you write your stories.

The Hard And Straight Group has tabled several Parliamentary motions expressing complete confidence in the best peacetime prime minister of the century. Myself and several of my colleagues have appeared widely on national television and radio to assure the nation that the Prime Minister's position is secure and that there will be no challenge to her leadership.

'Following yesterday's apostrophe s announcement by Mr Michael Heseltine comma the former Defence Secretary comma that he will stand against the Prime Minister for the leadership of her party comma the election will take place in six days' s apostrophe time. Stop.'

Well, I'm covered if he does win, I've got him already. He's in that cupboard in the corner. Thick with dust and fluff and stuff, but I gave him a once-over with a damp cloth. That was when I saw he was chipped. Funny. Looked as if he'd been thrown in there a bit rough, maybe.

A callow chap in her office has telephoned me and asked if there might be any Biblical texts relevant to this situation. One's facetious instanteous thoughts were 'Get behind me, Satan', and 'Either you are for me or against me'. To be perfectly honest, I think they were looking for something along the lines of Nostradamus rather than Holy Scripture. You know the kind of thing. 'And the one who wears blue and is marked not with the sign of man, and who rises in the west, shall she be cherished for ever.' I told him that divine revelation probably didn't include the kind of thing he had in mind. I said, however, that I would pray for the best outcome in the contest. He sounded disappointed.

*

'New par. The Prime Minister will herself be in Paris at a European Summit when the result is announced. Stop. This decision comma which recalls other jaunts sorry make that visits abroad during general elections comma is thought by some observers to be an attempt to emphasize that the party is considering the removal of an international statesperson. Stop.'

Ayurveda is a proven relaxation technique, with thousands of satisfied clients around the hemisphere, but I sense it is not working. I try to relax her with small talk about Paris, how I have never been there, how I would like to. But she says only 'More power! More power!' No, no, no, I say, we are having none of this nonsense. She repeats her demand in a louder voice. I say, look here, I am not one of your men. I am a trained ionized water and floral oils therapist. You know about votes, I tell her, but I know about volts. She doesn't laugh.

I can tell you, my dears, Paris is a challenge. Any summit, containing as it does both daytime tedium and evening relaxation, tests a wardrobe's flexibility. High heels under the conference table and flatties on the dance floor are the primary traps to be sidestepped on such occasions. We've set aside a lurexy number, which legend has it once won a compliment from Ronnie Reagan, for the visit to the ballet at Versailles on the evening of what we are all brightly telling each other will be her easy victory on the first ballot. For the summit business on the day of the voting, we're favouring a dark blue two-piece with discreet shoulder padding – Germany is such a big man, after all – of a kind which she has worn for big conference speeches, House of Commons debates. The costume's familiarity, its symbolism of the latest decade will, the theory goes, render her monumental, statuesque. Unmovable?

This morning – the day of the first, unnecessary ballot – I published an article in one of the media outlets which remains sound. On behalf of the Hard And Straight Group, I put forward the view that the attempted unseating – although it will certainly fail – of an elected Prime Minister who does not wish to go is undemocratic, unconstitutional, and, arguably, treason. I have put forward the proposal that if, by some mathematical aberration or other malevolent chance, these quislings should bring her down, Her Majesty The Queen must simply refuse to accept another first minister. This is constitutionally possible. The occupant of this position need not, historically, be leader of their party. Myself and my fellow members have arranged for a dozen red roses to be delivered to the British Embassy in Paris this afternoon. The message reads: 'For ever . . .'

In the Lobby of the House of Commons, I was approached by a totter for Her side. I made it quite clear that, although she had sacked me, I regarded this election as monstrous folly and would cast my vote where it morally belonged: for Britain's greatest peacetime (give or take a couple of small wars) prime minister. Within a quarter of an hour, I was bearded by a teller for the Challenger's team. Old bat gone barmy, I told them, two sandwiches short of a picnic. I would be voting for their chap. Thank God duplicity comes easily to politicians.

My daughter from my first marriage tells me that, this morning, I was for a few moments simultaneously on three television channels. There may be a lot of former ministers but there still do not seem to be quite enough to go around. One cheeky bugger of an interviewer – one of these new young chaps who keeps looking at you as if your flies are undone – said: 'I expect you'll be hoping for your old job back.' I muttered that that had nothing to do with it, as any sensible viewer would realize. On all three channels, I refused to state a preference for either candidate, on the grounds that the ballot is secret.

My constituents, inevitably, cruelly distracted by these events from their plan to have the nation renamed after her, are pressuring me to tell. 'Sir,' I told one such interlocutor. 'That matter is private, like a man's religion and his hat-size.' One of these smart-arse second-hand car salesmen the party now unfortunately attracts, he replied: 'Oh, is that a fact? Well, I do know you're an Anglican and a bighead. And I think I've guessed the third one as well.' I shall, of course, be voting for the challenger. My view is that this is too good an opportunity to miss, like Hamlet catching Claudius at prayer. But I have neither doubts nor bad dreams. Now might we do it, pat.

The guvnor says we ought to change her handle from Boadicea to Marie Antoinette, on account of her being for the chop in Paris. My view – and that of many of the police force – is that anyone who does this to her needs locking up (Office joke). She shows no particular signs of stress apart from occasionally checking her watch.

It is winter dusk and the courtyard of the British Embassy in Paris is bright with artificial light. Every half-minute I spot and hail a journalist I know. The illumination, from the rigs of television crews, for some reason makes me think of a murder investigation. In those television detective serials, when a body is discovered at night, they light the site like this. In trying to find a comparison for the tension of these moments, as we wait for the ballot result to be phoned through here, I am also drawn to the genre of the thriller. I mean particularly those moments towards the end of the film or episode when the hero attempts to still the ticking nuclear device. But, even as a child, you soon appreciate that the hero will survive. The difference is that, here, we really do not know if the heroine will wriggle free. She will learn the verdict in an upstairs room, flanked, apparently, by her press secretary and her private secretary. In the sweepstake on her fate – measured in the number of votes secured by her Challenger – I have drawn the figure of a hundred and sixty-eight, which is highly unlikely. It is figured that one hundred and twenty equals blood drawn, one hundred and forty major organ damage and one hundred and sixty fetch-a-stretcher. Whatever the result, you could sense, at the summit today, the myth ebbing away. The other leaders looked at her in that way of colleagues in an office when it is revealed or rumoured that some company upright hits his wife or does it with sheep. The faces say: I didn't know. Did you know? It is a withdrawal of awe.

'Yes, I'm sorry, Peter, I hope you can hear me in the studio. I've got to whisper because I am actually standing outside Committee Room 12. An MP has just rushed past me . . . his face is, well, inscrutable really, which isn't much use and yes, it's a hundred and fifty-two votes for . . .'

The number – one hundred and fifty-two – is shouted round the courtyard, then screamed back into telephones, so that the place suddenly sounds like the Stock Exchange. In the midst of this, there is a little whoop of pleasure from the journalist who's won the sweepstake. Two television crews are arguing over satellite time. Second ballot, everyone is saying, second ballot.

I said to my husband: 'There's no end to the dusting this might mean.' He said: 'It's not that I'm being unsympathetic but there'd be pluses.'

When the result was announced, I shouted, very loudly, 'Brutus!' One of the wets – the kind that reads books – murmured that he wasn't sure that I didn't mean Judas. I shouted, just as loudly, 'Judas!' to be safe. The view of the Hard And Straight Group is this: OK, you've had your fun. Very amusing. You've thrown your ball through the conservatory window. Now, let's pull ourselves together and end this silly game. On television tonight we will denounce the election rules as ridiculous.

I had requested of my 6 p.m. client – a most very well known actress – that I be permitted to keep a wireless playing by the bath. When I hear the news, I say, 'Oh my goodness, I do not believe they are doing this.' She says, 'Oh, Madame A, you can't mean it. Most people in this country have been praying for years you'd accidentally pull the wrong lever.'

I have a terrible feeling this means Krakatoa time tonight. However, the message is: lay out the gladrags for the ballet. Business as usual.

'New par. One former minister said colon quote she is a lame duck now endquote stop. A leading opposition politician riposted colon quote lame question mark at least stop. I have had ducks with more life served *à l'orange* that's 1 apostrophe endquote stop.'

A television reporter on the steps of the Palace is broadcasting live to London. A time for consideration, reflection, he is saying. The Prime Minister will be speaking to her advisers. We are not expecting any early reaction. At this moment, the great door of the Embassy swings open and she, with her weird Groucho crouching run, like someone picking up their car keys as they dash in from the rain – Nixon, incidentally, had a funny walk as well – advances down the steps behind him. The reporter is innocent of this. On a monitor in our corner, we hear the presenter in London yelling: 'She's behind you, she's behind you!' Never has the comparison of politics with a pantomime been more apt. Her chief press secretary is running after her, like a policeman chasing a streaker in a sports stadium. Barking 'Where's the microphone?' he barges journalists out of the way. She says that she will be allowing her name to go forward for the second ballot. She did not, she says, get quite the required majority, but nearly.

OK, OK, gather round. Don't let the attractions of gay Paris go to your head when you write your stories, gentlemen. Get it in perspective. The view of the Prime Minister is that it is the prerogative of her challenger, who failed to beat her outright, to withdraw. Her view is that, in the next round, one vote will be enough, as it is in every other election. She will be missing the ballet tonight but will attend a dinner in Versailles. The mood she's in? Oh, I'd say her only real cause for alarm is that the German Chancellor has promised to devote this evening to cheering 'er up.

'Boadicea to Versailles. Boadicea to Versailles.' The consensus view of Special Branch – confirmed by officers riding in her car – is that she has not been crying.

I will never forget that tableau: The Mad Woman on the Embassy Steps. I think it can be regarded as one photo-opportunity too many; another attempt to appeal to the people over her colleagues and the press. However, like that other late tableau – The Responsible Citizen Demonstrates the Evils of Litter – it failed. In fact the image conveyed all the symptoms of her decline: impulsiveness, a refusal to consult others, a wild-eyed belief in her own destiny. A wonderful, though unconfirmable, story is going around about the prelude to the sermon on the steps. It is said that, as soon as the result was announced, she declared her intention of going outside to spread forth her immortality. Her press secretary and private secretary advised against and formed a casual, but, given their size, significant, blockade of the door. At this, she expressed a desire to powder her nose, to which they gentlemanly acquiesced. Then she headed for the Ladies, turned and sped for the exit. Can this perfect symbol of her nature be true? Certainly, on the replay, her press secretary looks breathless, like a man in pursuit. I believe that, when they concern the celebrated, rumours have their own legitimacy and I present the story in that spirit.

'New par. The Prime Minister returned from Paris this morning stop. This afternoon comma a statement was issued on her behalf stop. It read colon quote I fight on comma I fight to win stop. However comma it is believed that party managers are still conducting a damage assessment exercise and that there may yet be pressure on her to stand down stop. Can you give me Home?'

I was approached in the House this afternoon by the Chief Whip. He said he wanted to sound me out about the way the wind was blowing. He said that he thought a rebel with a grievance – a reference, presumably, to my untimely ripping from the womb of power – might be the perfect weathercock. Her wobbles have made us cocky. So I told him I thought the wind was blowing through her head. This was a reference to a remark I have long treasured, made in 1979 by the press secretary of President Idi Dada Amin. 'The president is not well,' this poetic gentleman told the press. 'The wind is beginning to blow through his head.' The Chief Whip said – he's a dry old bugger – 'I'll not be marking you down as a definite for her, then.' He asked if I felt that my colleagues might be swayed by the promise of a reformed, listening Prime Minister. I said they might. But then, as I told him, the animal kingdom might equally be swayed by heavy off-the-record briefing that the skunk had discovered soap.

At a meeting of the Hard And Straight Group, we confirmed tonight our total faith in 'a Prime Minister in her prime'. A neat phrase, of my own invention. Shortly after this meeting, it came to our attention that, in individual discussions with her ministers this evening, grade one quislings were saying that they wanted her to stay but feared she could not win, while grade two quislings were threatening to resign unless she did. I used my car phone to ring a senior fellow member. 'OK, we're going nuclear,' I said. We demanded a meeting with Margaret at which we begged her to stay. We left with the strong impression that she would.

'New par. At the meeting of the cabinet at which she announced

326

her resignation to emotional colleagues comma the Prime Minister was said to have remarked colon quote It's a funny old world endquote stop.'

Separating them with tissue paper – blue, I thought, was best – I pack away her porcelain men, one by one. I wonder if she'll find space for them in her retirement home. (Apparently, it's in Dulwich, where my sister looked, but didn't like it.) My husband said it's a good job they're not the kind you can stick pins in.

I wonder if she would think it very funny if I asked about the possibility of putting a small plaque on the side of the bath.

For her going-away outfit, she has chosen a burgundy two-piece. There is no particular symbolism in this, I think, although I was educated by Jesuits and it is something like the colour the priest wore on Martyrs' days.

My colleagues and I in the Hard And Straight Group are pledged – let there be no doubt about this – that those who did this to her will be hunted down and punished. She was taken before her time, long, long before her time, by pygmies. This is, for us, an act with the private dimensions of a bereavement and the public dimensions of treason against the state. However, we know who Cassius was and Cassius, I think, knows that we know. Cassius now holds one of the major offices of state. But there will be no escape for him. A highly trained squad of fanatical columnists will isolate and eliminate him in the right-wing press.

And do not, either, make the mistake of thinking that this is the end for her. For the moment, she will be Queen over the water – although Dulwich may, I admit, be a little far in that direction – but she will return. The nation will, in time, appreciate the magnitude of its mistake. And Margaret will be magnanimous enough to accept their invitation, for humility was by no means the least of her manifold virtues. For the moment, we are intending to establish a Trust, ideally with charitable status, to sustain her ideas and legacy throughout the Free World. I am, whatever the so-called constitutional position, her backbencher, hers still. Always. At night, in my dreams, she comes with a machine-gun and, in erotic slow-motion, mows down those who broke her.

They announced it on the platform when I was waiting for a train to my sister's in Nottingham. 'The Prime Minister has resigned.' I don't know if any more details were given, because there was a great whoop, like when you're walking past the football ground and you know a goal's been scored. Only closer than that. And people were laughing and applauding on an intercity train waiting to pull out. And I thought – this is terrible, really – I thought of VE Day, that same feeling of relief, of strangers looking as if they wanted to shake hands or hug each other and only being English stopped them. And I thought of Snobby looking disapproving in the classroom all those years ago and there was somehow no way you could connect the two events. What makes me really mad is that, the way things turned out, this will convince the fellas that a woman isn't up to it. Back to suits and dandruff.

Let me, as a priest, look, from as objective a theological position as possible, at the success of what we might call, in shorthand, the Assisi Manifesto, that prayerful of promises made on her first day in office. After all, few previous political regimes have been built on so explicitly Christian an agenda, although, of course, deist regimes of other faiths are a burgeoning phenomenon.

1 'Where there is war, may we bring peace.' A tricky one. Her time in office was bordered by two large conflicts, the first of which (the Falklands) she won and the second of which (the Persian Gulf) she has left, as it were, unbegun. The American press, I notice, credits her with 'stiffening the President's

resolve' to go to war, so perhaps this one really ought to be chalked up to her too. Then, there's also Northern Ireland, the war that isn't there, to which none of us, in all honesty, gives a waking thought, but which continued throughout her eleven years.

I often think it's odd, the difference between the reaction of the Americans if someone who has read a page of *Das Kapital* even sneezes in what the nation thinks of as its 'backyard', a geographically elastic concept, and our unfussy acceptance of what is happening in what really does back on to our house. Well, pass or fail? Look again at the firmness of the Assisi words. Peace must replace war. There is nothing about going to war to secure a better peace or establishing peace without preconditions in line with such and such an accord. So, I fear, fail.

2 'Where there is hatred, may we bring love.' Again, by no means a straightforward one. To live a comfortable existence in the modern world, it is necessary to have a selective memory. Even so, I find it something of a shock to look back at a period which I have helped to represent in speeches as a time of unprecedented national optimism and prosperity and find myself forced to recall the three episodes of violence, apart from the two wars, which have marked her time in office: the race riots of 1981, the riot-shield policing of the miners' strike in 1984, and the bitter demonstrations against the poll tax of the last two years.

Has any modern elected politician unleashed hatred, a word I dislike but feel constrained to employ, on the scale that she did? Cartoons and television spoofs have become nastier and more furious during her decade. Her fierce certainty, chafing and irritating, produced a boil of strong response. Oh, it is true that she seems to have promoted an equally unprecedented level of popular devotion: the howling voices on the radio phone-ins during the days since her fall have the authentic timbre of mourning. So, a draw, high-scoring on both sides. But the

Church would not, I think, teach that creation of x quantity of love cancels out x quantity of hatred. Fail, then.

3 'Where there is discord, may we bring harmony.' Tell you an amusing story about that one. In the generally accepted translation, the final word is 'union'. Just before she announced the Assisi Manifesto, a colleague of mine had a phone call from her office, asking whether there was an alternative translation of the word. She didn't want to say 'union', because of its associations with industrial trade organizations, whom she, unfortunate word again, hated. 'Harmony' was suggested as a compromise.

However, this story makes it clear that, even when she said it, her mind was set on the destruction of union power. That may be a political achievement of great merit but, spiritually, she amended a prayer for pragmatic purposes. Equally, her handling of the cabinet cannot, with any semantic accuracy, be described as harmonious, given her propensity for sacking those who were not 'one of us' and encouraging even some of those who were to walk out. So, if we're marking the card hard, another fail.

Do you know something? I think she was right, in a way that she did not intend, when she hissed at my senior colleagues in the Church that religion and politics should not mix.

Finally – and I 'ope you'll miss my voice as much as I'll miss your faces – she will be driven home to Dulwich after seeing the Queen. Yes, Simon? The duck? I don't know what's going to happen to the fucking duck.

I have been asked, surprise, surprise, to write a piece summing up her eleven years. Liberal qualms prevent me from using – in print, at least – the comparison with an Eastern European country after Communism. But that's how it feels. Britain has the feel of Luxemburg or Belgium: a small and hesitant place dependent on tourism. We again have a leader – a shy man

330

with a smile and glasses – commensurate with her status as a nation.

I suppose that I will play around, in this piece, with some paradoxes. The oddness that a politician who was destroyed because of her refusal to countenance surrender of Englishness to Europe simultaneously seemed prepared to make the nation a satellite of America: finally, in the bloody war which seems to await us in the Gulf, presenting with pride the idea of being a kind of pecker-bird for the American military rhinoceros. The Iron Lady and her Uncle Sam. Why did she detest Europe so? I have a theory that it's because she has an English civilian's attitude to Germany. Male politicians of her generation, who actually fought against the Hun, are far more amenable to unity. She, though, spent the war under a kitchen table, filled with morale-raising stories about Hitler.

And there is also the paradox of someone who spoke so often about freedom being responsible for expensively preventing a book called *Spycatcher* from being published in her own country (though freely available everywhere else). This was despite the fact that the book claimed to expose the ultimate offence against democracy: the destabilizing of an elected British Labour government in the 1970s. This champion of freedom also frequently attempted to have television programmes on subjects which worried her removed from the schedules, the tapes seized from the studios before transmission or the producers censured afterwards.

I will also hope to argue – and can predict already the postmarks on the apoplectic letters which splutter in – that history may largely ignore her, relegating her to the second division of leaders. For what were her shibboleths? Home ownership? Listen now to the tramp of bailiffs to the doors. Hear the howl about the poll tax, the price of living in a house somehow rising quite as spitefully as the cost of buying one. Economic recovery? Cyclical, currently very glum. A place on the world stage? Her and whose army. A moral crusade? The doors of the divorce courts are not boarded up. In fact, more branches may be opening.

This would be the greatest paradox of all. That a politician three times elected, ruling for eleven years, regarded by her party and part of the country during that time with an adulation which makes the Mariolatory of the Vatican look apathetic, could leave such a small dent behind. Longevity, novelty of gender, and the ruination of the trade unions. For a lesser man, it might have been enough. But surely it must disappoint this theorist of Year Zero, this Conservative believer in permanent revolution.

There is also the possibility that history, far from ignoring her, will maul her. She provides a fascinating case-history in the additions and reductions demanded by high office in the modern world. Her body already extensively remodelled for the electorate, her mind made a journey of its own during those eleven years. Used in the time before her and Reagan to one-term presidents, two-year Prime Ministers, we had perhaps forgotten the radioactive fall-out from the core of a country and the dangers for those who sit close to it. We had forgotten the symptoms: the deafness that comes from hearing only syco-phants, the inability to imagine the lives of the lowest which comes from the pampered, nannied high life of leadership.

This is what interests me. Long after her policies and the local impact of her character are forgotten, she will represent a wonderful study in the destructiveness of power.

I would be silly to pretend that the offer of a knighthood was not some balm. I am organizing a fund for the creation of a statue: of her, not me, that is. The Hard And Straight Group is in touch with a sculptor of sound political views, who tells me he is looking at the possibilities of constructing it in iron.

Of course, it's the wife that's really made up about the knight-hood. For me, it will still be first-name terms at the Plough and Whistle. That's on the record, if you want.

They now must call me sir. I will call them Judas.

'New par. It has been traditional for prime ministers plural to reward their closest supporters plural in politics and the press through the honours system. Stop. Even so comma some eyebrows have been raised . . .'

My surgeon reckons he can wrap it up in four more skin grafts. We seem to be getting somewhere. Sometimes, passing a shop window, I sneak a glance. It's easier, anyway, now that the interest from the papers and the box has gone. There was a film about me. One of the reviewers said that it ought to stop politicians from starting a war for at least the next two decades. I was going to drop him a postcard now. I got rung up when this Gulf business started. I know a lot of the buggers out there. I just hope that if any of them cop it – and these guys have got stuff which makes the ammo the Argies had look like flyspray – I just hope they're remembered for longer than we were. And I'm glad it's not her in charge, stomping around shouting 'Rejoice! Rejoice!' like she did during our show. Out there in the Gulf, the towel-heads keep going on about a 'Mother of Battles'. I think that's what she'd like to have been called. And before any of the papers has me court-martialled, I'm not a pacifist. I'm a soldier who saw war. Do you know, there's only been one monument to an ordinary soldier and he was Unknown.

I've been talking to another lass, who was in our class. She said she wondered if Snobby would send a note to *The Old Granthamite* – that's our old girls' rag – saying: 'Margaret (Roberts) Thatcher (1936–1943) has been fully occupied running the country for the last eleven years but now plans to spend more time with her family.'

The new chap, there's no porcelain. Plastic cricketers. Bugger to dust.

Apparently I am not to be restored to a cabinet position, certain half-wits from the last regime surviving in the interests of party unity. It is a disappointment, particularly to my wife, but my opposition to Margaret was never about my own career hopes. Oh, no.

The Hard And Straight Group has discovered that Cassius – and other members of her cabinet – attended a supper – I hope they used long spoons! – at the house of a traitor before – this is the point – before the Prime Minister had decided to resign. We now believe that there was a conspiracy of ruthless men to remove her from the sacred office to which the public raised her. We have, however, seen that film about Watergate starring Robert Redford and we will use the same methods to secure the truth of these events.

The editor's got this thing about conspiracies. I said: look, there wasn't a conspiracy, just a mass coincidence of commonsense.

She said she wouldn't need full-time advisers in the future. However, when I'd got pushed of my memoirs, I might lend a spot of advice about the press and so on. She said she wouldn't be silent. There would be speeches and interviews, after a brief interlude of national mourning. She mentioned De Gaulle a lot. I said: I thought you'd always hated the Frogs.

Oh, lovely! There's no doubt at all that the purple number was the inspired choice. There's a perfect play-off with the black of the Number 10 door. And the camera flashes give her a sort of halo, which doesn't hurt. Here she comes, into her car. Oh, lawks, the poppet looks a little liquid. I suddenly panic about whether the mascara was the water-resistant sort.

The chariot door slams for the last time. The vultures and fuckpigs bang off pictures through the glass, as if she was a bomber or something. Raising my radio to my lips, flicking with

my cuff at my eye – I seem to have got something in it – I say:
'Boadicea home. Boadicea home.'

Teach Yourself American In Seven Days

'The New York sandwich, a mere piece of etymology, a disregardable slice of bread, under a square meal hidden, is an example of the way in which American things grow beyond their origins.'

ANTHONY BURGESS – *You've Had Your Time*

Teach Yourself American
In Seven Days

Before leaving to eat – he was already salivating as he began to balance the competing attractions of blood-raw rump steak and haemorrhaging hamburger – he decided to treat himself to some more American television.

Robert Oscott, although still forced by law to carry a British passport, appreciated, among many other cultural distinctions, the way in which America's use of the medium differed from Britain's. American television for adults had comforts generally only available in British television for children: presenters wearing outfits in primary shades spoke clearly through vast, reassuring smiles in items which rarely lasted longer than a minute.

Button-punching to his favoured frequency, he found the jauntiest of the network weathermen. Out on location in the Midwest, this jokey doughnut of a bloke was warning of prevailing winds. Only he didn't do it as the English would, with Physics-teacher talk of belts of low pressure and north-westerly gusts. He simply yelled at the camera: 'You think it's windy today? Listen, five minutes back, I had hair!' With this, the weatherman jerked off a baseball cap to expose his familiar growthless dome.

Chuckling, Oscott vaporized the weatherman, riding the remote control through the American President warning Iraq to get out of Kuwait or else – the Gulf Crisis was about to become the Gulf War, Operation Desert Shield to mutate into Operation Desert Storm – and then past the faintly eerie sepia-TV of a 1950s American comedy show, before settling on a baseball game in which his adopted team – the Los Angeles Raiders – appeared to be winning, although, as an Englishman, he feared it would be another few years before he was sure of the rules.

At the end of an inning – he was learning to lose the English plural usage from cricket: *innings* – Oscott killed the picture and took what he now called the subway to a, what was the word?, diner called Adam's Ribs. It was a gloomy cellar-like space below street level, decorated with early American beer and automobile posters. In both the Smoking and No Smoking sections, there was a juke-box of the old kind with thick pipes like a cathedral organ and a front like the fender of a big truck.

'Hi! I'm Sandy,' said a waitress after leaving him with the menu, a complimentary glass of 80 per cent ice and 20 per cent water, and the information that the specials today were a char-broiled tender baby chicken stuffed with apricots and chestnuts, which she herself was hoping to have later if there was any left, and monk-fish fillets steamed in a light raspberry mustard sauce, which a lot of the pre-theatre crowd were saying was delicious.

Oscott considered this kind of cuisine rather regrettably European in influence and favoured the broad, basic flavours of the native dishes, particularly the barbecued ribs which gave the restaurant its name – the owner was not actually called Adam – and the hamburgers. There was a fourteen-ounce serving in a wholemeal bun which he particularly relished. Eating it pulled at the little skin hinges in the corners of your mouth and made you think of holding open wide for the dentist.

When Sandy returned, he saw from a badge on her minimal red tunic – the rib-theme of the diner seemed to extend as far as the eaters being able to see those of the female staff – that she spelled her name Sandi.

'What can I get for you today?' asked Sandi.

'Let's see. I'll have Onion Loaf to start. And then a fourteen-ounce Pacific Heights, rare, very rare, with fries. Extra fries, if that's no . . .'

'Sir, you got it. Coleslaw or Summer Salad with that?'

'Coleslaw, please.'

'Would that be Lite 'n' Healthy mayonnaise or Regular with your 'slaw, sir?'

'Uh, Regular.'

'Can I get you anything to drink?' Canna getya ennthina dreeunk. He tried to guess from her delivery which state she had come from to this one. He was too shy to ask.

'I'll have a Stag, please.'

Stag was his present number one among American beers. A Pacific Heights was similarly top of his burger charts. In this design, the beef was topped with blue cheese, chilis, and fried banana.

Tonight, he found the Onion Loaf, a sort of oblong of onion rings stuck together, rather dry – it needed to be slipping in oil – but the Pacific Heights was the usual delight. After his final bite of bun and beef, he neatly swabbed up the blood pooled on the plate with French fries.

Sandi asked him if he wanted dee-zirt. He did, choosing a treat which the menu jokingly titled Don't Tell The Cardiologist! It consisted of strawberry shortcake soaked in rum, topped with four scoops of butter-pecan ice-cream and smothered with hot fudge sauce and whipped cream.

When he left, Oscott tipped Sandi handsomely, although he had been forced to ask her for sugar for his coffee, when it ought to have been on the table.

On the street, he couldn't find a cab and was forced to take a bus. This deflated him. In a cab, he could shut his eyes and pretend that the vehicle, though black and squat, was really wide and yellow, taking the corners and jumping the pot-holes of New York. A bus, particularly if you were forced to take the upper deck, was literally and lumpenly London-bound. This detracted from what had been a very satisfying evening of fantasy.

For this was the thing which Robert Oscott liked most about London in 1990: that, with network television coming by cable and satellite, the sleek City sandwich joints which sold greasy pastrami piled on rye, the underground restaurants where Californian and Brooklyn girls served you fat and haemorrhaging hamburgers, you could pretend to be in America.

Back in what he tried to remember to call his apartment in West London, he slumped on the sofa, glum that the red double-decker bus had so ruined his illusion. He had been planning to complete his American evening by masturbating over some magazine pictures of an actress newly famous in the States. Someone at work had said they were as close as you got to crotch shots without actually seeing the lips.

Oscott tried to recover the mood by punching through his cable and satellite channels. Even more so than the food, it was a sure method of entry to the pretence. British television was like visiting your mother. American television was like visiting your lover. And, although even the main British channels featured more and more American programming, cable and satellite were still the surest way of avoiding anything English and tasteful.

Born middle-class English in the late '50s, Robert Oscott had grown up watching the British Broadcasting Corporation, with its solemn charter to inform, educate, and entertain. His parents, a suburban solicitor and a suburban solicitor's wife, had considered the single British commercial channel vulgar and limited his viewing of it to news and the occasional wildlife documentary. The housemaster at his boarding school had taken the same view, rarely relenting to more than a sixth-form dispensation to view a Sunday night production of Ibsen or Molière on the BBC. Accordingly, it was not until Oscott attended university in the last years of the '70s – 'Keys', he would say, now, which any people worth impressing would know was Gonville and Caius, Cambridge – that he saw television advertisements in any quantity.

Suddenly, he had understood the origin of tantalizing mantras – 'Nice one, Cyril!', 'I'm with the Woolwich!', 'Course you can, Malcolm!' – recited by his class-mates and passengers on public transport. The discovery of the source was like the mastery of a foreign tongue. Perplexing memories were at once set in context. For example, after his first sexual encounter, aged seventeen at a party, with a friend of his older sister whom he thought a little chubby but impressively well-spoken, he had spurted rather too early. In fact, if he was honest with himself, it was borderline whether he had got it in at all.

'Ooops!' the girl had said, in a tone of voice which suggested that he had spilled his tea rather than his seed, before rubbing with her fingers near to the base of his testicles. This delicate attention rapidly magicked a second erection, which proved more usable. 'Only Heineken can do this!' she had murmured, straddling her clever construct. He had smiled, but was mystified. Heineken, he knew, was a beer, but could it also be the name of some German sexologist, who had created this arousal technique – he had read of one called Heimlich's Manoeuvre, for saving people from choking – or even a cream, although he had not seen her reach for one?

It was only eighteen months later in his college common room – a majority of the students was sardonically addicted to an evening soap opera set in the North of England – that he had finally understood. That particular German lager ran a series of commercials in which the pay-off was the supposed restorative properties of the brew. The revelation of this and other saleslines made conversation easier.

He had realized in his teens that, if your parents or your friends used, to general amusement, a phrase you didn't recognize, it was probably from some wartime radio comic or a writer like Jerome K. Jerome whom you thought you might get round to reading when you were older. Now he had broken another spoken code. If someone younger used a mystifying line, it was probably one used to promote a drink, a cheese spread, or a piece of kitchen equipment on television. Working as a banker in London in the 1980s, he had also been able to add a third rule of usage: anything incomprehensible said by an American was probably a reference to baseball.

Oscott had joined from university a broker's called Hanratty Forest Podge. Many of his generation of colleagues had the advantage of money running in the family – both as a profession and a consequence of their profession – but Oscott, willing to add long hours to the solid gloss of charm and manners lent by his education, had risen to be a junior partner by the time, in 1987, that the old English company was taken over by Potomac Johnson (US) to become Potomac Johnson Hodge.

Many of Oscott's colleagues resented the immigrant Americans in the City – with their neologisms, jogging, and obsession with the performance of the dollar – but he was exhilarated by them. Perhaps this was because, although Oscott had been obsessed by social background ever since realizing as a teenager that not everyone in life had the same start-line, he had recently come to feel that he would never, despite Keys and other openings, accumulate quite enough class kudos to get as far as he would like in Britain. The top men from Potomac Johnson, never once asking him which school he went to or whether he was by any chance one of the Norfolk Oscotts, held out the promise of an oasis of meritocracy in which the superior breeding of his British colleagues could be neutralized.

Oscott also convinced himself that instinct played a part alongside cynicism. He had always, for example, felt uneasy with the anti-Americanism which was standard among his circle, whatever their political direction. At Cambridge, a favourite student diversion had been sneaking in at the back of groups of US tourists – with their rhinoceros bottoms in vivid stretch slacks – and joining in the chorus of 'Oh, gee' and 'You gotta shot of that?' when the guide indicated an ancient date on a college lintel.

Oscott, however, had found this activity childish and would

argue: 'OK, they're gross, but so what? I mean, would you like it if those oiks who eat sausage and chips in Real English Pubs on the Costa del Smell were taken as representative of all our great nation?' He had also been the only voice to demur when, around the time of the takeover, another junior partner had said: 'The thing to remember about Americans is that they are essentially a nation of four-year-olds.' A final item of evidence in this respect was that, at university, Oscott had read a novel, of which the opening line was: 'I am an American, Chicago-born.' I am an American. I am an American. It had seemed to him one of the most resonant phrases he had ever encountered and he was suddenly heavy with envy that he would never be able to speak the words himself.

Now, as he scanned the channels, his big American dinner shifting and sifting in his stomach, he located a US game show on one of the satellite stations. The programme, one of his favourites, was called *Cash-Dash-Flash*. In it, contestants were asked questions on General Knowledge. If they gave an incorrect reply, they had to chase down a short hardboard corridor, like a rabbit run, and press a button before a large red light went on. If they succeeded, they were permitted another question. Five right answers qualified them to attempt a one-off query, called The Big Brain Teaser. Success at this stage brought them an accumulating dollar jackpot.

As Oscott watched, a woman shaped like a bean-bag, wearing a purple trouser-suit apparently chosen to blend with her hair-tint, bounded across the studio, where she was embraced by the host, an elderly comedian whose own hair, which resembled in shape and positioning a grey felt yarmulke, was probably younger than himself. The meeting between the bean-bag and the host was not what you might call a hands-on hug, which suggested that perhaps he was worried about becoming parted from his parting.

'Tell all the lovely people out there who yare!' roared the presenter.

'Stanley, I'm Clarice Jansen from Draycott, North Carolina,' trilled the bean-bag.

'Hey! Hey! Hey! That is one ace of a place!' commented Stanley, raising his voice above the shriek of the studio audience, who were already giving a big hand to North Carolina.

The internal restructuring of Oscott's supper now resulted in a fart, which achieved his always sought-for combination of loud noise but low odour. Feeling a little uncomfortable in the tummy area, he loosened his belt and flies.

'Clarice, how do you spend your time down there in North Carolina?' asked Stanley. Since the early '80s, Oscott had noticed, game-show hosts had started asking the job-question euphemistically, because of high unemployment.

'Stanley,' said Clarice. 'I'm happy to be a full-time homemaker.' There were a few shrill cheers. She paused for effect. 'And grandmother.'

The audience had simultaneous orgasms at this news. Stanley put his arm around as much of the guest as he could span.

'Ya kidding me! Ya look like ya just left high school!' he shouted. One of the things that Oscott most admired about the Americans was that they valued personal esteem above sincerity. English manners meant making people feel small; American manners meant making them feel big.

After some stuff about the ages of the grandchildren, the questioning began.

'Clarice – and listen, ya take ya time here – Clarice, which famous American author wrote *Uncle Tom's Cabin*?'

Clarice said something which sounded like Harry Beecham Stove, which was accepted, to the ecstasy of the audience.

'That's one down, Clarice. Listen, now, ya obviously got brain as well as beauty. Ya go for two now. Maybe ya go buy all those sweet little grandkiddies of yours something cute from your winnings. We certainly hope so. Clarice, what substance has the chemical formula – that's hey, like, a kind of scientific nickname, OK? – has the chemical formula haitch-two-oh?'

'Hydrogen!' guessed Clarice. A couple of intellectuals in the audience groaned, knowing that she was wrong. The rest were soon informed by an electronic sound not unlike the one which Oscott had produced naturally a few minutes previously. Clarice lurched between the wooden screens, her bulk forcing her to brush against the sides. She was less than half-way to the button when the light was activated.

'Dash – Flash – Which means no Cash!' screamed the host. Many of the studio audience joined in what was the pro-gramme's catchphrase, as did Oscott in West London. Wheez-ing and beetroot, Clarice, who looked alarmingly close to a stroke, was picked up and steered away by a tanned girl in a lurex swimsuit. Stanley reassured the viewers that she would receive an all-weather garden barbecue in consolation. Oscott, feeling sorry for Clarice, who had looked like an original Ameri-can rather than an immigrant stick-on, switched over to a news channel, where an American general was summarizing the latest successes against Iraq.

Oscott's girlfriend, Henrietta, whose friends called her Henry, was at her own flat that night. It wasn't that Oscott didn't like her – she was a dependable old-money ex-head-girl type who could be persuaded to do blow-jobs when drunk – but, on this particular evening, her absence was, he chuckled to himself, a relief. It meant that he was able to bring himself to a three-jerk spurt with the magazine, imagining himself sliding between the American thighs of the actress. It was one of his regrets that he had never yet had sex with an American girl. Part of the reason for this omission was that Oscott had, despite the intensity of his secret life, never been to America.

On the Tuesday, when the announcement was made, Oscott felt like a successful contestant in a game-show. Brind, whose business cards said J. Herbert Brind III, and who was the top Yank at the London end of Potomac Johnson Hodge, took the partners out to lunch. To Oscott's horror, the American had chosen Albion, a currently modish central London restaurant, in which the food was English in inspiration as, compounding the felony, was the wine. The waitresses wore a variation of Beefeater costume.

Either Brind had a sentimental attachment to Anglo-Saxonry, which seemed to be a weakness of even the jogging and top-dollar-orthodontry Americans, or he was thoughtfully accommodating British insularity by not asking his colleagues to dare anything beyond the local fare.

Certainly, one of those invited – a rather prissy guy (Oscott was gradually teaching himself not to say chap) called Alastair – seemed delighted by the choice.

'Best grub on the globe,' he spluttered, chewing a lamb-chop. He was eating it peasant-style, holding it to his mouth with his hands.

Oscott was eating with rather less relish a plate of Steak and Kidney Pie and sipping at a glass of Côte de Cotswold '87, when Brind gave a familiar pre-monologue cough and, the table falling silent, said: 'Since the merger, our guys have been getting to know you guys and, take it from me, we're mighty glad to have you guys on side. I guess your George III never thought that one day you guys would be a colony of ours . . .'

The guy who was called Alastair suddenly looked in need of medical attention. Brind continued: 'Listen, I'm only fooling when I say that, Al. Point I'm making is, Potomac Johnson HQ in New York, New York, have been on the line saying that their guys'd kinda like to get to know you guys like we guys do. That's a lot of guys, but I hope you hear what I'm saying.'

What he was saying, they heard next, was that all London partners at their level and in their departments would be visiting New York in March – it was now the end of January – to attend a Management Refresher Seminar. Someone asked Brind about the schedule of such a seminar. Brind was using the hand-written wine list to flap away smoke from a neighbouring table.

'When are you guys going to wise up to no-smoking zones? It's a fundamental civil liberties issue,' he said. And then: 'John, the schedule will be standard corporate in-flight refuelling, with an eye to future upgrades to vice-president status. We'd envisage role-playing, problem-solving, individual goal-counselling, group encounter therapy.'

Brind left them shortly afterwards, having declined the Sticky Toffee Pudding With Real Egg Custard which his junior colleagues had all ordered. He told them to take their time and that the tab was taken care of. The Americans rarely took longer than forty-five minutes over lunch but respected the different cultural traditions of the English partners.

'Jamm-eee,' said one of them, with a low whistle, when Brind had disappeared from ear-shot. 'One week, free board and broads, in the You Ess of Ay.'

Most of the others had visited America before, some on vacation (California or Florida) and one as a student at the Harvard Business School. Oscott's transatlantic virginity amused them.

'Of course,' said Oscott. 'Like anyone of my age, I've kind of been to America. I go there all the time. The telly, books, films . . .'

'The London Stock Exchange,' said someone.

'Yes. Well. Quite,' muttered the guy called Alastair. He, too, had never been to America before but nor did he now seem very pleased at adding the visa to his passport.

'Group Encounter. Goal-counselling. Role-playing,' he drawled. 'What, pray someone tell me, is role-playing?'

But Oscott, for one, understood.

It was in the Travel section of a West End bookshop, two days later, that he made his discovery. All the necessary broad-brush stuff about the States he already knew from his self-infusions, but he was low on geographical and logistical details. After all, a series like *Dallas* wasn't intended for those who were visiting Texas; it was compensation for those who never would. In the same way, Oscott had a head full of souvenirs and snapshots of New York, from shows like *Kojak* and *Starsky and Hutch*, now blessedly repeated all night on cable, and those Ed McBain books he always took to France in the summer, but he still felt he needed a Fodor's or a Frommer's for the street-grid and restaurant-addresses side of things.

Heading for the till with his Fodor's, Oscott stopped to browse beside the Berlitz's and other quick foreign phrase-trainers. He was toying with learning Japanese as further career insurance, but that language was obviously thought too complex for these cassette-and-pamphlet crammers and he was about to abandon the search when, in the rack displaying a series called Langopac, of which he had not previously heard, he saw it: Teach Yourself American In Seven Days.

He read the sell on the back of the box. 'In one week, you can learn to speak – and even begin to think! – like a native American. In short, fun-to-do exercises, Langopac takes you through the basics of (North) American English. Enjoy, buddy, OK!'

The last phrase rather jarred his eye. But then he noticed that each of the series included on the packet some such cheery final injunction: Hasta La Vista! or Soyez Courage, Mon Brave!

When he opened the package at home, Oscott found six cassettes and a booklet divided into the same number of sections. The sections, which were called Program Modules, had headings like 'Gimme A Burger (The Language Of Food)', 'Shooting The Breeze (Everyday Conversation)', 'Last Licks (Baseball and Sporting Imagery)', and 'Arse Stroke Ass (Anglo-American Variations)'. There was also an envelope marked World Map. The sheet of glossy paper inside was perhaps two feet wide and bore an impression of a flattened Earth noticeably different from the familiar one. The continent of North America occupied almost all of the central space, with the rest of the world – a midget Britain, a smudge of an Australasia, a button-sized Russia – grouped in the margins, like the planets around the earth in a standard poster representation of the galaxy.

For the next hour, Oscott inserted the cassettes at random in his Walkman, rewinding and fast-forwarding to take the flavour of the course. Each tape began with a snatch (a word which was itself discussed in the Anglo-American Variations section) of the celebrated song about tom-arrrr-toes and tome-ayyy-toes. This was followed by an introduction from a breathy male American voice which sounded a little like Ronald Reagan's.

The narrator's approach was simple and folksy, like a slightly lower-key version of the host of *Cash-Dash-Flash*. For example, in the cassette dealing with food, he said: 'Now, you may reckon, you folks that are planning to become adopted children of Uncle Sam, that a breakfast of Biscuits with Jelly sounds like no real first meal of the day for someone in long pants. Now you already know from earlier in the course that the American word *pants* translates as ...'

Here, a second male voice, not dissimilar from that of the heir to the British throne, cut in with the word: 'Trousers,' pronounced as *trizers*. The Reagan-soundalike resumed the narration: 'In the same way, the American meal of Biscuits with Jelly translates into English as ...' The prince-voice interrupted with: '... roll (or bap) with jam (or preserves).' Now the gravelly American accent added: 'So, you see, if the waitress offers you Biscuits with Jelly, don't think she's being fresh with you. Now, "fresh" ...'

A lot of the early material, Oscott already knew: like how, in America, 'fanny' meant what women and men had round the back, whereas, in Britain, it meant what women had round the front. Oscott could see that this might lead to problems in the bedroom for the visitor. (In the same connection, however it concerned him that, in the Pocket American-English dictionary included in the pack, 'French letters' was translated as 'epistolary novel'.) There were also small variations of accent and grammar: for example, a contrast between an English newspaper report that a politician [abbreviated later to 'pol'] had 'protested the ban Tuesday', said *toos-day*, and an English cutting, in which a politician had 'protested *against* the ban *on* Tuesday', pronounced *chews-day*.

More unusual was a cassette marked 'Manners'. The pseudo-Reagan crooned: 'It's always good to thank another human being for performing a service or courtesy for you. But, in the United States of America, these necessary pleasantries have particular rules of usage. In England, an expression of pleasure might take the following form . . .' Here, the sub-royal voice already featured was joined by another in a brief duologue, apparently based around the delivery of food in a restaurant, which proceeded: 'Your steak, sir.' / 'Thank you.' / 'Thank *you*, sir. Another glass of wine? / 'No, thank you.' / 'Thank you, sir.'

Chuckling archly, the narrator cut in: 'And thank *you* to our two actors. Didn't they sound just like Sir Laurence Oliver? Now, listen carefully to the same conversation, taking place in American.'

Two lighter, younger voices were now heard to speak: one male, one female. The man talked, Oscott thought, like a Californian, the type Hollywood used for movies about yuppie bankers. He suspected that the woman was black. Their dialogue was: 'Surf 'n' Turf coming up, sir.' / 'Thanks.' / 'Uh-huh. Fix you another beer?' / 'Uh, I'm all set, thanks.' / 'Uh-huh. Enjoy your meal.'

The narrator re-introduced himself with his artificial giggle. 'Experience shows that one of the ways in which even the most fluent non-native American-speakers give themselves away is by saying "Thank you" too often. Remember that the correct reply to "Thank you" is "Uh-huh." Repeat after me. Uh-huh . . .'

Oscott diligently joined in with the repetition-exercises. The most complex featured two voices – the English prince and the Los Angeles banker – alternating sentences of a short story. The redneck presenter explained: 'In the next exercise, a kinda cute love story helps the student to identify key differences between your language and ours.' Then the bilingual melodrama began: a duet for two usages, with gaps for the student to parrot each phrase back.

AMERICAN: Bobby-Lou's folks were at a movie.

ENGLISH: Roberta's parents were visiting a cinema.

AMERICAN: Which was swell, because her guy had a window to ball her on the love-seat with the eggplant drapes down.

ENGLISH: This was fortuitous, as it presented her fiancé with an opportunity to make love to her on the settee, with the aubergine curtains drawn.

AMERICAN: As soon as Bobby-Lou's folks had gotten their limo, he jumped her, junking her barettes and bobby-pins.

ENGLISH: No sooner had Roberta's parents departed in their taxi-cab than he made advances to her, throwing her hairslides and hair-grips to one side.

AMERICAN: He dropped his pants and nixed her panty-hose.

ENGLISH: He lowered his trousers and removed her tights.

AMERICAN: She eyeballed his lovegun. 'Goddam,' she said.

ENGLISH: She espied his penis. 'Good lord!' she said.

AMERICAN: It was like a squash. It made other guys' look like zucchini.

ENGLISH: It was like a marrow. It made other guys' look like courgettes.

AMERICAN: She went down on his dick like it was a popsicle.

ENGLISH: She performed an act of fellatio, as if his organ were an iced lolly.

AMERICAN: Later, he said: 'It's cool. I gotten some rubbers at a five and ten.'

ENGLISH: Later, he said: 'It's all right. I purchased some prophylactics at a corner shop.'

AMERICAN: He gotten tooled up. She was amazed it fit.

ENGLISH: He donned it. She was amazed it fitted.

At this point, the main narrator explained that the story of Bobby-Lou and her guy was continued on another cassette. Oscott hungrily fumbled for the second tape. His only complaint against the tale was that, as with many language courses, the vocabulary taught was sometimes of little practical application. But the story was an absorbing one. It was clear to Oscott, from early on in the next cassette, that perhaps the guy's rubber hadn't fit too good, 'cos Bobby-Lou was in schtuck. Oscott's other objection was that the English translations often contained words spoken only in the kind of books he had been forced to read at school.

AMERICAN: When Bobby-Lou told her pop she was knocked up, he damn near leaked in his knickers.

ENGLISH: When Roberta informed her pater that she had fallen wrong, he almost urinated in his plus-fours.

AMERICAN: 'Hey, I wanna termination,' she said.

ENGLISH: 'Actually, I plan to arrange an abortion,' she said.

AMERICAN: 'In my view that's your first-amendment right,' her pop replied.

ENGLISH: 'Do that and you'll lose your inheritance,' her pater responded.

AMERICAN: 'Pop,' she kvetched. 'I'm too young for a life of diapers and pacifiers and, anyway, it's no bigger than a pollywog.'

ENGLISH: 'Father,' she complained, 'I'm too young for a life of nappies and dummies and, anyway, it's no bigger than a tadpole.'

AMERICAN: On the sidewalk outside the medical center were an African-American and a differently-abled person.

ENGLISH: On the pavement outside the hospital were a black and a cripple.

By the end of the week, he was working slowly through the final cassette, which was labelled 'Mayun, whaddaya you all? (Dialect variations: Deep South, Bronx, Texan)', and had completed with ease all the unseen translation exercises ('Render this page of the *New York Times* into clear, concise English') at the back of the booklet. After the seventh day of the course, the student was merely required to repeat, after the narrator, five times each morning, the phrase: 'I am an American. I am an American.'

But, as the week of the Management Refresher Seminar approached – he already had air tickets and traveller's cheques in his combination-lock genuine Arizonan crocodile-skin attaché case – Oscott's preparation was not restricted to Langopac. He now ate only American food: guzzled pancakes with bacon and syrup for breakfast, lunched on the Six-deck meat and cheese sandwich that his local delicatessen called a Statue of Liberty, nibbled pecan-butter or chocolate-chip cookies with his morning and afternoon coffee, though always careful not to eat so many that he spoiled his dinner in Adam's Rib, where they had fortunately added Real Cajun Catfish in Beer Batter to the menu. He was like an athlete preparing for a major race, with the admitted exception that he became fatter and more breathless as his training progressed.

At night, if he was not too enervated by the stacked fats and calories in his system or from his Langopac exercises, he would speed-read a few more pages of a book he had arranged to have sent by air courier from New York. It was currently Number 1 on the *New York Times* Non-Fiction Bestseller List. Called *The Other 90 Per Cent: Finding Your Fifth Gear*, it was described on the cover, which depicted a silhouette of a man, woman and child jumping with arms stretched out towards the highest branch of an oak tree, as 'an inspirational self-help guide in the dazzling tradition of the same author's *The Fourth Gear: Finding Your Right Lane*'. The author was someone called Dr Judah K. Pamploma, Jr.

In his (her?) preface – the biographical notes on the jacket were no help with gender – Dr Pamploma chummily summarized the intention of the book: 'All people are different. Let's face it, that's one of God's greatest gifts to His creation. I count myself as a people person – and I'm kind of lucky like that, as my work as a professional goal-counsellor brings me a new person every hour of the working day – and I'm here to tell you that people come in all shapes and sizes and colors. God has a whole big bunch of different people-molds in his production zone up there and His production controller breaks the mold each time the clay is dry.'

Oscott, who had grown up in the Church of England, could find all this upfront talk of God a little off-putting, even though he had now completed the brief Langopac Program Module called 'God Bless America (Religion and the Life of the Mind).'

However, like any student desperate to achieve a particular result, he had read on. Dr Pamploma continued: 'And, if I can generalize, I would say that people, for all their infinite variety, kind of, in the end, lap up at the shores of two particular extremes. In the real bad, no-no zone, there are those who function on only 10 per cent capacity. And in the hey-hey, way-to-go, home-run zone, there are the folks whose throttle sticks at 110 per cent.'

Thankfully, Langopac had already rendered Oscott fluent in the baseball imagery of the previous sentences. He read on: 'A lot of people, when they come to me for consultation, are in the first zone; most of them, when, after a year or two of sessions, they feel ready to walk alone again on the mean streets of modern life, are in the second zone. But I say: why stop there? Even the 110 per centers have the chance of joining society's two hundred per centers. And then, of course, there are all those ten per centers who haven't attended my clinics or read my first coast-to-coast bestseller. Both sets of folks have the chance of reaching the top ten per cent of society's achievers, leaving behind the other ninety per cent. I guess that explains the kind-of-cute title of this book.'

Perhaps, in an earlier, English, incarnation, Oscott would have cynically reflected that Dr Judah K. Pamploma Jr had rather cannily expanded the market for his book by attesting to its usefulness for both notably high achievers and notably low achievers. But he did not think that now. Perhaps it was because, by this regime of eating and reading, he was colonizing his colon and his brain in much the way that Langopac was planting a new flag on his vocabulary.

Oscott was reading Chapter 2 ('Prioritize Your Goal Zones') in bed one night, when he had his first row, on this particular topic at least, with Henry.

'Robs . . .'
'Uh-huh . . .'
'What's coming over you?'
'You gotta problem, hon . . . ?'

'Well, actually, that's exactly the kind of thing . . .'

'Shoot!'

'The thing is, Robs, this probably sounds completely loopy, but you seem to be changing, not just the getting fat, heaven knows I could do with a few pounds off round the middle, but the way you talk and . . .'

'I guess I hear what you're saying but . . . jeez, spit it out, willya?'

'Robs, are you . . . please don't get angry with me, I'm saying this for your own good . . . Robs, I'm just terribly terribly frightened that you might be turning into an . . . well . . . American.'

'Damn right, sweetie. And call me Bob.'

'Barb?'

'Correct. Bob. Robs is what they do to banks, OK, darlin'?'

'Robert, what is this? *Why* are you trying to become an American?'

'Because my asshole folks never had the goddam sense to get me born there . . .'

'Boy-un?'

'Correct. Born.'

'Robs, this is silly. It's like some stupid Jekyll and Hyde thing . . .'

'Damn right, honey. 'Cept, in this case, it's Dr Small One and Mr Big Prong . . .'

'Well, I must say I hadn't noticed any tangible difference,' said Henry, tartly, turning over on her side and switching off the light. Listening for a few seconds, before he returned to *The Other 90 Per Cent*, Oscott thought: Goddam chick is sniffling.

He found, in fact, despite his robust sexual boasting to Henry, that his appetite for intercourse diminished as his bulk increased. Whacking off (he was learning not to say masturbation), over some bronzed Hollywood starlet, was quite satisfactory most nights.

He reflected on Henry's comparison with the story of Dr Jekyll and Mr Hyde, but soon rejected it. The whole point about that tale, surely, was that a respectable man had a disreputable side, whereas his own transformation was benevolent and even historically logical. He was becoming what he ought to have been born. He had read about trans-sexuals, men made convincingly concave between the legs by delicate surgery, and, while he found it hard to understand why any red-blooded guy would swap a plonker for a pouch, he found the image interesting. He regarded himself as a trans-cultural, a cross-thinker rather than a cross-dresser.

Oscott and the four other partners selected for the Management Refresher Scheme had been booked into Business Class. They were flying to New York from London via Zurich on a Swissair 747. Because of the Gulf War – a ground offensive to expel Iraq from Kuwait had just begun, after six weeks of air bombardment of Baghdad – there were fears of terrorist reprisals against the West. Potomac Johnson Hodge had been instructed by Potomac Johnson (US) that no employees were to fly American or British airlines until further notice.

'I must say I always thought the Swiss were rather prissy wimps until this moment,' said the partner called John, as Zurich disappeared at a steep and speeding angle beneath their plane. 'All banks and no tanks make Jacob a dull boy. But I think I'm beginning to see the point of neutrality.'

'Listen, bud, you listen good,' said Oscott. 'If these fuckin' yodellers in their leather pants ain't going to trouble to get up off their butts, doing zilch, zero, zed, militarily, in defence of truth, freedom, and democracy in the Persian Gulf, I reckon the minimum – zilch, zero zed – they can come across with is safe passage across the Atlantic for the citizens of the nations who are defending freedom down there in the sand . . .'

Oscott was aware that he might have got some of the constructions and colloquial expressions slightly wrong, but that was a common difficulty when you first learned a new language. Fluency came with usage. He also noticed that he was breathing heavily after this speech. He had already expended a great deal of energy being rude about the (goddam Frenchified) Swissair food.

'I say, old man,' said the guy called Alastair, leaning across the aisle, 'are you OK over there? You've been coming on like John Wayne ever since we checked in.'

This was the first day on which Oscott had come out in public as his new, American self. He had been nervous, much as he supposed a burly bank clerk called Brendon would be, reporting for duty for the first time, in skirt and heels, as Brenda. Thankfully, the English convention by which it was rude to comment on dramatic changes in the appearance or behaviour of another had allowed him a crucial two hours to settle down. By now, he felt confident enough to respond to Alastair with a robust: 'Don't you worry chickenshit about me, Al.'

'Now Ally mentions it,' said one of the other partners, 'are you absolutely convinced that that striped shirt actually goes with that checked suit . . . ?'

'Just leisure wear,' Oscott insisted.

'Did you say leeeez-her?' spat Alastair.

'Correct,' Oscott confirmed.

'Personally, I preferred the Harris tweeds,' continued the other partner. 'Although I can see that you'll have to have brought a completely new wardrobe . . .'

The in-flight movie, which was called *Dead Sorry*, was about a young Philadelphia widow whose husband comes back from the grave in order to give her a chance to say: 'Goodbye. I love you.' He had been killed in a car crash, speeding angrily away from the house after a row.

The other partners jeered and sneered throughout – and the guy called Alastair read a book called *New Trends In Cost Accounting* instead of watching – but Oscott sobbed uncontrollably at the ending, when the widow told her daughter: 'Remember only this, Jamie-Lou. Speak to everyone you meet, especially those you love, as if it might be the last time you ever see them alive.'

'Does Pop know I love him, Mom?' asked the little girl.

'Pop knows, Jamie-Lou,' replied Mom solemnly, at which point a lampshade in the living room fell over. The 'ghost' of the dead dad had previously told Mom that this would be a sign that his spirit was watching them.

'My God, that was so beautiful,' said Oscott. 'And so, like, spiritually deep.'

'Someone buy that chap a stiff drink,' said Alastair.

As they made landfall at Labrador, and the pilot pointed out to those on the right-hand side of the aircraft the first sights of North America, Oscott and the others were discussing the Gulf War. The guy called John said, tentatively: 'What I find amazing, looking back, is that moment, a sort of, don't laugh, golden moment, only last summer. I'm serious. When Eastern Europe was electing governments, Russia was seriously reforming, or so we thought, and we were all – weren't we? – worrying about what to do with all the money we wouldn't need to spend on guns. I suppose, when we're old and boring, tapping past the war memorials with our sticks, we'll always remember that summer of 1990, as a kind of mirage.'

Oscott snorted. He had restricted himself to contributing short, loud assessments of Iraqi military capability, usually ending with an exclamation like: 'And then it's Goodnight, Mustafa.'

'I really don't know what to believe now,' said the guy called John.

'You're talking like a goddam liberal,' snarled Oscott.

At Kennedy, immigration was the usual chore. Oscott, seamlessly into the role now, seethed at the indignity of having to sweat in the Other Nationalities pen. During heated exchanges with the US Embassy in London, before leaving, he had discovered that bureaucracy would take years to catch up with what chemistry and illusion had achieved so rapidly. Just as a trans-sexual would always have the wrong chromosomes, whatever medicine's deceptions, so Oscott was doomed to enter America, his new found land, with a visitor's visa.

When they reached their hotel, at 47th Street and 5th, part of one of those chains which permit you to think you are in America wherever you are in the world, Oscott, seeing that he had an hour before they were due to meet up in the bar, was thrilled to find that the bedroom television offered sixty channels. On one of them he found an edition of *Cash-Dash-Flash*.

'Jolene, you got four, you're going for a fifth, deep, steady breaths now, what is the name of former President Ronald Reagan's wife?'

'Stanley, is that a trick question? The former President was first married to the actress Jane Wyman, a leading featured actress in the series *Dynasty* . . .'

'Jolene, I admire your, uh, exactness but I have to repeat the question: what is the name of former President Ronald Reagan's wife?'

'Nancy. The former Hollywood actress Nancy Davis.'

'Jolene, you score five and qualify for the Big Brain Teaser . . .'

Jolene, a plain but relatively slight lady by the average standard of the series' contestants, started jumping up and down on the spot, punching her arms in the air and squealing: 'I dun beleeeve it! I dun beleeeve it!'

The pedantry which Jolene had displayed in her answers, the knowledge of the minutiae of trivia, was, in Oscott's experience, typical of those who competed. It was as if, having been poor at school, they were compensating now. These programmes were their exams, the prizes their qualifications.

For the Big Brain Teaser, Jolene was required to sit on a cheap throne which appeared to be a reconstruction of an electric chair in a prison death chamber. Polystyrene mock electrodes, painted silver, were attached to her temples.

'Jolene, your Big Brain Teaser. What are the first three words of the Constitution of the United States of America . . . ?'

Jolene began to bite her bottom lip, as if it might be made

of marzipan. Many in the audience were shouting the answer, so that the studio briefly resembled a political rally. At last, Jolene took up the cry herself: 'We the people, Stanley. We the people.'

Stanley kissed Jolene, supposedly on the cheek, but, in reality, somewhere in her green-tinted coiffure, behind the ear. Perhaps he had been warned by the network executives about the possibility of contracting Aids from the saliva of a guest. Now the American national anthem began to play in the studio and Jolene was handed a three-metre long, two-metre wide hardboard cheque, with a row of vivid illuminated light bulbs around the edges. The several zeros in her bounty were picked out in the same way.

Pleased for Jolene, Oscott switched off and joined the others in the George Washington Bar in the hotel lobby. He was sure, because of a halt in the conversation as he approached, that they had been discussing his new self but the realization did not disturb him as it might have done in his English life. He drank two Scuds, a cocktail with a bourbon base, which was named after a missile much in use during the Gulf War.

Oscott joined in conversation with his colleagues, but he was more interested in listening to the American exchanges around him.

'Listen,' one man was saying to another, 'I'm not going to kiss ass to make them buy our produce.'

He said it prow-juice. Oscott loved the aggression of American speech. He also, eavesdropping at two bar stools on the other side, noticed the way in which almost all professional Americans now spoke as if they were being interviewed on television. Even when, as in the discussion he was bugging, the substance was no more sombre than the whereabouts of a mutual acquaintance.

'What's he doing now?'

'I don't have that information.'

'Did he go back to Boston?' Bawston.

'I can't answer that.'

After another round of Scuds, they walked down 5th Avenue to a restaurant recommended in the Fodor's Oscott had purchased with his Langopac. He would have more time for sightseeing later in the week, but he was able now to catch sights like St Patrick's, the Catholic cathedral, its spire outclimbed by the surrounding skyscrapers, as if to prove the supremacy of Mammon over God. Even so, as an American, Oscott now believed in God and, in particular, His firm support for America and her allies in the Gulf War, which, according to that day's network news bulletins, America had just won.

The native visitor was disappointed by the state of the New York streets, both the lunar undulation of the road surface and the mess on what he now effortlessly called sidewalks. It occurred to him that a clever Middle Eastern terrorist should invent a garbage bomb: an explosive device packed in crumpled cardboard or sticky cellophane, which could be left without suspicion directly outside the doorways and windows of airlines and tourist offices.

The restaurant was a little pink and fussy in decor, but Oscott was able to order the kind of bright red bleeding meat he favoured. He was pleased to hear that other American diners were also resisting the menu's threatened departures from tradition.

'This salmon you've got,' growled a husband who looked as if he might have been in *The Godfather*. 'Is it, like, cooked good? ... what I'm saying is, we're not Japanese ... you see, some places in this town, they're cooking it raw, in the middle, like steak. ...'

'Sir, we cook fish very good here.'

Oscott noted that the waiter was not an American. He was pleased when the mafioso decided to have chicken instead.

That night, he didn't require a magazine to produce an erection before beating off: being in America was enough. In addition to all the information he had taken in from Langopac, he now knew the meaning of another American phrase: born-again.

*

They breakfasted in the hotel together next morning. The Management Refresher Course Induction Session was timed for 8.30 a.m. All the others were complaining about jet-lag, and a wakeful night, but Oscott, strangely, had slept solidly from local midnight to local dawn. Because it would be a long day, he ordered bacon and egg waffles with maple syrup, a side order of grits, followed by corn muffins and bilberry jelly.

While he ate, he read in a complimentary copy of a New York daily tabloid that a guest had died during a recording of *Cash-Dash-Flash*. The report said:

'Mildred L. Nicholson, 58, of Hoboken, NJ, was stricken by a sudden myocardial infarct while racing to avoid elimination from the game-show in a short dash against the clock which is a feature of the twice-daily quiz programme. She had answered four questions correctly, but had been prevented by her failure to identify the two sides who fought the battle of Waterloo [Great Britain and France] from an immediate progression to a financial jackpot.

Mrs Nicholson, a widow who is survived by four children and sixteen grandchildren, was pronounced dead on arrival at the Sammy Davis Jr Medical Center in Brooklyn. A family representative said that she had been taking medication for hypertension.

A spokesman for the producing network, NAB (North American Broadcasting), said that Mrs Nicholson had signed a standard indemnity document and that the company did not anticipate the question of compensation arising. An NAB Vice-President (light entertainment division), would, however, attend the burial service, as a mark of respect.

The host of *Cash-Dash-Flash*, Stanley F. Zucchini, 78, a former movie comedian, said: 'In a very real sense, I love every one of the guests on my show and, at this tragic time, I share the pain of Millie's [Mildred's] family, as I'm sure do our millions of viewers.'

An aide to the office of the Mayor of New York, who faces

a difficult re-election campaign in the fall, issued a brief statement: 'If Mrs Nicholson had known just a little more non-American history, she might still be alive. This merely serves to underline the mayor's repeated emphasis on the importance of a broad-brush approach to high school education.'

However, a representative of the dead woman's family responded later with a short, clarificatory statement: '*Cash-Dash-Flash* was mom's favourite show. She had overruled the advice of her doctors to take part in the recording and it is the view of those who loved her that she would have had no complaints that God decided to take her to Him in such circumstances and at this time.'

NAB said that a decision had not yet been reached on whether an edited version of the fatal programme might yet be transmitted.

Mrs Nicholson was the fifth game-show fatality of the present television season and industry executives are known to be examining a proposal that fitness exams be introduced for the big-prize series.'

'You look as if you're blubbing, you big Jessie,' growled the guy called Alastair.

'Don't you worry about me, Bud,' replied Oscott, but the report had, indeed, brought tears to his eyes. There was just so much that he admired in the story: the rash determination of Mrs Nicholson to seize her piece of fame, the cunning legal efficiency of the network, the dignity and religious faith of the dead woman's family. It seemed, to him, a very American tragedy.

Afterwards, all of the other visiting partners would be asked, by the investigating Vice-President (personnel division) of Potomac Johnson (US) in New York, whether Oscott had been behaving strangely that day. All of them commented on the apparent transformation in accent and dress but they did so hesitantly, as if they feared that they might be fantasizing from the shock of the events. Or, perhaps, it was merely a reluctance to tell an American that what they had really noticed about their colleague was that he had become a bit, well, you know, American.

All reported that he had been jaunty during the morning session, in which, to break down the inhibitions of the participants, each delegate had been asked to pretend to be a tree. Oscott had been a Giant Californian Redwood. Indeed, it was Alastair who had behaved most oddly at this point. When the exercise was described, he announced that he was a Christmas tree and, it being March, would be represented by an empty space on the floor. He then left the room until the game was over.

Oscott, the English visitors told the investigating Vice-President, had been in buoyant form at lunch-time for which, a print-out of the staff refectory computerized till revealed, he had eaten a sandwich of pastrami and meat-balls with melted blue cheese on rye.

He had participated vigorously in the afternoon's session, which was a Goal-Identification Brainstorming Seminar. The notes of the presiding Vice-President revealed that Oscott, asked as a final exercise to write his three main short-term goals and his three main long-term goals on a piece of paper, had been the first to hand in a completed sheet. His short-term goals were listed as: 1: Kick Ass, 2: Eat Pussy, 3: Hit Pay Dirt. His long-term goals were identified as: 1: Kick Ass, 2: Eat Pussy, 3: Hit Pay Dirt.

The day's sessions had ended with an individual meeting for each English delegate with the Potomac Johnson (US) company psychologist. A secret copy of the doctor's interim assessment, given to the investigating Vice-President, showed that Oscott had been adjudged: 'Arrogant, aggressive, intensely patriotic (no doubts at all about Gulf policy and aims) with a high sex-drive and a definite contempt for those in society who do not know what they believe or do not do what they desire. His recurrent dreams feature images of strong violence. Preliminary grading is A1. Fast-stream management advance is indicated.'

It was, however, generally agreed by all those present that Oscott's mood had changed when delegates and tutors were drinking Scuds in the private General Eisenhower Lounge of the Potomac Johnson (US) building. After a few drinks, a vice-president who had tutored the morning's role-playing session fell into conversation with Oscott.

This vice-president told the investigating Vice-President: 'He'd been a lively guy in class. I liked his energy. I said, listen, tell me, something's bugging me, where you from? You see, I hear some Boston, and some Bronx, but I'm getting Deep South and I'm getting Texas. Where you lived most of your life? London, he said. So, I say, Jeez, where were you born, then? He says Surrey. Apparently, that's, like, commuter belt. And he sees my puzzled expression and he looks, from his smile, like you've told him his dick's so big he's gonna have to stand in another room. And I said what's going on here, then? And he gives me stuff about how everyone back in England wants the kids learning French and German, because of what they call their European Community. And he says, I think our kids should be learning American. That's the language of the future. I'm setting an example, he says. And I think I laughed and said to him: listen, bud, you want to get your kids writing ideograms, like those pretty little Japanese pictures, right? Because that's the language of the future. I said: lemme tell you a story. I said I suddenly realized last week that, now, everytime I shake hands with a guy, like socially I mean, I give this little nod. And I realize it's because 95 per cent of the guys I see for business meetings are Japanese. So all day now, here, at one of America's biggest fuckin' finance houses, it's hello, bow, goodbye, bow. As a result of this I find I'm turning Japanese. Now I notice the guy's kinda looking deflated. But I go on. I say, do you have any idea of how much real estate those slit-eyed guys own now? Do you have any hold on how much of each US Treasury bond issue is bought by a guy with a name that sounds like a car or a hi-fi? I said – I was kinda into my stride – for New York, New York, read New York, Tokyo. I finished by saying that, like, I thought we'd said sorry now for Hiroshima and all, but those Nips obviously weren't hearing us. Then I saw that he was on his way out of the room. He said he was wanting to feel America under his feet. I'm damn sure that was how he put it.'

The New York police department homicide squad was, as often, too much in demand to react in anything more than a routine way to the incident. The attack had taken place near to Oscott's hotel. An English couple on vacation said that when the two men, who they thought were West Indian, had approached the corpulent young gentleman with their knives raised, the assailants had shouted something like: 'Give us your wad or we'll cut you.' It had been, they said, like a scene from *Hill Street Blues*.

They had heard the victim say something like: 'Hey, hey, hey, bud. I'm not a tourist, I'm an American. I am an American.' But, then, one of the, er, black, no offence, men had laughed and said something, which had sounded like: 'You're an American? Hey, that's why we're fuckin' killing you, brother!' Could that possibly be right? (The weary, coffee-swigging cop muttered that that sounded right.) Next, one of the two attackers had reached inside the corpulent gentleman's coat, extracted a wallet, and then – they insisted this had been the sequence of events – stabbed him repeatedly in the upper chest and dashed away. The couple said they hated to admit this now but they had been too frightened to go to the gentleman's aid until the police arrived. It was just that New York terrified them. The police told them that the dumb thing about the whole business was that the guy had probably been carrying mainly traveller's cheques, which were not much use to anyone else.

Oscott's death was reported in two lines at the bottom of a late page of a New York tabloid newspaper under the headline: 'Brit Hit.' The story read, in full: 'Visiting British businessman,

Robert Oscott, 30, died Tuesday in a fatal mugging incident in mid-town Manhattan, NY police said.'

Describing his death to friends as 'a tragedy more complicated than anyone begins to realize', Henrietta, Oscott's former girlfriend, inquired about the possibility of his being buried in America, but was over-ruled by Oscott's mother, who told her: 'He was always so very English.'

Oscott was laid to rest in an English country churchyard. After consultation, his family decided to ignore the request in his will that the theme tune from the television programme *Cash-Dash-Flash* should be played as the coffin left the church.

The guy called Alastair left the company to rejoin his family business, after his final assessment on the Management Refresher Course, which continued after Oscott's death, concluded that he had 'negative attitudes to twenty-first-century management concepts'.

The vice-president who had been the last person to speak to Oscott on the evening of his death was also asked to leave the company. It was felt that the comments which he had reported making to the delegate were 'unpatriotic, denigratory to the corporate image and potentially racist'.

Following an article in a weekend magazine about the bizarre circumstances surrounding Robert Oscott's death – the piece was headlined The Pretend American – sales of the Langopac Teach Yourself American kit, perhaps surprisingly, increased by nearly 500 per cent.

Potomac Johnson (US) flew over a senior vice-president (personnel deployment) from New York to attend the funeral. The executive was booked on Swissair because of continuing doubts about the safety of British travellers, despite what was seen as the successful outcome of the 1991 war in the Persian Gulf.

Author's Note

AT THE END of a book, which, particularly in its first two sections, so freely mixes fact and fiction, the reader may require some reassurances.

In *The Nice Man Cometh*, all dates and statistics relating to the performance at national level of the Social Democratic Party (SDP), and all speeches or remarks made by non-fictional political figures, are intended to be factual. However, the particular London constituencies involved in the story are made up, as are all the local party members featured in these scenes.

A more complex case is Graham Sterling's interview with Mrs Margaret Thatcher in chapter five, in which 'her' comments are taken from speeches made by the Prime Minister at around the time of the fictional conversation. Also, the crash of a London-Glasgow express in 1979 is invented and does not relate to any specific railway disaster.

Bloody Margaret draws on fact, gossip and speculation about the British premiership (1979–1990) of Margaret Hilda Thatcher. For example, the speech to the 1987 Blackpool conference featured in the text is, verbatim, the one which that Prime Minister delivered. The majority of the other, less concrete, details are either fact or (perhaps a necessary distinction) were reported in the tabloid newspapers. They have, however, been given comic spin.

Specifically, Mrs Thatcher is known to have collected porcelain but the specific collection featured in the story is a fantasy. She was also said by the popular press to have adopted a lame duck in the late 1980s. In the same way, she was indeed reported (without denial) to submit to controlled electrocutions in Shepherd's Bush.

However, the members of the PM's entourage herein depicted do not, in any instance, represent a particular individual. All are satirical amalgams. Even the bluff, Northern press secretary, whom some may confuse with a bluff, Northern press secretary who operated from Downing Street, is not intended to represent exact reportage of real lobby briefings. The working rule was to allow generalizations and extrapolations about political power which a pure documentary approach would rule out, but to avoid gratuitously malicious inventions about the actual Thatcher administrations or verifiable events.

The writing of what is known as 'faction' inevitably establishes a heavy debt to works of non-fiction. Particularly invaluable was *Chronicle of the 20th Century* (Longman, 1987) and the linked single volumes covering the years 1988–90. The skeleton established by these books was fleshed out from the national newspaper archives stored at the indispensable British Newspaper Library at Colindale, whose staff were unfailingly helpful. I have drawn mainly on contemporary accounts from the *Daily Telegraph*, the *Guardian*, the *Daily Mail* and (after 1987) *The Independent*. The journalists who amuse the characters on pages 94–95 are Michael White and Clive James.

Hugo Young's masterly Thatcher biography *One Of Us* (Macmillan, 1989) was, otherwise, the most important single source of facts. Also useful were *Thatcher* (Macdonald, 1983) by Nicholas Wapshott and George Brock and *Margaret Thatcher: Wife, Mother, Politician* by Penny Junor (Sidgwick & Jackson, 1983). *Thatcher's Britain* (Bantam, 1987) by Terry Coleman was an important account of the 1987 election. All quotations from speeches by Mrs Margaret Thatcher are taken from the texts collected in *The Revival of Britain* (Aurum, 1989) and *In Defence of Freedom* (Aurum, 1986). *American-English, English-American* (Abson Books, 1985) was also a helpful companion. In all cases,

the responsibility for the uses to which the information has
been put remains my own.

The form of *Bloody Margaret* owes something to Ryszard
Kapuściński's *The Emperor* (Quartet, 1983), Chinua Achebe's
The Anthills of the Savannah (Heinemann, 1987), and Phillip
Roth's *Our Gang* (Random House, 1973).

A handful of paragraphs previously appeared, in a different
form, in the *Independent* and the *Independent* magazine and I am
grateful to their editors, Andreas Whittam-Smith and Alexander
Chancellor, for permission to re-use them and for originally
sending me to cover many of the real events which feature in
the book.

I must also thank Diana Trollope and Frank Lawson for help
with research; Helen Lorenz and W. T. Ram for computer
assistance; Peter Symes, Andrew Gosling, Harriet Bakewell,
and Annie Venables of the BBC, for insights into election
procedures; Philip French, Peter Kemp, and John Spurling for
advice on dentists in literature; and my wife, Sarah Bull, for
typing and many other kindnesses.

Mark Lawson, London, May 1991.